THREE BY BOX

THREE BY BOX

The Complete Mysteries of Edgar Box

Random House New York

Copyright © 1952, 1953, 1954, 1978 by Edgar Box

All rights reserved under International and Pan-American Copyright Conventions. Published in the United States by Random House, Inc., New York, and simultaneously in Canada by Random House of Canada Limited, Toronto.

Library of Congress Cataloging in Publication Data

Three by Box.

CONTENTS: Death in the fifth position.—Death before bedtime.—Death likes it hot.
1. Detective and mystery stories, American.
I. Title.
PZ3.V6668Ti [PS3543.I26]   813'.5'4   78-57100

ISBN 0-394-50117-9

Manufactured in the United States of America
24689753
First Edition

CONTENTS

Death in the Fifth Position   3

Death Before Bedtime   151

Death Likes It Hot   311

DEATH IN THE FIFTH POSITION

I

"You see," said Mr. Washburn. "We've been having trouble."

I nodded. "What sort of trouble?"

He looked vaguely out the window. "Oh, one thing and the other."

"That's not much to go on, is it?" I said gently; it never does to be stern with a client before one is formally engaged.

"Well, there's the matter of these pickets."

I don't know why but the word "picket" at this moment suggested small gnomes hiding in the earth. So I said, "Ah."

"They are coming tonight," he added.

"What time do they usually come?" I asked, getting into the spirit of the thing.

"I don't know. We've never had them before."

Never had them before, I wrote in my notebook, just to be doing something.

"You were very highly recommended to me," said Mr. Washburn, in a tone which was almost accusing; obviously I had given him no cause for confidence.

"I've handled a few big jobs, from time to time," I said quietly, exuding competence.

"I want you for the rest of the season, the New York season. You are to handle all our public relations, except for the routine stuff which this office does automatically: sending out photographs of the dancers and so on. Your job will be to work with the columnists, that kind of thing . . . to see we're not smeared."

"Why do you think you might be smeared?" The psychological moment had come for a direct question.

"The pickets," said Mr. Washburn with a sigh. He was a tall heavy man with a bald pink head which glittered as though it had been waxed; his eyes were gray and shifty: as all honest men's eyes are supposed to be according to those psychologists who maintain that there is nothing quite so dishonest as a level, unwavering gaze.

I finally understood him. "You mean you are going to be picketed?"

"That's what I said."

"Bad labor relations?"

"Communism."

"You mean the Communists are going to picket you?"

The impresario of the Grand Saint Petersburg Ballet looked at me sadly, as though once again his faith had been unjustified. Then he began at the beginning. "I called you over here this morning because I was told that you were one of the best of the younger public relations men in New York, and I prefer to work with young people. As you may or may not know, my company is going to première an important new ballet tonight. The first major modern ballet we have presented in many years and the choreographer is a man named Jed Wilbur."

"I'm a great admirer of his," I said, just to show that I knew something about ballet. As a matter of fact, it isn't possible to be around the theater and not know of Wilbur. He is the hottest choreographer in town at the moment, the most fashionable . . . not only in ballet but also in musical comedies.

"Wilbur has been accused of being a Communist several times but since he has already been cleared by two boards I have every confidence in him. The United Veterans Committee, however, have not. They wired me yesterday that if we did his new ballet they would picket every performance until it was withdrawn."

"That's bad," I said, frowning, making it sound worse than it was: after all I had a good job at stake. "May I see their telegram?" Mr. Washburn handed it to me and I read:

> To Ivan Washburn Director Grand Saint Petersburg Ballet Company Metropolitan Opera House New York City: WE HAVE REASON TO BELIEVE THAT JED WILBUR IS A MEMBER OF THE COMMUNIST PARTY AND THAT COMMA TO PROTECT OUR CHERISHED WAY OF LIFE

AND THOSE IDEALS WHICH SO FINELY FORGED A NATION OUT OF THE WILDERNESS COMMA THE SUBVERSIVE WORK OF ARTISTS LIKE WILBUR SHOULD BE BANNED PERIOD SHOULD YOU DISREGARD THIS PLEA TO PROTECT OUR AMERICAN WAY WE WILL BE FORCED TO PICKET EVERY PERFORMANCE OF SAID WILBUR'S WORK PERIOD IN A TRUE DEMOCRACY THERE IS NO PLACE FOR A DIFFERENCE OF OPINION ON GREAT ISSUES CORDIALLY ABNER S. FLEER SECRETARY.

"A poignant composition," I said.

"We've had a bad season so far this year. We're the fifth ballet company to arrive in town this spring and even though we're the original Russian ballet it's not been easy to fill the Met. Wilbur is our ace-in-the-hole. It's his first ballet for this company. It's his first new work in over a year. Everyone is going to be on hand tonight . . . and *nothing* must go wrong. That will be your job, too, by the way: to publicize the première."

"If I'd had a few weeks of preparation I could have got *Life* to cover the performance," I said with that modesty which characterizes my profession.

Washburn was not impressed. "In any case, I'm told that you've got a good many contacts among the columnists. They're the people who make opinion, for us at least. You've got to convince them that Wilbur is as pure as . . ."

"The driven snow," I finished, master that I am of the worn cliché. "But is he?"

"Is he what?"

"Pure as . . . I mean is he a Communist?"

"How in the name of God should I know? He could be an anarchist for all I care. The only thing I'm interested in is a successful season. Besides, what has politics to do with *Eclipse*?"

"With what?"

"*Eclipse* is the name of the new ballet. I want you to go over to the Met and watch the dress rehearsal at two-thirty. You'll be able to get some idea of the company then . . . meet the cast and so on. Meet Wilbur, too; he's full of ideas on how to handle this . . . too damn many ideas."

"Then I am officially employed?"

"As of this minute . . . for the rest of the season, two weeks altogether. If we're still having trouble by the time we go on tour I'd like you to go with us as far as Chicago . . . if that's agreeable."

"We'll see," I said.

"Fine." Mr. Washburn rose and so did I. "You'll probably want to make some preparations between now and two-thirty. You can use the office next to mine . . . Miss Ruger will show you which one."

"That will be perfect," I said. We shooks hands solemnly.

I was halfway out the door when Mr. Washburn said, "I think I should warn you that ballet dancers are very temperamental people. Don't take them too seriously. Their little quarrels are always a bit louder than life." Which, in the light of what happened later, was something of an understatement.

2

Until my interview with Ivan Washburn I could take ballet or leave it alone and since in earlier days I was busy writing theater reviews for Milton Haddock of the *New York Globe*, I left it alone: besides, the music critic always handled ballet and what with doing Mr. Haddock's work as well as my own I had very little time for that sort of thing, between eight-thirty and eleven anyway. Mr. Haddock, God knows, is a fine critic and a finer man and it is a fact that his reviews in the *Globe* were more respected than almost anyone else's; they should have been since I wrote nearly all of them between 1947 and 1949 at which latter date I was separated from the *Globe*, as we used to say in the army. Not that I am implying Mr. Haddock, who was writing about the theater the year I was born, couldn't do just as well as I did . . . he could, but there is a limit to the amount of work you can accomplish on Scotch whisky, taken without water or ice, directly from the bottle if he was in the privacy of his office or from a discreet prohibition flask if we were at the theater: he on the aisle fifth row from the stage and I just behind him in the sixth row, with instructions to poke the back of his neck if he snored too loud.

In a way, I had a perfect setup; Mr. Haddock was fond of me in a distant fatherly way (he often had a struggle recalling my name) and I was allowed all the pleasure of unedited authorship for he never changed a line of my reviews on those occasions when he read them at all. The absence of public credit never distressed me; after all I was Harvard class of 1946 (three years must be added to my age, however, during which time I served the nation on at least one very far-flung battlefront) and most of my classmates are still struggling along in the lower echelons of advertising firms or working anonymously for *Time* and *Life* and worrying about their integrity as liberals in a capitalistic organization. Anyway I knew a good thing when I saw it but after three years of being the real drama critic for the *Globe* I began to feel my oats and I made the mistake of asking for a raise at the wrong time: a fault in timing which must be ascribed to my extreme youth and natural arrogance, to quote Mr. Haddock quoting the managing editor, and since I had unfortunately phrased my request as an ultimatum I was forced to resign and Mr. Haddock looked very sorry and confused the day I left, saying: "All the best, Jim." My name is Peter Cutler Sargeant II, but what the hell; I shook his hand and told him that everything I knew about writing I had learned from him . . . which pleased the old fool.

For over a year now I have been in public relations, with my own office, consisting of a middle-aged lady and a filing cabinet. The middle-aged lady, Miss Flynn, is my official conscience and she had been very good to me, reminding me that money is not everything and that Jesus is my redeemer. She is a Baptist and stern in the presence of moral weakness. I firmly believe that the main reason she consents to work for me is that I constitute a challenge to her better instincts, to that evangelical spirit which burns secretly but brightly in her bosom. She will save me yet. We have both accepted that fact. But in the meantime she helps me in my work, quite unaware that she is a party to that vast conspiracy to dupe the public in which I and my kind are eternally engaged.

"Miss Flynn, I have been hired."

"The dancers?" She looked at me, her gray lips tight. Women in tights are dancers to her, not ballerinas.

"For two weeks, starting now."

"I am very happy for you, Mr. Sargeant," she said, in the tone of one bidding a friend farewell on the banks of the Styx.

"I'm happy, too." I said. I then gave her a few instructions about my other accounts (a hat company in the Bronx, a television actress and a night school); then I left my one-room Madison Avenue office and headed for the Metropolitan Opera House, leaving my conscience behind.

Mr. Washburn met me at the stage door and escorted me past several open dressing rooms to a flight of steps which led down to the vast stage itself. Everything was in great confusion. Small fat women ran back and forth carrying costumes, while dancers in tights stood about practicing difficult variations with the intensely vacuous expressions of weight-lifters or of those restaurant cooks who scramble eggs in front of plate-glass windows. Workmen, carrying parts of scenery, shouted to one another and cursed the dancers who seemed always to be in their way. In the pit the orchestra was making an awful noise warming up, while, beyond, the great red and gold opera house was empty and still . . . a little ominous, I thought, for no reason at all.

"The rehearsal is almost ready to begin," said my employer as we moved out onto the stage, toward a group of dancers in tights and T-shirts, the standard rehearsal costume of both boys and girls, which was very nice I thought, looking at the girls. "I'll introduce you to the principals in a minute," said Mr. Washburn. "If you . . ." But then someone waved to him from the other side of the stage and he walked away, leaving his sentence unfinished.

"Are you the new boy?" asked a female voice behind me.

I turned and saw a very pretty girl standing behind me; she wore black tights and a white T-shirt through which her breasts showed, small and neat. She was combing her dark gold hair back. For some inscrutable reason she had a rubber band in her mouth; it impaired her diction.

"Well, I guess in a way I am," I said.

"You better get your clothes off. I'm Jane Garden."

"My name's Peter Sargeant."

"You better hurry. You've got to learn the whole thing this afternoon." She pulled her hair straight back and then slipped the back hair through the rubber band; it looked like a horse's tail, a very nice horse's tail.

"Shall I take them off right here?"

"Don't be silly. The boys' dressing room is on the second floor."

I then explained to her who I was and she giggled, but not in a squeaky manner: her voice was low and her eyes, I noticed, were a fine arctic blue.

"Do you know *anything* about ballet?" she asked, glancing anxiously toward the other dancers. They were not ready, however. The orchestra was still warming up. The principals hadn't arrived yet. The noise was deafening.

"Not much," I said. "Are you one of the leads?"

"Nowhere near being a lead. Although they've made me understudy in this ballet."

"To whom?"

"Why, to Ella Sutton. She's the star of the ballet . . . I mean of this particular one. Actually she's the second-ranking ballerina . . . after Eglanova."

I knew who Eglanova was. Everyone, I suspect, who has ever heard of ballet knows about Anna Eglanova. I had even read up on her that morning before my interview with Mr. Washburn, just so I wouldn't appear too ignorant. The program notes and the facts, however, did not coincide as I found out soon enough . . . even though the program is approximately correct; she *was* a star at the same time as Nijinski and she *is* a genuine Russian dancer from the old Imperial School, but she is fifty-one not thirty-eight and she has been married five times, not once, and she was not the greatest ballerina of the Diaghilev era; as a matter of fact she was considered the least promising of the lot: how were her contemporaries to know that she had joints like ball bearings and a pair of lungs like rubber water wings and that with this equipment she would outlive all her generation, existing finally as a legend whose appearance on a stage was enough to break up a whole audience, causing tears of nostalgia to come to the eyes of characters who never saw a ballet before the last war.

"Where is Sutton?" I asked.

"Over there, talking to Wilbur . . . in the wings."

Sutton was a good-looking woman, with hair dyed jet-black and worn severely combed back with a part in the middle: the classic ballerina fashion. She had large but good features and a vividly painted face; she was in costume, a full-skirted white dress with red roses in her hair. Her body was good for a female dancer though the muscles tended to bunch a little unpleasantly at the calves. Jane Garden's did not, I noticed.

"Why aren't you in costume?" I asked. "Isn't this the dress rehearsal?"

"My costume isn't ready. I wish they'd hurry up and start."

"Why don't they?"

"I suppose they're waiting for Louis . . . Louis Giraud, he's the first dancer and he's always late. He sleeps most of the time. It drives everyone crazy . . . especially Wilbur."

"Why doesn't he do something about it?"

"Who? Wilbur? Why, he's in love."

"In love?"

"Of course . . . everybody knows it. He's just crazy about Louis."

Well, this is ballet, I decided, making a mental note to keep Miss Flynn in complete darkness as to the character of my new associates.

"I wonder," I said thoughtfully, sincerely, "if you might perhaps have a minute after the show tonight . . . we might go somewhere and have something to eat. You see"—speaking quickly now, gathering momentum—"I have to learn an awful lot about ballet very fast. It would help if you were to explain it all to me."

"You're sweet," said Miss Garden with an unexpected smile, her teeth shone glacier-white in her warm pink face. "Maybe I will. Oh, here comes the conductor. You better get out of the way now . . . we're going to start."

Mr. Washburn collected me at that moment and we went around to the front of the house. Here I was introduced to a number of patrons and hangers-on, as well as the *régisseur* or director of the company, Alyosha Rudin, a nice old man, and the set designer whose name I didn't get.

Jed Wilbur, a thin prematurely gray young man, came out on stage and began to lecture the dancers in a high nasal voice. They looked very pretty I thought. The girls in gray with pink roses in their hair and the boys dressed like 1910. But all was not ready.

"Where's Louis?" asked Wilbur suddenly. "Doesn't he know this is dress rehearsal?"

"He's always late," said Ella, fixing one of her false eyelashes in place. "I suppose he's sleeping."

"Just resting my legs," said Louis, ambling out onto the stage with that funny duck-like walk all dancers have from continually turning their feet out. He was a big-boned man, about thirty and, for a dancer, rather tall and muscular, with black curly hair and blue eyes.

"Why can't you ever be on time?" complained Wilbur, the eye of love eclipsed by the greater love of art and reputation; this was obviously an important moment for him, a major work . . . all the critics would be out front tonight and maybe even Margaret Truman.

"I get here, Jed. Now you start." Ella glared at him. Wilbur muttered something disagreeable. Then the overture began.

The set was a handsome one. A blue sky, which was dark when the curtain rose, gradually filled with light as the music swelled and the *corps de ballet* (eight boys and eight girls) appeared. In the center of the stage was a large rock of gray canvas while at the top of the blue sky, about forty feet up, was a yellow Van Gogh sun.

The plot, if *Eclipse* could be said to have a plot, seemed to be about a girl (Sutton) who was in love with a boy (Louis) who liked all the girls in the company except her. So, frustrated and miserable, she took her revenge when, not having been laid as she so dearly wanted, she rushed furiously away from the happy boys and girls who at this point were indulging in some pretty sophisticated fornication on stage (so stylized, however, that one's grandmother would never suspect what was happening); for a few dozen bars Ella hid behind the rock while Louis did his solo. Then, when he was finished, she reappeared and with a look of sheer malevolence slowly ascended into the air, spinning like an avenging spirit until she had at last eclipsed the sun. It was quite a tour de force, I thought . . . in spite of the dress rehearsal which was sufficiently godawful to make everyone think that tonight's performance would be a technical triumph: Louis dropped Ella in the midst of a complicated lift shortly after her entrance and they never got back with the music again, while the *corps de ballet* plunged wildly about in the best St. Petersburg tradition, knocking into scenery and one another, justifying all the cruel remarks I'd heard made about them by the more refined balletomanes.

"What do you think?" asked Washburn when the rehearsal ended.

"Wonderful!" I said, like a press agent.

"I think . . ." began Mr. Washburn, but he was not allowed to finish because they were having a row on stage. The curtain had remained up and the lights were on again. Louis, stretched out with his back to the proscenium, was carefully wiping the sweat from his face with a piece of Kleenex. The boys and girls stood puffing at the rear of the stage while Ella and Wilbur quarreled.

"You've got to change it, Jed. I insist. I will *not* go sailing up on that damn thing again."

"It's the whole point to the ballet."

"So what? I won't do it. I get dizzy and I can't make those turns off the ground."

"We can have one of the workmen turn you backstage . . . he'll jerk the cable . . ."

"Oh, no he won't!"

"The idea never seemed to bother you before."

"The *idea* still doesn't bother me. I never realized how high it was until now."

"Why don't you get her a net?" suggested Louis.

"And that lift!" she said furiously, turning on him. "I could have broken a leg. You did it deliberately. I *swear* he dropped me deliberately."

Mr. Washburn let them fight it out a few minutes more; then he went up on the stage, accompanied by me, and quickly made peace. It was agreed that Ella *would* ascend by cable tonight, but more slowly than before, and, further, she would not have to turn in the air.

"Very statesmanlike," I said to Mr. Washburn, as we moved toward the dressing rooms on the north side of the stage.

"We always have these little disagreements before a première . . . divertissements I like to call them." Despite his attempt at lightness, however, he seemed not at all diverted. "Have you had any ideas yet about those pickets?"

I nodded. "I've already called Elmer Bush at the *Globe* . . . that's where I used to work . . . and he's doing a column called 'Witch-Hunt in the Theater,' all about Wilbur and the ballet."

"First-rate," said Mr. Washburn, obviously impressed. I made a mental note to call Elmer Bush and suggest such a column to him. For all I knew he might even do it.

"I would rather wait until after we see the pickets before I do anything more. I mean we may get a lead from them . . . you know, something about bad behavior, bullying is un-American, that kind of thing. By the way," I added, "speaking of bad behavior, does Miss Sutton often make scenes like this?"

"Not often," said Mr. Washburn, as we approached a dressing room with a dusty star on the door. "She usually saves them for her husband."

"Her husband?"

"Miles Sutton. He's the conductor . . . big fellow with the beard."

My head was beginning to spin. Everyone was related to everyone else, either officially or unofficially. I couldn't keep them straight. The ballerina Ella Sutton was the wife of the conductor Miles Sutton and the choreographer Jed Wilbur was in love with the lead dancer Louis Giraud and Jane Garden the understudy to Ella Sutton was my idea of a fine specimen while Anna Eglanova the prima ballerina stood before me naked from the waist up. It was disconcerting. I was standing beside Mr. Washburn in the doorway of her dressing room; her maid had suddenly opened the door and darted by, leaving her mistress exposed to our gaze.

"Come in, Ivan," said the great ballerina. "Who is the young man?"

"Peter Sargeant, Anna, our new public relations man."

"So young! Ah!" She sat down before her dressing table and began to arrange her hair. She looked young for fifty. Her body was firm . . . the skin like antique ivory and the breasts more like worn china door knobs than glands intended for the suckling of the young. Her neck was slightly corded and her face was ugly but exotic, with deep lines about the mouth, a beaked nose and narrow slanting Mongol eyes. Her hair was dyed dark red.

"I get ready now for *pas de deux,* Ivan." Her English was so heavily accented that it sounded to me like a different language altogether. In fact everything about her was different, including her casual disregard for the conventions.

"I think I better go," I said, a little hastily. "I've got some calls to make. I'm going to try and head the newspaper photographers off."

"Good plan," said Mr. Washburn.

"Nice boy," said Anna, as I left.

Halfway down the hall, a loud voice said, "Hey, baby, come in here."

Now, I am twenty-eight years old and shave every day of my life and, though I wear a crewcut in deference to my collegiate past, I flatter myself that I look every inch a man of the world. But Louis Giraud obviously had about as much respect for other men as Don Juan had for little girls so I controlled myself. I walked into his dressing room.

He was lying on a steel cot. He had an electric fan going just above his head and a pair of sweaty tights were hanging over the radiator to dry. He wore nothing except a towel around his middle.

I said, "Hi."

"You like the ballet tonight?" He spoke good English with only a faint French accent; he had started life as a longshoreman in Marseille. No one knew how he had got started in ballet but I suspect that the rumor a certain rich gentleman discovered him in a bordello and took him to Paris was probably true.

"I liked it pretty good," I said.

"Real lousy," said Louis, stretching his long knotty legs until the joints cracked. "I hate this ugly modern stuff. *Giselle* was good enough for Nijinski and it's good enough for me. All these people running around stage with funny faces. *Merde!*" He had a deep voice and he wasn't at all like the other boys in the company who were inclined to be rather tender: Louis had shoulders like a boxer. I decided I wouldn't like to tangle with him and so I sat near the open door, ready to make a quick exit if he should decide to tear off a quick piece.

"Well, it's a new medium," I said absently, noting the comic books and movie magazines on the floor by the bed. Each to his taste, I said to myself in flawless French.

"But it's not ballet." Louis looked at me and grinned. "Hey, why're you trying to fool me, baby?"

I measured the distance from my chair to the door: two long steps or one broad jump, I decided coolly. "Who's trying to fool you?" I asked, getting up slowly with a look of innocence which would have done credit to Tom Sawyer. He was too quick for me, though. I made a leap for the door but he got there first. It was a very silly moment.

"Now, look here, Louis," I said as he made a grab for me. We played tag a moment and then he grabbed me, holding me the way a boxer holds another boxer in a clinch and both of us trying not to make any noise, for different reasons. I wondered whether to knee him or not; the towel had fallen off. I decided against it for the good of the company. I would be fired if I did. On the other hand I was in danger of being ravished; I couldn't move without seriously injuring him and, on the other hand, I couldn't stand like this forever pressed against his front while he fumbled and groped with his one free hand, embarrassing me very much. He smelled like a horse. Controlling myself with great effort I said in a very even and dignified voice, "If you don't let go of me, I will break every one of your toes." And with that, fairly gently, I put one hard leather heel on top of his left foot. He jumped at that and, breathing hard, I slid out the door.

I was mad as hell for several minutes but then, since no damage was done, I began to see the funny side and as I walked across the stage to the other set of dressing rooms I wondered if I should tell Jane what had happened. For one reason and another I had decided not to when I came upon Miles and Ella Sutton, quarreling. He was standing in the door of her dressing room; she was sitting at her make-up table in an old gray bathrobe. I caught one quick glimpse of her as I walked by, as though on urgent business. I have found that people who hang around to watch fights usually end by getting involved.

As I walked by, however, I heard Miles Sutton threatening to kill his wife. It gave me quite a turn. I mean temperament is all very well but there are times when it can be carried too far.

3

Now that I look back on that night it is perfectly apparent to me that almost everyone, including myself, sensed that something serious had gone wrong ... but what? I knew of course that there was always a great deal of tension before a première and the childish bad temper of ballet dancers was familiar to me, by reputation anyway. Yet when the curtain went up on the blue-lit stage for the first ballet of the evening, *Swan Lake,* I had a knot in the pit of my stomach.

I remember taking a good look at the audience just before the house lights were dimmed and I remember feeling thankful that I didn't have to appear on a stage in front of all those people, for the interior of the Met, seen from the stage, is like the mouth of a great monster, wide open, yawning and red, with tiers of golden teeth.

I have always had a personal superstition that when something begins badly it will end well and vice versa. Since that night I have discarded the superstition of a lifetime for this particular evening began badly and ended tragically.

The pickets arrived at seven-thirty, twenty well-fed veterans of the First World War; they were quiet but grim and their placards suggested in red ink that Wilbur go back to Russia if he liked it so much there. I had already telephoned the photographers, tipping them off; all publicity is good is my conviction and I had a scheme by which we might eventually be able to make considerable capital out of the veterans. Mr. Washburn took a dark view of this but I reassured him. I even wrote him a little speech to make to the audience right after *Swan Lake,* before *Eclipse,* saying that Jed Wilbur was a hundred per cent patriot and so on.

The trouble began, officially, after *Swan Lake* when one of the girls collapsed in the wings and had to be carried up to her dressing room.

I was standing beside Alyosha Rudin to stage right when this happened.

"What's the matter with her?" I asked.

The old man sighed. "A foolish girl. Her name is Magda . . . a little heavy to be good dancer but she has the heart."

"You mean she has a weak heart?"

Alyosha chuckled. "No, she is passionate. Shall we go out front?"

On our way we passed Mr. Washburn. He was dressed in white tie and tails and his glittering skull looked pale to me in the dim light of backstage. He was very nervous. "I don't think I'll be able to go through with it," he said in a voice which trembled.

"With what?" I asked.

"The curtain speech."

"Courage, Ivan," said Alyosha. "You always say that; then when the time comes, you have the courage of a lion."

"All those people," moaned Mr. Washburn, moving toward the lavatory.

Alyosha was a pleasant companion and most knowledgeable of ballet; as he should be since, like Eglanova, he is a genuine Russian dating back to the Fall of Rome . . . perhaps even to the pyramids for he is very old with the classic Russian greyhound head: hair brushed back, long features and eyes like gray metal. He looked very old-world and distinguished in a smoking jacket of mulberry velvet. We found ourselves two seats in the front row.

"What was wrong with that girl?" I asked when we were seated. Already I was beginning to think of a press release . . . dancer upset by pickets: lover killed in Korea.

"She will have baby," said Alyosha.

"But she shouldn't be dancing if she's pregnant."

"The poor child. She must. She has no husband and her family doesn't know."

"Do you know who the father is?"

Alyosha smiled sadly; his teeth were like black pearls. "Sometimes it doesn't matter," he said gently.

Then the house lights were turned down and Mr. Washburn made his curtain speech; there was polite applause. Miles Sutton, looking nervous and sick, I thought (we were sitting right behind him), rapped his baton sharply on the music stand and the ballet began.

Artistically, everything went off quite well, according to the critics the next day. Both Martin of the *Times* and Terry of the *Tribune* thought *Eclipse* a triumphant modern work, praising Wilbur, Sutton's interpretation of the Bartok music, the set designer, Louis and, above all, the ballerina Ella Sutton who, they both felt, gave her finest performance: a dedicated artist to the very end for, when the cable broke thirty odd feet in the air, she maintained complete silence as she fell in fifth position onto the stage with a loud crash, still on beat.

Alyosha who was sitting beside me, gasped and said something very loud in Russian; then he crossed himself as the curtain swept down over the stage and the house lights went on. The audience was too stunned to react. Mr. Washburn came on stage but I missed his announcement for I was already backstage.

Ella Sutton lay in a heap in the middle of the stage, her body curiously twisted, like a contortionist's. A doctor had been summoned and he was kneeling beside her, his hand on her pulse. The dancers stood in shocked attitudes around the still figure.

Then Ella was pronounced dead (her back was broken) and she was carried to her dressing room. Alyosha ordered the dancers to change for the next ballet, *Scheherazade*. Mr. Washburn led the doctor away.

The impassive workmen struck the set and I suddenly found that I was alone on the stage. Not even Alyosha was in sight.

I wandered down the corridor which led to the north side dressing rooms, but I could find no one. I paused at Eglanova's room and looked in. It was empty. Everything was in a tangle: costumes, telegrams, press clippings, flowers fresh and dying, all the paraphernalia of stardom. On impulse, I entered, feeling like a small boy who has been deserted in a haunted house. I knew, if I waited long enough, that she'd reappear: her dressing room was the clubhouse of the ballet . . . at least of the top echelon who, I was told, usually came here to drink hot tea and lemon Russian style and discuss, with some severity, those not present. But the club was deserted. Not even Eglanova's maid was in sight.

A little worried, I turned to go when, quite by chance, I glanced at the wastepaper basket which stood just inside the door: something glittered underneath the make-up-stained pieces of Kleenex and the dead roses. I bent over and picked up a large pair of brand-new shears.

I have since tried, unsuccessfully, to recall what I thought at that moment. As far as I can recollect I thought, rather idly, that it was curious that a perfectly good set of shears should be thrown out like that, and in Eglanova's dressing room, too. I had perhaps some vague notion that her maid might have borrowed them from one of the grips and then had absently thrown them out. In any event, I took them out of the dressing room and placed them neatly on top of a tool chest near the north side entrance.

It wasn't until an hour later, after the performance was over, that I began to worry a little because, by that time, the assistant district attorney had arrived, accompanied by a medical examiner and a detective named Gleason who announced to the assembled company that someone had deliberately cut all but a strand of that wire cable with a pair of shears, or maybe a saw, and that Ella Sutton had been murdered.

The company was kept backstage until nearly dawn. The questioning was conducted by Gleason, an autocratic little man who forbade me to call the press until the first of what proved to be a long set of interviews was concluded.

4

We met, almost by accident on Seventh Avenue at four-thirty in the morning. She looked very demure, I thought, in a plain cotton dress, and carrying a briefcase which contained her ballet clothes. I stopped beside her on the corner and we both waited for the light to turn green. Lonely taxicabs hurtled by; the city was still and a gray light shone dull in the east, above the granite and steel peaks, beyond the slow river.

"Hello, Jane," I said.

For a moment she didn't recognize me; then, remembering, she smiled wanly, and her face pale by street lamp, she said, "Are you going to take me out to supper?"

"What about breakfast?"

"I never get up this early," she said; and we crossed the street. The light was green. A sudden gust of warm wind came bowling up the alley and I caught her scent as Edgar Rice Burroughs was wont to say: warm flesh and Ivory soap.

"Can I walk you home?" I asked.

"If you want to. I live on Second Avenue." We walked nine uptown blocks and seven crosstown blocks to the brownstone where she lived. We paused below in the street . . . the hot wind, redolent of summer and river and early morning, stirred her streaked blond hair as we stood before a delicatessen while the drama of courtship took place. The dialogue, I must admit, was similar to that of every other couple in this same predicament at this same hour in the quiet city. Should we or should we not? was the moon right? and was this wise? or was it love? Fortunately, being a well-trained girl of casual habits, this last point wasn't worried too much and at last we walked up the two flights to her apartment.

The dialogue continued as, both seated on a studio couch in her two-roomed apartment, we were momentarily diverted from my central interest by the murder and, though we were both dead-tired and stifling yawns heroically in deference to my lust, we talked of the death of Ella Sutton.

"I never thought such a thing could happen to anybody I knew," said Jane, lying back on the bed, a pillow under her head. One paper lantern illuminated the room with red and yellow light. The furniture was shabby Victorian, very homelike, with photographs of family and fellow dancers on the walls, over the mantel of the walled-up fireplace. The ceilings were high and the curtains were of faded red plush.

"Do you think it was really murder?"

"That awful little man certainly thought it was. Somebody cut the cable . . . that's what he said."

"I wonder who?"

"Oh, almost anybody," she said vaguely, scratching her stomach comfortably.

"Don't tell me now that *everybody* hated Ella . . . it would be much too pat."

"Well, almost everybody did. Oh, she was just terrible. But that's an awful thing to say . . . her being dead, I mean."

"I expect we'll be hearing a lot about how terrible she was," I said, moving closer to her on the couch, my cup of tea in my hand (tea was the fiction we had both agreed upon to bring us together).

"Well, she wasn't that awful," said Jane, in the tone of one who wants to think only good of others. "I suppose she had her nice side." Then she gave up. "God knows what it was, though. I never saw it."

"Perhaps God *does* know," I said, rolling my eyes upward. Jane sighed. I moved closer, the teacup rattling in my hand.

"She was such a schemer," said Jane thoughtfully. "She was conniving every minute of the day. That was why she married Miles . . . he was the conductor and very important to the company. So she married him and then lo and behold she began to get some leads . . . though the marriage was always a farce."

"Didn't she like him?"

"Of course not . . . and after the first few months he was on to her, too. Only she'd never let him get a divorce. He was too useful to her, a perfect front . . ."

"And then he killed her."

Jane shuddered. "Don't even think it," she said in a low voice. "He's so wonderful . . . I mean as a conductor; I don't know him very well outside the theater. Anyway he's a nice man and Ella was a bitch and I see no reason for him to get in trouble on her account," she concluded spiritedly, disregarding all ethics in her emotional summary.

"I suppose he's the likeliest suspect," I said. I was curious about the whole affair, as anyone would be. It was an unusual experience to be involved in a murder during one's first day on a new job. Yet, aside from the novelty of my situation, it had occurred to me dimly that some end might be served by this event, that I might somehow be able to make use of this tragedy, an ignoble sentiment certainly but then I belong to an ignoble tribe which trades on the peculiarities and talents of others, even on their disasters.

"I guess so," said Jane unhappily. "Lord knows he hated her. On the other hand so did a lot of people. Eglanova, for instance."

"Why? What did she have against Ella?"

"Don't you know?" And for the first time (but not the last) I received that pitying dancer's glance which implied that though I might not be entirely a square I was none the less hopelessly ignorant of all that really mattered: the dance and its intricate politics. I said I didn't know, humbly.

"Mr. Washburn was all set to fire Eglanova this year. She's practically blind you know. It's got so even the audience notices it . . . why they even applaud her when she finishes a pirouette in the right direction . . . then she's always losing her partner in *Giselle*. She's lucky she's got Louis. He adores her and he follows her around on stage like a Saint Bernard. If she had any other partner she'd've ended up among the violins in the orchestra pit long ago."

"So Washburn was going to get rid of her?"

"I should say so. Only he acted as though she were retiring of her own free will. We were to end this season at the Met with a Gala Eglanova Evening, to celebrate her thirty-one years as a star; only now . . . well, I suppose she'll have to go the next season. You see Ella was all set to take her place."

"Can't they get somebody else?"

Jane looked as incredulous as any girl can at five in the morning after a tough night's performance and a questioning by the police. "You don't seem to realize that this is the oldest ballet company in the world and that it has to have a *prima ballerina assoluta* and there are only a half dozen of those in the world and they're all engaged like Markova, Fonteyn, Danilova, Toumanova, Alonso . . . or else too expensive for Mr. Washburn," she added, deflating somewhat the pretensions of the Grand Saint Petersburg Ballet. I knew already, from personal experience, that Mr. Washburn was a tight man with a dollar.

"So Eglanova might have cut that cable?" The memory of those shears still bothered me; I tried to think of something else . . . I had not yet mentioned finding them to the police . . . or to anyone.

"Oh, don't be silly," said Jane. But she had no other comment to make about this theory.

"She must've been awfully ambitious," I said sleepily; my eyes beginning to twitch with fatigue.

"Ella? Oh, I'll say she was. She wanted to do *Swan Lake* at the Met on opening night . . . instead of on Wednesday matinees and every night in all cities with a population under a hundred thousand. And she would've too."

"Was she that good?" It was hopeless to ask one dancer about the talents of another but I was thinking of something else now. I paid no attention to what we were saying. My hand was now on top of hers and I was so close to her that I could feel through my own body the quickened beating of her heart.

Jane told me very seriously that Ella had been a good actress and a good technician but that she had always been remarkably unmusical and that if she had not been married to the conductor she would probably never have become a star.

"Did she get on with Louis?" I asked, my lips so close to her cheek that I could feel the warmth of my own breath come back to me.

"I don't think he ever let her get away with anything. He's just as vain as she was only in a nice way. Everybody likes Louis. He pads, you know."

"He what?"

"You know . . . like a falsie: well, they say he wears one, too, when he's in tights."

"Oh, no, he doesn't," I said, remembering my little tussle with the ballet's glamour boy.

"You too?" She sat bolt upright.

"Me too what?"

"He didn't . . . go after you, too, did he?"

"Well as a matter of fact he did but I fought him off." And I told her the story of how I had saved my honor.

She was very skeptical. "He's had every boy in the company . . . even the ones who like girls . . . I expect he's irresistible."

"I resisted."

"Well . . ." And then it began.

5

"Jane." There was no answer. Light streamed into the room but she wore a black mask over her eyes, and nothing else . . . the sheets lay tangled in a heap upon the floor beside the bed. It was another hot day I could tell. Yawning, I sat up and looked at my watch which I had placed on the night table; I've always taken it off, ever since a girl from Vassar complained that it scratched. Ten-thirty.

I lit a cigarette and studied the body sprawled next to me in a position which, in any other woman, would have been unattractive. In her case, however, she could be suspended from a chandelier and she would look good enough to take home right then and there.

I leaned over and tickled her smooth belly, like pink alabaster, to become lyric, warm pink alabaster, gently curved, with hips strong and fatless and lovely breasts tilted neither up nor down nor sagging, but properly centered, the work of a first-rate architect: not one of those slapdash jobs you come across so often in this life. She sighed and moved away, not yet awake. I then tickled the breast nearest me and she said, very clearly, "You cut that out."

"That's not a very romantic way to begin the morning," I said.

She pulled off her mask and scowled in the sunlight which streamed into the high-ceilinged dusty room. Then she smiled when she saw me. "I forgot," she said. She stretched.

"I'm scared to look at the papers," I said.

She groaned. "And I thought it was going to be such a perfect day. It's so hot," she added irrelevantly, sitting up. I admired her nonchalance. She was the first girl I had ever known who had been agreeable and affectionate without ever once speaking of love. I decided that I was going to like ballet very much.

"I have a headache," she announced, blinking her eyes and pressing her temples with her hands.

"I got just the cure for it," I said, rolling toward her.

She took one look and said, "Not now. It's too hot." But her voice lacked conviction and our bodies met as we repeated with even greater intensity the act of the night before, our breath coming in short gasps until, at the climax, there was no one else in the whole world but the two of us on that bed, the sunlight streaming in the window and the springs creaking, our bodies making funny wet noises as the bellies pushed one against the other.

When it was over, Jane went into the bathroom and I lay with my eyes shut, the sweat drying on my body, as blissfully relaxed as that young man in the painting by Michelangelo. But then, in the midst of this euphoria, I decided that I should call Mr. Washburn and get my orders for the day. It was early of course for our business and, in ordinary times, no one would be stirring at this hour during the season but today with a murder on our hands . . . a murder. . . . It wasn't until that moment, lying contented and exhausted on a strange girl's bed that I realized the significance of what had happened, of what the sudden death of Ella Sutton might mean to all of us, including me, the newcomer, the fool who had found a pair of shears and. . . .

I got Mr. Washburn on the line. "Been trying to locate you," he said and I could tell from his voice that he was worried. "Get over to the Met at eleven, will you? The police are going to talk to us, to the principals."

"I'll be there, sir."

"Did you see the papers this morning?"

"Quite something, weren't they?" I said, implying I had read them which I had not.

"Made the front page . . . even of the *Times,*" said my employer in a voice which sounded almost joyous. "We'll have to change our strategy . . . but I'll go into all that when I see you."

I then called Miss Flynn at my own office.

"I tried to reach you at your home, Mr. Sargeant, *but there was no answer.*" Miss Flynn is the only human being I have ever known who could talk not only in italics but, on occasion, could make her silences sound as meaningful as asterisks.

"I was busy all night . . . working," I said lamely.

"I hope you will try and get some rest today, Mr. Sargeant."

"I hope so, too. But you know what happened . . ."

"Yes, I saw some mention of it in the *Times*. One of those dancers was murdered."

"Yes, and we're all being questioned. It's going to be quite a public relations job."

" * * * * * * * "

"I probably won't get to the office today . . . so refer my calls to me at the office of the ballet."

"Yes, Mr. Sargeant."

I then gave her some instructions about the night school, the hat company and the television actress who had just been voted Miss Tangerine of Central California by an old buddy of mine who lived out there and was a member of the Chamber of Commerce of Marysville.

Jane was dressed by the time I had finished . . . like all girls connected with the theater she could be a quick changer if she wanted. I told her that I had to join Washburn and the principals at the opera house. While I dressed it was agreed that we meet after tonight's performance and come directly here . . . presuming, of course, that there would be a performance. I had no idea of what the police attitude would be.

"I'll go take class now," she said, pinning her hair up. "Then I suppose I should go and see poor Magda."

"Magda who?" I had forgotten.

"The girl who fainted last night. She's a good friend of mine."

"The one who was pregnant?"

"How did you know?"

"Everybody knows," I said, as though I had been in ballet all my life. But then curiosity got the better of me. "Who was the father?"

Jane smiled. "I thought you would have found that out, too. *Everybody* knows."

"They forgot to tell me."

"Miles Sutton is the lucky man," said Jane, but she wasn't smiling now and I could see why.

II

I don't know when I'd seen so many gloomy faces as I did that morning in Eglanova's dressing room. Mr. Gleason of the Police Department had assembled the company's brass there, with the exception of Eglanova herself and Louis, neither of whom had yet arrived. But the others were present . . . including Miles Sutton who looked as though he hadn't slept in a week, his eyes glassy with fatigue, and Jed Wilbur who kept cracking his knuckles until I thought I'd go crazy and Mr. Washburn in a handsome summer suit, very grave, and Alyosha looking fairly relaxed, as well as the stage manager and a few other notables who stood about the room while Detective Gleason, a round pig of a man with a cigar, obligingly revealed to us the full splendor of the official mind.

"Where are those two dancers . . . Egg-something and Giraffe?"

Egg and Giraffe . . . pretty good, I thought, giving him an A for effort.

"They will be along shortly," said Mr. Washburn soothingly. "After all, this is very early for them to be up."

"Early!" snorted Gleason. "That's a funny way to run a business."

"It is an art, not a business," said Alyosha mildly.

Gleason looked at him suspiciously. "What is your name again?"

"Alyosha Petrovich Rudin."

"A Russian, eh?"

"Originally."

The detective scowled a xenophobe's scowl but made no comment. He had us where he wanted us but then again we were pretty hot stuff, too, and we had *him* if he got too frisky. I was quite sure that Mr. Washburn was in hourly contact with City Hall.

"Well, we'll start without them. First, I think you should all know that there's been a murder." He consulted a piece of paper which he held in his hand. "Ella Sutton was murdered last night at ten-thirty, by falling. The cable which was holding her thirty-eight feet above the stage was severed, except for one strand, by a party or parties as yet unknown, between the hours of four-thirty and ten P.M. . . . We have, by the way, what we believe to be the murder weapon: a pair of shears which are now being tested for fingerprints and also for metal filings, to see if they correspond with the metal of the cable." He paused and fixed us with a steely eye, as though expecting the murderer to burst into hysterical sobs and confess everything; instead it was I who almost burst into hysterical sobs, thinking of those damned shears and how I had handled them. I had several very bad minutes.

"Now, I'll be frank with you," said Gleason, who was obviously going to be no such thing, now or ever. "We could close down your show while we investigate but, for one reason and another, we've decided to let you finish up your last two weeks here, just as you planned, and we'll investigate when we can. Believe me when I say it's a real break for you." I turned to Mr. Washburn, the intimate of Kings and Mayors, but he was looking very bland indeed. "I want to warn you folks, though, that none of you is to take French leave, to disappear from the scene of the crime during your last week, or later, if we haven't wound this case up by then . . . and I think we will have, by then," he added ominously, looking, I swear, right at me, as though he'd already found my fingerprints on what was now called The Murder Weapon. I felt faint. Love and a possible accusation of being a murderer need a full stomach, coffee anyway.

"To be frank with you," said Gleason, obviously bent on being a good fellow, "it seems very likely that the murder was committed by someone closely connected with the theater, by someone who knew all about the new ballet and who had a grudge against Miss Sutton . . ." Bravo, I said to myself. You are cooking with gas, Gleason. I began to insult him in my mind . . . for some reason I was perfectly willing to let the murderer go undetected. Sutton was no great loss but then, of course, I am callous, having been an infantryman at Okinawa (wounded my first day in action, by a bullet in the left buttock . . . no,

I was *not* running away; the bullet ricocheted, I swear to God, and I was carried from the field, all bloody from my baptism of fire).

"I will," said Mr. Gleason, "interview each and every one of you, starting right now and continuing through the entire company, including the stagehands . . . every one, in short, who was backstage." He unfolded a long sheet of paper, a list of names. "Here is the list in the order in which I want to see you people. Will you have it put some place where the other members of the company can see it?" Mr. Washburn said that he would and motioned for the stage manager to take it outside and put it on the bulletin board.

When the stage manager returned, he was accompanied by Eglanova and Louis. Eglanova looked very distinguished in a black lace dress of mourning with a white feathered hat on her head, while Louis wore a pair of slacks and a sport shirt like the *Tennis Anyone?* juvenile he occasionally resembles.

"So sorry," said Eglanova, swooping down upon the Inspector. "You are the police? I am Madame Eglanova . . . this is *my* dressing room," she added, intimating that we had all better get the hell out of there.

"Pleased to meet you," said Gleason, obviously impressed.

"And I am Louis Giraud," said Louis with great dignity, but it didn't come off because Gleason was too busy explaining things to Eglanova who was carefully maneuvering him to the door, like a stalking lioness. In a few minutes we were all out of there and Gleason repaired to an office on the second floor to commence his interviews . . . the first, naturally enough, was Miles Sutton. I was number seven on the list, I noticed. Lucky seven?

I cornered Mr. Washburn outside in the street; we both had gone out, automatically, for the afternoon papers. "I've got something to tell you," I said.

"I want to hear only good news," said Mr. Washburn warningly. "I have had enough disaster to last me the rest of what, very likely, will be a short life. My heart is not strong."

"I'm sorry to hear that, sir, but I think you should know something about those shears."

"Those what?"

"The things the police thought the murderer cut the cable with."

"Well, what about them?"

"It just so happens that I found them last night in the wastebasket in Eglanova's room."

"What were they doing there?" Mr. Washburn was deep in the

Journal-American . . . we were still on the front page.

"Somebody put them there."

"Very likely . . . I wonder why they always spell Eglanova's name wrong? According to this account, it's all a Communist plot."

"Mr. Washburn, *I* moved those shears . . . I picked them up and I took them out of that dressing room and put them on top of the toolbox backstage."

"Very tidy. You'd be surprised at the size of our bill for tools every month . . . especially things getting lost. By the way, the box office reported that we're sold out until closing night. You better get *that* in the papers tomorrow."

"Yes sir, but I . . ."

"You know this may not be such a bad thing . . . I mean, of course, it's perfectly awful and God knows where I'm ever going to get a ballerina for next season . . . but it's certainly put *Eclipse* on the map. Everybody will want to see it from here to San Francisco, a real draw." At this moment, I found Mr. Washburn a trifle materialistic, even for an old-fashioned opportunist like me.

"Maybe Eglanova will go with the company again next year," I suggested, forgetting my own peril for a brief moment.

"But she wants to retire and we should let her," said Mr. Washburn, starting in on the *World-Telegram and Sun;* he made Eglanova's retirement sound like her choice rather than his.

"I hear Markova is tied up with her new company."

"True . . . she's too expensive anyway."

"And so are Toumanova, Alonso, Danilova and Tallchief," said I, repeating what Jane had told me the night before.

"Editorial in the *Telegram,*" said Mr. Washburn gravely. "They want to know if Wilbur is a Communist."

"I had forgotten all about that," I said truthfully.

"Well, I haven't. The Veterans Committee telephoned to say that their pickets would be back tonight and that they would have new placards, calling us the Murder Company as well as the Red Company."

"That's a laugh!"

"I am not sure on whom, though," said Mr. Washburn, studying the *Post* which had by far the best and sexiest pictures of Sutton, and no mention of the Red menace.

"Is Wilbur worried?"

"He seems to be. I'm supposed to have a talk with him this afternoon. Well, that's that," he said, handing the paper to me.

Outside the stage door a policeman in plain clothes lounged; he looked at us suspiciously as we entered.

"An armed camp!" exclaimed my employer with more gusto than I for one thought proper under the circumstances; our roles were reversed now: I was the one bothered by the publicity and investigation while he was the one who was meditating happily on free promotion and the coming tour with the customers flocking to see the "murder" ballet.

"By the way," I said, "who's going to dance the lead in *Eclipse* tonight . . . you have it scheduled, you know, and I should get a release out for the morning papers."

"Good God! Where's Wilbur?" The stage manager, hearing this, went to find the beleaguered choreographer.

"How would this Jane Garden do? I'm told she's very fine," I said, getting in a plug for the home team.

"It's up to him . . . after all we've got three soloists."

"I think she'd be great in it." Then, changing from my youthful, eager manner to that somewhat more austere manner which is more nearly me, I said, "About those shears that I found in Eglanova's room."

"What about them?" We went through the whole thing again and, for the second time in five minutes, he was upset.

"What I want to know is should I tell the police right now that I found the shears in her room and put them outside on the tool chest, or should I wait until the Inspector arrests me for murder, after finding my prints all over The Murder Weapon."

Mr. Washburn looked exactly like a man being goosed by the cold horns of the biggest, roughest dilemma this side of the Bronx Zoo. Needless to say, between sacrificing his star and his temporary press agent, he chose yours truly, as I suspected he would, to be offered up as a possible sacrifice to Miss Justice, that blind girl with the sword. "You can do something for me, Peter," he said, in the cozy voice of an impresario talking to a millionaire.

"Anything, sir," I said, very sincerely, looking at him with honest cocker spaniel eyes . . . little did he suspect that I was contemplating blackmail, that my mean little mind had seized upon a brilliant idea which would, if it worked, make me very happy indeed and if it didn't . . . well, I could always take a lie-detector test or something to prove that I hadn't eased Ella Sutton into a better and lovelier world.

"Say nothing about this, Son. Not until the season is over . . . just a week away. That's all I ask. I'm sure they won't go after you . . . absolutely sure. You have no motive. You didn't even know Sutton. On top of that . . . well, I have a little influence in this town, as you know. Believe me when I say there won't be any trouble."

"If you say so, Mr. Washburn, then I won't tell the police." I then asked that Jane Garden be given the lead in *Eclipse* (she was understudy anyway), and she got it. Perfidy had paid off.

"I suppose she'll be all right," said Wilbur a few minutes later when he'd been advised of this casting. "She's up in the part at least. I'd much rather have a dark-haired girl, but . . ."

"Garden should be very good," said Mr. Washburn. "You'd better rehearse her and Louis this afternoon."

"I'll go telephone her," I said, and I did. At first, she didn't believe it but then, when she did, she was beside herself and I knew we were going to have a pleasant time . . . champagne in bed, I decided, as I hung up.

My second official interview with the Inspector went off well enough.

"How old are you?"

"Twenty-eight."

"Where were you born?"

"Hartford, Connecticut."

"In the service?"

"Three and a half years . . . Pacific Theater of Operations . . . Army."

"What sort of work did you do upon discharge?"

"Went back to college . . . finished at Harvard."

"Harvard?"

"Yes, *Harvard.*" We glared at one another.

"What sort of work after that?"

"I was assistant drama critic on the *Globe* until a year ago when I opened my own office . . . public relations."

"I see. How long have you known, did you know, the deceased?"

"Who?"

"Miss Sutton . . . who do you think I meant? Mayor La Guardia."

"I'm sorry if I misunderstood you, Mr. Gleason." Oh, I was in splendid form, putting my head right into the noose, but what the hell . . . tonight there'd be champagne. "I met Miss Sutton the day I came to work for the ballet . . . yesterday afternoon."

"As what?"

"As special public relations consultant . . . that's what it says on that paper in front of you."

"Are you trying to get funny with me?"

"Certainly not." I looked offended.

"How well did you know the . . . Miss Sutton?"

"I met her yesterday."

"You never saw her outside of work then?"

"Not very often."

"How often?"

"Never, then."

"Well, which is it, never or occasionally?"

"Never, I guess, to speak of . . . maybe now and then at a party before I'd met her . . . that's all I meant."

"It would help if you say what you mean the first time."

"I'll try."

"Did she have any enemies that you know of?"

"Well, yes and no."

"Yes *or* no, please, Mr. Sargeant."

"No . . . not that I know of. On the other hand, I gather that nobody liked her."

"And why was that?"

"I'm told she wasn't very easy to work with and she was unpleasant to the kids in the company, especially the girls. She was set to be the big star when Eglanova retired."

"I see. Does Egg . . . lanova look forward to retiring?"

"Wouldn't you after thirty years in ballet?"

"I'm not in ballet."

"Well, neither am I, Mr. Gleason. I know almost as little about this as you."

Gleason gave me an extremely dirty look but I was full of beans, thinking about how I had handled Washburn.

"Was her marriage to Miles Sutton a happy one?"

"I suggest you ask him; I've never met him."

"I see." Gleason was getting a little red in the face and I could see that I was amusing his secretary, a pale youth who was taking down our conversation in shorthand.

"Now then: where were you at the dress rehearsal yesterday afternoon?"

"Backstage mostly."

"Did you notice anything unusual?"

"Like what?"

"Like . . . never mind. What were your movements *after* the rehearsal?"

"Well, I went out and had a sandwich; then I called up the different newspapers . . . about the Wilbur business. I got back to the theater about five-thirty."

"And you left it?"

"Not until after the murder last night."

"Who did you see when you returned at five-thirty, who was backstage?"

"Just about everyone, I suppose: Mr. Washburn, Eglanova, Giraud, Rudin . . . no, he wasn't there until about six, and neither was Miles Sutton now that I think of it."

"Is it customary for all these people to be in the theater such a long time before a performance?"

"I don't know . . . it was a première night."

"Eglanova was not in the première, though, was she?"

"No, but she often spends the day in the theater . . . so does Giraud. He sleeps."

"By the way, do you happen to know who will take Sutton's place tonight?"

I paused just long enough to sound guilty; I kicked myself but there was nothing to be done about it. "Jane Garden . . . one of the younger soloists."

But he missed the connection, I could see, and not until all the interviews had been neatly typed up and my fingerprints had been discovered on the shears would he decide that I had cut the cable so that Jane could dance the lead in *Eclipse*.

He asked me a few more questions to which I gave some mighty flip answers and then he told me to go, very glad to see the last of me, for that day at least. I have a dislike of policemen which must be the real thing since I'd never had anything to do with them up until now, outside of the traffic courts. There is something about the state putting the power to bully into the hands of a group of subnormal, sadistic apes that makes my blood boil. Of course, the good citizens would say that it takes an ape to keep the other apes in line but then again it is piteous indeed to listen to the yowls of those same good citizens when they come afoul the law and are beaten up in prisons and generally manhandled for suspected or for real crimes: at such moments they probably wish they had done something about the guardians of law and order when they were free. Well, it was no problem of mine at the moment.

I found Jane already downstairs in her rehearsal clothes. I gave her a big kiss and then, when she asked me if I had had anything to do with her getting the lead in *Eclipse* and I said that I certainly had, I got another kiss. She asked me all about the investigation.

"Everybody's being pumped," I said. "They just got through with me. You better go look on the bulletin board and find out what time they'll want to see you." We looked; and she was to be questioned at six o'clock.

"What did he want to know?"

"Just stuff. Where I was when it happened . . . who else was around, and gossip."

"What did you tell him?"

"Not much of anything . . . in the way of gossip: it's his job to find out those things."

"I suppose it is."

Wilbur and Louis appeared, both in work clothes. "Come on, Jane," said Louis. "We got work." He winked at me. "How're you doing, baby?"

I called him a rude but accurate name and marched off to telephone the newspapers about Jane's coming debut as a soloist . . . it wouldn't get in till tomorrow but then, perhaps, we might be able to get a few of the critics out to report on her the next night. Needless to say, we were scheduled to do *Eclipse* at every single performance until we closed. After I had made my calls and arranged for some photographs of Jane to be sent around by messenger, I left the building with every intention of going to get something to eat . . . I was getting light in the head from hunger and the heat. I was so giddy that I almost stepped on Miles Sutton who was lying face down in the corridor which leads from the office to the dressing rooms.

2

"What's going on here?" were, I am ashamed to say, my first words to what I immediately, and inaccurately, thought to be a corpse, the discarded earthly residence of our conductor who lay spread-eagled on his belly in front of the washroom door.

The figure at my feet moaned softly and, thinking of fingerprints, I nevertheless was a good Samaritan and rolled him over on his back, half expecting to see the hilt of a quaint oriental dagger sticking through his coat.

"Water," whispered Miles Sutton, and I got him water from the bathroom; he drank it very sloppily and then, rolling up his eyes the way certain comedians do when their material is weak, he sank back onto the floor, very white in the face. I trotted back into the bathroom, got another cup of water, returned, and splashed it in his face. This had the desired effect. He opened his eyes and sat up. "Must've fainted," he whispered in a weak voice.

"So it would appear," I said; at the moment there was very little the conductor and I had in common. I stood there for several seconds, contemplating him; then Sutton pulled out a handkerchief and dried his beard. His color was a little better now and I suggested that, all in all, it might be a good idea for him to stand up. I helped him to his feet. He lurched into the washroom; I waited until he came out.

"Must be the heat," he mumbled. "Sort of thing never happened before."

"It's a hot day," I said . . . it was remarkable how little we had to say to each other. "Do you feel O.K. now?"

"A bit shaky."

"I don't feel so good myself," I said, hunger gnawing at my vitals. "Why don't we get something to eat across the street? I'm Peter Sargeant, by the way; I'm handling publicity. I don't think Mr. Washburn introduced us."

We shook hands; then he said, dubiously, "I don't suppose I should hang around here. They may want me for the rehearsal."

"Come on," I said, and he did. Very slowly we walked down the brilliant sunlit street; shimmering waves of heat flickered in the distance and my shirt began to stick to my back. Miles, looking as though he might faint again, breathed hoarsely, like an old dog having a nightmare.

"Must have been something you ate?" I suggested out of my vast reservoir of small talk.

He looked rather bleak and didn't answer as we walked into an air-conditioned restaurant with plywood walls got up to look like the paneling in an old English tavern; both of us perked up considerably.

"Or maybe you got hold of a bad piece of ice last night." This was unworthy of me but I didn't care. I was thinking of food.

We got ourselves a booth and neither of us spoke until I had wolfed down a large breakfast and he had had several cups of coffee. By this time he was looking less like a corpse. I knew very little about him other than that he got good notices for himself and orchestra, that he conducted the important ballets with more than usual attention to the often eclectic performances of the Grand Saint Petersburg stars who have a tendency to impose their own tempo on that of the dead and defenseless composers. I disliked his face, but that means nothing at all. My character analyses based on physiognomy or intuition are, without exception, incorrect; even so I have many profound likes and dislikes based entirely on the set of a man's eyes or his voice. I did not like Sutton's eyes, I might add, large gray glassy eyes with immense black pupils, and an expression of constant surprise. He fixed me now with these startled eyes and said, "Did you talk to the Inspector?"

"Just for a little bit."

"What did he ask you?"

"Nothing much . . . the standard questions . . . where were you on the night of May twenty-seventh kind of thing."

"Such an awful thing to have happen," said the husband of the murdered woman with startling conventionality; well, at least he wasn't hypocrite enough to pretend to be grief-stricken. "I suppose everybody's told him we weren't getting along, Ella and me."

"I didn't," I said, righteously, "but obviously he knows. He wanted me to say that you hated her . . . I could tell by his questions."

"He practically accused me of murder," said Miles; I felt very sorry for him then not only because of the spot he was in but because I was quite sure that he *had* murdered her . . . which shows something or other about mid-twentieth-century morality: I mean, we seem to be less and less aroused by such things as private murders in an age when public murder is so much admired. If I ever get around to writing that novel it's going to be about this sort of thing . . . the difference between what we say and what we do—you know what I mean. Anyway, *I* didn't make the world.

"Well, you are a perfect setup," I said, cold-bloodedly.

"Setup?"

"Everybody in the company knew you wanted a divorce and that she wouldn't give it to you . . . I heard all about it my first hour with the company."

"That doesn't mean I'd kill her."

"No, but a cretin like Gleason would think that you were the logical one . . . and you are."

"I'm not so sure of that."

"What do you mean?"

"Well, there are others." He looked purposefully vague and I felt very compassionate; he *was* in a spot.

"Who?"

"Well, there's Eglanova." That did it; my instinct was right. Miles had cut the cable and then planted the shears in Eglanova's wastebasket. I wondered if he had managed to implicate her in his interview with Gleason.

"What did she have against Sutton?" Not that I didn't know.

"She was being retired against her will and Ella was the only available dancer with a big enough name to head the company . . . All the others are either tied up with contracts or else cost more than Washburn will pay. With Ella gone, he would have to let Eglanova dance another season."

"It seems awfully drastic," I said mildly.

"You don't know much about ballerinas," said Miles Sutton with the exhausted air of one who did. "Eglanova doesn't want to retire, ever; she feels she's at her peak and she would do anything to stay with the company."

"But that's still going a bit far."

"She hated Ella."

"So did just about everybody; they didn't all kill her . . . or maybe they did . . . formed a committee and . . ." But, no, this was getting a little too feckless, even for me. I subsided.

"Besides, who else could have done it? Who else would benefit as much by her death?" Well, you would, lover, I said to myself, you you you, wonderful you in the shadow of the electric chair. He must've read my mind, which isn't as difficult a feat as I sometimes like to think. "Aside from me," he added.

"So far as we know."

"So far as *I* know, and I should know . . . I was married to her seven years."

"Why wouldn't she let you have a divorce?"

He shrugged, "I don't know. She was like that . . . a real sadist. She married me when she was just a *corps de ballet* girl and of course I helped her up the ladder. I suppose she resented that. People usually resent the ones who help them."

"Why didn't you just go ahead and divorce her?"

"Too complicated," said Miles, evasively, looking away, tugging at his wiry orange beard. "By the way, will you be at the inquest tomorrow?"

I said no, that this was the first I'd heard of it.

"I have to be there," said Miles gloomily. "The funeral's after that."

"Church funeral?" I made a mental note to call the photographers.

"No, just a chapel in a funeral home. I got her a lot out at Woodlawn."

"Very expensive?"

"What? No, not very . . . the funeral home handled everything. Awfully efficient crowd."

"It's a big racket," I said.

"I know, but it saves all sorts of trouble."

"Open or closed casket at the service?"

"Closed. You see there was an autopsy this morning."

"What did they find?"

"I don't know. Gleason didn't say. Probably nothing."

"You know," I said, suddenly struck by a novel idea, "it might have been an accident after all."

Miles Sutton groaned. "If only it were! No, I'm afraid they've already proved that those shears did the trick. Gleason told me that the metal filings corresponded to the metal of the cable."

A cold chill went up my spine, and it wasn't the Polar Bear Airconditioning Unit for Theaters, Restaurants and Other Public Places. "What about fingerprints?"

"They didn't say."

"Fingerprints are pretty old-fashioned now, anyway," I brazened. "Every kid knows enough not to leave them around where the police might find them."

"Then Jed Wilbur could have done it," mused Sutton. "He never got along with Ella."

"But, as I keep pointing out, even in a ballet company dislike is insufficient motive for murder."

"Maybe he had a motive," said Miles mysteriously, kicking up some more dust. I'll say this for him, if Miles did his act with the police the way he did with me he'd keep them busy for a year untangling the politics and private relationships of the Grand Saint Petersburg Ballet.

"Well, motive or not, he's not the kind of person to endanger his career. That gentleman is the opportunist of all times. If he was going to knock off a dancer he wouldn't do it on the opening night of his greatest masterpiece . . ."

"Even so," said Miles, reminding me of the giant squid in those underwater movies . . . spreading black ink like a smoke screen at the first sign of danger. "And what about Alyosha Rudin?"

"What about him?"

"Didn't you know?"

"Know? Know what?"

"He was Ella's lover before she met me. He got her into ballet when she was just another chorine."

"Well, I'll be damned." This was a bit of gossip I hadn't heard.

"He's been in love with her all these years . . . even after she married me."

"Why would she marry you to get ahead when she had the *régisseur* of the company in love with her?"

Miles chuckled. "He wouldn't help her . . . thought she couldn't dance classical roles worth a damn . . . which was quite true, then. She was just another little girl who hadn't studied enough. But he didn't take into account her ambition, which I did. I got her solos in spite of him and she was always good. She was one of those people who could do anything thing you gave her to do well, even though you might have thought she'd fall flat on her face."

"And Alyosha?"

"He was surprised how well she turned out."

"And he stayed in love with her?"

"So she always said."

"He seems a little old for that kind of thing."

Miles grunted to show that I was too young to know the facts of age. Then we paid our checks and went back to the theater. A crowd of newsmen met us at the door. Miles scooted inside quickly and I paused to butter them up a little, promising them impossible interviews in my dishonest press-agent way; they were on to my game but we had a pleasant time and I *was* able to tell them about the funeral the next day; I promised them full details later, time and place and so on.

I watched the end of the rehearsal. I knew that, as a rule, rehearsals which involve just the principals don't take place on the stage but at the West Side studio; in this case, however, Wilbur had insisted on rehearsing Louis and Jane on stage to the music of one piano. He wanted to get Jane used to the stage, immediately.

She looked very efficient, I thought, as I sat on the first row and watched her move through the intricate *pas de deux* with Louis; she acted as though she had been dancing leads all her life and I experienced a kind of parental pride. Wilbur seemed pleased; especially with the way she did her turns fifteen feet above the stage, scaring the life out of me as I recalled the night before . . . it was just possible that we had some homicidal maniac in the company who enjoyed seeing ballerinas take fatal pratfalls. If Jane was at all aware of any danger she certainly didn't show it, as she pretended to eclipse the sun with a transfigured expression that I had seen on her face only once before, that morning when she had slid blissfully into a hot bath.

"All right, kids, that's enough for today. You'll be fine, Jane," said Jed Wilbur as she came floating down out of the ceiling. "Remember to take it a little slower in your solo. Keep it muted, lyric. Remember what you're doing . . . when in doubt go slow. The music will hold you up. You have a tendency to be too sharp in your line, too classical . . . blur it a little." And the three walked offstage. I headed for the office where we had the largest sack of mail I think I have ever seen . . . requests for tickets, for souvenir fragments of the cable, as well as advice from ballet lovers on how to conduct the investigation; I'll say one thing for the balletomanes, they really know their stuff; they follow the lives and careers of their favorites with rapt attention and remarkable shrewdness. Many of the letters that I glanced at openly suggested that Miles Sutton and his late wife had not been on the best of terms . . . now how could strangers have known that? From the columnists?

Mr. Washburn summoned me into the inner office, a spacious room with a thick carpet and a number of Cecil Beaton photographs of our stars, past and present, on the walls. He looked fit, I thought, in spite of the heat and excitement.

"The police have been very agreeable," he chuckled, handing me one of those special filtered cigarettes which I particularly dislike. I took it anyway. "They have consented not only to let us finish our season but, after the inquest tomorrow, to conduct the investigation a little more discreetly than had been Gleason's intention." Mr. Washburn looked like a very satisfied shark at that moment . . . one who had been swimming about all day in the troubled waters of City Hall. "There'll be two plainclothes men backstage at every performance and, of course, no member of the company is allowed to leave New York . . . *and* they all must be available at a moment's notice, leave messages where they can be found."

"What's our policy about the funeral tomorrow afternoon?" I asked, after I had first assured my employer that his wishes were, as always, my command.

Mr. Washburn frowned. "I suppose the principals had better attend. I'll be there of course . . . you, too."

"And the press?"

He gave me a lecture on the dignity of death, the privacy of sorrow; after which he agreed that the press should be fully represented at the last rites.

Then I asked if I should give Jane the full star treatment and he said we should first wait and see what the reviewers would have to say about her . . . needless to say they were all turning up again tonight. After that, he gave me some routine orders, ending with the announcement that Anna Eglanova would tour another year with the company, her thirty-second year as a star.

"When did you sign her?"

"This afternoon. She changed her mind about retiring, as I knew she would." He was very smooth.

Neither of us made any mention of the murder. Mr. Washburn had taken the public line that it had all been an accident, that no one connected with his company could have done such a thing but that of course if the police wanted to investigate, well, that was their right. In private he also maintained this pose and for all I knew he really believed it. In any case, his main interest was the box office and that had never been so healthy since Nijinski danced a season with the company a long time ago. If someone had the bad taste to murder a fellow artist he would wash his hands of them.

3

I was almost sick to my stomach during that night's performance . . . experiencing double stage fright for Jane: first, because it was her big chance, as they say in Technicolor movies, and second, because of that cable.

Everyone in the audience was also keyed up. They looked like a group of wolves waiting for dinner. There was absolute silence all through the ballet . . . even when Louis, who is after all a big star, came on stage with that pearly smile which usually gets all the girls and gay boys.

Jane was better than I thought she would be. I don't know why but you never regard your lover as being remarkably talented; you never seem to think her able to do anything at all unusual or brilliant unless, of course, she's a big star or very well known when you first meet her, in which case, you soon discover that she's not at all what she's cracked up to be . . . but Jane floored me and, I am happy to say, the critics, too. She lost the music once or twice and there was a terrible moment when Louis fumbled a lift, when she sprang too soon and I thought they would land in a heap on the stage but both recovered like real professionals and by the time she began her ascent by cable I knew that she was in, really there at last.

I don't need to tell you that I watched her rise in the air, slowly turning, with my heart thudding crazily and all my pulses fluttering. Even when the curtain fell I half expected to hear a crash from backstage. But it was all right and there she was, a moment later, standing on the stage with Louis, the *corps de ballet* behind them, as the audience roared its excitement, relief, disappointment . . . everything, every emotion swept over that stage like surf on a beach. She took seven curtain calls, by herself, and received all four of my bouquets as well as two others, from strangers.

I ran backstage and found her in Sutton's dressing room (now hers) with most of the company congratulating her, out of relief as well as admiration. I think they were all afraid that something might happen again. . . .

Then the stage manager ordered everybody to get upstairs and change and I was left alone with Jane in the dressing room, among the flowers and telegrams from those friends who had been alerted.

"I'm glad it's over," she said at last, her eyes gleaming, still breathing hard.

"So am I. I was terrified."

"Me too."

"Of that cable?"

"No, just the part. I didn't have time to think of anything else. You have no idea what it's like to come out on a stage and know that every eye is on you."

"It must be wonderful."

"It is! It is!" She slipped out of her costume and I dried her off with a towel . . . her skin glowed, warm and rich, like silk. I kissed here, here and there.

4

There is no need to describe my evening with Jane. It was a memorable one for both of us and, next morning, the sun seemed intolerably bright as we awakened, showered, got dressed, ate breakfast . . . all in a terrible hung-over silence which did not end until, of mutual accord, still without a word, we each took an Empirin tablet and together threw out the three empty champagne bottles (Mumm, Rheims, France);

then I spoke: " 'April,' " I said thickly, " 'is the cruelest month.' "

"This is May," said Jane.

"And twice as cruel. I have a strange feeling that during the night the spores of some mysterious fungus or moss, wafted down from the planet Venus, lodged themselves in my brain, entering through some unguarded orifice. Everything is fuzzy and blurred and I don't hear so well."

"You sound like you're still lit," said Jane, putting on a pink negligee which she had once bought at a sale to make herself look seductive over the morning coffee. Wearing only jockey shorts, I posed like Atlas before the full-length mirror on the bathroom door.

"Do you think I'd make a dancer?"

"You've made me, darling," she said.

"Shall I wash your mouth out with soap?"

"I'm sorry. It won't happen again."

"Not even on alternate Wednesdays?"

"That's matinee day . . . when I do *Eclipse,* twice." And that was the end of our little game. In case you should ever have an affair with a dancer I recommend total resignation to the fact that the Dance comes first; not only in their lives (which is all right) but also in *your* life (which is not, unless you're a dancer, too, or connected with it the way I am). After a time you will gradually forget all about the other world of Republicans and Democrats, Communists and Capitalists, Hemingway, the D. and D. of Windsor and Leo Durocher. I suppose in a way it's kind of a refuge from the world, like a monastery or a nudist colony . . . except for the tourists: the lives of dancers are filled with the comings and goings of little friends and admirers, autograph hounds and lovers, and you never know who is likely to turn up backstage in hot pursuit of one of the girls, or boys. I've been very surprised, believe me, at certain respectable gentlemen who have unexpectedly revealed a Socratic passion for one of our dancing boys. If I should ever decide to go into the blackmail game I could certainly get some handsome retainers!

Midway through an analysis of her last night's performance in *Eclipse,* the phone began to ring: friends and relatives of the new star . . . so I left her to enjoy their admiration.

It was another hot day, windless and still, with not a cloud in the harsh blue sky. I walked to our office, keeping in the shade of buildings, enjoying the occasional blasts of icy air from the open doors of restaurants and bars.

The newspapers were very gratifying. We were still on the front page, or near it, and the *Globe* had a feature article on the life of Ella Sutton, implying, as did nearly all the other papers, that an arrest would soon be made, that the murderer was her husband . . . naturally, they all kept this side of libel; even so it was perfectly clear that they thought him guilty . . . all except the *Mirror* which thought it was a Communist plot. The *Globe* carried a six-column story of Ella's life with pictures of her from every phase of what turned out to be a longer and more varied career than even I had suspected. Dancers are such liars (and so are press agents, God knows) that as a result the facts of any star's life are so obscure that it would take a real detective to discover them, or else a good reporter with access to a first-rate morgue, like the *Globe's*.

There was nobody in the office; except one secretary, another sack of mail, and so many messages marked urgent that I didn't bother to look at any of them; instead, I just relaxed and read the true story of Ella's life. I was surprised to note that she was thirty-three years old when she crossed the shining river so abruptly, that she had been dancing professionally for twenty years, in burlesque, in second-rate musical comedies and, finally, in the celebrated but short-lived North American Ballet Company which was to ballet in the thirties what the Group Theater was to the drama . . . only a good deal more left wing than the Group, if possible. There was a photograph of her at that time all done up like a Russian peasant woman with her eyes looking north to the stars. When the North American folded, she danced for a time in night clubs; then, just before the war, Demidovna emerged on our startled ken, to be rechristened the next year Ella Sutton, prima ballerina but never *assoluta*. It was a good piece and I made a mental note to call the *Globe* and find out who had written it . . . the by-line Milton Haddock meant nothing, I knew.

The next few hours were occupied with business . . . the ballet's and my own. Miss Flynn implied that my presence in my office might make a good impression. I promised to drop by later. It wasn't until I had finished my twentieth phone call and dispatched my eleventh bulletin to an insatiable press that Mr. Washburn phoned me to say that the inquest had been held without excitement and that I had better get over to the funeral home on Lexington Avenue where Ella Sutton was to make her last New York appearance.

All the principals were there when I arrived, including the photographers. Eglanova wore the same black lace dress and white plumed hat that she had worn the day before and she looked very cool and serene, like a figure carved in ice. Louis had broken down and put on a blue suit and a white shirt, but no tie . . . while Alyosha, Jed Wilbur and Mr. Washburn all managed to look very decorous indeed. Miles looked awful, with red gritty eyes and a curiously blotched face. His hands shook and once or twice during the ceremony I thought he would faint . . . now just what was wrong with him? I wondered. He seemed not always to remember where he was and several times he yawned enormously . . . one photographer, quicker and less reverent than his fellows, snapped Miles in the middle of a yawn, getting the picture of the week for, when they ran it the next day, the newspapers commented: husband of murdered star enjoying a joke at funeral. I don't need to say that everything connected with the death of Ella Sutton was in the worst possible taste and, consequently, we had the most successful season in the history of American ballet.

The service was brief, inaccurate and professional. When it was over, the casket and at least a ton of flowers were carried out of the room by four competent-looking young thugs in ill-fitting cutaways and the long journey to Woodlawn began, three limousines transporting the funeral party. If Ella had had any family they did not choose to appear and so she was buried with only her ungrieving husband and her professional associates at her grave. I must admit that there are times when I hate my work, when I wish that I had gone on and taken my doctorate at Harvard and later taught in some quiet university, lecturing on Herrick and Marvell, instead of rushing about with side shows like this, trying to get the freaks in to look at some more freaks. Well, another day another dollar as the soldiers in the recent unpleasantness used to remark.

"How is the investigation coming?" I asked Mr. Washburn as we drove back to town; Alyosha sat silently on the back seat with us while two girl soloists sat up front with the driver.

"I'm afraid I'm not in Mr. Gleason's confidence," said Mr. Washburn easily. "They seem very busy and they seem quite confident . . . but that's all a part of the game, I'm told . . . to pretend they know who it is so that the guilty party will surrender. Not that I, for one minute, think any member of the company is involved."

Mr. Washburn's unreality had a wonderfully soothing effect on me; I responded just like a prospective patron.

We both were rudely jolted out of this quiet mood when, upon arriving at the theater, a plain-clothes man announced that Gleason would like to see me. I exchanged a startled glance with Mr. Washburn who turned visibly gray, thinking no doubt of those shears, of

Eglanova's being involved in a scandal, of no season this fall because of no star.

Gleason, smoking a slobbery, ill-smelling cigar, looked every inch a Tammany man. His secretary sat at another desk, shorthand pad before him.

"Come in, Mr. Sargeant." Oh, this was bad I thought.

"How are you today, Mr. Gleason?"

"I have some questions I want to ask you."

"Anything you want to know," I said graciously.

"Why didn't you mention at our previous interview that you had handled those shears?"

"What shears?"

"The Murder Weapon."

"But I don't remember handling them."

"Then how do you explain the fact that your fingerprints are on them . . . yours and no one else's?"

"Are you sure they're my fingerprints?"

"Now look here, Sargeant, you're in serious trouble. I suggest for your own good you take a more constructive attitude about this investigation or . . ." He paused, ominously, and I saw in my mind's eye the rubber hose, the glaring Klieg lights and finally a confession thrust under my bloody hand for that shaky signature which would send me to the gates of heaven for the murder of a ballerina I had never known, much less killed. It was too terrible.

"I was just asking, that's all. I mean you never did fingerprint me . . ."

"We have ways," said the Inspector. "Now what were you doing with those shears between dress rehearsal and the murder?"

"I wasn't doing anything with them."

"Then why . . ."

"Are my fingerprints on them? Because I picked them up off the floor and put them on top of the tool chest."

Gleason looked satisfied. "I see. And are you in the habit of picking up tools off the floor—is that your job?"

"No, it's not my job, but I *am* in the habit of picking things up . . . I'm very neat."

"Are you trying to be funny?"

"I don't know why you keep accusing me of trying to amuse you . . . it's the last thing I'd try to do. I'm just as serious about this as you are. More so, because this scandal could louse up the whole season,"

I added, piously, speaking the language of self-interest which men of all classes and nations understand.

"Then will you kindly explain why you happened to pick up The Murder Weapon and place it on that tool chest."

"I don't know why."

"But you admit that you did?"

"Of course . . . you see I stepped on them and almost fell," I lied: how many years for perjury? threescore and ten; can I get there by amber light? yes, and back again.

"Now, we're getting somewhere. Why did you step on them?"

"Don't you mean where?"

"Mr. Sargeant . . ."

I spoke quickly, cutting him short, "I'm not sure just where I was." (This uncertainty might save me yet, I thought, watching that grim youth take down my testimony . . . well, I wasn't under oath yet.) "Somewhere near the dressing rooms. I damn near fell. Then I looked down and saw those things at my feet and so I picked them up and put them on the box."

"What time was this?"

"About ten-thirty."

"*After* the murder?"

"Well, yes."

"Didn't you think it peculiar that a pair of shears should be lying out in the open like that?"

"I had other things on my mind."

"Like what?"

"Well, Ella Sutton, for instance . . . she had been killed a few minutes before."

"And you made no connection between the shears and her death?"

"Of course not. Why should I? For all we knew at the time, the cable might have broken by itself."

"When you did discover that the cable had been cut, why didn't you tell me at our last interview that you had handled The Murder Weapon?"

"Well, it just slipped my mind."

"That is no answer, Mr. Sargeant."

"I'd like to know what you want to call it then?" I was getting angry.

"Do you realize that you could be under suspicion right now for the murder of Ella Sutton?"

"I don't realize any such thing. In the first place you'll find that my fingerprints are on the cutting end of the shears, not the handle . . . also the fact that there are no other prints on it means that whoever *did* cut the cable had sense enough to wipe the shears clean."

"How do you know there were no other prints?"

"Because you said there weren't . . . and, in case you still aren't convinced, I may as well tell you that I had less motive than anyone in the company for killing Sutton. I told you I didn't know the woman, and that's the truth."

"Now, now," said the Inspector with a false geniality that made his earlier manner seem desirable by comparison. "Don't get hot under the collar. I realize that you had no motive . . . we've checked into all that. Of course it doesn't do your girl friend any harm, having Ella Sutton gone, but that of course would hardly be reason enough for murder . . . *I* realize that."

He was playing it dirty now but I said nothing; he had no case and he knew it. He was only baiting me, trying to get me to say something in anger which I would not, under other circumstances, say . . . something about Miles or Eglanova, or whoever they suspected. Well, I would disappoint him; I composed myself and settled back in my chair; I even lit a cigarette with the steadiest hand since the 4-H Club's last national convention.

"What I would like to know, though, is the exact position of the shears, when you first stumbled over them."

"That's hard to say. The north end of the stage, near the steps which go up to the dressing rooms."

"Whose rooms are there?"

"Well, Sutton's was, and Eglanova's, and the girl soloists share a room. The men are all on the other side."

"Tell me, Mr. Sargeant, who do *you* think killed Ella Sutton?" This was abrupt.

"I . . . I don't know."

"I didn't ask you if you knew . . . we presume you don't know. I just wondered what your hunch might be."

"I'm not sure that I have one."

"That seems odd."

"And if I did I wouldn't be fool enough to tell you . . . not that I don't want to see justice triumph and all that, but suppose my guess was wrong? . . . I'd look very silly to the person I'd accused."

"I was just curious," said Gleason, with that same spurious air of good fellowship and I suddenly realized, like a flash, that, motive or not,

I was under suspicion . . . as an accomplice after the fact or during the fact or even before it for all I knew. Gleason was quite sure that I was, in some way, on the murderer's side.

This knowledge froze me and the rest of our talk was mechanical. I do remember, however, wanting to ask him why he hadn't arrested Miles Sutton yet. It was very strange.

III

"And then I told him that I thought I'd stumbled over the shears backstage, on my way to the dressing rooms."

"Good boy." Mr. Washburn was properly appreciative, having no reason yet to regret that favor he'd granted me the day before at the point of a gun or, rather, of a pair of shears.

"I wish, however, to record my serious unease, Mr. Washburn. I didn't like Gleason's questions. Just between us and the *New York Globe* he is about to pull something."

"But, my dear boy, that's what he's paid for. He will have to make an accusation soon or the city will be angry with him. That's the price of office."

"I think he suspects *me*."

"Now don't be melodramatic. Of course he doesn't."

"I don't mean of the murder, but . . . well, of being connected with it. My story about finding what is officially known as The Murder Weapon just didn't go down. He knows it was left some place else."

"You don't think . . ." My employer looked alarmed.

"I just don't know." And we left it at that.

On the way back to the office, I stopped off at Eglanova's Fifty-second Street apartment. She had invited me to come see her and I knew that she was always at home to those she liked, which was almost anyone who would pay a call on her.

She had the whole second floor of a brownstone to herself; it had been her home for twenty years and, consequently, it seemed now like a room from a Chekhov play: Czarist Russian in every untidy detail, even to the bronze samovar and the portraits of the Czar and Czarina, signed, on the piano, a grand affair, covered with an antique lace shawl and decorated with several more silver-framed photographs, of Karsavina, Nijinski and Pavlova. "They are my family," Eglanova was accustomed to say to casual visitors, waving her long sinewy hand at the photographs, including the Russian Royal Family as well as the dancers. Over the mantel was the famous painting of Eglanova in *Giselle*, her greatest moment in the theater . . . 1918.

Her maid opened the door and, without comment, ushered me into the presence.

"It is Peter!" Eglanova, wearing an old wrapper, sat by the bay window near the piano, looking out at a bleak little garden in the back where one sick tree grew among the tin cans and torn newspapers. She put down the copy of *Vogue* she was reading and gave me her hand. "Come sit by me and keep me company."

I sat down in a papier-mâché Victorian chair and she said something in Russian to her maid who appeared, a moment later, from the kitchen with two ordinary drinking glasses full of hot tea and lemon. "It is just right thing for hot day," said Eglanova and we toasted each other gravely. Then she offered me some candy, rich creamy chocolates which made me sick just looking at them. "All boys like candy," she said emphatically. "You sick maybe? or drink too much? American boys drink too much."

I agreed to that all right . . . if anything causes this great civilization of ours to fall flat on its face it will be the cocktail party. I thought of those eighteenth-century prints of Rowlandson and Gilray and Hogarth, all the drunken mothers and ghastly children wallowing in gin in the alleys . . . it makes you stop and think. I thought longingly for several seconds of a gin and tonic.

"I couldn't take class again today . . . too hot. I perish." Contrary to vulgar legend the lives of great ballerinas are not entirely given up to a few minutes of graceful movement every night followed by champagne drunk out of their toeshoes till dawn, in the company of financiers . . . no, most of their time is spent in filthy rehearsal halls, inhaling dust, or else in class, daily, year in year out, practicing, practicing even after they are already prima ballerinas. It occurred to me, suddenly, irrelevantly, that Eglanova was the same age as my mother.

"I think Jane Garden is taking class this afternoon."

"Such darling girl! I hear she is your *petite amie*. So good for both of you."

"Oh sure . . . it's wonderful." News travels fast, I thought.

"I'm so happy to see good children happy. Every night?"

"What?" for a moment I didn't understand; then I blushed. "Except on Wednesday, I guess, when she's too tired."

"Just like me!" Eglanova laughed, a wonderful deep peasant laugh. "My husband Alexey Kuladin (he was prominent lawyer in Russia before) could never understand about Wednesday . . . I tell him about matinee but he would say: what difference?" She chuckled; we drank tea and Eglanova asked me more questions about what Jane and I did and what my habits had been previous to our affair. I told her a number of stories, mostly true, and she loved them. She was like one of those old women you read about who brood over an entire village and are never shocked no matter what happens . . . good witches. She made everything seem completely natural which, of course, it is or should be . . . she even regarded Louis with delight. "Where does he get the energy? where?" I had just told her about my run-in with him. "He works hard most of the day and at performance. Then he goes out and he drinks, oh, like an American, or maybe Russian . . . then he picks up one tough boy; then maybe another later on, not counting the people in the theater. It is wonderful! Such vitality! So manly!"

I wasn't convinced of the manly end of it but then it all depends on how you look at such things . . . he certainly acts like a man and there may be, who knows, not much difference between nailing a boy to the bed and treating a girl in like manner; it's all very confusing and I intend one day to sit down and figure the whole thing out. It's like that poem of Auden's, one of whose quatrains goes:

> Louis is telling Anne what Molly
> Said to Mark behind her back;
> Jack likes Jill who worships George
> Who has the hots for Jack.

Kind of flip but the legend of our age. Anyway, it may all be a matter of diet.

Eglanova wolfed down a couple of chocolates; I tried to recall if she were married at the moment but when I attempted straightening out in my mind the various marriages and divorces and widowhoods, some known and others suspected, I found I could not remember even half the names, mostly Russian ones, of her husbands and protectors . . . as they used to call boyfriends in the wicked days before the First World War.

"She will be lovely dancer," said Eglanova, her mouth full of chocolate.

"Jane? I think so, too."

"She is warm . . . here." Eglanova touched her liver, the source, she said, of a woman's deepest emotion. A man's was somewhere south of the liver and much less reliable as a center of intensity and artistic virtue.

"Do you like her in *Eclipse?*"

"Very much. So strong. Is bad ballet of course."

"Bad?"

"Very bad. Just tricks. We do all those things in nineteen twenty. We groan and suffer on stage for not enough love. We act like machines. We did everything then. Now American boys think it modern. Ha!" She gestured scornfully, sweeping the copy of *Vogue* off onto the floor.

"When did you see it?"

"Last night only . . . I was in final ballet so I went around front."

"Sutton did it well, too."

Eglanova's face darkened. "Such tragedy!" she murmured intensely.

"The funeral was pretty awful."

"Disgusting! Miles is fool!"

"I guess he was too broken up to make much sense about the arrangements."

"Broken up? But why? He loathed her."

"Still . . . it's a terrible thing to have happen."

"Ah!" She looked menacing. "If ever woman needed murder she did. But Miles was fool."

"Why?"

Eglanova shrugged. "How can he get away? It is so obvious. I know . . . you know . . . they, the public, know."

"But why don't the police arrest him?"

She spread her hands, yellow diamonds gleamed in dusty settings. "It is like ballet. You go slow. You introduce themes. Male solo. Female solo. *Ensemble. Pas de deux.* They know what they must do."

This unexpected coldness was too much for me. "You sound as if you want him to be found out."

"It is not what *I* want . . . no, he is fool. His only hope was they could not prove he did it. But they always can once they know. Today they almost did."

"When?"

"This morning at the . . . what they call it?"

"Inquest?"

"What funny word! Yes, they make it clear they watch him. He will not conduct tonight . . . or ever!" she added . . . this time like a wicked witch placing a curse.

"You sound as if you hated him."

"I? *I* hate Miles? He is best conductor I have had since Paris. I shall grieve when he is gone . . . you may be confident. No, I am angry with him. He wants to kill wife . . . fine! I am all for it . . . like nature: get rid of what does not make you happy. If he tell me first, if he come to me for advice, I say, certainly go kill her but do it natural . . . so you won't be caught. What is point of getting rid of nuisance only to be put away yourself? I have contempt for bad artists. He is hysterical fool. He lose his head. She refuses to give him divorce so he rushes backstage and cuts cable. Then he *is* in trouble."

"Perhaps he didn't do it?"

"Oh yes he did . . . Miles is only person who is big fool enough to do it that way. I push her out window in fit of anger. Ivan or Alyosha would poison her. Jed Wilbur would shoot her . . . Louis he would strangle her. Psychology!" said Anna Eglanova, winking solemnly at me.

"You seem to have thought a lot about it."

"Who has not? Remember I am the one who must dance with that assistant conductor leading the orchestra always two bars behind me who am *always* on beat. *I* am martyr to this man's foolishness."

"Are you glad of the new season?"

Eglanova sighed, "Ah, Peter, I am old, I think. Thirty-one years is a long time to do *Swan Queen.*"

"But you'll never retire?"

"They will carry me protesting from the stage!" she laughed. "They will have to kill me, too. And I tell you one thing . . . no fall from a cable would break *these* tough bones!" and she slapped her thighs.

Alyosha Rudin, in a white suit, stood in the doorway, bowing. "Shall I go away?" he asked gallantly.

"My old friend has caught me in a compromising situation! Defend your honor, Alyosha! challenge him! I demand it!"

He smiled and took my hand, forcing me gently back into my chair. "Don't get up. I will sit here." And he pulled up a deep leather chair and joinded us by the bow window. "I am too old for duels."

"How he has changed!" mocked Eglanova.

"But only for the better, Anna, like you."

"For that I give you chocolates." He actually ate one, I saw, marveling at his constitution . . . in this heat a lettuce leaf seemed too heavy for my stomach.

"I have been with Miles," said the old man. "He is in terrible state. I think he will have a breakdown, or worse."

"His own fault."

"Be charitable, Anna."

"I am not responsible for his condition. I told him six months ago to divorce Ella no matter what she said . . . go ahead, I say, you have one life; you don't live forever . . . go ahead, I say, and divorce her whether she likes it or not. What can she do? That's what I told him."

"But, Anna, obviously she *could* do something otherwise he wouldn't have waited like this; and then . . ."

"Killed her! Such big fool!"

"We know no such thing."

"Oh, we don't 'know no such thing,' " mocked Eglanova. "Tell that to this fat and ugly man who smokes cigars . . . tell *him.*"

"I know it looks very bad."

"Oh . . . but I forget. The little one . . ."

"Magda? Her family is with her. What more?"

"Ah, what more indeed!"

"Then you know about Magda?" They both looked surprised, as though I had suddenly asked where babies came from.

"There are no secrets here," said Alyosha gently.

"And now, can you not understand why I am furious with that idiot? It is all right to kill the wicked, to kill oneself, but *not* to hurt an innocent, oh, that is not moral . . . I swear that is wrong . . . Alyosha, tell me, tell him, that it is wrong."

"Sad . . . too sad," murmured the old man, accepting tea from the maid.

"Has Miles been to see her?" I asked.

"I think so," said Alyosha, "as often as possible . . . but it's not been easy."

"The police?"

Alyosha nodded. "It is the end of Miles if they find out and they will certainly find out . . . something which is known to fifty people is hardly a secret."

"The fool got desperate," said Eglanova, pointing her feet. "She would not free him and there was the other girl *enceinte* . . . such mess!"

"Why was he afraid to divorce Ella?"

"Who can tell," said Alyosha uneasily.

"Who can tell? Ha! I can tell . . . in this room at least. She would have exposed him. *She* was capable of that . . . he told me once that she'd threatened to make public private things if there was divorce against her."

"What private things?" I asked.

"Anna!" Alyosha's usually gentle voice was harsh and warning . . . the way it was at rehearsal when the *corps de ballet* was off.

"Why make such secret? It is obvious to all but a baby like this. Miles takes drugs . . . not little ones like so many music people, no, big ones, dangerous, expensive ones. The sort that will kill you. *I* should know. My husband Feodor Mihailovitch died from opium at the age of thirty. He was big man, bigger than you, Peter, but when he died he weighed five stone . . . how much is that? seventy pound!"

2

Miles Sutton was not at the theater that night. According to the note on the bulletin board, he was home, sick, and until further notice the orchestra would be under the direction of Rubin Gold, a bright nervous young man with insufficient experience and a regrettable tendency to follow the music instead of the dancers.

After taking care of my usual chores at the box office, getting all the movie stars in their seats and one thing or another, I went back to Jane's dressing room, my first glimpse of her since our hung-over morning.

She was just getting into her tights when I marched into the dressing room. "Good God! You frightened me."

"You don't expect your buddy to knock, do you—or send a note back?"

"Of course not." She went on with her dressing in spite of a number of distracting things which I thought of to do to her just then, those little peculiarities of behavior which are always a lot of fun at the time but might look alarming to a man from Mars, or even to a man from the police department. "I don't know why I'm so jittery," she said. "But I tell you I *know* something's going to happen."

"You mean to the cable?"

She yelped and looked at me furiously. "Don't even *suggest* such a thing! No, I was thinking of Miles. Everybody says the police are ready to arrest him."

"What's been puzzling me is why they didn't do it a long time ago."

"I don't know . . . not enough evidence . . . oh, darling, I just feel awful."

I had a brave masculine moment, holding her in my arms while she shuddered a bit and gave way to some healthy old-fashioned female nerves; then, remembering that she was a dancer and not a woman, she broke the clinch and began to paint her face.

"Did you see Magda today?" I asked.

She nodded. "The poor thing's out of her mind . . . her family isn't much help either. They're very Boston and though they're perfectly nice to her you can see they think it's the end of the world, her carrying the bastard child of a murderer . . . oh, it *does* sound awful, doesn't it?" Intently, she placed a set of eyelashes in place.

"How come you never lose them?"

"Lose what?"

"Eyelashes . . . Sutton used to lose them every performance according to legend."

Jane laughed. "I thought you asked me why I never lost babies . . . I stick them on with a special mess . . . all the girls use it. Oh!" She turned around suddenly. "Did I tell you that they are going to give me *Coppélia?*" This called for a number of congratulatory words and deeds and the time passed pleasantly until Jane had to go backstage and do a few pre-performance knee bends and pirouettes. I walked with her as far as the long wooden bar near the tool chest; then I left her.

I paused for a moment and watched Eglanova in *Giselle* . . . it's not my favorite ballet and it's certainly not my favorite role for her. I am told she was once very fine in it but now she seems coy and unconvincing, too old and wise-looking, too regal, to play the part of a girl gone soft in the head for love.

During the intermission, I headed for Sherry's, the bar upstairs at the Met, where I found Mr. Washburn taking his ease in the company of my old employer, Milton Haddock, who was his usual noble drunken self, dressed casually in tweeds, horn-rimmed spectacles (old school, pre-junior executive: they curved); he looked very distinguished in a sottish way.

"Wonderful to see you, Mr. Haddock!" I exclaimed, pumping his hand.

"Why, hello there, George. Haven't seen you in a long time."

"Not since New Haven."

He clutched at the clue. "*Streetcar Named Desire*, wasn't it? I remember now. You were at that party afterwards . . . some party. The Scotch flowed like the Liffey." And he swallowed some more of it since Mr. Washburn was providing same gratis.

"And to think this is the man I worked for for four years," I said jovially to Mr. Washburn, regretting those three fours: after all it was *my* prose style which made Milton Haddock the trenchant critic he is today, the adder of the Rialto . . . or at least the garter snake of Forty-fifth Street.

"My God . . . it's Jim," said Haddock, recognizing me at last. He patted my arm, spilling my drink in the process. "Here . . . I'm sorry . . . let me fix it for you." And he dried my sleeve and cuff with his handkerchief, after which he carefully folded the handkerchief and put it away . . . to suck on later, I decided, in case he ran out of the stuff in the flask.

"I don't suppose you two have seen each other in a long time," said Mr. Washburn.

"Not in a coon's age," said Mr. Haddock, looking at me fondly with those foggy blue eyes of his. "Right in the middle of the news, too, aren't you, Jim? Wonderful place for a young man to be when a hot story breaks . . . and such a story! Falling sandbag kills opera star in the first act of *Lakmé* . . . one of the dullest operas, by the way, I have ever sat through. I mean if it had to ruin an opera it might just as well have been that one, don't you agree, Mr. Bing?" At that point I gave Mr. Washburn the high sign and we quietly crept away while the dean of New York drama critics had a chat with himself about the relative merits of the great operas.

"Why didn't you warn me?" asked Mr. Washburn.

"How could I? I didn't even know you knew him . . . after all, he never covers the ballet."

"He did a story on Ella, thought he'd come by and have a chat. Awful experience." Mr. Washburn shuddered as we stood and watched the last half of *Eclipse* run smoothly to its spectacular end. The audience ate it up and, beside me in the dark, I could hear Mr. Washburn applauding.

Jed Wilbur met us backstage; he looked less harried than usual and

I supposed that the success of his ballet had bucked him up considerably.

"It is very, very fine," said Mr. Washburn, slowly, taking Wilbur's right hand in both of his and looking at him with an expression of melting admiration and wonder . . . the four-star treatment.

"Glad you liked it," said Jed, in his high thin voice. "Glad *they* liked it, too. Did you see the notices the new girl, Garden, received? Gratifying, very gratifying."

"She danced well . . . but the part! Ah, Jed, you have *never* made such a fine ballet before in your whole life."

"It isn't bad," said Wilbur with that freedom from modesty and the commoner forms of polite behavior which makes dance people so refreshing and, at times, so intolerable. "I though the *pas de deux* went well tonight."

"Lyric!" exclaimed Mr. Washburn as though all words but that accurate one had failed him.

"But the *corps de ballet* was a little ragged, I thought."

"They are not used to such dynamic work."

"By the way, I'm ready to talk about the new ballet."

"Have you really thought it out? . . . will it be ready by the time we open in Chicago?"

"I think so . . . I'm ready to begin rehearsals, if you are."

"What music? Something old and classical, I hope. They are the best, you know, the masters."

"A little piece by Poulenc . . . you'll have no trouble getting the rights."

Mr. Washburn sighed, thinking of royalties to a living composer. "My favorite modern," he said bravely.

"I knew you'd be pleased. I'm calling the ballet *Martyr* . . . very austere, very direct."

"Brilliant title . . . but it's not, well, political, is it? I mean this isn't the best time . . . you know what I mean."

"Are you trying to censor me?" Jed Wilbur stood very straight and noble, nostrils flared.

"Now, Jed, you know I'm the last person in the world to do such a thing. Why, I put the artist's integrity ahead of everything . . . you know that, Peter here knows that."

"Yes, sir," I murmured.

"But what *is* it about, Jed?"

"Exactly what the title says."

"But *who* is the Martyr?"

"A girl . . . It's all about a family."

"Ah," said Mr. Washburn, relieved. "Marvelous theme . . . seldom done in ballet. Only Tudor, perhaps, has done it well."

"This is better than Tudor."

"I'm sure it is."

"What happens in the ballet—what's the argument?"

"It's very simple," said Jed Wilbur, smiling. "The girl is murdered."

Mr. Washburn's eyebrows went up in surprise; mine went down in a scowl. "Murdered? Do you think, under the circumstances, that's a . . . well, an auspicious theme for this company?"

"I can always take it to Ballet Theater."

"But, my dear boy, I wasn't suggesting you *not* do it, or that you change the theme. I was only suggesting that, perhaps, in the light of recent events . . ."

"It would be fabulous," said the dedicated Mr. Wilbur, revealing an unexpected sense of the commercial for one so pure.

"Well, you're the doctor," said Mr. Washburn jovially. "Who will you need?"

"Most of the company."

"Eglanova?"

"I don't think so . . . unless she would play the part of the girl's mother."

"She wouldn't do it, I'm afraid. You can use Carole for that, the heavy one . . . she's good in character. What about the girl?"

"Garden, I think," said Wilbur, and I found myself liking him: what a break this would be for Jane—to have a new ballet made for her by a choreographer like Jed Wilbur! Things were looking up. "I'll need all the boys. Louis can be her husband . . . a very good part for him, by the way . . . lot of fire. Then there are two brothers and her father. One brother plays games with her . . . they have, as children, an imaginary world all their own. The boy is a dreamer and he loses her to the other brother who is a man of action who loses her at last to Louis. But, of course, all the time, she belongs to her father (a good part for old Kazanian by the way) and her mother hates her. When she marries Louis there is terrible trouble in the family . . . a little like Helen of Troy, perhaps, and, to end the trouble, the girl is murdered."

"Who murders her?" asked Mr. Washburn.

"The father, of course," said Jed Wilbur evenly.

Neither of us said anything for a moment. Then Mr. Washburn chuckled. "Obscure motivation, isn't it?"

"No, very classical . . . guilt, jealousy, incest."

"Wouldn't he be more inclined to kill the girl's husband?" I suggested, appalled at the implications.

"He was a rational man . . . he realized that the boy was only fulfilling his nature . . . the boy had no connection with him; the girl had; the girl betrayed him *and* the brothers . . . the mother, too."

"I'll be very interested to see how you work this out," said Mr. Washburn with greater control than I would have had, similarly confronted.

"By the way," I said to Wilbur, "the *Globe* wants to know if you have any statement to make about this Communist deal."

"Tell them I'm not a Communist . . . that two boards have cleared me already." Wilbur seemed more relaxed now and I wondered why . . . after all, the pickets were at this very moment marching up and down the street outside with placards denouncing not only him but us. We found out soon enough. "I've been signed to do the new Hayes and Marks musical this fall. . . . You can tell the *Globe* that." And Mr. Wilbur marched off in the direction of Louis' dressing room.

"I guess that clears him," I said. Hayes and Marks, sometimes known collectively as Old Glory, are the most successful, the most reactionary musical comedy writers on Broadway. To be hired by them is a proof of one's patriotism, loyalty and professional success.

"The little bastard," said Mr. Washburn, lapsing for the first time in my brief acquaintance with him, into the argot of the street. "I knew there'd be trouble when I hired him. I was warned."

"What difference does it make? You've got at least one good ballet out of him and by the time you open with *Martyr* in New York next year the whole scandal will be forgotten. From what I hear the police are going to arrest Miles any minute."

"I wonder why they don't?" mused Mr. Washburn, suggesting also for the first time that a member of his company might, after all, have been guilty of murder. It was obvious this exchange with Wilbur had shaken him.

"I know why," I said boldly.

"You know?"

"It's those shears . . . they aren't sure about them . . . they can't figure what my role in all this is."

"I'm sure that's *not* the reason."

"Then what is?"

"I don't know . . . I don't know." Mr. Washburn looked worried as the dancers trooped noisily by, costumed for *Scheherazade*. "Oh," he said, as we both watched one blond trick march past us, rolling her butt, "Lady Edderdale is giving a party for the ballet tonight . . . just principals, no photographers, except hers, of course. You be there, too, black tie . . . right after the last ballet. I'm not so sure that it's a good policy to be going out to parties so soon after an accident, but she's much too important a patron to pass up."

I was thrilled, I have to admit. She gives the best parties in New York . . . a Chicago meat heiress married to a title . . . I wondered idly if I might find myself a rich wife at the party—every wholesome boy's dream of heaven. Thinking of marriage, I asked Mr. Washburn whether Eglanova was married at the moment or not.

He laughed. "She has a Mexican divorce at the moment . . . I know it for a fact because I helped her get it when we were playing Mexico City."

"Who was she married to then?"

"Don't you know? I thought you would have noticed it in her biography . . . but, no, come to think of it, we haven't used it in the program for nearly five years. She was married to Alyosha Rudin."

IV

Once a Lady always a Lady, as the saying goes; especially in the case of Alma Shellabarger of Chicago who married the Marquis of Edderdale when she was twenty and then at twenty-four married someone else and after that someone else and so on until now, at fifty, she had no husband, though she still uses the title of Marchioness in spite of all the other names she has been called along the way. No one seems to mind, however, because she gives great parties even though her income is not as large now as it was when she appeared in the fashionable world with a face like a bemused horse and all that Shellabarger cash, from slaughtered pigs and sheep. Nevertheless, her blood-drenched income is adequate . . . though there is no longer the Paris house or the Amalfi villa or the Irish castle . . . only the Park Avenue mansion and the Palm Beach house, where lavish parties are given, in season. I am told that at her dinners neither pig nor sheep is served, only poultry, fish and game . . . real sense of guilt as any analyst would tell you at the drop of a fee.

Mr. Washburn and I arrived before the rest of our company. As a rule, he waits until Eglanova is ready and then he escorts her; but tonight, for some reason, he couldn't wait to get out of the theater. Both of us were hot in our tuxedos . . . his white and mine black, an obvious clue to our respective incomes. Fortunately, the house was cool . . . a gust of freshened air met us in the downstairs hall, a vast room with gray marble columns, marble floor and Greek statuary in niches. A footman took our invitations and led us up a flight of stairs where, so help me, a butler announced our names to a hundred or so decorative guests in a drawing room which looked like the waiting room at Penn Station redecorated by King Midas . . . the guests looked as though they might be waiting for trains, too, I thought, as we moved toward our hostess who stood beneath a chandelier at the room's center, all in green and diamonds, receiving her guests with a half-smile and mumbled greetings as though she weren't quite sure why she was there, or why *they* were there.

"Dear Alma," said Mr. Washburn, beginning to expand as he always does in the presence of money.

"Ivan!" They embraced like two mechanical toys, like those figures which come out of old-fashioned clocks every hour on the hour. I bowed over her hand in the best Grand Saint Petersburg Ballet style.

"You poor dear," said Alma, fixing my employer with yellow eyes. "What a disaster!"

"We must take the good with the bad," said Mr. Washburn gently.

"*I* was there!" breathed Alma Edderdale, shutting her eyes for a moment as though to recall, as vividly as possible, every detail of that terrible night.

"Then you know what it was like . . ."

"I do . . . I do."

"The ghastly fall . . ."

"Can I ever forget?"

"The end of a life . . . a great ballerina's life."

"If there was only *something* one could do." That did it, I thought. Mr. Washburn would immediately suggest an Ella Sutton Memorial Ballet, sets, costumes and choreographer's fee to be paid by that celebrated patroness, the Marchioness of Edderdale. But Mr. Washburn is as tactful as he is venal.

"We all feel that way, Alma." Then he paused significantly.

"Perhaps . . . but we'll talk of that another time. Tell me about *him*."

"About whom?"

"The husband. The . . . well, you know what they say."

"Ah . . . quite broken up," said Mr. Washburn evasively, and I withdrew, moving toward the bar in the next room where, among other things, they were serving a Pommery '29 worth its weight in uranium. I knocked off two glasses before Jane arrived, looking very young and innocent in a plain white dinner dress, her hair drawn severely back ballerina-style. She was like the daughter of a country minister at her first grown-up party, only she looked perhaps too innocent to be the real thing. She caused a mild stir, her appearance at least: this gang hadn't absorbed her yet, made her a legend the way they had Eglanova who now stood, between Alyosha and Louis in the doorway, like some bird of paradise poised on the edge of a hen coop. In the excitement of Eglanova's entrance, Jane and I met near the bar and toasted one another in Pommery.

"How did you like it tonight?" she asked, breathless and young, like a bride in an advertisement (and, like the model in question, well paid for her characterization).

"Wonderful party," I said, enjoying myself for the first time, publicly at least, since my wild ballet season began. "Best stuff I've ever tasted. And the air-conditioning! Wonderful job . . . like an autumn day."

"You misunderstood," said Jane firmly, with the bright monomaniacal stare of a dancer discussing the Dance. "I meant my performance."

"I'm afraid I didn't catch it. I was at the office most of the night, before I came here."

She rallied bravely. "You . . . *didn't* see me tonight?"

"No, I had to get some pictures off to the papers . . . the new ones of you, by the way," I added.

"I got eight curtain calls."

"That's my girl."

"And three bouquets . . . from strangers."

"Never take candy from strange men, little girl," I chanted as we moved toward a tall French window which looked out on an eighteenth-century garden, all of five years old.

"I wish you'd seen it. Tonight was the first night I really *danced*, that I forgot all about the variations and the audience and that damned cable . . . that I really let go. Oh, it was wonderful!"

"You think you're pretty good, huh?"

"Oh, I didn't mean that!" She was anxious: nowadays in the theater good form (or actors' notion of good form) is everything. Everyone dresses carefully and quietly, no practical jokes, no loud voices and, above all, no reference to self . . . just smile and blush if you are congratulated for having won a Donaldson Award, look blank when someone mentions the spread on you in *Life,* murmuring something about not having seen it yet. In a way, I prefer the grand old egotists like Eglanova: she hardly admits that there is another ballerina in all the world . . . and even Louis has been known to ask reviewers: "Who is this Youskevitch you talk to me about?" But anyway Jane had a storm of modesty which quickly passed and then, the Dance taken care of for the rest of the evening, we cruised the party.

About one o'clock we separated with an agreement to meet back at her apartment at two-thirty on the dot. Neither of us is very jealous . . . at least not in theory, and I wandered about the drawing room, saying hello to the few people I knew. I was pretty much lost in this crowd. It's not the gang I went to school with, the sons of those dull rich families who seldom entertain and who traipse off to Newport, Southampton, Bar Harbor and similar giddy places this time of year; nor is it the professional newspaper and theater world wherein I sing for my supper . . . rather, it is the world of unfixed money: obscure Europeans, refugees from various unnamed countries, the new-rich, the wilder old-rich, the celebrated figures in the arts who have time for parties and finally the climbers, mysterious and charming and busy, of all ages, sexes, nationalities, shapes and sizes. It takes a long time to straighten everybody out. I haven't even begun to see my way clear yet but I probably will in a few more years. Some people of course never do add things up right. Lady Edderdale is still among the more confused, after thirty years of high life.

Beneath a portrait of the lady of the house (the work of Dali) stood Elmer Bush with whom I have a nodding acquaintance . . . through no fault of mine I am not his bosom buddy: his column, "America's New York," is syndicated in seventy-two newspapers as well as being the *New York Globe*'s biggest draw on the subway circuit. He was of course too important ever to visit the office, so the only time I met him was at first nights when he would always come up to Milton Haddock and say: "It looks like a bomb from where I sit. What do *you* think, boy?" and Milton would grumble a little and sometimes I would be introduced and sometimes not.

"Hello there, Mr. Bush," I said with more authority than usual since I was, after all, sitting in the middle of the best piece of news in town.

"Why if it isn't old Pete Sargeant himself," said Mr. Bush, his face lighting up as he saw his next column practically composed already. He gave a polite but firm chill shoulder to a blond middle-aged star of yesteryear who had obviously got the Gloria Swanson bug; then we were alone together in the middle of the party.

"Haven't seen you in a coon's age!" said Elmer Bush, showing a row of capped teeth: he has the seventh highest Hooper in television with a program called "New York's America" which is, they tell me, a combination of gossip and interviews with theater people. . . . I never look at television myself because it hurts my eyes. Anyway, Elmer is big league, bald and ulcerous, the perfect symbol of metropolitan success for an earnest hard-working boy like me trying to get ahead in "the game."

"Well, I've been pretty busy," I allowed in my best bumpkin manner.

"Say, what about that murder you got in your company?" and the benign features of Elmer Bush ("just a friend of the family in your own living room giving you some *real* stories about *real* people in the news," . . . just old horse-shit Bush, I thought) shone with friendship and interest.

"Some mess," I said, because that's exactly what he would have said had our roles been reversed.

"Well, it keeps the show in the news . . . that's one thing. Hear my broadcast about it Wednesday night?"

"I certainly did," I lied. "Just about the best analysis I've seen so far."

"Well, I didn't really try to analyze it . . . just straight reporting."

Had I blundered? "I mean the way you put it, well, that was some job . . ."

"Get the facts," said Mr. Bush, smiling mechanically. "When are they going to arrest the husband?"

"I don't know."

"He *did* do it?"

"Everyone thinks so. He certainly had a good enough reason."

"Bitch?"

"Very much so."

"I saw the man who's on that case yesterday. What's his name? Gleason? Yes. Used to know him years ago when I was covering the police courts. He was mixed up in the Albemarle business . . . but that was before your time. Anyway, he made it pretty clear to me, unofficially of course, that Sutton would be arrested in the next twenty-four hours and indicted as quick as possible . . . while public interest is high. That's the way they work." And he chuckled. "Politicians, police . . . the worst hams of all. But I still don't know why they've held off so long."

"Pressure," I said smoothly, as though I knew.

He pursed his lips and nodded, everything just a bit more deliberate than life, made sharp for the television camera. "I thought as much.

Not a bad idea to string it out as long as possible either . . . for the good of all concerned. Are you sold out? I thought so. Take a tip from me! *This* will put ballet on the map." And with that message he left me for a dazzling lady who looked like Gloria Swanson and who, upon close inspection, turned out to be Gloria Swanson.

"How're you doing, baby?" inquired a familiar voice behind me . . . needless to say I gave a bit of a jump and executed a fairly professional pirouette . . . never turn your back on the likes of Louis, as Mother used to say.

"I'm doing just fine, killer," I said, showing my upper teeth.

"Such good boy," said Louis, holding my arm for a minute in a vise-like grip. "Some muscle!"

"I got it from beating up faggots in Central Park," I said slowly; he doesn't understand if you talk fast.

Louis roared. "You kill me, baby."

"Don't tempt me."

"Come on out on that balcony . . . just you and me. We look at moon."

"Not on your life, killer."

"Why're you so afraid of me?"

"Just two guesses."

"But I tell you you won't feel nothing. You'll like it fine."

"I'm a virgin."

"I know, baby, that's what I go for. Last night . . ." But before he could tell me some lewd story concerning his unnatural vice, Jed Wilbur approached us, pale and harried-looking, like the White Rabbit in *Alice in Wonderland*. He too was got up in a dinner jacket . . . it was the first time, I think, that I had ever seen him in a suit, wearing a tie. I was not able to continue my sartorial investigation, however, for Louis broke off what had promised to be our big balcony scene and rushed off in the direction of the main hall, as though he had to get to the john real fast. I could see that Wilbur was in some doubt as to whether to chase his beloved and corner him in some barricaded lavatory or to tarry a bit with me instead. He chose the latter course.

"I wonder where Louis is off to?" he asked.

"Call of the wild, I guess."

"What was he talking to you about?"

This was abrupt and I was almost tempted to remind Jed Wilbur that it was none of his business. But then he is the leading choreographer of the minute and I am, for this minute at least, a minion of the ballet and so I swallowed my thimble-sized pride and said, "Just idle chatter."

"In other words making a pass." Wilbur sounded bitter.

"But that's natural. I mean for him it is. He has to get into everything he sees."

"Male and under thirty." Wilbur sighed and I felt sorry for him . . . unrequited love and all that. He fidgeted with his ready-tied bow tie.

"Well, that's the way he gets his kicks," I said, idly dropping into an Army attitude; while I talked to Jed I looked over his shoulder at the room, recognizing several famous faces, one of whom, belonging to a Senator, was talking very seriously to Jane who obviously had no notion of who he was. I smiled to myself as I recalled the day before when she asked me, very tenderly and shyly, whether Truman was a Democrat or Republican.

"Why does everyone at parties look over everyone else's shoulder?" asked Wilbur suddenly, capturing my attention with a bang.

"Oh . . ." I blushed. "Bad manners, I guess."

"*Some* commentary on our society," said Wilbur, in a voice which smacked a little of the soapbox. "Everyone trying to get ahead every minute of the day . . . rushing, rushing, rushing, afraid of missing a trick."

"This is a competitive town," I said with my usual profundity, sneaking a glimpse over *his* shoulder at Eglanova who was surrounded by some rich-looking bucks, laughing as though she was quite prepared to slip off a shoe and guzzle champagne from it.

"You're telling me," said Wilbur and he looked over his own shoulder in the direction that Louis had taken . . . but our Don Juan was nowhere in sight. No doubt he was having his way with one of the busboys behind a potted palm downstairs. Thinking of Louis always puts me into a good mood . . . that is when he's not around to make me nervous . . . he just makes me laugh, for no particular reason. But then Lady Edderdale, surrounded by outriders, rode down on us, diamonds whispering against green satin.

"Mr. Wilbur? We haven't met. I must have been in the other room when you arrived. I've so much wanted to meet you."

Jed took her outstretched hand, bewildered. "Yes . . ."

"*I* am Alma Edderdale," she said, smiling a blinding smile, like sun on a glacier; she withdrew her hand.

"We've met," I said quickly, to cover the moment's confusion. "With Mr. Washburn."

"Of course. Can I ever tell you in words, Mr. Wilbur, my reaction to *Eclipse?*"

Wilbur suggested in a confused voice that she give it a try . . . stated more politely of course.

"It was my one wonderful, *mystical* experience in the ballet . . . not including the classics which I have seen so long that I can no longer remember how they first affected me. But in *modern* ballet . . . ah!" Words failed her. They failed Jed, too.

"It's generally thought to be Mr. Wilbur's best work," I gabbled.

"And of course what happened that first night! Mr. Wilbur, *I* was there. I saw." She opened her eyes very wide, great golden orbs, swimming in jaundiced tears.

"Very awful," mumbled Wilbur.

"And to have had it happen then . . . at that wonderful moment! Ah, Mr. Wilbur . . ." The passage of several boisterous guests made escape possible; I slipped through them and wandered off to find Jane. But she had vanished . . . the Senator, too. I settled for Eglanova who was seated on a love seat with an old man and surrounded by younger ones, all rather sensitive I noted with my shrewd and merciless eyes . . . I can tell one of our feathered friends at twenty paces: a certain type anyway. The Louis kind nobody can spot until they're coming at you . . . then flight is in order, if they're bigger than you.

"My darling Peter!" Eglanova was mildly lit, not yet weepy and Czarist the way she gets when she is really gone on vodka . . . twice a year: at Russian New Year and backstage the last night of every season in New York . . . her *last* season, she always moans, so they say. She gave me her hand to kiss and, feeling good on all the Pommery I had drunk, I kissed it soulfully.

"I have had such good time with young men." She waved to include them all. They giggled. "I never go home now."

"It's late, Anna," said Alyosha, suddenly joining us.

"Tyrant! Tomorrow I do one *pas de deux* . . . no more."

"Even so." Then he spoke in Russian and she answered in Russian, both speaking rapidly, seriously, the good humor of the party-mood gone. I thought Eglanova's face went quite pale though it was impossible to tell since her make-up was like spar varnish . . . perhaps, it was the way her eyes opened very wide and her face fell, literally sagged, as though whatever force had been holding it tight across the bone suddenly gave way. Then, with a stage gesture, she got up, swept a half-curtsy to her admirers and, without saying a word to any of us, left the room on Alyosha's arm. I saw them at the door saying good night to Lady Edderdale.

I looked about the room for Jane but she was gone. I wondered if she had gone home early . . . or perhaps had decided in a puckish mood to have a Senatorial fling. Well, she could look out for herself, I decided, and went downstairs to the bathroom. I was just about to go in when I saw Mr. Washburn come trotting across the black and white marble floor.

"I was looking for you," he said, stopping short, breathing hard. "We've got to get out of here."

"Why? What's the matter?"

"I'll tell you outside. Come on." He looked furtively about as though afraid the footmen were eavesdropping. They were not. Even so, as we went out the door, he looked back over his shoulder, like a man fearing pursuers; I looked, too, and saw no one except Louis coming out of the head with a blond footman, both looking pleased as hell. They did not see us.

We headed east on Seventy-fifth Street, toward Lexington Avenue.

"What's going on? What's up? Where're we walking to?"

"It's quicker, walking," said Mr. Washburn grimly, prancing ahead of me like a fat mare.

"But where?"

"To Miles Sutton's apartment. He lives just the other side of Lexington."

"What's the matter?" But I knew: Gleason had arrested him at last, or was about to.

"He's dead," said Mr. Washburn.

I think I said: "Sweet Jesus!"

2

We walked up three flights of stairs which smelled of damp and cabbage; at the top of the third flight was an open door with a curiously formal card on it: "Mr. and Mrs. Miles Sutton" . . . obviously a Christmas present from an old aunt. The apartment was a three-roomed affair, very modern: you know the kind . . . two walls battleship gray and two terra cotta in the same room with fuchsia-covered furniture. This was where the happy couple had lived until the present season when Miles moved out, not returning until after Ella was dead.

In the front room several detectives stood, looking important as they always do in the presence of someone else's disaster. They were very tough with us until Gleason, hearing the noise of Mr. Washburn's protests, shouted from another room, "Let them in."

"In there," said one of the detectives, motioning to a door on the left.

We found Gleason in the kitchen. A photographer with a flash bulb was taking pictures of the corpse, from all angles. Two unidentified men stood by the sink, watching.

"Oh, my God!" And Mr. Washburn, after one look at the body of Miles Sutton, hurried out of the room. We could hear him vomiting in the bathroom. I didn't feel so good myself but I have a strong stomach and I have seen a lot of things in my time, during the war, and I'm not easily upset . . . even so all the wine I had drunk that night at the party turned sour in my belly as I looked at Miles Sutton. It was one of the damnedest things I have ever seen. He was slumped over a gas stove, his arms hanging at his sides and his legs buckled crazily under him . . . he was a tall man and the stove didn't come up to his waist. But the horrible thing was his head. He had fallen in such a way that his chin had got caught in one of the burners on top of the stove . . . which might not have been so bad except for the fact that the gas had been lit and his hair, his beard and the skin of his face were burned until now his head resembled a shapeless mass of black tar. The room was full of the acrid odor of burnt hair and flesh.

"O.K.," said the photographer, getting down from a kitchen chair: he had been shooting a picture from directly overhead. "It's all yours."

The two men by the sink moved forward and lifted the body off the stove. I looked away while they lugged the large corpse out of the kitchen into the living room. Gleason and I, still without a word to one another, followed the procession into the living room.

A moment later Mr. Washburn joined us, very weak at the knees. Without further invitation, he sat down in an Eames chair, careful not to look at Miles Sutton who was now laid out on a stretcher in the middle of the room. Detectives scurried about, searching the room, taking photographs.

Gleason lit a cigar and glared at us.

"How . . . how did it happen?" asked Mr. Washburn in a low voice.

"It ruins the whole case," said Mr. Gleason, savagely chewing on his cigar.

"Poor Miles . . ."

"It makes no sense."

"Inspector, could you . . . would you *please* put something over him."

"You don't have to look at it," snapped Gleason, but he motioned to one of the detectives who found a sheet and covered the body.

"That's better," said Mr. Washburn.

"We were going to arrest him this evening," said Gleason. "We had a perfect case . . . in spite of everyone's refusal to co-operate with us." And he looked at me with bloodshot eyes . . . when Irish eyes are bleary, I hummed to myself.

"How could such a thing have happened? I mean . . . well, it's impossible."

"That's our business: the impossible."

"How could someone have got in that position . . . I don't understand." Mr. Washburn sounded querulous.

"That's what we're going to find out . . . the medical examiner here," he gestured to one of the men standing by the door, "says that he's been dead for about an hour."

"It must've been an accident," said Mr. Washburn.

"We'll know after the autopsy. We're going to do a real job, you can bet your life. If there's been any monkey business, we'll find out."

"Or suicide," suggested Mr. Washburn.

Gleason looked at him contemptuously. "A man decides to kill himself by lighting a gas stove and putting his head on the burner like it was a pillow or something? For Christ's sake! If he was going to kill himself he would've stuck his head *in* the oven and turned on the gas. Anyway he was about to cook something . . . we found a pan beside him on the floor."

"Unless somebody put it there . . . to make it look like an accident," I suggested, to Mr. Washburn's dismay.

The detective ignored me, though. "I wanted you to come here, Mr. Washburn, to tell me which members of your company were at the party tonight."

"All the principals . . . Rudin, Wilbur . . . everyone."

"Who?"

Mr. Washburn, unhappily, gave him all the names.

"Where was the party held?" When Mr. Washburn told him, Gleason whistled, putting two and two together in a manner marvelous to behold . . . there's nothing quite like watching a slow reflex in action.

"That's just a few blocks from here?"

"I believe so," said Mr. Washburn.

"Anyone could have come over here and killed Sutton."

"Now look here, you don't know he was killed . . ."

"That's right, but then I don't know it was an accident, either."

"Just how could anybody kill a grown man by pushing his head on a stove?" I asked.

"It could be done," said Gleason, "if you knocked him out."

"Is there any sign he was knocked out?" I asked.

"The examination hasn't been made yet. In the meantime, Mr. Washburn, I want you to have the following people ready to see me tomorrow afternoon at the theater." And he handed my employer a list of names.

"How soon will you know . . . what happened, whether he was knocked out or not?"

"By morning."

"Morning . . . oh, God, the papers." Mr. Washburn shut his eyes; I wondered why publicity should bother him at this point.

"Yes, the papers," said Gleason, irritably. "Think what they'll say about *me*? 'Suspect killed or murdered on eve of arrest.' Think how that'll make *me* look!" I wondered if perhaps Gleason might not have political ambitions . . . Gleason for Councilman: fearless investigator, loyal American.

My reverie was broken, however, by the appearance of a dark, disheveled woman who pushed her way past the detectives at the door and then, catching sight of the figure on the floor, screamed and drew back. There was a moment of pure confusion. The woman was taken into a back room by the medical examiner who spoke to her in a low, soothing voice which had startlingly little effect on the sobs. Magda was hysterical.

"Was *she* at the party?" asked Gleason, turning to Mr. Washburn, the sobs muffled now by a closed door.

"No, no . . ." Mr. Washburn looked about distractedly, as though ready to make a run for it.

"She's been sick," I volunteered.

"I know she has," said Gleason. Then the sobbing stopped and presently the door to the bedroom opened and Magda, supported on one side by the doctor, joined us. Whatever shot the doctor had given her was obviously working like a charm for she was in complete control of herself now . . . even when she looked at the sheet-covered figure on the floor, she remained calm.

"Now," said Gleason, in a voice which was, for him, gentle, "why did you come here tonight?"

"To see Miles." Her voice was emotionless; she kept staring at the white sheet.

"Why did you want to see him?"

"I . . . I was afraid."

"Of what?"

"Of his being arrested. You were going to arrest him, weren't you?"

"He was guilty."

She shook her head, slowly. "No, he didn't kill her . . . but I told you that once, when you came to see me."

"What did you intend to do tonight? Why did you come?"

"I wanted to . . . to get him to run away, with me, the two of us. We could have gone to Mexico . . . any place. I wanted . . ." But she didn't finish her sentence; she looked dully at Gleason.

"You couldn't have got away," said Gleason quietly. "He couldn't have got away. You see, he was watched every minute; didn't you know that? Why, there was even a man watching this building tonight."

Mr. Washburn gave a start. "You mean . . ."

Gleason nodded, looking very pleased with himself. "I mean, Mr. Washburn, that at one-ten you were seen entering this building and at one-twenty-seven you left it, in a great hurry. What were you doing here?"

Mr. Washburn shut his eyes, like an ostrich heading for a sandpile.

"What were you doing here?"

"I came to talk to Miles." Mr. Washburn opened his eyes and his voice was even and controlled: he was still the intrepid Ivan Washburn, the peerless impresario . . . he could take care of himself, I decided.

"And did you talk to him?"

"Yes, I did . . . and if you're implying that I killed him you are very much mistaken, Inspector Gleason."

"I implied no such thing."

"Don't even think it," said Mr. Washburn, coolly, as though he were saying: if you go after me I'll see that you end up pounding a beat in Brooklyn. "I had some business I wanted to talk over with Miles. That's all."

"What kind of business?"

"His contract, if you must know. I told him that it would not be renewed. That we would tour without him."

"What was his reaction to this?"

"He was upset."

"Why did you tell him this tonight? Why didn't you have him come to your office tomorrow? Or you could have written him."

"I wanted to tell him myself. He was a friend of mine, Mr. Gleason . . . a very good friend."

"Yet you were prepared to fire him?"

"I was indeed."

"Why?"

"Because I suspected that sooner or later you would arrest him and that, even if you didn't, too many people thought he was a murderer . . . too many of our backers, to be blunt about it."

"I see . . . and you left in the middle of a party to come tell him this?"

"We both seem agreed that I did," said Mr. Washburn.

"Could anyone else have visited Sutton this evening?" I asked, eager to get my employer off the hook.

Gleason ignored me. "Did you notice anything unusual about the deceased?"

"He was not deceased when I arrived, if that's what you mean, and he was very much alive when I left."

"I meant did he act peculiar in any way, say anything which might throw light on what subsequently happened." Excellent sentence, Gleason, I said to myself; he was beginning to face up to the fact that none of his "deceased" talk was going to get him anywhere with this gang.

"He objected to my firing him and he said that he did *not* kill his wife no matter what the police thought and that he would welcome a trial."

"So he told us," said Gleason. "And we were perfectly willing to give him a chance to tell all, under an indictment, of course. But then what did you say?"

"I told him that I was convinced of his innocence, but that no one else was, that I would be only too happy to take him back *after* a trial, presuming he was acquitted."

"You got the feeling, then, that Sutton was looking forward to a trial?"

"No, I didn't."

"But you said . . ."

"As a matter of fact, he was terrified of appearing in court. As you know he took drugs and he was positive that the prosecution would throw all that at him . . . I *can* tell you that he was not afraid of the murder charge . . . I don't know why but he wasn't; it was the drug thing that disturbed him: the idea not only of being sent to jail for it, or whatever the law is, but, worse, of having it taken away from him even for a few days during the trial . . ."

"He was going to give all that up when we were married," said Magda in a tired, faraway voice. "There's a place in Connecticut where they cure you. He was going to go there. We were to spend our honeymoon there." She stopped abruptly, like a phonograph when the needle's lifted.

"Then when you left the . . . Sutton he was alive and angry."

"I'm afraid so . . . angry, I mean."

"Did anyone else come to see him in the last hour?" I repeated.

"*I'm* asking the questions," snapped Gleason.

"Was that fire escape watched?" I asked, just to be ornery. "The one outside the kitchen window."

"So you noticed there was a fire escape, eh?"

"I did."

"Were you at the party, too?"

"Yes . . . remember, Mr. Gleason, I'm the one without a motive."

Gleason gave me a warning or two about the possible dangers into which my insouciance might yet lead me.

While we had been talking, the detectives had ransacked the apartment and the photographer had taken pictures of everything in sight. They were now ready to push off. Gleason, receiving a signal from his chief lieutenant, stood up, rubbing his hands together as though washing them of the guilt of others.

"I will see all of you, tomorrow. Can you get home alone?" He turned to Magda.

"Yes . . . yes," she said, stirring in her chair.

"You better see her home, Macy." The detective in question nodded and helped her to her feet.

"I hope," said Mr. Washburn, "that this turns out to be the end of the whole ugly business."

"Or the beginning," said Gleason darkly.

"I presume that you had a case against him. Now that he is dead . . . suicide, accident, who knows how he died? . . . the fact remains that a man about to be arrested for a murder has died and so the case . . . Oh, Lord, look!" Mr. Washburn leaped back and we all turned to stare at the figure on the floor. The sheet which covered him had caught fire from the still smoldering head and a yellow flame, like a daffodil in the wind, blossomed on the white sheet. I was not there, however, to see it put out; I had followed, as quickly as I could, Mr. Washburn's blind dash down the stairs to the street outside.

3

For once I didn't really want to see the newspapers; neither did my employer but of course we read them all, together, in absolute silence. "Death Company" . . . "Slain Dancer's Husband Suicide" . . . "Mystery Death of Murder Suspect" . . . "Second Death in Jinx Ballet" . . . Needless to say, we had all the front pages to ourselves. When we had finished the lot we looked at one another. Fortunately, at that moment, Alma Edderdale saw fit to telephone and I left the office and headed for the Met.

A crowd had gathered at the stage door, for no particular reason . . . just to be as near as possible to a couple of murders and, better yet, to be near a murderer. I pushed my way through them and went immediately to Jane's dressing room. She had been asleep when I got home from Sutton's apartment the night before and she had been asleep when I left in the morning, at nine o'clock, to help Mr. Washburn with the reporters who had, for three hours, made our lives miserable at the office.

She was mending one of her costumes; the day was cruelly hot and she wore no clothes.

I gave her a long healthy kiss, tilting her chair back so far that she kicked the air gracefully with her long legs, to keep her balance.

"Is it true?" she asked, when we were done and I was again composed.

I nodded. "Has Gleason seen you yet?"

"I don't see him till four something. He killed himself, didn't he?"

"I suppose so."

"But . . . like that! Did you see him?"

I shuddered, remembering. "I'll say. It was the awfullest sight . . . worse than the war . . . at least then you were usually looking at people you didn't know, and there were so many of them . . ."

"But the papers act as if he'd been murdered."

"I don't believe it."

"But how could he kill himself in that way?"

"He might've passed out . . . you know he was taking an awful lot of the stuff, whatever it was he took . . . you remember my telling you how I found him passed out in the hall the day after Ella died."

"Let's hope this is the end of the whole mess."

"I hope so, too." But I knew that we hadn't come to the end of the trouble . . . I'd taken to calling it "the trouble" in my mind, like one of those Negro spirituals.

"How're the kids in the company holding up?"

"Scared to death," Jane smiled. "They're positive we've got a maniac around . . . they go everywhere in pairs, even to the john."

"And the thing I always liked about dancers was that they had no imagination."

"Sometimes I think you're against ballet."

"I am . . . I am," I said, locking the door. "But I'm not against you . . ." And I headed for her with an insane leer, scaring hell out of her. Then, before she had time to complain, I was out of my clothes and we were together on the floor, doing it like Mamma and Poppa as Eglanova would say . . . she likes the old-fashioned, heart-to-heart method, with no thrashing about . . . so do I, on hot days at least, when anything else would use up too much energy. After we finished, we lay side by side for a bit on the cool dirty floor.

"We shouldn't have done that," said Jane, at last.

"Why not? We missed last night. At least I did."

"I did, too."

"Are you sure you didn't have a frolic with that Senator?"

"With who?"

"That big middle-aged job with the gray hair you were talking to at the party . . . the red face."

"Oh him! Was he a Senator?"

"I should say so."

"He told me he was a broker named Haskell."

"I hope you got your money in advance."

"Don't be dirty."

A knock on the door brought us both to our feet in a flash. "Wait a second," called Jane in the cool voice of one used to keeping her head in crises. Since I had not taken off my shoes and socks, I was able to dress with a speed which did credit to my military training. Jane slipped into a bathrobe and opened the door while I sat down before the dressing-table mirror and dried my sweaty face with a handkerchief as Magda entered.

"I'm sorry," she said. "I didn't know . . ."

"Come on in," said Jane briskly, offering her the third and last chair. "How do you feel?"

"Awful . . . naturally."

"I thought you were too sick to come to the theater?"

"I am," said Magda, and she did look ill. "I wanted to come, though. To talk to you, to my friends here. You have no idea what it's been like this last week with my family around and everything, not being able to see Miles . . ." Her voice broke a little. "The family wouldn't let me see him but he came once, anyway, when they were out and we talked and made plans and then I went to see him last night."

"Have you seen Gleason yet today?" I asked quickly, before she could start weeping.

"Yes."

"What does he say—what about the autopsy?"

"He wouldn't tell me but I told him that someone had killed Miles . . . I don't know how but someone did."

"But why? If somebody else murdered Ella then they certainly wouldn't murder Miles just as he was about to be arrested for Ella's murder."

"Oh, but they would," said Magda. "You see, Miles knew who killed Ella." I must say this gave us both a jolt.

"How do you know he did?"

"Because he told me so the last time I saw him. He told me not to worry . . . that if they tried to charge him with murder he would tell everything."

"But he didn't tell you who it was?"

Was it my imagination or did she pause just a second before she answered? Before she said: "No, he didn't tell me."

"Did you tell Gleason all this?"

"Oh yes . . . I told him a lot more, too."

"The sooner it's finished the better," said Jane emphatically, taking out her sewing kit and going to work on the torn costume.

We talked a little more and then, seeing that the girls had a lot to discuss, I wandered onstage where Alyosha was giving some directions to the electricians. He looked very dapper in a Lord Byron shirt, magenta slacks, with a silk handkerchief tied about his lean neck and his monocle screwed in one eye.

"We must have everything right for tomorrow," he said to me as the electrician walked away. "Anna will do *Swan Lake*."

"And for once, it won't be her 'last' performance," I said.

Alyosha smiled. "No, she won't be able to weep this year. Ten more years I give her. She is at her peak."

Well, you better get her some contact lenses, I said to myself, trying to imagine the old star at sixty reeling about the stage in *Giselle*.

"Have you seen Wilbur today?"

I said that I hadn't.

"I was told he was to start rehearsing the new ballet today . . . if he is he should send out a call for the dancers he wants. They are all eager, naturally."

"I think he intends to use most of the company, but not until the season closes."

"If you see him, though, tell him to let me know which dancers he will want . . . he is not used to our system."

I said that I would and we parted.

My interview with Gleason was more amiable than usual.

He looked very hot in a white crumpled suit which made me think of a photograph I once saw of William Jennings Bryan when he was down in Tennessee fighting evolution.

Where were you at such and such a time and did you for any reason leave the party before such and such an hour? No sir I did not sir. We got through the preliminaries without a blow. Then the first of the brass tacks.

"Where, Mr. Sargeant, did you find those shears?"

"I found them, now that I think of it, in Eglanova's dressing room . . . someone had put them in the wastebasket. I took them out."

"Why didn't you tell us this before?"

"I wasn't sure it had any bearing on the case."

"Aren't *we* to be the judges of that?"

"Certainly . . . I didn't remember at the time. So many things had happened." I'm no fool . . . I've watched some of those investigations over television: all you have to do is say you can't remember, or that you've suddenly remembered, and you're legally safe.

"It might have made it easier for us if you'd been able to remember at the time."

"Well, I didn't."

"I wonder if you realize how serious all this is, Mr. Sargeant." For some reason Gleason had decided to handle me with tenderness.

"I do . . . It was a dumb thing, wasn't it? For someone deliberately to put the shears in her wastebasket to throw suspicion on her . . . I mean, if she *had* cut the cable she'd never keep The Murder Weapon in her own dressing room."

"Very sound reasoning," said the detective; if I hadn't already been acquainted with his simple mind I would have thought he was indulging himself in a bit of irony at my expense.

"What did the autopsy turn up?" I asked, disregarding all his previous statements to the effect that it was not my place to ask questions.

"If you would just let us . . ." He began with a show of patience.

"Mr. Gleason," I lied, "I have the representatives of all the wire services, foreign and domestic, as well as reporters from every daily in town, waiting at my office for some word from Anthony Ignatius Gleason as to the outcome of the autopsy this morning . . ." That did the trick . . . Gleason for Mayor, Honest, Courageous, Tireless.

"As a rule the district attorney's office handles releases to the press but since the boys are so eager you can tell them that Miles Sutton had a heart attack and fainted, falling face forward onto the lighted stove. He was not attacked or poisoned . . . unless you can call a system which looked like a drugstore poisoned."

"That's certainly a load off my mind," I sighed. "Everybody else's, too."

"It would seem," said Gleason, "that the case is closed."

"Seem? Weren't you going to arrest him for murder?"

"Oh yes."

"He did kill her, didn't he?"

"We believe so."

"Then tell me; why did you wait so long to arrest him? What couldn't you prove?"

Gleason blinked and then, quite mildly, answered: "Well, it happened that of all the people involved Sutton was the only one who had an alibi . . . the only one who could not, if his story was true, have gone backstage between five and eight-thirty and cut the cable."

I whistled.

"There are times when a good alibi can be more suspicious than none at all. But we managed to break it. I won't say how because we weren't entirely sure but we had a theory and we thought we could prove it in court."

"Then I can tell the papers that the case is finished?"

Gleason nodded. "You can tell them that."

"They'll want to interview you."

"They know where to find me," he said quietly . . . Gleason for Governor, Man of the People.

Needless to say, my announcement to the press that afternoon caused a sensation. Everyone in the company was wild with excitement and relief and I felt like a hero even though I was just the carrier of the good news from Aix to Ghent.

After the last reporter had cleared out of the office, grinding the last cigarette butt into the expensive carpet, I sat back and enjoyed a few minutes of much needed solitude. The two secretaries in the next room made a restful steady noise of typing: "Miss Rosen and Miss Ruger, the talented duo-typists, made their Manhattan debut last night at Town Hall with a program which featured Samuel Barber's *Concerto for Two Typewriters with Black and Red Ribbons.*" I seldom get a chance to be alone any more . . . it wasn't like college or even the army when I would have long stretches of being by myself, when I could think things out, decide what to do next, figure just where I stood on any number of assorted topics like television, Joyce, deism, marionettes, buggery and Handel's *Messiah*. Maybe I should take a long rest . . . I'd saved up quite a bit of cash and . . . but my dream of solitude was shattered by a telephone call from Miss Flynn.

"I have had an inquiry from the Benjamin Franklin Kafka Foundation; they would like to know if you could handle their account for the next six months. I indicated that I would communicate with you."

I asked what sum they had suggested and when she told me I said that I would accept. We talked business for a few minutes. Then she suggested that I come by the office and read the mail.

"I'll be over this afternoon. The case is finished, by the way."

"That should be nice for the dancers."

"For all of us."

"Are you to continue *with those clients much longer?*"

"Only another week."

" * * * * * * *"

I did not get over to my office that afternoon, however, for just as I hung up the telephone Miss Ruger announced that the Executive Secretary of the Veterans' Committee awaited my pleasure.

"Show him in," I said.

A thick burly veteran of the First World War rushed toward me; I slipped behind my desk, afraid of being tackled.

"The name's Fleer, Abner S. Fleer."

"My name is . . ."

"I'll come straight to the point . . . no use mincing matters, is there? When you got something to say say it, that's what I say."

"Shoot!" I said, showing that I could talk straight, too.

"We've been picketing your show, right?"

"Right."
"I'll bet you'd like us *not* to picket your show, right?"
"Wrong."
"Wrong?"
"It happens to be a very useful form of promotion, Mr. Frear."
"Fleer. That remains to be seen. Veterans are staying away . . . I can tell you that."
"Even without the veterans we are sold out not only for this season, but also on the road. We go to Chicago next week."
"Only because you've been cashing in on the other immoral goings-on in your show."
"You're referring to the murder?"
"I am indeed."
"Well, a man killed his wife and now the man is dead of a heart attack . . . so that's all over."
"We have reason to believe that your company is a hotbed of Reds and other undesirables."
"What makes you think so?"
"Mister, we have spent close to a hundred thousand in the last year to root Reds and other perverts out of our way of life, in government, entertainment and the life of everyday . . . and we're doing it. We have reason to believe this man Wilbur is a party member."
"If you can prove it why don't you get him indicted? Or whatever the procedure is."
"Because these fellows are slippery. Oh, we've been tipped off but that's a long way from getting a gander at his membership card."
"Then why don't you wait until you *have* got it . . . save a lot of bother."
"There's a moral issue involved. It may take us years to track him down . . . in the meantime he is corrupting our cherished ideals with his immoral dances. We want to put him out of commission right now and we're appealing to you as fellow Americans to help us."
"But I'm not convinced he *is* a Communist and neither is Mr. Washburn."
"We can show you reports from a dozen sources . . ."
"Malicious gossip," I said righteously.
"Are you trying to defend this radical?"
"I suppose I am. He is a great choreographer and I don't know anything about his politics and neither do you."
"By the way, Mister, just what are *your* politics?"

"I am a Whig, Mr. Fleer. The last President I voted for was Chester A. Arthur." On this mighty line, I got him out of the office, still shouting vengeance on all who attempted to sully our way of life.

I was pretty shaken by this interview with what was very likely one of the last perfect examples of Neanderthal man on the island of Manhattan. I went back into Mr. Washburn's office to get a drink . . . I knew that he kept a bottle of very good brandy in a bottom drawer of his Napoleonic desk. Since he wasn't in, I took a mouthful right out of the bottle; then, carefully, I put it back in the desk and idly glanced at the papers on his desk. One of them was a letter from Sylvia Armiger, the English ballerina . . . a short note which I naturally read, saying that she would be unable to succeed Eglanova for the '52 season, that she was already under contract, but many thanks and so forth and so on.

The old bastard, I thought, amused by Washburn's duplicity. Even with Sutton gone he was still trying to replace Eglanova. I was less amused, though, when I noticed the date on the letter . . . it was ten days old. It had been written *before* Ella Sutton's murder.

VI

The last night was a triumph. The box office reported that we had beaten all previous standing-room records for the Met and the audience was in a frantic mood, drowning out the music with almost continual applause for the stars who danced, I must say, with more skill than usual. If the audience was disappointed that the cable didn't break in *Eclipse*, they didn't show it for they called Jane back on stage seven times after the ballet. *Swan Lake* was magnificent in spite of several veterans who saw fit to heave a couple of firecrackers onto the stage . . . as well as a stink bomb which fortunately didn't go off.

Backstage, after the audience had left the theater, a great deal of vodka was stashed away by the Russian contingent . . . those members of the company born in Europe and their hangers-on . . . all singing and laughing and drinking vodka among the trunks and costumes. Eglanova was roaring drunk, weeping and laughing, her talk a mixture of Russian and English, all very confused.

Jane and I left early. Mr. Washburn caught us at the door and grandly gave me the next day off . . . after extending my contract another week. Jane, however, had to report at three-thirty the next day for rehearsal with Wilbur.

We spent the morning in bed, reading the newspapers and talking to people on the telephone, to dancers who were also spending this wonderful morning in bed, in various combinations. It was very cozy, like being part of a large family with, at the moment, no serious feuds to shatter the pleasant mood.

None of us could get over the fact that the investigation was finished, that Gleason was no longer a part of our lives.

"But," as Jane said in her most professional voice over the telephone to one of the boy soloists, a Greek god with a voice like Bette Davis, "where are we ever going to get another conductor as good as Miles?"

"I think Gold's working out fine," I said, when she had hung up the telephone and was sitting cross-legged beside me on the bed, idly pinching my belly, trying to find a serious fold of flesh to complain about: she has always thought I do too little exercise . . . the reason, I always tell her, why I can eat everything and stay slim while she exercises, eats like a horse and has to watch her weight.

"You don't have to follow him," she said irrelevantly, breathing deeply, rib-cage thrust forward, chin held high, breasts moving all of a piece, not quivering like jello the way most breasts do in this age of starch.

I grunted and shook her hand off my stomach as I read about our company, on page twenty-seven, in the *Globe:* "Murdered Dancer's Husband Dead" . . . "Suspected of Murder." An interview with Gleason followed, on page twenty-eight, without photograph.

"Kind of nice *not* to be on the front page," I said.

"Don't say that or you'll be thrown out of the press agents' guild or whatever it is that makes people like you the way they are."

"The bitch goddess."

"The what?"

"The ignoble concern with ephemeral reputation which has created people like me . . . professional criers, drumbeaters, trumpeters of brazen idols with feet of clay."

"Oh, shut up. Does John Martin say anything in the *Times* about us?"

"He says that the Grand Saint Petersburg Ballet is leaving town next week for a five-month tour."

She grabbed the *Times* away from me and read the column on "Dance" with the desperate concentration of a ballerina hunting for a good notice.

"Certainly a plug for Eglanova," she said at last, critically.

"Well, she's had a lot of them in her day."

"Wouldn't it be wonderful if she retired of her own free will?" said my good-hearted girl.

"I don't see why. She'd be miserable. She doesn't want to teach. I think it's real fine the old woman can keep going like this . . . and still be a big draw all over the map."

Jane scowled. "It's so hard on the rest of us . . . I mean, it keeps everybody back."

I snorted. "Listen to her! A week ago you were one of those lousy cygnets in *Swan Lake* pounding up and down the stage with three other girls in a Minsky routine and now you're thinking of the day when you'll succeed Eglanova."

With one long liquid line as a certain ballet critic might have described it, Jane Garden dealt me a thunderous blow with the pillow. After a stiff fight, I subdued her at last . . . quite a trick considering she is a solid girl and, in spite of her lovely silklike skin, all muscle.

"It's not true!" she gasped, her hair like a net over the white sheet as I held her tight on her back.

"Delusions . . . that's what it is."

"Everybody feels the same way. Ask any of the girls."

"Vicious group . . . ambitious, untalented."

"Oh!" And she twisted away from me and sat up in bed, breathing hard as she pushed her hair out of her face.

"It wouldn't surprise me one little bit if you knocked off Ella just to get her place in the company."

Jane laughed mournfully. "I don't need to tell you that our company works on the caste system. I was number seven ballerina before Ella died."

"But now you're number two because you knew that if Ella was out of the picture I'd see to it you got her part."

"Everything *has* worked out nicely," said Jane, beaming.

"You have no conscience."

"None at all. Especially now that the case is over."

"Were you afraid of being caught?"

"Well, seriously, I didn't feel so good when poor Miles died."

"Why?"

"Well, darling, I was there."

"There?"

"I saw him about an hour before he died . . . I stopped off on my way to the party."

"Good God!" I sat up in bed and looked at her . . . "Did you tell Gleason that?"

"No, I didn't. I . . . I suppose I was afraid."

"You little fool. . . ." I was alarmed. "Don't you realize that he had that building watched, that Miles was being watched every minute of the day and night no matter where he was? Did you go in the front way?"

"Did I go in . . . ? Of course I did. What do you think . . ."

"Then he knows that you were there and that you didn't mention it when he questioned you. What do you think he'll make of that?"

"But . . . Miles did do it, didn't he? The case is closed?" she asked in a small voice. I sometimes think that dancers have less brains than the average vegetable.

"I don't know that he did and neither do the police. I have a hunch he didn't but I may be wrong. Even so, no matter what the papers say or Gleason says, those boys are still interested in what happened to Ella . . . and maybe to Miles, too."

"I think you're exaggerating." But she was scared.

"By the way, if I'm not being indiscreet, just what were you doing at Miles' apartment that night?"

"I had a message for him, from Magda."

"Who paid a call on him later, after he was dead."

"I know . . . but she wanted me to see him and tell him something. Her family was watching her like a hawk and she told me she wasn't able to get away and would I please go and see him."

"This was before Don Ameche's invention of the telephone or the establishment of a national post office."

"I wish you wouldn't try to be funny."

"I couldn't be more serious."

"Then act like it."

"I am acting like it . . . God damn it . . ." We snarled at each other for several minutes; then she told me that Magda had not been able to leave her room for several days, that her family did not let her near the phone. Except for one stolen visit, Miles was not allowed to see her; as a matter of fact, the family had been reluctant to let her see even Jane.

"What did Magda want you to tell him?"

"What difference does it make now? . . . the whole thing's finished."

"Come on . . . what did she want you to tell him?"

"It was about the child. She wanted to know if Miles would like her to have an abortion."

"What did he say to that?"

"He said no, that they were going to get married as soon as the trial was over."

"How was he when you saw him?"

"High as a kite . . . he didn't make much sense . . . he kept rambling about the new ballet . . . I mean about *Eclipse* and Mr. Washburn . . . he was angry at him. I don't know why."

"Had Washburn been to see him?"

"No, not then."

"How did you know he *did* see him that night?" I was like a district attorney, ready for the kill. But it didn't work.

"Because I saw Mr. Washburn outside in the street when I left and he asked me how Miles was, if he was high or not."

"That was an awfully busy street that night, with half the company running in and out of Miles' apartment."

"Oh, stop trying to be smart. You sound like a movie."

"That may be," I said somberly. "Was Mr. Washburn upset when he saw you?"

"He was surprised; after all, we were both supposed to be at the party."

"He didn't swear you to secrecy . . ."

"Oh, stop it, will you? I don't think it's funny."

"I don't either. As a matter of fact it may be very serious . . . your having gone there without telling Gleason about it."

"He didn't ask me. After all, I didn't lie to him."

"What did he ask you?"

"Just a lot of questions . . . general things."

It was no use; when Jane decides to be vague it is like collecting fragments of quicksilver from a broken thermometer to get a straight story out of her.

"You better go and tell Gleason what you told me."

"I certainly won't now that everything's finished."

"Then don't say I didn't warn you."

At three o'clock I went to the office of the ballet and she went to rehearsal and neither of us was in a good mood. I was both angry and worried at what she had done. I wondered whether or not I should tell Gleason myself. For a number of reasons I decided not to. I *did* wonder if Mr. Washburn had told Gleason. This possibility had not occurred to me before; now, when I thought of it, my worry turned to alarm.

I found Mr. Washburn in his office playing with some silly putty which an admirer had given him; in case you haven't come across it, silly putty is a pink substance which, if rolled in a ball, will bounce better than rubber, which will shatter if you hit it with a hammer and which will stretch to an unbelievable length if you pull it . . . there is no point to silly putty and I took it as a serious sign that Mr. Washburn should now be stretching a long pink rope of it, like bubble gum, across his Napoleonic desk.

"I told you you could have the day off," said my employer, unabashed, beginning to plait the substance. Had his mind snapped under the strain?

"I thought I'd drop by and take care of a few things. Toledo wants some photographs, so I thought . . ." I watched, fascinated, while Mr. Washburn made a hangman's noose.

"Wonderful house last night," said Mr. Washburn. "The best so far."

"Good press this morning."

"Gratifying . . . gratifying. Did you ever see this stuff before?"

"Yes."

"Wonderful idea . . . relaxes the nerves." He rolled the putty into a ball and bounced it on the carpet where it sank deep; Mr. Washburn had to duck under his desk to retrieve it.

"By the way," I asked, "have you decided if you'll open the Chicago season with the new Wilbur ballet?"

"Mid-season . . . we'll do it our third week. I haven't picked the day yet."

"Shall we do anything about Miles' funeral tomorrow?"

Mr. Washburn draped the silly putty over his upper lip like a mustache, only it looked more like some awful cancerous growth; he frowned. "Better do nothing about it, Peter. The quicker this business is forgotten the better. Besides, it's going to be a family affair. A couple of aunts and a grandmother appeared on the scene, from Jersey, and they're in charge."

"Are you going?"

Mr. Washburn shook his head and returned the silly putty to its egg-shaped plastic container. "I don't think I will. I passed word on to the others that I thought it might be a good idea for them not to go either . . . papers would be sure to print a picture of Eglanova at the funeral, and give it space."

"Then I won't go either." I was relieved. I don't like funerals. Then I asked him, very casually, if he had said anything to the police about seeing Jane at Miles' apartment the night he died.

Mr. Washburn looked at me gravely. "She was a very unwise young lady not to tell the police she was there."

"Did *you* tell them?"

"No, I didn't. Which was unwise of me I suppose, but I have no intention of losing Garden just as she's begun to dance like a real ballerina. Under the circumstances I don't think the police are very much interested. After all, it's to their advantage to have the case finished."

"I suppose you're right."

"By the way, what did you tell that man from the Veterans' Committee yesterday?"

"I told him that it was up to them to prove Wilbur was a Communist."

Mr. Washburn chuckled. "You will be happy to know that you have been accused of being a Communist-sympathizer, a party-liner, a fellow-traveler and a degenerate by one Abner Fleer . . . have you got anything to say in your defense?"

"Nothing at all . . . except that I was driven into the hands of the enemy by Mr. Fleer and his kind in the days of my youth; even before my America First button had begun to tarnish, I found myself disenchanted with the keepers of the flame."

"I sympathize with you. The charges against Wilbur are getting serious, though. The columnists are beginning to take up the question, and, frankly, I'm worried about Chicago. It's not like New York. The Veterans' Committee is a joke here but out there it carries a lot of weight and we may be in trouble if they decide to blackball us."

"What can we do?"

"I wish I knew."

"Couldn't we take an ad and say that he's already been cleared twice?"

"We'll have to do something like that. Think about it, anyway. That's your big assignment for the next week . . . getting Mr. Wilbur, and us, off the hook."

"I'll think of something," I said with the same air of quiet confidence which has made a fortune for any number of movie actors, con-men and politicians.

Eglanova, in a summer dress and a set of sables (the day was hot but she wouldn't be Eglanova without sable), swept into the office. We both rose and Mr. Washburn leaned across the desk and kissed her hand.

"Such wonderful last night!" she exclaimed, glowing with pleasure. "Such applause! Such loyalty! I weep to remember it."

But her narrow mascaraed eyes were dry, the lashes as artfully curled as ever.

"Darling Anna! You are the *prima* of our time . . . the ultimate."

"Such nice thing to say, Ivan. Of course last night I *tried*. That makes difference. But those *awful* people!" She scowled, looking like Attila the Hun or maybe Genghis Khan contemplating traitors. "Who *are* these people anyway? Who are people who throw things when Eglanova dances? Ivan, you must do something."

"They weren't throwing things at you, Anna. They were throwing them at Wilbur."

"Even so they hit *me* when I dance Swan Queen. If they don't like Jed, why don't they throw things during *Eclipse*?"

Mr. Washburn laughed. "I expect they intended to but they got their signals mixed. In any case, we won't have trouble with them in Chicago . . . rest assured." Eglanova did not look as though she were resting assured but she changed the subject.

"Dear Peter," she said, turning at me and smiling a dazzling smile, "I must thank you for not telling police about those big scissors. It was sweet of you . . . very brave. I thank you." And she patted my arm.

"I told her," said Mr. Washburn. "I told her that you didn't want to incriminate her."

I mumbled something graceful and incoherent.

"So strange," sighed Eglanova. "Why would Miles want to put scissors in my room? *I* who am last person to harm fellow artist."

Both Mr. Washburn and I expressed wonder at the murderer's intention; then, aware that some ballet plot was afoot, I excused myself. I was sure, even then, that Mr. Washburn had told the police about having seen Jane at Miles' apartment.

2

Jane and I were very cool with one another that evening and even cooler the next morning when we got up early, at ten o'clock, and made breakfast. She was angry at my having scolded her and I was alarmed at her bad sense; the fact that the night had passed without lovemaking didn't put me in a very good mood either.

It wasn't until we had finished a pot of coffee between us, that I told her what Mr. Washburn had said.

"Well, there wasn't any reason for him to say I was there." She looked sulky and she wore her dressing gown which was a bad sign . . . usually neither of us wear any clothes around the apartment.

"Except that he could get into trouble, too, for not mentioning it

... but I've got a hunch he *did* tell them ... if only because they know already."

"I think you're making an awful fuss about nothing ... that's what I think," said Jane, massaging her calves.

"How was the rehearsal?"

"Tough." She sighed. "It isn't like a rehearsal with Alyosha ... I'll say that. Wilbur screams at you and half the time I think he makes up the ballet as he goes along."

"I wonder if it'll be any good?"

"I suppose so. They say this is the way he always works."

"He wasn't like this during *Eclipse,* was he?"

"He was pretty noisy ... of course I wasn't there too much of the time. He worked mainly with the principals ... especially Louis."

"How's the big affair coming?"

"Not so well ... I don't think Louis likes him very much."

"But he likes Louis?"

"Madly. You should see the way he looks at him, like a spaniel or something."

The telephone rang. Jane answered it. She said "yes" several times then she said, "Come right over." And hung up.

"Who was that?"

"Magda. She's given up her apartment and she's going to move in here."

"I see." I turned to ice, thinking of my own lonely apartment downtown.

"I thought I'd let her stay on here after we go to Chicago. She'll look after the apartment and everything."

"And for the next week?"

"Well, I mean it's only a week ..."

"And I can go home?"

"But think of all she's gone through ... not a friend in the world except me. As a matter of fact, she may be pretty sick starting tomorrow."

"Why?"

"She's found a doctor who'll ... you know ... fix her, take care of the baby."

"What about her family?"

"They've gone back to Boston, thank God."

For a number of reasons, none charitable, I thought it best not to complain. With the air of a martyr surveying the flames, I packed my suitcase while Jane telephoned all her friends to discuss Magda, the ballet, Jed Wilbur and the doings of rival companies.

We were both dressed and ready to leave when Magda appeared, looking dumpy in a linen suit and carrying a suitcase. The two girls embraced tenderly.

"I hope I'm not being too awful . . . I mean moving in like this," said Magda, looking at me with red-rimmed eyes. She had obviously been weeping steadily for over a week now. I never felt more uncompassionate toward anyone in my life, at that moment anyway.

"Of course not," I said, with an attempt at cheeriness. "I think it's wonderful . . . now that your family's gone."

"We were just going to rehearsal," said Jane. "Why don't you make yourself at home. I'll be back at five."

"Do you think they'd mind if I went too? I'd like to sit and watch awhile . . . see what the new ballet's like." She sounded very wistful. "I can get my other bags later."

"That's a fine idea," said Jane who seemed more pleased with this new arrangement than she had any reason to be. So I grabbed the suitcase, bade the ladies farewell and took a cab for my Ninth Street apartment. Then, after a visit with Miss Flynn at my own office, I walked to the studio.

The Grand Saint Petersburg Ballet operates a school over in Hell's Kitchen, on the West Side. They occupy the fifth floor of a terrible old building which should have been condemned long ago. Their section, however, has been done up handsomely, very modern, and they have four classrooms as well as a large studio which is often used for rehearsal, sparing Mr. Washburn the unnecessary expense of hiring halls which he occasionally has to do during the season.

I arrived at about three-thirty and visited some of the classes before I went to the room where Jed Wilbur was creating like mad with Jane and most of the company.

There was a very chic-looking reception hall where the dancers often sit about in tights waiting for their hour in class, a long hall decorated with mobiles and paintings of dancers, with a desk at one end where Madame Aloin, formerly of the Paris Opera, sits in splendor and receives visitors and incoming telephone calls.

I said good afternoon to Madame Aloin who gave me a stately nod; then I wandered into the nearest classroom. Here a number of dismal tiny tots were being run through a set of exercises by a bored, overweight dancer who had once been celebrated before his thyroid had begun malfunctioning. The mothers, a row of somber ladies, gray and determined, glared at me as the piano plunked one two one two. I shut the door.

The next two classrooms were more interesting: lovely blond girls in black tights practicing intricate variations with a group of muscle-bound sissies. Somewhat aroused, *wanting* to be aroused since I was angry at Jane, at the celibacy she had arranged for me, I went to the fourth classroom which was empty, a cube of a room, like the rest, with mirrors at one end and a waist-high bar at the other end where the dancers did exercises, and tall windows which went almost to the floor. In one corner of this room is a door which opens into the rehearsal hall, a sneak entrance often used by the stars when they want to get out quickly, when they see the bores, the balletomanes, waiting for them at the main door.

The rehearsal looked like a panic. Most of the *corps de ballet* was there, in tights and T-shirts, drenched with sweat, as the piano banged out a phrase of Poulenc, over and over, while Wilbur shouted excitedly at them, his thin gray hair on end and his face flushed.

"Lift with the music! Lift with the music . . . it's not that difficult. Listen . . . there is your phrase. Lift the girls on the second beat, start it then, finish on the fourth. Da da dum dada . . . hear? Da da *lift* . . . da da *lift*! Now try it again."

I sat down on the long hard bench by the door and watched the *corps de ballet* go through its paces. They all looked tired and wretched in the heat. I was glad I wasn't a dancer.

Jane seemed worried as she did her solo in front of the company who were, in the meantime, doing a complicated movement behind her. Louis, who was not in this particular part, came ambling over to me with his usual grin. "Hi, baby . . . long time no see." For some reason, Louis, when he learned English, absorbed a great deal of Nineteen-twenty slang which sounds very funny coming from him, with his French accent and all. He sat down beside me, his knee shoved hard against mine. I moved away.

"You want to go up to Harlem with me tonight? I got a couple cute numbers there . . . oh, you like them fine."

"I got enough where I am, honey," I said, falling into his way of talking.

"That's too bad. We could have a swell time, you and me . . . up in Harlem."

"Not my idea of a swell time."

"What sort of boy are you? American boys all like . . ." and he made an obscene gesture. I glanced around nervously but nobody was watching us . . . the music covered our voices and Wilbur was giving the dancers hell.

"I guess I'm un-American," I said.

"Maybe you like real young boys . . . maybe I'm too old for you."

"Louis, you're my idea of heaven . . . honest to God you are, but I'd feel selfish having you all to myself when the fellows in the company need you so much more than I do. Why I wouldn't even know how to begin to appreciate you."

"I teach you in one plenty fast lesson." And I moved away as that sinewy leg slammed against mine. Then Wilbur saw his love and with a look of real alarm said, "Louis! That's your cue." And our hero bounded to his feet and joined Wilbur and Jane in the center of the room. *"Adagio!"* shouted Wilbur to the pianist; the boys and girls relaxed, wilted in decorative attitudes against the bar, talking to each other in low voices while Louis and Jane did their *pas de deux*.

I got up and stretched my legs. Magda came into the hall and smiled wanly at me.

"How is it going?" she asked.

"Damned if I can tell. Looks like a riot from where I'm sitting."

"It usually works out," she said vaguely, sitting down. "How does Jane look?"

"Worried," I said flatly; I was angry with Miss Garden.

"Such a responsibility, having a new ballet being made for you."

"And a few other people."

Eglanova and Alyosha entered the room, like an old king and queen come to watch the heirs-apparent at play. They nodded regally to Wilbur and the company and then they sat down on the bench, very straight. I joined them.

I chatted with Alyosha while Eglanova and Magda watched Wilbur at work.

"Such great confusion," said Alyosha. "No one can tell what it is. I hope he is nearly done, though."

"Why?"

"He must go to Washington on Wednesday." Alyosha did not bother to disguise his pleasure.

"To be investigated?"

"Exactly . . . very secret hearing, but I found out . . . now it is not so secret!" Alyosha laughed.

"Does Wilbur know?"

"I'm sure he does. So I hope the ballet will be ready in case he doesn't come back from Washington for a few days." Or years, I could hear our régisseur say to himself. Old Alyosha was, I knew, afraid that he would be retired one of these days, be replaced by one of the bright young men, like Jed Wilbur.

"Looks like the veterans have carried the day," I said.

"Pretty girl!" said Eglanova as Jane did some glittering *chaîné* turns into Louis' arms.

"In ten years she will be ready to take your place," said Alyosha gallantly.

"Dear friend!" said our star, her eyes black slits as she watched Jane do her stuff.

Then the door to the hall opened and Mr. Washburn peered in at us; he gestured for me to join him. I slipped out of the hall and joined him in the reception room.

"More trouble," he said with a sigh.

"About the hearings in Washington?"

"Exactly. I think it'll be in all the papers tomorrow. I was trying to hush it up but now it's too late. The F.B.I. is mixed up in the case."

"He's not guilty, is he?"

"I don't think so. I don't think that they have anything important. They only want to question him . . . but that's enough to get all the witch-hunters in this town against us. Not to mention Chicago."

"What can we do?"

"Make it appear that he's testifying of his own free will . . . which I suppose he is, in a way. We'll try and make a big thing of his turning informer . . . you know what I mean: ex-liberal telling what he knows about Communism in the theater."

"Seems kind of sick-making."

"So what? We've got a long tour ahead of us and I've tied up a good deal of money in Wilbur." You and Alma Edderdale and twenty other patrons, I thought.

"Have you talked it over with Wilbur?"

"Oh yes . . . just before rehearsal this afternoon. He's going to follow the same line. He doesn't want trouble . . . especially if he's innocent, and signed to do the new Hayes and Marks musical in the fall . . ." he added irrelevantly.

"What do you want me to do then? Get in touch with the papers directly? Or work through the columnists?"

"Get to the papers directly; but first you'll have to handle Elmer Bush. He's on his way over to look around, he says, but of course he's going to try and get some kind of exclusive out of Jed or me. Now I'm going to keep out of sight and I'm going to keep Jed away from Bush, if possible. Your job is to head him off . . . even if you have to hint that Jed has got some wild revelations for the committee in Washington."

"I'll do what I can," I said, like the Spartan youth with the fox at his vitals.

"Good fellow," said Mr. Washburn, hurrying down the hall to the classroom of tiny tots where he intended, obviously, to hide out until Elmer Bush, a symphony in blue: shirt, suit, socks and tie, appeared in our reception hall, causing a bit of a stir among the dancers who were sitting on the benches waiting to go into class . . . it was five minutes to the hour.

"Why, hello there," said Mr. Bush, flashing that television smile of his, the dentures superbly wrought and fitted. "Washburn or Wilbur around? . . . old friend of mine, Ivan Washburn." In spite of his fame and power he still had the reporter's nervous habit of trying a little too hard to establish friendship with persons in high and interesting places, for the moment interesting, for the moment news.

"They aren't here right now, Mr. Bush . . . is there anything I can do for you?"

"Call me Elmer," said the great man mechanically, taking in the room with a reporter's eye, a lecher's eye too, for his gaze paused longer than necessary over one of the girls, a slim brown-haired number with a T-shirt. "Nice place you people have here. Terrible neighborhood, though. Been fighting for years now to get it cleaned up. Made absolutely no headway. When do you expect Wilbur?"

It took me a moment to separate the question from what had promised to be a thoughtful Elmer Bush report of city-planning. "Well, you know he's pretty busy with that new ballet."

"They're rehearsing it here."

Since this wasn't a question, but a statement, I had to agree. "But nobody's allowed in the studio while he's working. He's very difficult."

"We'll see how difficult he is when that committee gets through with him in Washington."

"How did you know about that . . . Elmer?" I asked, very folksy, my eyes round with admiration.

"Never ask an old reporter to tell his sources," chuckled Bush, pleased with the effect he thought he was making.

"Why, *I* only heard about it an hour ago."

"That so? Then tell me this . . . how do you people plan to get your big wheel off the spot?"

"Well, for one thing we happen to know he's not a Communist and for another thing he's going to tell all he knows about the Reds in the theater."

"It's a closed hearing, too," said Bush thoughtfully. "Got any idea about some of the names he's going to mention?"

"Nobody very big," I invented glibly. "A few of the old North American Ballet Company people, that's about all."

"You've been having a busy time, haven't you, Pete," said Bush, suddenly focusing his attention on me for the first time in our long if superficial acquaintanceship.

"I'll say."

"They really wind that Sutton case up?"

"I think so . . . don't you?"

"Haven't heard anything to the contrary . . . worked out very neatly, from the police's point of view . . . no trial, no expense for the state . . . perfect case." While we talked I kept trying to edge him into the empty classroom before the hour struck, before four o'clock when Wilbur would take a break, on the dot, because that's a company rule even the most temperamental choreographers have to obey. But Mr. Bush wouldn't budge: the secret perhaps of his success. At four o'clock the door to the studio opened and thirty tired and messy dancers came charging out, heading for the dressing rooms, the drinking fountain, the telephone . . . I have a theory that dancers, next to hostesses, spend more time telephoning than any other single group in America.

Elmer Bush kept on talking but his eyes looked like they were on swivels, like the chameleon who can see in all directions. At first he couldn't spot anybody; then I waved to Jane who was standing by the door to the empty classroom, adjusting the ribbon to one of her toeshoes. It was five after four. She waved above the noisy crowd of dancers, parents and tiny tots (all the classes let out on the hour) and, breathless, came to us through a sea of sweating dancers.

"This is the young ballerina in *Eclipse*, Mr. Bush . . . Jane Garden."

They shook hands and Jane was pretty enough to distract Bush's attention long enough for Mr. Washburn to sneak past us, in the shadow of the corpulent teacher of dance with whom he pretended to talk. Before he got to the door, however, the first policeman had arrived.

3

It took them four hours to question the *corps de ballet*, parents, even the tiny tots, most of whom were whining loudly at this unexpected turn of events. But by the time Gleason had arrived, only the principals were left, all seated glumly in the studio, on that hard bench.

The body of Magda had been taken immediately to the morgue and though none of us had seen it the rumor was that she had been pretty badly smashed by her fall from the window of the classroom adjoining the rehearsal studio.

A policeman stood in the door of the studio, watching us as though we were wild animals. Inspector Gleason did not present himself to us upon arrival; we heard his full-throated Irish voice, however, as he had a desk set up for himself in the empty classroom. Here he received us, one by one.

We talked very little during those hours. Mr. Washburn, with remarkable presence of mind, had summoned his lawyer who waited now with a brief case full of writs calculated to circumvent any and every vagary of justice.

Eglanova, after one brilliant outburst of Imperial Moscow anger, had settled down to a quiet chat with Alyosha, in Russian. Alyosha was more nervous; he continually screwed and unscrewed his monocle, wiping it with a silk handkerchief. Jane, who sat beside me, wept a little and I comforted her. Wilbur, after a display of Dubuque, Iowa, temperament, settled down for a long tense quarrel with Louis, a quarrel which had nothing to do with Magda. For some reason Madame Aloin had been placed under suspicion as well as the pianist, a worm-white youth who acted exactly the way you would suppose a murderer at bay to act. Mr. Washburn was not with us long, since he was the first witness to be called. I might add that Elmer Bush had contrived to remain with us in the studio, after first phoning his numerous staff: this was one exclusive he was sure of . . . television star or not he was the same Elmer Bush who, twenty years ago, was the best crime reporter in the country. He chatted with everyone now . . . first with one; then with another, conducting a suave investigation which, I swear, was a good deal brighter than the one the taxpayer's burden was conducting in the next room.

"Come on, baby," I whispered to Jane, my arm around her. "Don't take it so hard. It's just one of those things . . ." I whispered stupidly, soothingly, because after a while she stopped and dried her eyes with a crumpled piece of Kleenex.

"I can't believe it," she said, shaking her head. "Not Magda . . . not like that."

"Tell them everything, Jane . . . everything. This is serious. Tell them about your being at Miles' place."

"Poor Magda . . ."

"You'll do that, won't you?"

"What? Do what?" I told her again and she looked surprised. "But what's that got to do with Magda?"

"It may have everything to do with her, with all of us. Promise you'll tell Gleason the whole story."

"If you think I ought to."

"I do. I'm sure all three of these things are connected."

"So am I," said Jane unexpectedly.

I was surprised . . . she had always been very unrealistic about the trouble . . . almost as bad as Mr. Washburn and his "accident" theories. I asked her why she had changed her mind.

"Something Magda said today . . . something about Miles . . . I don't remember exactly what it was but she . . . I think she knew who killed Ella. I think Miles must have known all along and told her that day when he went to see her, when she was sick and her family happened to be out."

"She—didn't tell you who it was?"

"Do you think I would be sitting here like this scared to death if she had? I'd be right in there with that policeman, telling him I wanted somebody arrested before . . . before this happens again." She shuddered suddenly and I felt cold myself. I looked about the room wildly, wondering who it was. Which of these people was a murderer? Or had someone who wasn't even here killed Ella and Magda, a maniac in the *corps de ballet* . . . ?

"I wonder just what happened?" I asked, changing the subject.

"I know," said Elmer Bush smoothly; he had sat down next to me without my knowing it . . . what a break this was for him: witness, or near-witness to a murder, a flashy, glamorous murder. He could hardly keep a straight face, hardly disguise his delight at what had happened. "A terrible tragedy," he said in a low voice, the one used to announce the death of forty passengers on a transatlantic airliner, or corruption in Washington.

"How did it happen?"

"She was pushed through the window . . . one minute after four o'clock," said Elmer and the tip of his tongue, quick as a lizard's, moistened his lips.

"By party or parties unknown," I said.

"Exactly. Her purse was found on the floor; her body on the sidewalk seven stories below."

"The purse . . ."

He finished my sentence: "Had been searched. Its contents were scattered over the floor. Whoever did it must've grabbed the purse away from her and then, quick as a flash, shoved her through the window and searched the handbag for something . . ."

"Robbery?" suggested Jane weakly.

We both ignored her. "I wonder what they were looking for?"

"When we know that," said Elmer slowly, in his best doom voice, "we will know who killed Ella and Miles Sutton."

I remember hoping at the time that the three murders were totally unconnected, just to prove this unctuous vulture wrong.

"Tell me," said Elmer gently, turning to Jane, "did she seem at all odd to you when you went into that room together?"

"Sweet Jesus!" I cried softly, turning to Jane. "You weren't with her, were you? You weren't there, too?"

"Always on the spot," said Jane with a faint attempt at lightness.

"Does Gleason know this?"

"I plan to tell him . . . honest I will, Peter."

"He knows anyway," said omniscient Elmer. "Did she say something which might throw any light on what happened?"

"No, she didn't."

"Why did you go in there with her?"

"Now listen, Bush," I snapped, "stop playing Mr. District Attorney. She's gone through enough."

"That's all right, Peter." She rallied a bit. "Magda wasn't feeling well. She's going . . . she *was* going to have a baby and she suddenly felt sick. I took her in there when the rehearsal was over . . . it was the only place on the floor where she wouldn't be crowded. Then I left her and talked to you. . . . Maybe she fell. She could have, you know. Those windows . . . well, look over there: they almost go down to the floor."

"Fell? After first emptying her purse over the studio floor?" Elmer shook his head. "Somebody shoved her. Was there anybody else in the room?"

Jane shook her head wearily. "I said it was empty."

"Anybody could have gone in there," said Elmer Bush, staring at the door at the far end of the room, behind which we could hear the distant rumble of Gleason's voice as he questioned Mr. Washburn.

The interviews went fairly fast. Eglanova, Alyosha, Wilbur, Louis, Madame Aloin, the pianist, Jane, myself. By the time my turn came around, it was already dark outside and the overhead fluorescent lights had been turned on, a ghastly blue light, reflected by tall mirrors.

The first thing I noticed was the window. For some reason I had supposed that it had been open when she fell out. It hadn't occurred to me that she would have been pushed through a pane of glass . . . which is what had happened.

Gleason looked much as ever and I noticed the same pale secretary was on hand taking notes; otherwise, the room was empty . . . no police, no furniture, no rifled handbag.

We got through the preliminaries quickly. I could see that he was not very much interested in me . . . possibly because Elmer had already told him that I was with him in the hall when the murder took place . . . what was that wonderful word they use to describe someone being pushed through a window: defenestration?

He wanted to know what, if anything, Magda had said to me that morning.

"She didn't talk much to me . . . I know she told Jane about her abortion. She was going to have it tomorrow; that was her plan."

"In the meantime she was going to live with Miss Garden?"

"That's right."

"Ordinarily you live in Miss Garden's apartment?"

I blushed. "For the last week or so," I said. "Do you plan to book me for lewdness?"

Gleason showed his teeth in a friendly snarl. "This is homicide, Sargeant, not the vice squad." He enjoyed saying my last name; he made it sound like a police rank, a subordinate rank. "We have reason to think the deaths of Ella Sutton and Magda Foote were the work of the same person."

"I think so, too."

"Why?"

"Because a few days ago at the theater, Magda told us, Jane and me, that she knew Miles was innocent and that he knew who had killed Ella. I asked her then if he'd told her and she said no he hadn't but I thought she was lying . . . I'm positive she was lying. I'll bet anything Magda knew."

"If she knew why didn't she come to us?"

"I don't know why. For one thing, she probably didn't care whether you ever caught Ella's murderer or not . . . after all she hated Ella and Miles' death was an accident, wasn't it?"

"As far as we know. Why wouldn't Miles Sutton have told us who killed Ella when he knew he was our number one suspect, that we were going to arrest him the second we could break his alibi . . . and we broke it, finally."

"According to Magda, he wasn't going to say anything until the trial . . . or until you arrested him. I think he hoped you wouldn't be able to pin it on anybody."

"That wasn't very realistic."

"I'd hardly call a man as far gone on drugs as Miles realistic . . . remember that whoever killed Ella was doing him a service. He wouldn't turn the murderer in . . . unless it was to save his own neck."

Gleason asked me some more questions, about members of the company, about Magda, pointless questions, or so they seemed to me . . . and probably were in fact because it was quite obvious that the police were completely at sea. I was then told to come back the next day for questioning, to stay in New York City at an address where I could be reached at a moment's notice . . . I gave them Jane's address.

She was waiting for me in the reception hall. Everyone had gone except Louis and herself and Wilbur. Louis had apparently just come from the shower room for his hair was gleaming with water, the celebrated black curls damp and straggly. Jane was also in her street clothes, looking very pale, her face not made up. Wilbur was talking excitedly, "As if I didn't have enough trouble without all this. A major investigation hanging over my head . . . I was supposed to go to Washington tomorrow . . . and a half-finished ballet and now one of those goddamned murder investigations this company seems to specialize in. I wish to hell I'd stayed in musical comedy. Nothing like this ever happened there."

"Shows we were just waiting for you, Jed," said Louis amiably. "It was all Mr. Washburn's idea to knock you off so Alyosha would remain the greatest living choreographer."

"Much help you've been through all this," said Jed spitefully. Jane and I got out before the lovers quarreled.

We both took it for granted that I was not going to go to my place after what happened. Jane was terrified at the thought of being alone.

"I'm sure it's a lunatic," she said, when we were back at the apartment, eating cold cuts and drinking beer from the near-by delicatessen.

"How do we know he isn't going to murder everybody in the company while the police sit by and let him kill us, one by one?"

"Come on, kid," I said, as calmly as possible. "Get a grip on yourself. Your old buddy is right here with you."

"I'm still frightened," she said, chewing a piece of liverwurst thoughtfully. "Not just of the murderer either."

"The police?"

She nodded.

"Did you tell Gleason about having been at Miles' apartment?"

"I told him everything."

"Then you have nothing to fear," I said heartily, beginning to slip out of my clothes.

"Pull the shade down," said Jane.

"You *are* jumpy." As a rule we never put the shade down or put the lights out either. But I went over to the window and drew the curtains; they stuck a little and by the time I had pulled them together I had seen the plain-clothes man across the street, watching the apartment.

I remember thinking how unusual it was to be making love to a girl who was thought by some to have murdered two, maybe three people.

V

Medical examination, inquest, more questioning . . . it promised to be a long day. When I was not participating in the official rites of investigation, conducted as solemnly as a church service by Gleason, I was at the office holding Mr. Washburn's hand and battling some thirty newsmen who had appeared at nine o'clock in the morning (proving we were news) and stayed in the anteroom chatting with our duo-typists most of the day, complaining about the meager handouts they got from me. The police were saying nothing and I had silenced the members of our company. Even so there were a dozen wild theories in the air and the editorial in the afternoon *Globe* demanded that the murderer be instantly produced . . . if not, the *Globe* suggested balefully, there might be some changes made in the office of the Commissioner.

I was almost afraid to read the columns that afternoon. The news stories were all right: they just reported the facts, which were few . . . Third Murder in Ballet Mystery. But the columnists, in their own libelous way, were hinting pretty strongly that someone highly placed in the ballet world, in our company, had done the three murders. Needless to say, in spite of the official theory, everyone was convinced that there was a connection between the deaths of Miles and Ella and Magda. The *Globe* had the inside story. Beloved Elmer Bush had seen to that. His column made the front page . . . an exclusive report by An Eyewitness.

"Little did I think, as I talked with the beauteous Magda, that a few moments later she would lie broken and alone in the street below. She must have known even then what fate had in store for her. There was something other-worldly in her manner, a remoteness, a true serenity. I think she wanted to join her friend Miles Sutton in a better world, to be as one with the father of her unborn child. Yet as we stood talking to one another in that busy rehearsal studio, a murderer was watching us, plotting her destruction. Did she know his (or her?) identity? Yes, I have reason to believe she did . . ."

"I don't want to hear any more," said Mr. Washburn, draining his third shot of brandy.

"It's more of the same," I said, putting the paper down on the floor, to join the pile by my chair. We were in his office. One of the duo-typists had brought us sandwiches for lunch and the newsmen had momentarily deserted us. We were taking no calls and reading no mail.

"I wonder if we shouldn't take that South American tour . . . we could leave next week . . . well, in two weeks' time anyway. First Guatemala City then Panama, Bogotá, Rio, Buenos Aires . . ." Naming these remote places seemed to soothe my employer who sat now sniffing his empty brandy glass, his eyes bloodshot and glazed.

"I'm afraid the police wouldn't let us go," I said gently.

He pulled himself together with a visible effort. "You take over," he said, as though I hadn't been in charge all along, since nine anyway. "I'm going down to City Hall. After that, I'll be at the studio in case you want me."

"The rehearsals still going on?"

"Oh yes. Gleason was very decent about that. In fact, he's moved into one of the classrooms . . . the one where . . . He stopped. "I suppose he wants to be on the scene."

"Try and stop them," I said, as Mr. Washburn placed his panama squarely on the center of his long head, the brim parallel to the floor.

"Stop who?"

"The police . . . when you see them. I think they're going to make an arrest."

"What makes you think so?"

"First, because I've read the papers today. They want an arrest. And, second, because Jane is being watched by the police."

"I'm sure they don't suspect her."

"It's a toss-up, Mr. Washburn, between her and Eglanova."

He shuddered. "Don't say that. Don't even think it."

"I'm perfectly willing not to think it but some of these columnists won't be so obliging. They've done everything except name names. 'Jealous ballerina' . . . that's their line, and that could mean only one of two people."

"Let's wait until we come to this bridge," said Mr. Washburn, with the air of a man ready to fall into a river. Then he left the office.

But I couldn't wait. I wasn't really worried about Jane. She was obviously innocent and if they indicted her they wouldn't be able to convict. I was confident of that. But even if justice prevailed she would be marked all her life as the girl who had been accused of a murder. I can still remember what happened to a certain musical comedy star back in the Thirties.

I sat at Mr. Washburn's desk for several minutes, more worried than I'd ever been in my life. Idly, with a pencil stub, I began to write names: Eglanova, Wilbur, Alyosha, Washburn, Louis . . . I stopped; then I wrote Jane's name at the bottom. I made a box around it, carefully, an elaborate doodle, like a wall protecting her. I was confident that one of those six had been responsible for the murders. But which one? I had to admit to myself that for all I cared the murderer could go free. The Suttons and Magda meant nothing to me; if someone disliked them or feared them enough to want to kill them, well, that was hardly my business. A callous way of looking at things but you must remember that I liked the suspects, most of them anyway, and I wished them no harm . . . I'm not a crusader or a reformer and I have no passion for justice: not the crazy way the world is now at least. Official murder, private murder . . . what's the difference? Not much, except when you're involved yourself or someone you care about is. The more I thought about it the madder I got.

I was very grim when I wrote "Why?" at the top of the page; then, next to it, I wrote "How?" Just trying to be methodical made everything seem much better. At least it was all in front of me . . . like a crossword puzzle, or a double acrostic. If I could only fill in the blanks under each column I might be able to figure it out without leaving my desk . . . as you see, I have that happy faith in logic which only a liberal arts education can give.

Eglanova. Why? Well, she didn't want to retire. She knew that Mr. Washburn could not get another ballerina with her pull at the box office for at least a year . . . except Ella Sutton. That was motive enough for someone of Eglanova's dedication. As for Miles and Magda, I was convinced that their deaths were connected with Ella's, that they had been killed because they knew who the murderer was . . . which took care of the "Why?" of their deaths. So the only important motive was the original one: who wanted to kill Ella Sutton; who had the strongest *known* motive? The answer was Eglanova. When could she have done the murders? Presuming that Miles had been murdered in some mysterious way. Well, she was at the theater from dress rehearsal to performance, almost continuously. She could have cut the cable any time. And Miles? She was at the party Alma Edderdale gave and she could have left at any time, gone to his apartment and climbed the fire escape without being seen by the police. But even as I checked her in, made it possible for her to have visited Miles, I felt a certain misgiving: it was not in character. Anna Eglanova might in a rage eliminate a rival, but I could hardly see the great ballerina skulking up a fire escape in the middle of the night. Of course everything is possible. As for Magda . . . well, any of my six suspects could have pushed her out of that window. There was such confusion when the rehearsal broke up that someone could have followed Magda into the classroom, grabbed the purse, shoved her out the window and slipped back into the studio, all undetected.

Sadly, I crossed out "How?" at the top of the page. It wouldn't work, or rather it worked too well: no one had an alibi. Each time the doughty six had been in the same place at more or less the same time and all had equal opportunity to commit the murders. So, instead of "How?" I wrote a large question mark over the column next to "Why?" Here I recorded the mysteries.

Opposite Eglanova's name I wrote "Shears." If she had sliced the cable, why did she leave the shears in her own dressing room? That was a problem which I left unsolved as I moved on to the next name on the list.

Wilbur. Why? God knows. He didn't get on with Sutton but obviously if he hated her, for some reason as yet unknown, he would hardly have come to work in the same company with her, create a whole new ballet around her. Was he jealous of her? No. He didn't like women to begin with; nor did their love interests overlap. Professional jealousy? None that I could see. Something in the past, perhaps? Mysteries? Why did he quarrel with Ella the afternoon of the day she was killed?

Alyosha. Why? Love for Eglanova and hatred of Ella his ex-mistress. That was clear-cut, a perfect crime of passion. He had been married to Eglanova, left her for Ella who had deserted him; then he went back to Eglanova, as official slave and acolyte, and now, seeing that Eglanova was soon to be succeeded by Sutton, he lost his head and removed Ella from this vale of tears. Mysteries? Why would he put the shears in Eglanova's dressing room, implicating her if he'd done the murder for love of her? My head began to ache. Those goddamned shears . . . they made a mess of every theory. Then a new idea occurred to me. Suppose the person who had done the murder had put the shears some place else and then another villain had, for malicious reasons, put them in Eglanova's room from which I moved them again . . . button button who's got the button?

Washburn. Why? Well, he is the most devious man alive. For all I know he may have wanted to get rid of both Sutton and Eglanova, and he saw this as a perfect way to take care of them. Among the mysteries was the fact of that letter I found from Armiger, the English ballerina. Why had Mr. Washburn wanted to engage a big star when the succession had already been arranged, when it had been all but announced that Sutton was to succeed Eglanova for the next season? And what was Mr. Washburn really up to at Miles' apartment that night?

Louis. Why? I could think of no reason. There was an old rumor in the company that Ella fancied him but since he was so obviously interested in the other side he could hardly have been disturbed by her love for him, presuming that glacier had ever experienced such a tender emotion. I made a note to ask Louis about Ella; it was possible that he had some unsuspected slant on her character. More and more I was convinced that her character would provide the clue to the puzzle.

Jane? Well, despite the mysterious visit to Miles and her incriminating presence in the classroom with Magda, she had no motive. She was not in line to succeed Sutton even though she was the understudy in *Eclipse*. She had no professional reason for wanting Ella out of the way and after living a while with her, I was fairly sure she had no private reason as well; their private lives had never touched, as far as I knew.

Gloomily, I studied the page, awaiting revelation. None came. The thought that my hypothesis might be wrong was chilling. I was going on the theory that X had killed Ella, that Miles had found out and was on the point of revealing X's identity to the police when X, getting wind of this, jammed Miles' head into the gas burner, not knowing that Miles had somehow gotten a letter or document off to Magda, his proof that X had done the murder. Then X had made a date with Magda to meet her at the studio to discuss the letter . . . perhaps, even to buy it from her. When she wouldn't hand it over X had seized the purse which contained whatever it was the murderer wanted and shoved

Magda through the window. That was my theory, the police's theory, too. But suppose Miles had killed Ella and then died of a heart attack and that Y, for reasons unknown, killed Magda? Or suppose . . . But I made up my mind not to think of any more difficulties. First, I would follow the obvious line; if that failed . . . well, it *wouldn't* fail. As I look back on it now, I think my confidence in myself at that point was remarkably unjustified.

I had reason to believe from Gleason's behavior that morning at the inquest that he was planning to make an arrest in the next twenty-four hours . . . Elmer Bush had said as much in his column and he had undoubtedly got it from the horse's ass. I looked at my watch. Three-thirty. I had less than a day in which to find the murderer.

I spent about twenty valuable minutes on the telephone, lining up the suspects, making appointments for spurious reasons. Then I told the duo-typists that they would see me no more that day. If the press wanted news, I recommended they contact Gleason, or Elmer Bush. Miss Flynn wished me luck.

Eglanova's maid let me in without comment. I sometimes wonder if she knows any English. From the bathroom I heard Eglanova's voice above a Niagara of bathwater. "Peter! I am right out in one minute!"

The maid withdrew and, feeling like a Pinkerton man, I covered the living room and the bedroom with the speed of an Electrolux vacuum cleaner. Needless to say, I found nothing of interest. The rooms were an old-fashioned clutter of photographs and bric-a-brac and antimacassars, establishing, as her legs did not, that Eglanova was an Edwardian, a displaced person in time.

"If I keep you waiting, I am sorry," she said, sweeping down on me in a creation of mauve satin, her head wrapped in a towel. "I wash my hair. First, soap and water. Then gasoline. Gives marvelous luster. Even during the war I use gasoline. I tell authorities Eglanova's hair important, too. They give me little coupon book . . . so nice of them. And people say Americans are barbarians!" She sat down in her usual place by the window. I sat opposite her. The inevitable hot tea and lemon was brought us.

"You like nougat?"

I shook my head and watched, fascinated, while she devoured two large awful-looking pieces of nougat. "From admirer," she said, her mouth full. "He sends me nougat from Rome, Italy. Only place for nougat . . . and Parma violets: I eat pound of violets at one sitting once when I dance in Florence."

"I'll stick to tea."

"You never be big and strong," she said and took a swig of tea. Outside the sun glared, like a globe of brass in the afternoon.

I decided the direct approach was best. "I think they're going to arrest Jane."

Eglanova blinked, as though I had made a move to strike her. Unsteadily, she put her tea beside the gaily painted nougat box on a marble-topped table. "What . . . why you think this?"

"She's being watched every second by a plain-clothes man . . . the way they watched Miles when he was to be arrested."

Eglanova smiled wryly. "They watch me, too, Peter. I am no fool. I know all along they suspect me. I have engaged two lawyers . . . in case."

"Yes, they suspect you, too, but they're making a case against Jane. Like a fool, she went to see Miles the evening he was killed, or died. She was with Magda in that classroom before Magda died."

"But, child, she is so safe! She had no reason to kill Sutton. She never has reason. Surely even that brute who asks questions must know this thing."

"I'm sure he knows it and I'm also sure that he has to arrest somebody or there'll be trouble for him and the police department, from the papers, from the public."

"So they give her trial and she is innocent."

"In the meantime her reputation is ruined. All her life people will say: 'Oh, yes, she was mixed up in that ballet murder.' Because by the time the case falls flat, the real murderer will have covered his tracks and the case might never be solved and she'll always be suspected. People will say a smart lawyer got her out of it. You know the way they talk. They always want to believe the worst."

"Poor little Jane."

"I want to stop it before we really have to say poor little Jane."

Eglanova laughed. "And I help you? They arrest poor Anna Eglanova instead?"

"They would never arrest you."

"I am not so sure of that. Of course I did not kill this vile woman but I tell you one thing: if I did kill her I would do such good job there be no talk of murder. I know ways," and looking like a real murderess she shut those Asiatic eyes of hers until they were like black slanting lines drawn on her white face.

"Then who did kill her?"

"Meaning if I did not? Ah, you are not gallant."

"No, I didn't mean that."

"I don't know. I think sometimes I know but I am afraid . . . very afraid."

"Think back to the night at the theater. Can't you remember anything which might help us, you and Jane and me?"

"I try. God, how I try all time! I go to Greek church and pray something happen . . . that whole thing be forgotten by a miracle. But no miracle, and I remember nothing. I am in dressing room almost all time. I go for little dinner across the street. I come back. I stay in dressing room. Why I never even know where cable is until afterward. After all, I am not in ballet. I pay no attention to ballets in which I am not dancing. I had no idea I was connected with whole thing until Ivan told me about shears and how you save me embarrassment. For which I am so grateful."

"Then try and help now."

"I pray for miracle. Otherwise I can do nothing." She had never seemed so oriental to me before . . . like a peasant woman in Samarkand.

"Who do you think killed Ella?"

She looked away, very pale. "Don't ask me this question."

"But you want to help."

"Not like this . . . not to hurt people I care about."

"If you don't help, Jane will be hurt . . . maybe you will be, too."

"I have good lawyers," she mumbled, looking away, out the window at the sunlit yard, at the garbage pails gleaming dully in the light.

"And so has Jane," I lied. "We've already discussed what their strategy will be if she is indicted. They intend to incriminate *you* as the person with the greatest single motive." This was wild but it had the effect I wanted.

Her head jerked around toward me and the narrow eyes opened wide . . . I saw, I think for the first time, that Eglanova's eyes were as gray as metal, as silver as steel.

"Let them. I am not afraid."

"Not even of the publicity, of the months in and out of court? Because they won't be able to convict her and they'll indict you next and maybe they'll be able to make the conviction stick, lawyers or no lawyers." It is not possible for a white face to turn pale but if it were I could have seen the change right then and there . . . as it was her face sagged.

"Then they find out truth," she said at last, slowly, looking at me all the time with those silver cat's eyes of hers."

"And the truth?"

"Don't you know? Can't you guess? It is so plain. It is why I have not slept for weeks. Why I grow sick. Why I almost fall off *arabesque* in *Swan Lake* on the last night . . . I am so weak . . . not because those terrible men throw things at stage, like I said, but because I am frightened for some person I adore!"

"For whom?"

"For Alyosha."

I said nothing for several minutes and Eglanova, as though shocked herself by the enormity of what she had said, drank tea quickly, a thin trickle of it on her chin.

"Why did he do this?" I asked at last, softly, respectful of the panic which had brought her to make such an admission.

"We were married," she said at last. "For a number of years. I am bad on time. I don't remember how many years, but a long time, in this country, after I come with Grand Saint Petersburg from Paris. Then we grow apart. He is old man and I am young woman. He is tired and I am in my prime so we part, on good terms. I have my private life but I do not marry again. Alyosha falls in love with Ella and he loves her a long time, but like an old man . . . a mistake I tell him but he doesn't listen, no, he thinks he can hold this little *corps de ballet* girl, but of course, she sees better opportunity and marries Miles, poor stupid Miles, who is fooled by tricks as old as woman. Then she becomes great star and Alyosha hates her, worse even than Miles. And he comes to me and I comfort him . . . we have no bitterness, Alyosha and I. He is like a brother to me always. When Washburn tries to replace me with Sutton, Alyosha is just like a madman . . ."

"And Alyosha killed Ella?"

She nodded, not looking at me. "I think that is what happened."

"Do you mean to tell me that after he killed Ella he put the murder weapon in your room . . . to throw suspicion on you?"

"I don't know . . . I don't know . . . I don't know what happened after that . . . maybe he uses something else to cut with. I only tell you all this now because I have very little time, because I can dance only one two more seasons and because I have so little time I cannot be involved for many months in courts, with lawyers. I put dance ahead of Alyosha . . . ahead of me, child, ahead of everything. It is the big thing . . . and though I love Alyosha I never ask him to kill this Sutton."

She stopped abruptly and put her empty tea glass on the table with a click. "He was not wise but he is old man and very bitter. You should have seen him the way he was in Russia . . . yes, I am almost old myself. I remember him when he was young dancer . . . so handsome, such man! you have never seen such man! Women, men, children they fall in love with him, follow him in streets everywhere he goes. Then we leave Russia and go on tour and all Europe loves him. Not because he is such good dancer like Nijinski but because he is so beautiful, because he is so good . . . but that was a long time ago, child. We are old now." And I saw the tears in her eyes. She did not speak to me again and so, with a murmured good-bye, I left her.

3

I had made a date to see Jed Wilbur after rehearsal, at four-thirty. I arrived at the studio just as the place was breaking up. It looked strange seeing our dancers in their tights running in and out between plain-clothes men in double-breasted suits with snap-brim hats worn like uniform caps.

I said hello to Jane who was standing by the drinking fountain reading the rehearsal schedule with a preoccupied frown.

"How did it go?" I asked.

She jumped. "Oh, it's you. I'm like a cat today. It went O.K. Nobody was thinking about the ballet except Wilbur."

"What's the ballet like?"

"I don't remember a thing." She shuddered. "That policeman! He gives me the shivers. For some reason he's decided that I know a great deal more about all this than I do. He's been asking me questions all morning. Where was I at such a time, how well did I know Ella . . . as if I had anything to do with this mess. I couldn't get it through his head that my only connection with the murder was through Magda who was a friend of mine and not much of a friend . . . I mean she latched onto me during her troubles with Miles just because I'm so goddamned sympathetic."

"I don't suppose it's any use my telling you again what a mistake you made in going to Miles' apartment that night, and not telling Gleason about it . . ."

"No use at all. What are you doing right now?"

"I have to see Wilbur on business. Then I'm off to dinner with some people . . . newspaper people. I don't know when I'll be back."

"Try and finish early. I'm going to be home all evening. I don't know when I've ever been so jittery."

I said that I would and she disappeared into the ladies' dressing room. I was about to go into the studio where I could see Wilbur talking to some dancers, when Louis hove-to, flashing that ivory smile . . . uncapped teeth, by the way.

"What's new, baby?"

"About that Harlem deal," I said. "I'd like to go up there some time."

"That's a good boy. I knew you come around." He gave me a sweaty hug. "We go tonight . . . unless you rather go straight on to my place."

"I'd like to see Harlem first. I'm writing a book."

"That's a hot one," said Louis who liked only comic books about Superman and Prince Valiant and Terry and the Pirates. We made a date to meet at eleven in the Algonquin lobby.

I avoided Gleason who was, I gathered, in the classroom sifting evidence. Wilbur had obviously forgotten our appointment but he was pleasant enough and suggested I go to his apartment with him while he changed clothes.

Jed lived in a small apartment in one of the drearier housing projects on the East Side . . . one of those red brick fortress jobs with tiny windows, the perfect place for a true liberal to get that anthill feeling, that sense of oneness with everyman.

I sat in his living room while he showered and dressed. I cased everythin , much the way I had in Eglanova's apartment, and with the same result. It is difficult to search a room for nothing in particular; on the other hand, you get some feeling of the owner's character. In this case, a rather negative feeling. Everything was functional, 1930-modern, lots of chrome and natural-wood finishes and no decorations other than an abstract painting on the wall, so abstract that it would take an art-lover more dedicated than I to tell whether it was good or bad. In the bookcase were twenty or thirty books on ballet, and nothing else. I was quite sure that the inevitable reference works of the left wing could be found in the bedroom, hidden away while the heat was on.

"I've never been so tired," said Wilbur, coming back into the room wearing a T-shirt and a pair of slacks which hung loosely from his thin body. "Want a drink?" We had bourbon and water.

Then he sat at the other end of the gray and gold couch and looked at me expectantly.

"It's about these Washington hearings," I said. "I wanted to know when you were going down and when you'd be back and how you'd like us to handle the publicity . . . especially for Chicago where we may run into trouble. You see, Mr. Washburn has dropped the whole public relations end in my lap and I don't quite know how to handle it." I was dazzlingly glib.

"I wish I knew what to say," said Wilbur, twisting a lock of hair. "Because of this murder business I can't go away yet. It takes precedence, I gather, over a Congressional subpoena. I suppose, though, that as soon as they arrest whoever they're planning to, I'll be able to go down, testify, and be back in a couple of days. Don't worry; they won't find anything. Try and convince that fool Washburn, if you can. I'm sure he thinks I'm a Russian spy."

"He's an alarmist."

"This mess all dates back to my connection with the North American Ballet. Two of the dancers were party members and the rest of us were sympathizers . . . I've already admitted that a hundred times. Unfortunately this is a competitive business and people have been trying to knock me off for years. If you get to the top they'll use any stick to beat you with. This Communist scare was made to order for my enemies. But I'll lick them yet; if I have to go through a thousand investigations." Wilbur was properly truculent and I couldn't help but admire his spirit. He was not going to knuckle under; the toughness that had got him where he was hadn't deserted him. I felt, though, that he tended to over-dramatize the situation . . . I mean, after all, who really gives a damn about a choreographer, a dancing master, a twinkle-toes expert; it's a minor art form in a second-rate theater, for which sentiment I could probably be run out of town.

"Have you much to do with Gleason?" I asked, before he could go into the inevitable "I-am-a-suffering-artist-who-has-struggled-to-bring-beauty-into-the-world" routine that so many of our talented cornballs slip into at a moment's notice.

"Gleason?" He looked bewildered, the autobiography of Jed Wilbur, mid-twentieth-century choreographer, halted at the first chapter. "You mean that Inspector? No, not since yesterday when he had us all in. I've got enough to worry about without getting mixed up in these murders. Do you realize that they may not let us go to Chicago next week? That my ballet may not be ready even if we do go, what with all these damned interruptions? It was godawful today . . . I can tell you that. The company was worse than usual . . . if that could be possible. It was like running through molasses. I'll tell you one thing, though, which I haven't even told brother Washburn; if we're not allowed to go to Chicago I'm going to break my contract. I've already talked to my lawyer and he says that I've a legal right to."

"I'm sure Gleason will have solved the case by then, before the Chicago opening."

"I hope so." Wilbur poured himself another drink.

"Who do you think did it?" My question was abrupt.

"Did what? The murders? I haven't the slightest idea. Tell me did that ape from the Veterans' Committee show up today . . . what's his name, Fleer?"

"I don't think so. Mr. Washburn and I sent away most of the callers . . . including the press."

"He has a personal grudge against me. I swear he has. This is downright persecution. Why, of all the liberals in New York, in the theater, did he have to go after me? The one who really cares just about as much about politics as . . . as Eglanova."

"After all you said yourself the reason . . . I mean, you're the first in your profession. You're a big target. If they could knock you off that would really be something for them . . . a real victory. Justify their whole existence."

This neatly tendered wreath of laurel was received in grateful silence as he absorbed my statement about his pre-eminent position in the ballet: Wilbur . . . then Tudor, Balanchine, Ashton, Robbins. This brief meditation put him in a good humor. His expression grew more gentle, almost relaxed.

I repeated my earlier question.

"Who killed Ella and the others? Well, I'm not sure that any opinion I would have would be worth a damn. You see, I'm new to the company. I don't have much idea of all the politics and so forth. . . . As a matter of fact, I've been so involved in my own mess that I haven't paid as much attention to all this as I probably should. But just remember that it isn't easy to create two ballets, defend your reputation and worry about a few murders, too. I figure if I survive the next month I'm going to Bermuda for the rest of the summer, right after the Chicago première. I can't take much more."

"But you have known all the people involved for a long time. The ballet's a pretty small world no matter which company you're with."

"That's true. But ballet companies are like families. They are different on the inside . . . no matter how well you know them from the outside."

"You knew Ella a long time?"

"Oh yes. In fact, except for Louis, she was the person I knew best in the company."

"How long did you know her?"

"You sound just like that policeman." He smiled at me.

"I'm pretty concerned. This is my bread and butter. You can always go on to another company, to Broadway. I'm on a salary, and there aren't many jobs around as pleasant as this."

"I see what you mean. O.K. . . . Ella Sutton. How long did I know her? Since nineteen thirty-seven, when she was in the North American Ballet. She joined it the month it folded; even so she danced several leads and got her first recognition."

"Did you see much of her after that?"

"Very little. We never worked together from that day until she got Washburn to hire me to make some new ballets for her."

"I didn't know Ella was responsible for hiring you."

"She was indeed. I suspect she was the most ambitious dancer in the history of ballet. She felt she had mastered the classics and the Grand Saint Petersburg chestnuts; she wanted to branch out . . . to prove she was a great dramatic dancer like Nora Kaye. So she got Washburn to hire me . . . for which I could kill her. . . ." He laughed, suddenly aware of what he had said. "If somebody hadn't taken care of that already. As far as I'm concerned, in spite of the success of *Eclipse*, my little association with your company has taken ten years off my life."

"Did you like Ella?"

"Certainly not. She was a bitch, not at all the kind of woman I like," he said, making a perfunctory effort to show his aversion to Ella was not a general one, did not include the entire sex . . . which of course it did. "But she was one marvelous dancer. I felt, working with her this season, that she might easily have become the finest ballerina of our time . . . and I've worked with the whole lot, with just about every important dancer in the world."

"Who do you think killed her?"

He frowned; then he finished his drink. "You know," he said at last, "I've gotten so nervous lately with all these investigations that I hardly dare open my mouth to say it's a warm day for fear some bastard will twist what I say around and use it against me."

"Well, there're only two of us here. You need two witnesses, don't you, to prove a statement? You can tell me what you think, if you want to."

"Then I may as well say what I think . . . not what I *know*; and if you quote me on this I'll deny it till I'm blue in the face. From what little I know of this company and the way it's put together, I'd say the Russians did it."

"Eglanova?"

"And Alyosha . . . one or the other or both. I mean who else had any real motive? Aside from Miles, and I still think maybe *he* did it; though that makes Magda's death seem a little crazy . . . which makes me also think that the whole thing might be the work of a lunatic. God knows we have enough of them in ballet—and more than our share in this company."

"I don't think Eglanova would ever take such a chance."

"It wasn't much of a chance since she knew Miles would be blamed for it, as he was. Or maybe she had Alyosha do it for her. He certainly hated Ella . . . though I suppose if he did it he wouldn't have planted those shears in Eglanova's room. That's more the sort of thing *she* might've done, an obvious stunt to make herself seem victimized. But that's all theorizing. Ideally, I'd be very happy if the police just gave up, or arrested the janitor, somebody who didn't have a thing to do with ballet but if they have to arrest the old girl, or Alyosha, I wish they'd hurry up and do it so I can go to Washington and clear myself. I don't want anything to affect my chances for the fall, with that musical . . . it's the biggest chance I've had in the commercial theater and I'm looking forward to it . . . and not just to the money either. . . . It's a chance to do something big . . . something nobody else has done before."

He talked awhile about the great things he intended to do; I then asked him if the rumor I'd heard about Louis' going into musical comedy was true.

"Where did you hear that?"

"Some of the boys in the company . . . you know how they chatter."

"We talked about it once. I don't think he wants to leave the ballet."

"He'd be good in musicals," I said.

"You never can tell." Then Wilbur steered the subject back to himself and before I left he had given me a number of pronouncements to give to the press about his political status.

4

It was almost seven o'clock when I met Alyosha at the Russian Tea Room on Fifty-seventh Street, a favorite meeting place for the ballet, where the Russians often sit for hours at a time drinking tea and eating pressed caviar.

I found Alyosha at his usual table, just inside the main room. He was going through his mail when I joined him; he was as dapper as ever, his monocle in place, a glass of vodka at his elbow. I remember thinking at the time that if he was a murderer, he was certainly a cool one. Except for the marks of fatigue which were standard equipment for the members of the Grand Saint Petersburg Ballet Company that season, he could not have been more relaxed as he motioned me to the chair opposite him.

"I'm sorry I'm late," I said, ordering bourbon. "But I've been at the office, trying to keep the newspapers in line."

"They are like wolves," said the old gentleman, placing a cigarette in his long onyx holder. "They smell blood and they want more of it."

"I know one thing: they're crazy for an arrest."

"And this Inspector plans to give them one, I am sure."

"The wrong one, too, I'll bet."

"Undoubtedly," said Alyosha sadly.

"I wish I could head them off."

"How?"

"I don't know. I only meant I *wished* I could . . . because of Jane."

"Is she involved?"

I was quick enough, fortunately, to get out of that one. I did some extraordinary feints and maneuvers. "We're going to be married," I said. "And all this is making things so difficult for us . . . her being in Wilbur's new ballet . . . the strain of doing *Eclipse* night after night, terrified that someone may do the same thing to her that they did to Sutton. Well, it isn't the most wonderful climate for love."

"Love makes its own climate," said Alyosha with a warm smile. "Let me congratulate you."

"Thank you . . . I appreciate that . . . But don't say anything to the company about it . . . for now."

"I shall be very discreet." He toasted me in tea and I toasted him in bourbon. We talked for a while of love and marriage and he told me about himself and Eglanova. "What a divine woman she is! I have never known any woman so without vanity or meanness. Oh, I know that seems strange since she is such an egotist about her work, but that is natural. . . . It is the ballet she cares about, not Eglanova. In a way it is like the priesthood for her, for us. You Americans are not quite the same thing. You think of money and glamour and all that, not of the thing itself, the dance, the work, the magic. In a way our marriage was perfect."

"But it ended."

"All things must . . . in our world sooner than later. I was infatuated with someone else and so it ended. Yet Anna never reproached me, not once."

"With Ella?"

"Yes . . . I am afraid everyone knows. I made a fool of myself, but I don't blame *her*. We were such different people. I thought first of ballet then of her and she thought only of herself: she thought because I loved her I'd give her the great roles but I saw that she wasn't ready and I refused, thinking that ballet came first with her, too, that she would know, as I knew, that she wasn't ready. So she married Miles and suddenly, pouf! like that, she *was* ready: overnight she was a great ballerina. Sad woman . . . she ended the way she deserved."

"Did you hate her so?"

"For a long time but not in the last year. I felt something would happen . . . I am not superstitious but I think sometimes a terrible deed casts a shadow before it. I saw the shadow some time ago. I knew she would not be allowed to live much longer . . . and I was sorry for her. After all, I had loved her once."

"I have some news," I said, interrupting this mystical reverie.

"News?" He put the onyx holder down and looked at me politely.

"The police are going to arrest the murderer tomorrow."

"How do you know?"

"I found out this afternoon . . . through the grapevine . . . the warrant is being prepared now."

"But they *can't* do this to her . . . they can't!" He fell with the grace of a dying swan into my little trap . . . unless of course I had fallen into *his* trap: at the moment, I wasn't sure which, but I bluffed it through.

"I'm afraid they can. After all, even a great dancer like Eglanova is at the mercy of the law."

"I know, but we must stop them." He let his monocle drop; he was suddenly haggard-looking. "She mustn't be brought to trial."

"But if she's innocent she'll be let off."

"Innocent!" he groaned.

"Do you think she really killed Ella?"

"Who else?" His voice was strained and it quavered; he sounded very old.

"Did you talk to her about it?"

"Never. We have never discussed Ella alone together since it happened. I knew. She knew that I knew, from the beginning. There was never anything to say."

"Did you talk like this to Gleason?"

"Of course not. I made up lies! oh, such lies, such confusion! They may never straighten out all the things I tell them."

"Even so they will arrest her tomorrow."

"Then we must get Ivan. We must engage lawyers. The best in America . . . I am told in this country with a good lawyer you can escape anything."

"It's been known to happen. She already knows the police suspect her, but they may arrest her any minute."

"I should be with her now."

"I'm not sure that'd be such a good idea." For the moment, I didn't want any of these people getting together and comparing notes; if they did I might find myself in serious trouble. "You see the police are watching her and if they think you might be an accomplice of some sort your testimony in her favor won't be worth a cent."

"Even so . . ."

"Besides, she told me she was going to be with her lawyers this evening. Wait until tomorrow. That's the only thing to do, the only really intelligent thing to do . . ." I talked for several minutes, trying to divert him; then, still unsure as to whether I had or not, I left.

5

Mr. Washburn arrived ten minutes late for dinner with me at a little French restaurant on Fifty-fifth Street. A place with good food and dim lights.

"Elmer Bush is going to drop by in an hour," said Mr. Washburn, sitting down, not even bothering to say good evening.

"Is that a good idea?"

"Good idea or not we have to see him. He's in charge around here, just as much as Gleason." This last name, on his lips, became a curse.

We ordered a light cool dinner. The room was dark but not air conditioned... it was a little like being in a cave somewhere in Africa.

"The police are going to make an arrest, aren't they?"

He nodded.

"Jane?"

"I'm doing everything I can to stop it. I've been at City Hall all afternoon. I've talked to the Mayor, to the Governor up in Albany."

"I suggest you find her a good lawyer."

"Benson will represent her... I've seen to that, at company expense." I knew then he was serious; Mr. Washburn doesn't like to spend money.

"Jane doesn't know yet, does she?"

"I don't think so. *You're* the one who sees her."

"She's home now. She suspects they might... it's so damned awful, so stupid! Didn't you explain to Gleason that there is no motive, absolutely none? That regardless of circumstantial evidence, the state is going to look damned funny when they try to convict her?"

"He seems confident."

"But can't you stop him? A trial like this could ruin her."

"I can't do anything more than get her acquitted. She *will* be acquitted... I'm sure of that."

It's a good thing, I suppose, that I have a great deal of self-control because my impulse at that moment was to rush straight to Gleason's office and tell him exactly what I thought of his investigation.

"Besides," said Mr. Washburn, "I have reason to believe that the trial will be speeded up so that Jane will be through in time for our Los Angeles opening."

I was beginning, dimly, to see the plot. "You seem very confident," I said, "that by the time the trial is over the police will have lost interest in the case... that Eglanova will be out of danger." I was now fully aware that Jane was to be the lightning rod for the whole company in general and for Eglanova in particular.

"I don't know what you're talking about," said my employer sharply and I shut up. There was plenty of time for saying what I had to say.

We ate the first course in silence; then, when the entrée arrived, I asked, very casually, "Tell me, Mr. Washburn, why you were trying to get Armiger to take Eglanova's place, before Ella was killed."

I suppose if I had spat in his face I would have made less effect; he sat back in his chair abruptly and his chin jerked up, like a boxer off guard.

"How did you know I'd written her?"

"I saw her answer on your desk one day."

"I'm not sure I approve of your reading my mail."

"It was accidental, believe me. I don't usually read other people's mail. I've been wondering, though . . . been wondering quite a bit lately whether that might tie in with the murders. You see, it's more important to me to get Jane off the hook than it is for you to save Eglanova."

"You haven't mentioned seeing that letter to anyone, have you?"

"Not yet. But I plan to tell Gleason about it tomorrow . . . any stunt I can think of to throw him off the track."

"It could be misinterpreted." Mr. Washburn was worried.

"It would provide a mild diversion. They might even suspect you."

Washburn snorted. "As if I would make such trouble for myself! All I have to do is *fire* a ballerina . . . it couldn't be simpler. I don't have to kill them . . . though there are times when I have been greatly tempted."

"Why did you write Armiger?"

"Because right after we opened in New York, Sutton told me that she and Louis were planning to quit the company and go into musical comedy, into night clubs, to make money. I was furious, of course; I did all I could to stop her, promised her more money than Eglanova gets . . . everything, but she said she'd made up her mind."

"Then that clears you."

"Not entirely," said Mr. Washburn very distinctly, his eyes on mine. "I found out after I wrote to Armiger that Ella had said nothing to Louis about this plan of hers . . . or rather they had discussed it but neither, according to him, had decided to leave the company. For some reason she wanted to upset me, to get me to promise her more money which I did and which I was bound to give her after Eglanova left. That's the way the situation was when she died. She hadn't told me she would stay with us but I knew, after talking to Louis, that she would. . . ."

"But in the meantime you had written that letter to Armiger."

"To several other dancers, too."

"Very messy."

"I sometimes wish I had stayed in Bozeman."

"Stayed where?"

"Bozeman, Montana. That's where I was born. . . . I still own property there. I came East about twenty years ago and my ex-wife got me into ballet." This was an unexpected confidence. As a rule, Mr. Washburn never made any reference to his life before the ballet, nor could one find out much about him before his ballet days. I know. I tried soon after I joined the company; out of curiosity, I looked him up and found almost nothing at all. His birthplace is recorded, officially, as San Francisco, the child of Anglo-Russian parents; his mother was supposed to have been a dancer called the "Pearl of the Baltic." None of this of course was true . . . a real New York biography! much glamour and no facts.

"In a way," said Mr. Washburn after a brief reminiscence or two on his early days, "this may be a blessing for all of us."

"What may be?"

"Their putting Jane on trial. They haven't a chance in the world of making any case against her stick because she is so obviously innocent and, let's face it, of almost all the people involved in this business she is the one least likely to be hurt by a trial. They might make a case against Eglanova or Alyosha or even against me, and make it stick regardless of how innocent we are in fact . . ."

"But is Eglanova innocent?"

"I have never allowed myself to think of her or anyone else connected with my company as a murderer."

"Then you should allow yourself to think right now that somebody we both know *is* responsible for those murders and that Jane is scheduled to take the rap for that somebody. It might be a good policy for us to co-operate with Gleason and help him catch the real murderer instead of trying to confuse him the way you've been doing for the last few weeks, helping him make a case against Jane whom you know is innocent."

"I've done no such thing. I . . ."

"Then why did you tell Gleason about seeing Jane at Miles' apartment? Especially when you made it a point to tell me you *hadn't* mentioned it to Gleason." This was wild but I had to take chances; it worked.

"I didn't want to upset you and then have you disturb Jane when she was working on a new ballet. Of course I told Gleason. How would it have looked if I hadn't? He knew anyway."

"I don't like this . . ."

"In which case you may want to find a job somewhere else." said Mr. Washburn looking at me coldly, a piece of lettuce sticking to his lower lip.

"I have other jobs," I said brazenly. "Which is fortunate . . . especially if they start investigating those letters you wrote Armiger and the other dancers."

"Are you trying to blackmail me? Because if you are . . ."

"Christ no!" I said. "I'm just trying to make a little sense out of the mess you and the others have made. I don't know why but it seems that everybody connected with this company has a constitutional aversion to telling the truth which is very nearly miraculous . . . I mean just by accident the truth will sometimes out, but not in this set. I'm sick to death of all the shenanigans . . . yours, too, Mr. Washburn."

"A fine speech," said Elmer Bush appearing out of the shadows.

"A little joke," said Mr. Washburn easily, getting to his feet. "How are you, Elmer? Let me order you a drink."

"The boy may be right," said Elmer, accepting a gin and tonic from a waiter. "Sometimes it's best to be direct."

"He's very much upset, as he should be."

"Over that girl? Well, he has every reason to be," said Elmer Bush, giving me his serious television gaze, the one denoting sympathy, compassion.

"What do you mean?" I asked, knowing exactly what he meant.

"You better get her a good lawyer; she'll need one, starting tomorrow."

"I've got Benson for her," said Mr. Washburn. "And of course we'll take care of the bond."

"She's innocent," I said, wearily.

"Perhaps," said Elmer Bush, "but the police and the press both think she killed Ella to get her part in the ballet."

"Thin motive, isn't it?"

"They may have evidence we know nothing about," said Elmer, looking as though he knew all sorts of things nobody else did . . . which was possible. If it was, I had another puzzle dropped in my lap . . . and there wasn't much time to unravel all the threads, to work everything out.

"Do you mind," said Mr. Washburn, turning to me with icy formality. "Elmer and I . . ."

"I'm on my way," I said, getting to my feet. I gave them a brisk good night. Then I headed down the street to the Blue Angel. There, sitting in a booth at a black table under a red light, I pulled out my sheet of paper and began to go over the names, solving some of the old mysteries, adding the new ones I'd come across during the evening, making brief notes on my conversations with the suspects. While making those notes, I figured out who killed Ella Sutton. There was the solution in front of me, in black and white. The only bad thing was that I didn't have one bit of evidence to prove what I knew. I was very pleased with myself; I was also scared to death.

VII

I doubt whether I will ever forget that evening I spent with Louis; we did New York from the Village to Harlem in something under nine hours, from eleven-thirty that night to eight-thirty the next morning when I crawled off to bed.

We met at the Algonquin. From there we went to a bar in the Village . . . Hermione's I think it's called.

I thought I knew a great deal about our feathered friends, the shy, sensitive dancers and so on that I've met these last few years in New York, but that night with Louis was an eye-opener . . . it was like those last chapters in Proust when everybody around starts turning into boy-lovers until there isn't a womanizer left on deck.

"You'll like this bar," said Louis with a happy grin as he marched me into a long blue-lit tunnel, an upholstered sewer, with a number of tables in back and a bar in front. Heads turned to look at us; there was a hiss of recognition when they saw Louis. He's hot stuff in these circles.

We pushed our way to the back of the bar and a mincing youth, a waiter, found us a table right by the stage, a wooden platform about four feet square with a microphone in front of it and a piano beside it. The stage was empty. A tired little man sat at the piano, banging away.

"They have a swell show here," said my guide.

"What will it be, big boy?" said Mae West, behind me; I turned and saw that it wasn't Mae West . . . only our waiter who despite his debutante slouch managed to give a vivid impersonation of that great American lady.

Louis ordered gin and I ordered a coke, to Louis' horror but I was firm . . . I had no intention of getting tanked tonight, for a number of reasons, all good.

The pianist, getting a look at Louis, played a hopped-up version of *Swan Lake* in his honor and a more godawful noise I've never heard. He was rewarded with a big smile from the French Nijinski.

"Nice, isn't it? They know me here even though I only get down this way maybe once twice a season."

"Tell me, Louis, how does it feel to be famous?" And believe it or not he told me; it was the last time I ever tried irony on that boy . . . on any dancer because, for some reason or another, they are the most literal-minded crew in the world.

When he had finished telling me what it was like at the end of a ballet when the applause was coming up out of the darkened house ("like waves"), our waiter eased by with drinks as I watched, fascinated. Most queens walk in a rather trotting manner with necks and shoulders rigid, like women, and the lower anatomy swiveling a bit; not our waiter, though . . . he was like Theda Bara moving in for a couple of million at the box office, in the days when a dollar was a dollar.

"Here's your poison," he said in that slow Mae Western manner of his.

"That's a boy," said Louis and he swallowed a shot of gin which he immediately chased with a mouthful of water. He grimaced. "Lighter fluid," he said.

"What did you expect, lover, ambrosia?" Obviously a literary belle, our waiter . . . and what a joy it was to hear her say "ambrosia"!

"Just a little old-fashioned gin."

"You want some more?"

"The real stuff."

The belle looked at him beneath sleepy lids which even in the dim light I could see had been heavily mascaraed. "Are you *that* dancer?"

"That's me." And Louis flashed the ivory smile.

"That's what Mary said when you came in but I said, no, this one's too old."

One for the belle, I said to myself, as Louis' smile vanished. "Get the gin," he said, suddenly rough and surly.

"I didn't mean any offense," said the belle, with a smile of triumph; she ambled off swaying like some tall flower in a summer breeze.

"Bitch," said Louis, in a bad temper. But then two admirers came over, college boy types, very young and drunk.

"Hey, you Louis Giraud aren't you?" asked one of them, a crewcut number, short and stocky. The other was a gentle-looking blond.

"Yes," said Louis, obviously taking no chances after his experience with the waiter.

"See, what did I say?" said the short one to the tall one.

"He's kidding you," said the blond.

"No, he's not," I said, just to be helpful; Louis was beginning to look very tough indeed.

"Giraud's right calf is about half an inch thicker than his left," said the blond.

I could tell by the gleam in his eye that he was a balletomane.

"Please show us," said the short one. "I got a bet. . . ."

Louis, exhibitionist to the last, pulled up his trouser legs to reveal those massive legs, like blue marble in this light; sure enough one calf was bigger than the other. They both touched him very carefully, like children in a museum. "I win," said the short one and he pulled the taller one away, with some difficulty now that Louis' identity had been established.

"Nice boys," said Louis, with his old good humor. "Like little pussycats, fuzzy and nice."

"They don't look much like pussycats to me," I said austerely.

"Why don't you come off it, baby? Stop all this girl-business."

"I can't help it, Louis. I got a weak character."

"I could teach you a lot," said Louis with a speculative look; before he could start the first lesson, however, the belle returned with another shot of gin.

"Compliments of the management, Miss Pavlova," said the belle insolently.

"Why don't you go stuff . . ."

"That's no way to talk to a lady," said the belle, with a faraway Blanche Dubois smile.

But then the chief entertainer Molly Malloy came over, a man in his late thirties with small regular features; he was wearing a crimson evening gown and a blond wig like Jean Harlow.

"Hi, there, Louis, long time no see," said Molly in a husky voice, not precisely female but on the other hand not very male either. He sat down at our table, drawing all eyes toward us. I felt very self-conscious.

"How're you doing, Molly? I've been tied up all season . . . haven't been able to get out once."

"That's not what I hear. This your new chick?" asked Molly, giving me the eye.

"Yeah," said Louis, beaming. "Pretty cute piece, huh?"

"Well you always get the best, dear. And I know why." There was much vulgar laughter and I looked politely away, looked toward the bar where youths and old men of every description were furtively nudging one another, all engaged in the maneuvers of courtship. It was a very interesting thing to watch.

"You still doing the same act, Molly?"

"Haven't changed it in ten years . . . my public wouldn't let me . . . even if I could. Tell me, dear, about all that excitement you've been having uptown: all those dancers murdering each other. Who did it?"

"Damned if I know," said Louis, and he changed the subject, the way he had with me all night whenever I tried to get the conversation around to the murders, tried to question Louis about one or two things which had to be cleared up before I could get the proof I needed. But Louis wasn't talking. And I wasn't giving up . . . not if I had to get him drunk, a hard job but, under the circumstances, a necessary one since I'd heard he talks a lot when he's drunk and there's truth in the grape, as the ancients used to say.

"Well, dear, it's been a real sensation . . . let me tell you. And such publicity! If it doesn't sell tickets my name isn't Molly Malloy." I couldn't help but wonder whether or not his name really was Molly Malloy. "Come here, Miss Priss," said Molly sternly to our waiter who obeyed with the air of a royal princess dispensing favors, or maybe Saint Theresa scrubbing floors. "Another gin for Louis Giraud the dancer, another Coke and a Tom Collins . . . understand?"

"You don't have to act like I was deaf," said the aggrieved, petulantly; another round was brought us and when Louis finished his third shot of gin he was definitely in a joyous mood . . . just next door to drunkenness and indiscretion. I bided my time.

Then Molly Malloy went into his act, to the delight of the initiates though it was pretty bewildering to me, full of references to people I never heard of, and imitations of celebrated actresses which weren't remotely like the originals, or anything else for that matter. He finished the act with a torch song and, when that was over, disappeared through a door behind the stage to much applause. Beneath clouds of blue smoke the pianist continued to play; voices sounded louder and the mating at the bar grew more intense and indecorous.

During Molly's last number, Louis had taken my hand in his and held it like a vise. After a while I stopped trying to pull away; it wouldn't last forever I knew. That's what I always tell myself in difficult situations, like the war . . . fortunately he soon got tired of kneading my palm and let it drop. I sat on my hands for the next half hour.

"Swell place," said Louis, after Molly left the stage.

"Swell," I said.

"I came here on my first night in New York . . . maybe ten years ago. I was just a kid from Europe . . . didn't know a word of English. But I got by." He laughed. "Right away a nice old gentleman took me home and since any French boy can make better love than any American, I got me a home real quick; then, later, I go into ballet here . . . to keep busy. I like work . . . work, sleep and . . ." He named his three passions.

"When did you meet Mr. Washburn?" I asked casually.

"When he came backstage at the old ballet company where I was working. I had done one beautiful *Bluebird*; I guess maybe the best damned *Bluebird* since Nijinski. Every company in America was after me. Washburn had the most money so I joined him and he made me *premier danseur*. I like him fine. He treats me like a king."

"Don't you ever get tired of those old ballets?"

"I hate all new dancing," said Louis, diverted momentarily from his usual preoccupation with pussycats and such like.

"Even Jed Wilbur's?"

Louis shrugged. "He's the best of that kind, I guess. I don't get much kick out of dancing in them, though . . . in *Eclipse* and now the new one."

"Where the father kills the girl, isn't it?"

"I think that's the story. To tell you the truth I don't pay much attention. I just do what they tell me. At least he lets me do things I like to do . . . *tours en l'air*, that kind of thing. He keeps me happy."

"I wonder what the story means?"

"Why don't you ask Jed? He'll talk your ear off about it. I just go to sleep when he starts getting arty with me."

"You sound like Eglanova."

He snorted. "We got that in common then. I love her. She's like a mother to me, ever since I've known her: Louis, you do this, Louis, you do that . . . Louis, don't go out with sailors, Louis, don't snap your head when you finish pirouette, Louis, don't take such deep bows after ballet . . . I never had any mother," said Louis, and for a minute I thought he was going to have a good cry.

"It's terrible," I said, "the way Mr. Washburn tried to get rid of her before Sutton was killed."

"He's a bastard," said Louis, gloomily licking the edge of his gin glass. "He can't help it. He was just made that way . . . all the time doing somebody dirty . . . not that he isn't good to me, as long as I'm hot with the audience. The second I have a little trouble, get bad reviews or something awful, good-by Louis, I know him."

"He's a businessman."

"Ballet is art not business," said Louis making, as far as I knew, his first and last pronouncement on ballet. "But you should've seen his face when he came to find out if me and Ella were going to quit the company for sure and go into night clubs. He looked like somebody had just belted him one. 'Now, Louis, you know we're old friends . . .' that was his line to me; so I strung him along awhile then I told him that Ella was just bluffing him."

"Do you think she was?"

"At least as far as I was concerned, I didn't have any intention of leaving the company, even though I've thought about it a lot. We had talked a little about it then and just lately Jed has been trying to talk me into doing that big musical of his this fall, but I said no; I mean the money's very nice except that the government gets it all . . . then you're out of a job maybe six months of a year with no money coming in and it isn't so swell. No, I like to know I got a regular amount coming in every week, ten months a year." I hadn't realized before that Louis was quite so money-conscious, so shrewd.

"I wonder why Ella told Washburn that, about your quitting the company together?"

"Just to worry him a little, to raise her price. She knew he couldn't find another dancer to take her place. As a matter of fact, just between you and me, I think she was planning to leave ballet in a year or so, but alone. I think she wanted to go in musicals and I got a feeling that was why she was so keen on getting Jed to join the company. Oh, she wanted to do a real modern ballet and all that but she wanted to work on him to get her a Broadway job. She had an eye for all the angles."

"I thought Jed joined the company because of you."

"You're pretty fresh, *petit gosse,*" said Louis with a grin, pinching my thigh until I just about yelled with pain. "I wasn't talking about why

Jed joined us; I was talking about why Ella wanted him to, why she sold Washburn on the idea." I rubbed my leg until the pain went away. One day I am going to beat the hell out of Louis, if I can; if I can't I'll do a lot of damage first.

"Jed's sure got it bad for you," I said in an earnest, slightly breathless tone of voice.

"Funny, isn't it?" said Louis, with a sigh, stretching his arms and controlling a yawn . . . it was stifling in the bar, a single fan made a racket but did not cool the warm smoke-filled air. "He's been after me for years. Used to write me crazy letters even before we started working together."

I waved to the waiter who, without asking, brought us another round; before he left he gave Louis a lightning grope and Louis didn't like it but, as I pointed out, he was just getting some of his own medicine. He didn't think that was very funny but after he'd swallowed some more gin he was in a better mood. I tried to get him to talk about Mr. Washburn but he wanted to talk about Jed. "I'm a lone wolf," he said, wiping his sweaty face with the back of his hand. "Lots of guys get themselves a nice pussycat and settle down but not me . . . I used to be a pussycat for some older guys, when I was real young, but I didn't like it much and besides it isn't dignified for a man like me to be kept by somebody else, and that's what Jed's got in mind. He wants me to settle down with him and be his boy while he makes dozens of ballets for me until I'm too old to get around a stage. Even if I liked the idea of going to bed with him, which I don't and never have, I couldn't go for that kind of life and, as for his making ballets for me, well, that's what he's doing right now with Mr. Washburn paying for them in cash, not me paying for them in tail . . . I tell him all this a thousand times but he doesn't listen. He's made up his mind I'm his big love and there's nothing I can do about it. You'd think somebody who'd been around dancers as long as he has wouldn't feel that way, like a little girl, but he's got a one-track mind. He came to us just because I was in the company . . . not because Ella wanted him or because Washburn offered him a lot of money. Believe me it's been hell dodging him, too. I can't take my clothes off but what he isn't in the dressing room wrestling around. I finally convinced him that Ella, who was making eyes at me this season, and me were having a hot affair and I suppose he fell for it since I've been known to play the other side, too. I let Ella in on the secret and so we pretended we were having an affair which was fine until I found out she expected to have a real one . . . you could've knocked me over with a feather when she suggested the idea one afternoon, right after the season opened. I said no and from that time on till she died we were having trouble and I mean *trouble*. She used to do everything she could to break me up on stage and off. I hate to admit it but I was kind of relieved when that cable broke."

So were a lot of people, I thought, sipping my third Coke. . . . I was getting more and more wide awake and, perhaps as a result of the caffein I was drinking, more and more keyed up.

Molly, in black satin and a dark wig, joined us. "Going to make a real night of it, dear?" he asked.

"First real bender this season," said Louis, looking happy.

"Well, I must say you couldn't pick a better place, and in better company," said Molly giving me the eye. "You a dancer, honey?"

I said that I was, in the *corps de ballet*.

"My, they're much more butch than they used to be," said Molly, turning to Louis. "What's happened to the mad girls who used to be in your company?"

"Flew away," giggled Louis. "Spread their wings and flew away. . . . psst! like that, all gone."

"Well, it's a new look," said Molly, giving me a tender smile. We had a great deal more to drink and then we left Hermione's. I was wide awake and a little jittery while Louis was roaring drunk, throwing passes almost as fast as I could catch them and throw them back.

At four in the morning we ended up in a Turkish bath in Harlem. I was very innocent; I figured that if Louis tried to give me a rough time I'd be safe in the baths since they were, after all, a public place with a management which would come to my help if he got too horny. I was mistaken.

We undressed in separate lockers, like a beach house, then we went upstairs to the baths: a big swimming pool, then steam rooms and hot rooms and, beyond these, a dark dormitory with maybe a hundred beds in it where you're supposed to lie down and take a nap after your pores have been opened by the heat. Only nobody takes a nap.

Standing by the pool in a strong light, I was very embarrassed not only by what was going on but by Louis who was staring at me, taking inventory. "Where'd you get those muscles, baby?" he asked, in a low husky voice.

"Beating up dancers," I said evenly. But I wasn't too sure of myself. Louis looked like one of those Greek gods with his clothes off, all muscle and perfect proportions, including the bone head. Our presence caused even more of a stir than it had in the different bars. Fat old gentlemen came strolling by; one old fellow could hardly walk he was so old . . . he wheezed and puffed and he looked like a banker, very respectable, very ancient, yet here he was, operating like mad, or wanting to.

"Let's go in the steam room," said Louis and, ignoring the pinches and the pawing, we got through the old gentlemen to the steam room where a number of youths, black and white and tan, were carrying on, dim shapes in the steam which hid everything over a foot away. All around the steam room was a concrete ledge or shelf on which the various combinations disported themselves, doing a lot of things I never thought possible. It was like being in hell: the one electric bulb in the steam room was pink and gave a fiery glow to the proceedings. For the first time that night I was tempted to give up, to run away, to let the whole damned murder case take care of itself. Only the thought of Jane kept me in that steam room.

We climbed up on the ledge out of the way. Louis stretched out beside me while I sat straight up, legs crossed, and he made love noises. It was pretty terrible. Fortunately, he was drunk and not as quick as usual and I was able to keep his hands off me. For several hours I had been trying to clear something up but I couldn't. He was either on to me or else he was too drunk to make sense.

"Come on, baby, lie down," he mumbled through the steam as dark shadows moved by us, shadows which would abruptly become curious faces; then, seeing us together, seeing my furious scowl, would recede into the ruddy mist.

"I told you one million times, Louis, I don't like it," I said in a low voice.

He sat up, his face so close to mine that I could make out the little red veins which edged the bright blue irises of his eyes. "You don't think I don't know all about you," he said. "You think I don't know about Jane?"

"What about Jane?"

"You know as well as I do. Everybody in the company knows . . . no use your trying to bluff."

"What're you talking about?"

"About Jane and Ella."

"What about them?"

"Stop looking so dumb . . . Ella had a big thing with Jane, didn't you know that? Just last year. Everybody knew. Ella was crazy for Jane.

As long as I knew Ella, Jane was the only person she ever got excited over, except maybe me and that was just because I wouldn't have anything to do with her."

"I don't believe it."

"Then go ask Jane . . . she'll tell you. Maybe she'll tell you about the fight they had . . . if she doesn't, the police will."

2

The sun was shining when I got back to the apartment. I was staggering with fatigue and I was aware of nothing as I fell into bed beside Jane who did not wake up.

Two hours' sleep is not as good as eight but it's better than none. At least I didn't feel that my head was full of feathers when Jane woke me at ten o'clock.

"What happened to you?" She was already dressed.

I groaned as I sat up, shaking the sleep from my eyes. "Hunting a killer."

"Did you find one?"

I nodded grimly, wide awake. "In spite of the fact, nobody's been very co-operative . . . including you."

"Here's some coffee," she said, handing me a cup from the table by the bed. Then: "What do you mean?"

"You and Ella," I said, looking straight at her. "I didn't know you went in for that sort of thing."

She turned very pale. "Oh my God," she breathed and sat down with a thump on the bed. "How did you find out about that?"

"Then it's true?"

"No, not really."

"It either is or it isn't."

"Well, it's not. I've been so scared somebody would rake all that business up . . . the police don't know, do they? Gleason didn't tell you, did he?"

"No, I found out from one of the dancers last night. I gather everyone knew about it except me."

"It's not one of the things I most enjoy talking about," she said with some of her usual spirit.

"I can see why not."

"And not for the reason you think. It all started about two years ago when Ella needed an understudy in one of the lousy new ballets we were doing then . . . this was before she was such a star: so I was given the job and she offered to teach me the part . . . something which is pretty rare with any dancer but unheard of with someone like Ella. It took me about five minutes to figure it out. From then on, for the next few months, it was something like you and Louis, only worse since I had to work with her. I turned her down a dozen times; then, finally, after being as nice as I could be under the circumstances, I lost my temper and we had a knockdown fight which did the trick: she never bothered me again . . . never spoke to me again as a matter of fact, off stage anyway."

"Then why does everybody think you were carrying on with her?"

"Because she told them we were, because she got everybody in the company to believe that I was the one who had gone after *her* and that she had been the one who finally threw *me* out."

"Jesus!"

"That's what I say. Well, even though everybody knew what an awful person Ella was, they tended to believe her since after all, she had so many affairs with men, too, and I wasn't at all promiscuous," she added primly.

"This may make it kind of tough," I said, putting on my shirt.

"I don't see why they have to bring all that old stuff up now. What does it have to do with Ella's being killed?"

"Well, they're pretty thorough in these matters, the police are . . . they'll probably trot out every scandal they can find in the company, if only to make the headlines."

"I had a premonition about this," said Jane, gloomily packing her rehearsal bag.

"I wish you'd told me sooner."

"I was afraid you wouldn't believe me . . . you *do* believe me, don't you?" I gave her a big kiss and we both felt better after that.

"Of course I do. Only a complete hayseed like you could manage to do so many things wrong."

She shut the rehearsal bag with a snap. "I almost forgot . . . somebody searched the apartment yesterday."

"Take anything?"

"Not as far as I could tell."

"The police . . . probably just a routine checkup."

"I'll be glad when they make their damned arrest and stop bothering us."

"That's just because you want to dance Eglanova's roles."

She smiled wanly. "I've been wondering, though, who they will get for the rest of the season."

We took a taxi across town to the studio; we were followed, I noticed, by two plain clothes-men in another cab. I said nothing to Jane about this.

Mr. Washburn was at the studio and he greeted me as cordially as ever, as if the unpleasant exchange of the night before had never taken place. "I hear you were out late," he said, when I joined him in the reception room, near Madame Aloin's desk. Dancers in tights, detectives, tiny tots, and mothers all milled about. None of the company, though, was in sight.

"How did you know?"

"I saw Louis this morning. He was here for the nine o'clock class."

"How on earth does he do it? I didn't get to sleep until eight and he was still going strong when I left him."

"Where were you?"

"In Harlem."

"Then I suppose he came straight to the class instead of going to bed . . . he often does that when he's been drinking, to sober up."

"Iron man," I said, with real admiration. "Is he still here?"

"He's rehearsing with the rest of the company. How is Jane?"

"She doesn't suspect anything."

"Well, try and keep the papers away from her today. One of them says right out that she's guilty, for personal as well as professional motives."

"They don't mention her name, do they?"

"No, but they make it clear."

"I suppose somebody tipped them off about Jane and Ella."

Mr. Washburn looked solemn but I could see he was pleased. "So you've found out about that."

"Yes . . . have the police?"

"Of course, I didn't want to be the one to tell you."

"Very thoughtful."

"Yes, I think it *was* thoughtful of me. There was no use in upsetting you with gossip like that. Now that you know, however, I may as well tell you that we're going to have a hard time keeping it out of the trial . . . the state will build its case on that affair, so Bush tells me."

"When are they going to arrest her?"

"Today, I think; Gleason is in that classroom having a conference.

I've told our lawyer to stand by. He's at the office now, waiting. It's terrible, I know, but there's nothing left for us to do but live through it."

"Have you found someone to take Jane's place in *Eclipse?*"

"No," said Mr. Washburn emphatically; I knew he was lying.

"Well, don't hire anybody yet . . . don't even write one of those letters of yours."

He winced slightly at this reference. "Why not?"

"Because I know who really did the murder."

He looked like one of those heifers which Alma Shellabarger's old man used to hit over the head with a mallet in the Chicago stockyards. "How . . . I mean what makes you think you know?"

"Because I have proof."

"Be very careful," said Mr. Washburn harshly. "You can get into serious trouble if you start making accusations you can't back up."

"Don't worry," I said, more coolly than I felt. "I'll be back in an hour." I was gone before he could stop me.

At the office I ran into Elmer Bush who had somehow got his signals mixed and had expected to meet Mr. Washburn here. "See the old rag this morning?" he asked brightly, referring to that newspaper which had once given me a berth.

"Too busy," I said, pushing by him into my office; he followed me.

"Happen to have a copy of it right here," he said. "I say in it that there will be an arrest by noon today."

"Do you say whether the right person will be arrested or not?"

"No, I leave it up in the air," said Elmer, chuckling.

"You'll find Mr. Washburn over at the studio," I said coldly, going quickly through the heap of mail on my desk.

"I've got some advice for you, boy," said Bush, in a serious voice.

"I'm listening." I didn't look at him; I was busy with the mail.

"Keep out of this. That girl of yours is in big trouble. There're a lot of things you don't know . . . just take my word for it. I've been around a long time. I've had a lot more experience dealing with the police . . . I know what they're up to. They never act in a big case like this unless they got *all* the dope, unless they're sure they got their suspect signed, sealed and delivered. I like you, Pete; I don't want to see you get torn apart by these wolves. I know you like the girl but there's more in all this than meets the eye . . . more than most people, even real friends like Washburn, are willing to tell you."

I looked up. "Do you mean to say that I have body odor, Mr. Bush?"

"I was only trying to do you a good turn," said Elmer Bush, very hurt. He left me alone with my ingratitude.

I looked at my watch; I had less than an hour before the rehearsal broke up, at which time I was fairly sure the arrest would take place. I took out my sheet of paper and went over it carefully: all the mysteries had been solved and the answer to the puzzle was perfectly clear. Short of a confession on the part of the guilty party, however, I was not going to have an easy time proving my case. If worst came to worst, though, I could always announce my theory, get the police to hold up the arrest and then let *them* do the proving, which they could do, in time . . . I was sure of that.

I got on the telephone and called an acquaintance of mine at the rival ballet company's office . . . he's been the press agent over there for years. Since we've always been friendly, he told me what I wanted to know . . . it helped a little.

It was not until I was out in the street that I recalled I had not shaved or changed my clothes in two days and that I looked incredibly seedy, according to the plateglass window in which I caught an unflattering glimpse of myself. I had not been to my own apartment in several days, not since the afternoon when I had packed my clothes and stormed out of Jane's place.

I let myself in and picked up the suitcase which still lay in the middle of the living-room floor. Then I opened it.

At first I thought someone was playing a joke on me. The bag contained a woman's nightgown, nylon stockings, brassière, panties . . . I examined them all with growing bewilderment. It was not until I discovered the sealed envelope that I realized what had happened, that this was Magda's suitcase.

I had a long talk with Gleason. It lasted for forty minutes and ended just as the rehearsal did, which was good timing for the company was at least able to get through its rehearsal before the killer was arrested.

I purposely held the final bit of evidence back until I had explained, to Gleason's annoyance, how I had put the puzzle together. I'm afraid I was a little smug in my hour of triumph.

"You see," I said in the same quiet, somewhat bored tone a professor of English I had had at Harvard was accustomed to use with his students, "we all were led astray by the later deaths; we didn't concentrate on the first murder enough, on the character of the murdered woman which was, naturally, the key to the whole business." I paused in the middle of this ponderous and obvious statement to fix the

Inspector with my level gaze, as though I expected him to question what I had said. He didn't. He just looked at me, waiting. His secretary's pencil was poised above his shorthand pad. After a suitable pause, I continued.

"Curiously enough, what I considered to be your somewhat morbid interest in the shears, The Murder Weapon as they are officially called, turned out to be, finally, the first clue I had to the killer's identity; in my pocket I have the final evidence. Between the first clue and the last, however, there is an extremely complex story which I am sure that you never suspected, in its entirety at least . . . I didn't either, I must admit." I am not sure but I think that at this point, I put the tips of my fingers together.

"Ella Sutton was an ambitious girl, as we all know, and an excellent artist. Her tragedy began (and I think it has all the elements of a classic tragedy: a beautiful, clever, gifted woman rising to glory only to be struck down because of one fatal flaw in her temperament . . . greed)." I was having a very good time; I had shifted now from the slightly bored professor of English to the more suitable role of classic moralist, a Sophocles sitting in judgment. "Her tragedy, then, began in 1937 when she joined the North American Ballet Company where she met Jed Wilbur, an eager young choreographer, and Alyosha Rudin who, though he was with the present company, was more active in the whole ballet world in those days than he is now. She made, as I construct the case, two friends at that time: Jed, who was not only her choreographer but her political mentor as well, and Alyosha who fell in love with her and, when the North American Ballet folded, was able to take her into this company. Both men had a great influence on her. With Wilbur, she joined the Communist Party . . ."

"You realize what you're saying?"

"Yes, Inspector. They joined the Party and belonged, for a time, to the same cell. Ella, however, was not very much interested in politics, or anything else which didn't help her to get what she wanted professionally . . . she was a true artist when it came to her work: she would do anything to get ahead. I believe she became a Communist to impress Jed, who was indifferent to her sexually; and she became Alyosha's mistress to please him . . . even taking a Russian name for a while in an attempt to make people believe that she was a White Russian born in Paris. All of this you can find in old interviews.

"As you probably know, she quickly lost interest in Alyosha who adored her but cared for the dance more; he refused to push her ahead in the company as fast as she thought she should go. She deserted him finally and married the next most powerful person, from an artistic point of view, Miles Sutton, the conductor. Their marriage was never very happy. She had a bad temper and she was a natural conniver. I suspect much of the trouble she had with the men in her life came from the fact that she was either quite indifferent to sex or else she was, in actual fact, a Lesbian. In any case, she went quickly to the top, and, finally, this season, she got her dearest wish when she prevailed upon Washburn to fire Eglanova. Meanwhile, however, Ella had made a great deal of trouble for herself. She had got involved with Jane Garden in an abortive affair . . . she was genuinely attracted to Jane who is not, contrary to your recent theory, a Lesbian . . . that's one of those things I would know better than you without *any* evidence. And Ella had decided to shed Miles and marry Louis, partly out of attraction (she seemed always to care only for men and women who would have nothing to do with her) and partly because it would be a glamorous marriage or alliance: the king and the queen of ballet.

"Everything might have worked out perfectly if Louis had ever shown the faintest interest in her, but he didn't and there were bitter quarrels. Miles, who now no longer lived with Ella, fell in love with Magda and, as you know, got her pregnant. Even in ballet circles that sort of thing presents a problem and he did his best to get Ella to divorce him. She took it all very lightly . . . it was the sort of thing that amused her and she made it clear that he would have to work his problems out on his own time. I think she was indignant, deep down, that he had preferred another woman to her even though they no longer lived together, even though she despised him . . . naturally, he could have killed her. But he didn't. So, by the time *Eclipse* was to be premièred, Ella had infuriated Miles and Magda, Louis, Mr. Washburn by threatening to leave the company and take Louis with her, Eglanova by succeeding her, Alyosha for deserting him and for getting his beloved Eglanova fired, Wilbur for having blackmailed him into joining the company. . . .

"Now when I had found out all these things, it occurred to me that the person who killed Ella would, naturally, be the one with the most urgent motive or, failing that, the one whose monomania was equal to hers. The most urgent motive was her husband's and I was just as sure as you were that he killed her. But we were all wrong. That left Eglanova, Alyosha, Louis, Wilbur, Mr. Washburn and Jane. I knew Jane hadn't done it. Mr. Washburn, despite a rather sinister nature, had no motive, other than exasperation. Eglanova and Alyosha seemed likely candidates, for nearly the same reason. Louis had no apparent motive. Wilbur had an excellent one.

"Ella needed Wilbur for two reasons: she wanted a modern ballet and she wanted to go into musical comedy. They had grown apart over the years and when she first had Washburn approach him the answer was no. He didn't like the Grand Saint Petersburg Ballet and he had no intention of leaving his own company, or Broadway. Ella then went to see him and told him, in her definite way, that if he didn't accept Washburn's offer she would give evidence in Washington that he had been, and for all anybody knew now, was still a member of the Communist Party . . . and she had proof. She was the sort of girl who never let go of anything which might one day prove useful. Needless to say, Wilbur joined the company. But like everyone else connected with this mess, he had more than one iron in the fire: you see, he had been in love with Louis for years. Which was, as far as he was concerned, the one good thing about his predicament, about his giving in to Ella.

"Everything might still have turned out all right if Ella had not gone too far and if Louis had been a little brighter. The Grand Saint Petersburg doesn't have much of a reputation for chic but it is a money-maker and Wilbur was allowed a free hand and he did create for Ella what many people think is his best ballet—*Eclipse*. As for Ella's going into musical comedy, well, there was nothing wrong in that either. She could have gotten a job with any management in town on her own . . . so there was no reason why Wilbur shouldn't sponsor her. The complication arose when Ella became interested in Louis, and Louis, who was not at all attracted to Wilbur, used Ella as an excuse for his own coldness, saying that she was the one woman he had ever loved and that they were to be married. Poor Wilbur took this as long as he could. Louis would even pretend to make love to Ella in his dressing room when he knew Wilbur might be within hearing distance.

"The crisis came to a head the afternoon of the day Ella was killed. Wilbur told her he wasn't going to stay in the company another minute, that he was going to break his contract. She told him if he did she would expose him as a Communist and that would be the end of his career. So, believing that he would lose his career as well as his love to Ella, he cut the cable; then he put the shears in Eglanova's dressing room since she seemed as likely a suspect as any."

I stopped, expecting some outcry from the Inspector, but there was none. "Go on," he said.

"Fortunately for Wilbur, Miles was immediately suspected and, as fortunately, Miles died a natural death before he was arrested. The case would have ended there except that Miles had known all along that Wilbur was the real murderer . . . Wilbur never knew that Ella, a very efficient woman, had somehow managed to get hold of his membership card in the Party years ago and, with an eye to the future, had kept it. She was a very shrewd woman . . . the more you study her life the more you have to admire her for the sheer audacity she displayed. If she had been able to identify a bit more with her friends and victims she'd still be alive . . . might even have ended up being adored by everyone like old Eglanova."

"Why didn't Sutton give up this card?"

"He would if you'd tried to arrest him. He was not rational . . . no man as heavily doped as he was could be. Besides, he must have regarded Wilbur as a benefactor. I do know, though, that he discussed the whole thing with Magda that day he went to Magda's apartment and he either gave her Wilbur's membership card then, or else told her where it was in case something should happen to him. If he didn't give it to her then she could have got it the night she came to his apartment. No matter *how* she got it, the card was in her possession at the time of her death."

"Why didn't she bring it to us?"

"The same problem . . . why should she? She had nothing against Jed. The death of Ella didn't disturb her one bit and she realized that now with Miles dead the case was over. And it would really *have* been over if, for some reason we may never know, Magda hadn't become suspicious of Jed. She began to think that perhaps Miles had not died naturally. She made a date to talk to him; she told him that she had the Party card and he asked her for it. They were to meet after the rehearsal. I admire the way he went through that rehearsal, not knowing what to expect from Magda who was sitting there with the rest of us on the bench, waiting for him to finish. After the ballet they went into the empty classroom . . . or rather Wilbur joined Magda there after Jane had left her . . . a break for him, the room being empty. She told him that she had the card with her; they quarreled. She demanded to know whether Miles had died naturally or not. There was some sort of scuffle and he grabbed the purse and, either accidentally or on a sudden impulse, he pushed her through the window. Then, taking the card out of her purse, he rushed back into the studio."

"Then *he* has the card?"

"Yes. Magda, however, the day she died came to Jane's apartment as you know, intending to move in. Since the apartment is a small one I was forced to move out . . . which naturally irritated me. So, shortly after Magda arrived, I left . . . after first shoving my own suitcase under the bed and taking hers with me to my own apartment where it remained unopened until an hour ago."

"What was in that suitcase?"

With a look of quiet triumph I handed Mr. Gleason the photostatic copy Magda had had made of Jed Wilbur's membership card in the Communist Party, dated 1937.

4

It was a blissful evening. I had sold the exclusive story of my apprehension of the murderer to the *Globe* for what is known in the trade as "an undisclosed amount," meaning a good deal . . . to the fury of one Elmer Bush whose own story on the arrest of Jane Garden had to be killed at the last minute at great expense, and now Mr. Washburn was entertaining Jane and myself at the Colony Restaurant for dinner.

"You know," said my erstwhile employer expansively, offering me a cigar, "though it may sound strange, I always suspected Jed. You remember how I repeatedly maintained that no one connected with my company could have done such a thing? Well, in a sense, I was right . . . it was the newcomer who was responsible, the outsider."

"Very sound, Mr. Washburn," I said, glancing at Jane who glowed in coral and black.

"But what made you suspect him . . . when did you get on to him?"

"The evening I went to see him in his apartment and tried to get him to talk about the murder. At first he wouldn't, which was suspicious. But then, after much coaxing, he did suggest that perhaps Eglanova had done the murder and then put the shears in her own dressing room to make herself appear victimized. Well, I knew that only three people in the company knew where those shears had been found originally . . . you, Eglanova and myself. Only the murderer could have known that they had been placed in her wastebasket because it was the murderer who had put them there. Very simple."

"Isn't he wonderful?" sighed Jane. I preened myself.

"Now isn't that remarkable," said Mr. Washburn with a gentle smile.

"Remarkable?"

"Why, yes. You see I told Wilbur about those shears . . . or rather I mentioned it to Eglanova in Wilbur's presence. I felt at that time it would make no difference since the case seemed solved . . . Miles was dead and the police were satisfied. I must say it was fortunate, all in all, that you were able to locate Wilbur's Party card. Otherwise he would have said that he'd learned about those shears from me."

"That may be," I said evasively, feeling a little sick to my stomach. "Anyway, it's all over and he's confessed."

"*And* you did a bang-up job," said Mr. Washburn, riding high on the wind he had knocked from my sails. "Not only did you save this little lady from an unpleasant experience but you have cleared the whole company of these crimes. I am more grateful than I can say."

To this tribute, I made chivalrous answer.

"We are also fortunate that the arrest didn't take place earlier because now, I am happy to say, the new ballet is in good enough shape for the Chicago opening. A real bit of luck under the circumstances. It'll be a sensation . . . the *Murderer's Ballet* . . . I can see the papers now."

Reflecting sadly that the Ivan Washburns of this world always win, Jane and I went home to celebrate. A row of Miss Flynn's asterisks could alone describe our bliss.

DEATH BEFORE BEDTIME

To V. W.

I

"You know, I've never gone to bed with a man on a train before," she said, taking off her blouse.

"Neither have I," I said, and I made sure that the door to the compartment was securely locked.

"What innocents we are," she sighed; then; "I wish I had a drink."

"I think you're an alcoholic." I was very severe because Ellen Rhodes is an alcoholic, or at least well on her way to becoming one: but of course her habits are no concern of mine; we are just playmates of the most casual sort.

"I wish you'd call the porter . . . he could get us something from the club car."

"And have him see us like this? a young man and a young woman enjoying an intimacy without the sanction of either church or state. You're out of your mind."

Ellen sighed as she unsnapped her brassiere. "There are times, Peter, when I suspect you of becoming a solemn bore."

I enjoyed, with my usual misgivings, the sight of her slim nude body. She was a lovely girl, not yet twenty-five, with only one marriage (annulled at seventeen) to her credit. Her hair was a dirty blond, worn long, and her eyebrows and eyelashes were black, naturally black, and the brows arched. Her skin was like ivory, to worry a cliché . . . and her breasts were small and jiggled pleasantly from the vibration of the train as she arranged her clothes in the closet of our compartment. I watched her back with some pleasure. I like backs . . . only aesthetically: I mean I don't make a thing of it, being old-fashioned; yet I must say there is nothing that gives me quite such a charge as a female back, especially the double dimple at the base of the spine, the center of balance a dancer friend of mine once assured me; although in her case the center was a trifle off since she was usually horizontal when not dancing.

"Darling, will you get my bag out from under the bed? The small one. I seem to recall having hidden the better part of a fifth in there just before we left Boston."

"Very provident," I said, disapprovingly, but I got the bottle for her and we both had a drink, sitting side by side on the bunk, my bare leg touching hers.

"I feel better," she said, after gulping a shot. And indeed she even looked better . . . her eyes shining now, and her face wonderfully rosy. "I love blonds," she said, looking at me with embarrassing intensity. "I wish I were a real one like you . . . a strawberry blond exactly. . . ." But then we rolled back onto the bunk. From far away a conductor shouted: "New Haven!"

"Ellen."

She moaned softly, her face entirely covered by hair.

"We're almost there. The train's just leaving Baltimore."

"Oh." She sat up and pushed the hair out of her eyes and blinked sleepily at me.

"I hate men," she said simply.

"Why?"

"I just do." She frowned. "I feel awful. I hate the morning."

" 'Morning in the bowl of night has flung the stone which put the stars to flight. . . .' " I quoted sonorously as we dressed.

"Is that poetry?"

"Indeed it is," I said, pushing up the shade and letting in the cold white light of a December morning. "Picturesque Baltimore," I remarked, as the train passed slowly through that city of small shabby houses with white doorsteps.

"Coffee," said Ellen, sitting down with a thump; she is a miraculously fast dresser for a woman . . . a quality I find both rare and admirable in the opposite sex.

If the waiter thought anything amiss when he served us breakfast in the compartment, he did not betray it; not that I minded particularly, nor for that matter did Ellen . . . rather, I had a job at stake and I didn't want to be caught in a compromising position with the daughter of my new client, the incomparable, the reactionary Senator Leander Rhodes, the only adult American male to be called Rhodes without the inevitable nickname Dusty.

"Now I feel better," said Ellen, after she'd finished two cups of black coffee, the alcoholic fumes of the night before dispelled.

In the year that I had known her she was either just coming out from under a hangover or else going into one, with a moment or two, I suppose, of utter delight when she was in between, when she was high. In spite of the drinking, however, I liked her. For several years she had been living in New York, traveling with a very fast set of post-debutantes and pre-alcoholics, a group I occasionally saw at night clubs or the theater but nowhere else.

I am a hard-working public relations man with very little time for that kind of living. I would never have met Ellen if she hadn't been engaged for eight weeks last year to a classmate of mine from Harvard. When the eight blissful weeks of engagement to this youth were up, she was engaged to me for nearly a month; I was succeeded then, variously, by a sleek creature from the Argentine, by a middle-aged novelist, and by a platoon of college boys to each of whom she was affianced at one time or another and, occasionally, in several instances, at the same time. Not that she is a nymph. Far from it. She just likes a good time and numerous engagements seem to her the surest way of having one.

"Won't Father be surprised to see us together!" she said at last.

"Yes." I was a little worried. I had never met Senator Rhodes. I had been hired by his secretary who had, I was quite sure, known nothing about my acquaintance with Ellen. My contract with the Senator was to run three months with an option in March and then another after that . . . by which time, if I were still on the job, the National Convention would be meeting and the Midwest's favorite son Lee Rhodes would go before the convention as the people's choice for President of the United States, or so I figured it, or rather so I figured Senator Rhodes figured it. Well, it was a wonderful break for the public relations firm of Peter Cutler Sargeant II, which is me.

Ellen had been more cynical about it when I told her the news in Cambridge where we had been attending a Harvard function. In spite of her cynicism, however, we had both decided, late at night, that it would be a wonderful idea if we went straight to Washington from Boston, together, and surprised the Senator. It had all seemed like a marvelous idea after eight martinis but now, in the cold light of a Maryland morning, I was doubtful. For all I knew the Senator loathed his daughter, paid her liberally to keep out of Washington . . . nervously, I recalled some of Ellen's exploits: the time last spring when she undressed beneath a full moon and went swimming in the fountain in front of the Plaza Hotel in New York, shouting, "I'm coming, Scottie . . . Zelda's coming!" in imitation of that season's revival of Scott Fitzgerald . . . imposing on the decorous 1950's the studied madness of the 1920's. Fortunately, two sober youths got her out of there before the police or the reporters discovered her.

"What do you think your father's up to?" I asked, resigned to my fate: it was too late now to worry about the Senator's reaction to this combination.

"Darling, you know I hate politics," she said, straightening one eyebrow in the window as frame houses and evergreens flashed by.

"Well, he must be planning something. I mean, why hire a press agent like me?"

"I suppose he's going to run for the Senate again."

"He was re-elected last year."

"I suppose he was. Do let's send George and Alice a wire, something funny . . . they'll die laughing when they hear we're on a train together."

"You know I think it's quite wonderful your father's done as well as he has considering the handicap a daughter like you must be to him."

Ellen chuckled. "Now that's unkind. As a matter of fact he simply adores me. I even campaigned for him when I was fifteen years old. Made speeches to the Girl Scouts from one end of the state to the other . . . I even spoke to the Boy Scouts, lovely young creatures. There was one in Talisman City, an Eagle Scout with more—"

"I don't want to hear any of your obscene reminiscences."

She laughed. "You *are* evil, Peter. I was just going to say that he had more Merit Badges than any other Scout in the Midwest."

"I wonder if he's running for President."

"I don't think he's old enough. You have to be thirty-five, don't you? That was ten years ago and he was seventeen then which would make him . . . how old now? I could never add."

"I was referring to your father, not that Eagle Scout of infamous memory."

"Oh, Daddy. Well, I don't know." Ellen was vague. "I hope not."

"Why not?"

"It's such a bore. Look at the time poor Margaret Truman had, trailed by detectives and guards everywhere."

"If you were a nice girl like Miss Truman you wouldn't mind."

"Oh . . . !" And Ellen Rhodes said a bad word.

"There would be all sorts of compensations, though," I said, trying to look on the bright side. "I think it would be very pleasant having a father who was President."

"Well, I don't. Besides, I don't think Mother will let him run. She's always wanted to go back to Talisman City where we came from originally."

"That would be nice for you."

Ellen snorted. "I'm a free spirit," she said, and, all things considered, she was, too.

2

We parted at the Union Station. Ellen went home in a cab and I walked across the square to the Senate Office Building, a white cake of a building in the shadow of the Capitol.

Senator Rhodes' office was in a corner on the first floor, attesting to his seniority and power since he was, among other things, Chairman of the Spoils and Patronage Committee.

I opened the door of his office and walked into a high-ceilinged waiting room with a desk and receptionist at one end. Several petitioners were seated on the black leather couches by the door. I told the woman at the desk who I was and she immediately told me to go into the Senator's office, a room on the left.

The room was empty. It was a fascinating place, and while I waited I examined everything: the vast mahogany desk covered with party symbols, the hundreds of photographs in black frames on the wall: every important political figure since 1912, the year Leander Rhodes came to the Senate, was represented. Leather chairs were placed around a fireplace on whose mantel were arranged trophies and plaques, recording political victories . . . while above the mantel was a large political cartoon of the Senator, handsomely framed. It showed him, his shock of gray unruly hair streaming in the wind of Public Opinion, mounted upon a spavined horse called Political Principle.

"That was done in 1925," said a voice behind me.

I turned around quickly, expecting to find the Senator. Instead, however, a small fat man in gray tweed, wearing owl-like spectacles, stood with hand outstretched, beaming at me. "I'm Rufus Hollister," he said as we shook hands. "Senator Rhodes' secretary."

"We've had some correspondence," I said.

"Yes, sir, I should say so. The senator's over in the Capitol right now ... important vote coming up this morning. But sit down for a minute before we join him and let's get acquainted."

We sat down in the deep armchairs. Mr. Hollister smiled, revealing a handsome upper plate. "I suspect," he said, "that you're wondering exactly why I engaged you."

"I thought Senator Rhodes engaged me."

"He did, he did, of course ... I was speaking only as his ... proxy, as it were." He smiled again, plumply. I decided that I disliked him but then I usually dislike all men on first meeting: something to do, I suppose, with the natural killer instinct of the male. I tried to imagine Mr. Hollister and myself covered with the skins of wild beasts, doing battle in the jungle, but my imagination faltered: after all we were two Americans living in rooms centrally heated and eating hygienically prepared food got out of cans ... the jungle was remote.

"In any case," Hollister was saying, "I thought I should brief you a little before you meet the Senator." He paused. Then he asked: "What, by the way, are your politics?"

Being venal, I said that I belonged to the same party as my employer; as a matter of fact, I have never voted so even if I did not entirely admire the party of Senator Rhodes I hadn't perjured myself.

Mr. Hollister looked relieved. "I don't suppose, in your business, that you're much interested in politics."

I said that, aside from my subscription to *Time* magazine, I was indeed cut off from the great world.

"You don't have, then, any particular choice for the nominating convention?"

"No, sir, I do not."

"You realize that what I tell you now is in the strictest, the very strictest confidence?"

"I do." I wondered whether or not I should cross my heart; Mr. Hollister had grown strangely solemn and mysterious.

"Then, Mr. Sargeant, as you may already have guessed, The Senator's Hat Is In The Ring."

"The what?"

"Senator Rhodes will announce his candidacy for the nomination for President on Friday at a speech before the National Margarine Council."

I took this awesome news calmly. "And I am to handle the publicity?"

"That's right." He looked at me sharply but my Irish, piggish features were impassive: I saw myself already as Press Secretary to President Rhodes: "Boys, I've got a big story for you. One hour ago the President laid the biggest egg. . . ." But I recalled myself quickly to reality. Mr. Hollister wanted to know my opinion of Leander Rhodes.

"I hardly have one," I said. "He's just another Senator as far as I'm concerned."

"We, here in the office, regard this as something of a crusade," said Mr. Hollister softly.

"Then I will, too," I said sincerely. Before he could tell me why the country needed Lee Rhodes, I remarked that I happened to know his daughter, that, by chance, I had come down on the train with her. Was it my imagination, as they used to say in Victorian novels, or did a cloud cross Mr. Hollister's serene countenance? As a matter of fact, it was worse than a cloud: it was a scowl.

"Is Miss Rhodes *in* Washington?"

"I believe so. Unless she decided to go back to New York."

"A charming young lady," said Mr. Hollister, without conviction. "I've known her since she was a tiny tot." The idea of Ellen Rhodes as a tiny tot was ludicrous but I was not allowed to meditate on it. Instead I was whisked out of the office and into the reception room; then into a further office filled with gray women answering the Senator's voluminous mail. I was introduced to all of them; next, I was shown an empty desk which I could call my own, close by one of the tall windows which overlooked the Capitol. I noticed that none of the typists was under fifty, a tribute, I decided, to Mrs. Senator Rhodes.

"Now if you like we'll go over to the Senate."

I have never been inside either the Senate Office Building or the Capitol before and so I am afraid that I gaped like a visitor from Talisman City at the private subway which whisked the Senators in little cars from the basement of their building to that of the Capitol.

After we got off a crowded elevator, Mr. Hollister led me down a long marble corridor to a green frosted double glass door beside which stood a uniformed guard. "That's the floor of the Chamber," said my escort, in a low reverent voice. "Now I'll see if I can get you into the cloakroom."

As I later discovered, this was the holy of holies of the Senate, almost as inaccessible to a non-Senatorial visitor as the floor itself. Some quick talk got us in, however.

The cloakroom was a long room with desks, couches and a painted ceiling, very ornate, a little like Versailles; swinging glass doors communicated directly with the Senate Chamber from which could be heard a loud monotonous voice.

"Senator Rhodes," whispered Mr. Hollister proudly, pushing me back against the wall, out of the way of the statesmen who wandered in and out, some chatting together in small groups, others reading newspapers or writing letters. It was like a club, I thought, trying to summon up a little awe, trying to remember that these were the men who governed the most powerful country in the world.

Mr. Hollister pointed out several landmarks: Senator O'Mahoney, Senator Douglas, Senator Byrd . . . I stared at them all. Then the swinging door opened and Leander Rhodes, the Great Bear of the West as he liked to hear himself referred to, appeared in the cloakroom, his face red from speechmaking, his gray hair tangled above his bloodshot eyes, eyes like his daughter's I thought, recalling irreverently her face on the pillow beside me that morning. But no time for that.

"Ah, Sargeant. Glad to see you. Glad to see you. Prompt. I like promptness. Secret of success, punctuality." Since neither of us could either prove or disprove this statement, I murmured agreement.

"Been to the office yet? Yes? Good scout. Let's go to lunch."

It took us quite awhile to get from the cloakroom to the Senate Dining Room. Every few yards or so, the Senator would pause to shake hands with some other Senator or with some tourist who wanted to meet him. He was obviously quite popular with the voters; the other Senators were a bit cool with him, or so I thought, since he was, after all, by reputation anyway, a near-idiot with a perfect Senate record of obstruction. He regarded the administration of Chester A. Arthur as the high point of American history and he felt it his duty to check as much as possible the subsequent national decline from that high level. He was a devout isolationist although, according to legend, at the time of the First World War he had campaigned furiously for our entry into that war, on the side of the Kaiser.

I suppose I shouldn't, in actual fact, accept jobs from men for whom I have so little respect but since it never occurred to me that Lee Rhodes had a chance in the world of getting nominated, much less elected, President, I saw no harm in spending a few months at a considerable salary to see that his name appeared in the newspaper, often and favorably.

The lunch was excellent, served in an old-fashioned dining room with tile floor where the Senators eat . . . there is a Pre-Civil War feeling about the Senate Dining Room . . . especially the menu, the remarkable cornbread, the legendary bean soup which I wolfed hungrily, trying not to stare too hard at Senator Taft, who sat demurely at the next table reading a newspaper as he lunched.

"Suppose Rufus here has briefed you?" said Senator Rhodes, when coffee arrived and all around the room cigars were lit, like Roman candles.

I nodded, holding my breath as a wreath of blue Senatorial smoke crossed the table and settled about my neck.

"Day after tomorrow, Friday, that's the big day. Making announcement then. Want it well covered. Can you do that?"

I told him that all speeches by such a celebrated statesman were well covered by the press. He took my remark quietly, adding that he wanted *Life* there, or else. I said that *Life* would be there.

"Get yourself located yet?" he asked, after we had exchanged a number of very businesslike remarks. I said that I hadn't, that I'd only just arrived on the morning train.

"Stay with *us* then; for a few days," said the Senator generously. "Got plenty of room. Give us a chance to talk strategy."

"I'd appreciate that, sir. By the way I happen to know your daughter slightly. I came down on the train with her this morning."

Was it my imagination . . . no, it wasn't; the Senator sighed rather sadly. "A wonderful girl, Ellen," he said mechanically.

"She seems very pleasant."

"Like her mother . . . a wonderful woman."

"So I've been told."

The Senator rose. "I'll see you this evening then, at the house. Got a committee meeting now. Rufus will show you around. Remember: this is a kind of crusade."

3

A crusade was putting it lightly. It was an unscrupulous and desperate effort of one Leander Rhodes to organize the illiberal minority of the country into a party within his party . . . and, I suspect, if you'd been younger and a little more intelligent he might very well have got himself into the White House. As it was, from what little Rufus Hollister would tell me, the Senator had some impressive backing; he also had some very sinister backing. I disguised my alarm, though, and by the time I took a taxi to the Senator's house on Massachusetts Avenue, Mr. Hollister was convinced that I too was a crusader for Good Government and True-Blue American Ideals.

The house on Massachusetts Avenue was an heroic imitation of an Italian villa, covered with yellow stucco and decorated with twisted columns and ironwork balconies. The Senator, I soon discovered, was a very wealthy man though the source of his income was not entirely clear to me. Mr. Hollister spoke vaguely of properties in Talisman City.

A butler showed me to my room on the third floor and, as I went up the marble staircase, I caught an occasional glimpse of ballrooms, of parquet floors, of potted palms, all very 1920 Grand Hotel *chic*. Dinner would be announced in an hour, I was told. Then I was left alone in a comfortable bedroom overlooking the Avenue.

I was dozing blissfully in a hot bath, when Ellen marched into the bathroom.

"I've come to scrub your back," she said briskly.

"No, you don't," I said, modestly covering myself. "Go away."

"That's hardly the way for my fiancé to act," she said, sitting down on the toilet seat.

"I haven't been your fiancé for almost a year," I said austerely. "Besides, the bride-to-be is not supposed to inspect her groom before the wedding."

"You give me a pain," said Ellen, lighting a cigarette. She wore a very dashing pair of evening pajamas, green with gold thread, quite oriental-looking . . . it made her look faintly exotic, not at all like a simple girl from Talisman City. "By the way, I told Mother we were engaged. I hope you don't mind."

I moaned. "What is this allergy you have to the truth?"

"Well, it *was* the truth a few months ago . . . I mean time's relative and all that," she beamed at me. "Anyway it should help you with my father."

"I'm not so sure," I said, recalling the Senator's look of pain at the mention of his only daughter.

"The house is full, by the way," said Ellen, exhaling smoke. "Some of the dreariest political creatures these old eyes have seen in many a moon."

"Constituents?"

"I suppose so. One's rather sweet . . . a lovely boy from New York, a newspaperman. He's doing a profile of Father for some magazine, very Left Wing I gather, and of course poor Father doesn't have the remotest notion that he's being taken for a ride. Did you ever see the piece the *Nation* did on him?"

I said that I hadn't; I asked her the name of the lovely boy who was doing the profile. "Walter Langdon . . . a real dream. I had a quick drink with him in the drawing room, before I dashed off to make violent love to my prospective groom."

"I have a feeling that our engagement isn't going to last very long."

"You may be right. Oh, and you'll never guess who's here . . . Verbena Pruitt."

"My God!" I was alarmed. Anyone would be alarmed at meeting the incomparable Verbena, the President of the Daughters of the War of 1812 as well as National Committeewoman for her party, one of the most powerful lady politicos in the country.

"She's from Daddy's state, you know. She has the hairiest legs I've seen since that football game at Cambridge last week."

"I had better get myself a hotel room quick," I said, letting the bathwater out and standing up, my back turned modestly toward Ellen as I dried myself.

"How do you keep so slim?" asked the insatiable Ellen.

"No exercise is the secret," I said flexing a muscle or two in an excess of male spirits.

"You're really not bad at all," she said thoughtfully. "I wonder why we ever fell out." She rose and came toward me, a resolute expression on her face.

"None of that," I said, making a dash for the bedroom. I had my trousers on before she could violate me further. She relaxed and we went on talking as though nothing had happened. I dressed more slowly.

"Then there's an old buddy of Father's staying here, Roger Pomeroy and his wife, a poisonous creature. I don't know what *they're* doing here. He's an industrialist back in Talisman City, makes gunpowder or something like that. . . ."

"Sounds like a chummy gathering."

"Grim . . . awfully grim. That tiresome Rufus Hollister, Father's secretary, also lives in. I have often said that he was the reason I left home. Did you ever feel his hands? like an uncooked filet of sole

... which reminds me I'm hungry, which also reminds me I desperately need a drink. Do hurry . . . here, let me tie your tie . . . I love tying a man's tie: gives me such a sense of power when I think with just the slightest pressure I could choke him to death."

"Darling, have you ever been analyzed?"

"Of course. Hasn't everyone? I went every day for three years after my annulment . . . Mother insisted. When it was over I was completely normal; I had passed my course with flying colors: no more inhibitions, no frustrations, an easy conscience about alcohol as well as the slightly decrepit body of a middle-aged analyst named Breitbach added to my gallery of conquests." She finished tying my tie with a flourish which made me jump. "There! You look such a lamb."

4

The drawing room was a large draughty affair with French windows which looked out on a bleak garden of formal boxwood hedges and empty flower beds, black with winter. Several people were seated about the fire. Two men rose at our entrance. A woman in black lace rose, too, and approached us. It was Mrs. Leander Rhodes.

"Mother, I want you to meet my fiancé, Peter Sargeant."

"I'm so happy to see you, Mr. Sargeant. I've heard such a great deal about you . . . such a coincidence, too . . . the Senator engaging you without knowing about you and Ellen." She was an amiable-looking woman of fifty, thin and rather bent with, as far as I could tell through the swatches of black lace, no bosom and no waist. At her throat old-fashioned yellow diamonds gleamed. Her eyes were black; only her wide full mouth was like her daughter's. "Let me introduce you around," she said; and she did.

Verbena Pruitt was worse than I'd expected: a massive woman in mauve satin with henna-dyed hair, bobbed short over a red fat neck, large features, small pig eyes and a complexion not unlike the craters of the moon as seen through a telescope. She gave my hand a vigorous squeeze. So did Roger Pomeroy, a tall silver-haired man of distinction. His wife, Camilla, a fairly pretty dark woman, smiled at me winningly, one heavily veined hand at her smooth neck, fondling pearls. Ellen's lovely boy Walter Langdon, a red-haired youth, mumbled something incoherent as we shook hands. He was obviously uncomfortable. And well he should be, I thought righteously, coming into a man's house like this with every intention of axing him later in a magazine.

"The Senator and Rufus should be along soon," said Mrs. Rhodes, as a maid brought martinis. Ellen gulped one quickly, like a conjurer; then she took another off the tray and held it in one hand, occasionally sipping it in a most ladylike way. Whom was she trying to impress, I wondered. The lovely boy? or her mother? or the assorted politicos?

At first, I thought that possibly I was the one who was ill at ease but, by the time dinner was over and we were all seated in the drawing room having coffee beneath a virile painting of Senator Rhodes, I decided that something was obviously going all wrong and I surmised that it had to do with Ellen's unexpected visit to Washington. Yet she was a perfect lady all evening. She was a trifle high by the time dinner was over but she spoke hardly at all . . . in fact, I'd never before seen her so restrained. The Senator was in good form but I had a feeling that the funny stories he told, and his loud rasping laughter were mechanical, a part of the paraphernalia of public office rather than sincere good spirits. He eyed Ellen and myself suspiciously all evening and I began to wonder just how long my job was going to last. I cursed Ellen to myself, fervently, furiously . . . her announcement that we were engaged had messed up everything.

The other guests seemed uneasy, except for Verbena Pruitt who matched the Senator laugh for laugh, joke for joke in a booming political voice.

Brandy was served with coffee and Senator Rhodes, turning to Roger Pomeroy whom he had ignored most of the evening, said, "Got some good cigars in the study. Want one?"

"No thank you, Lee," said the other. "I've had to give up the habit . . . heart."

"None of us are getting any younger!" snorted Miss Pruitt over her brandy, a hairpin falling softly to the carpet. . . . His eye is on the hairpin, I thought irreverently.

"I'm sound as a bell," said the Senator striking his chest a careful blow. He did not look very sound, though. I noticed how pale he was, how one eyelid twitched, how his hands shook as he lighted a cigar for himself. He was an old man.

"The Senator has the stamina of ten men," said little Sir Echo, Rufus Hollister, smugly.

"He'll need it, too, if he's going after that nomination," said Miss Pruitt with a wink. "Won't you, Lee?"

"Now who told you I was interested in the nomination?" said Senator Rhodes with an attempt at roguishness, not much of an attempt at that; he was obviously paying very little attention to us. He seemed preoccupied with some perplexing problem. His gray eyes looked unfocused.

While Verbena Pruitt and the Senator sparred, I talked to Mrs. Pomeroy who sat beside me on the couch. "Such a marvelous man, the Senator," she said, her eyes glowing. "Have you known him long?" I shook my head, explaining my presence in the house.

"We've known the Rhodeses for just years, back in Talisman City. Were you ever there? No? It's a wonderful *residential* town, almost Southern in a way, if you know what I mean. Except we're getting quite a bit of industry there . . . my *husband* is in industry."

"That's very nice," I said.

"We have a *government* contract," said Mrs. Pomeroy importantly. She chattered on about herself, about their hometown, about the gunpowder business, about the latest developments in gunpowder: the new process Pomeroy Inc. had developed. While she talked I watched Ellen making time with lovely boy Langford on the couch opposite us. She was talking to him in a low voice and I could tell by the gleam in her eyes and the flush of confusion on his youthful puppydog face that before this night was over he would be forced to revise his estimate of the Rhodes family since, I was quite confident, long before Aurora showed her rosy head in the east, he would be engaged to the daughter of the house. He was a gone goose . . . for a few weeks anyway. I wondered if Mrs. Rhodes was on to her daughter. If she was she hardly showed it. She completely ignored her, speaking for the most part to Mr. Pomeroy and Rufus Hollister who sat on either side of her, their voices pitched a register below those of Senator Rhodes and Miss Pruitt who were now speaking of various scandals attendant upon the Denver Convention of 1908.

Just before midnight, Mrs. Rhodes stood up and announced that she was going to bed but that the others should take no notice of her if they wanted to remain up. "Good nights" were said and the hour for breakfast set. I was wondering whether I should go straight up to bed or wait for some sign from Ellen, when the Senator beckoned to me. "Like to have a little chat with you," he said. "We can go up to my study." I said good night to everyone. Ellen hardly noticed us go; she was already beginning to unravel poor Langdon, right there on the couch . . . all very ladylike, though: only an experienced eye like mine could tell what she was up to.

The Senator's study was a corner room on the second floor with windows on two sides, oak paneling and bookcases filled with law books (which looked unopened), bound copies of the *Congressional Record* (fairly worn), and thick scrapbooks of newspaper clippings, much used, dating from 1912. There were photographs on the walls . . . less political, however, than those in his office. Photographs of his family at various moments in their lives . . . even one of Ellen as a bride. This surprised me since, as I remembered the story, she had eloped with an undesirable and had been brought home before, in the eyes of the law at least, he had soiled her.

The Senator seated himself at a desk in front of the windows. I sat down in a leather armchair beside the unlit fireplace; the room was chilly, I thought. I remember shivering.

"I must tell you frankly," said the Senator, looking at me severely, "that I didn't anticipate this . . . situation."

"What situation?" I acted innocent.

"This business with my daughter . . . this 'engagement.'"

"Sir, there is no business with your daughter," I said, sitting up very straight.

"What do you mean, sir?" He was obviously going to out-courtesy me; our manners became more and more antebellum. "My daughter gave me to understand that you and she were to be married."

"She is mistaken," I said; the job was over, I decided sadly.

"You mean that you refuse, sir, to marry my daughter?"

"I mean, Senator," said I, suddenly weary of the whole farce, "that I have never in my one year's acquaintance with your daughter thought of marrying her nor has she ever thought of marrying me."

He looked at me as though I were Drew Pearson investigating the inner workings of the Senate Committee on Spoils and Patronage. He blustered. "Do you mean to imply my daughter is a liar?"

"You know perfectly well what she is," I snapped.

Leander Rhodes sagged in his chair; he looked a hundred years old at that moment. "Young man," he said huskily, "I have misjudged you. I apologize."

"It's nothing, sir," I mumbled. I felt genuinely sorry for the old bastard. He sighed heavily; then he lit another cigar.

"I'll tell you a little about the coming campaign," he said. I was enormously relieved: I wasn't fired after all. "On Friday I shall announce my candidacy. So far the only two candidates officially in the field are both conservatives . . . neither is quite so conservative as I am, however, and neither has my following in the Midwest, among the farmers and small business people. Now I have been in this game long enough to know that high ideals are not enough if you want high office; you have to compromise to win and I want to win and I am willing to compromise with both Labor and the Left Wing, two elements which have never supported me before. You follow me?"

I said I did, perfectly. I was beginning to revise my estimate of him. He was not entirely a fool. Had he been in the fashionable liberal camp I should probably have thought well of him . . . there were men far less astute than he who enjoyed a good deal more esteem.

"Now I anticipate a deadlock at the convention. . . ." For the next few minutes I was told political secrets which any Washington journalist would have given an arm to know. I found out what the President was going to do and what was going on in the inner circles of both parties . . . it was all very grand. "I am taking you into my confidence, young man, because unless you are up on the facts you'll be of no use to me, and you have a lot of work to do. Fortunately, we have money. I am backed in this by some of the richest men in America and we'll spend all that the law'll allow . . . and then some." He smiled for the first time since I'd met him: long yellow teeth, like a dog's. . . .

It was almost one-thirty when our conference ended. "I feel we understand each other," said the Senator, shaking my hand as he led me to the door.

"I do, too, sir," I said sincerely, not adding, however, that I understood Leander Rhodes so well that I was tempted to take the next train back to New York and start a crusade against him. I had not realized the extent of his cunning nor had I suspected he had so many large sinister interests behind him. It was a chilling interview, even for a political innocent like myself: I realized, as I walked down the hall, that Huey Long had been a ward heeler compared to Senator Rhodes.

In my confusion, I went downstairs to the drawing room instead of upstairs to my bedroom. The butler was still up, to my surprise, collecting the remains of the coffee cups and brandy glasses. He looked at me expectantly but I only smiled vaguely at him and then, seeing a package of cigarettes on the couch opposite me, I walked over and picked them up, determinedly, as though I had come downstairs for them. The butler and his tray vanished. I stood for a moment, looking into the coals of the fire. The phrase "Man on horseback" kept going through my head. What a terrible man he was! I thought impotently, and what should I do? just how far from virtue should self-interest propel one? It was very perplexing.

"Oh, you gave me a start," said a female voice.

I jumped myself; it was Verbena Pruitt in a dressing gown of flesh-colored silk, a vast tent-like affair which made her seem more than ever like a mountain of festering flesh; her thin gray hair was done in paper curlers and I noticed that she had a bald spot the size of a Cardinal's cap on the back of her head.

"I was looking for my cigarettes," said the apparition. "I thought I left them on the couch over there."

I felt like a thief: the lady's cigarettes in my coat pocket. Had I been of strong character, I should have admitted guilt and handed them over to her. But, as usual, I took the easy way. "Perhaps they fell down behind the cushions," I said and I began to search for them with great stage gestures, scrutinizing the backs of cushions with an idiot stare.

"It's unimportant," said Verbena Pruitt. "The butler probably took them. They always do. Anything they can get their hands on." She glanced thoughtfully at the row of bottles on a tray near the fireplace.

"Can I get you anything?" I asked eagerly.

"Perhaps a mouthful of that brandy," said Miss Pruitt smiling; I noticed with alarm that her upper teeth had been removed for the night . . . so richly fat was her face, though, that it made hardly any difference. Only her speech was somewhat impaired. I wondered if I should attempt some pleasantry or not about the mouthful . . . did she want me to carry it to her in *my* mouth? I let it go. The Verbena Pruitts of the world were, as far as I was concerned, an unknown and dangerous quantity, capable of any madness. I brought her a stiff shot of brandy, and one for myself.

"That *is* nice," she said, tossing off half of it in such haste that a bit of the essence trickled down her tier of chins, like Victoria Falls.

We sat down on one of the couches. I could hardly believe it. Here I was alone at night in an empty drawing room with the First Lady of her Party seated beside me, wearing an intimate garment of the night, her hair in curlers and her teeth waiting for her upstairs in one of the bedrooms. It was the sort of moment every boy dreams of, in nightmares.

"Tell me, my dear young man, what your function is . . . in relation to Senator Rhodes."

"I am to handle his publicity."

"Not an easy job," said Miss Pruitt cryptically, touching her bald spot bemusedly with a hand like a bloated starfish.

"I'm afraid not."

"Lee has many enemies."

"I can see why."

"You what?"

"I mean I can see why . . . considering the principles he stands for and so on," I extemporized hastily.

"Of course. Still most of the press is against him . . . I can't think why except you know what smart alecks those newspaper people are . . . just between you and me and the lamppost. . . . I hope you won't quote me." She smiled, terribly.

"I know what you mean," I said, averting my eyes.

"Lee has such courage," she added irrelevantly, sniffing her brandy like a terrier at a rat's hole. "Take tonight. He actually thinks he can win over that young Communist from New York who's writing a piece about him. He is fearless . . . but he should keep people like that at a distance."

"Perhaps the Senator needs someone to save him from himself," I suggested.

"How right you are, Mr. Schroeder."

"Sargeant."

"I mean Mr. Sargeant. Then you must remember that I'm not exactly *pro*-Rhodes." This last information was said with a shrewd wink which struck me as being oddly unpleasant.

"I thought you were on his committee." Rhodes had given me to understand that Miss Pruitt would deliver the women of America on Election Day.

"Wheels within wheels," said Verbena Pruitt rising to her feet. "But now I must be off to my beauty sleep." And, like Lady Macbeth, she sailed out of the room.

I finished off my brandy slowly. Then, wondering whether or not I should look in on Ellen, I walked up the dimly lit staircase. I was just recalling that I had no idea where her bedroom was when a figure stepped out of the shadows on the first landing. I gave a jump.

"Hope I didn't startle you," said Rufus Hollister smoothly, emerging from the darkened doorway, where he had been standing, into the faint lamplight. He was still dressed.

"Not at all," I said.

"The Senator just phoned me . . . on the house phone. He's working late . . . never lets up . . . secret of his success . . . nose to the grindstone." I was pelted with saws.

"I'll see you in the morning," I said, edging away. I didn't get very far, though. The next thing I knew I was on the floor, in Mr. Hollister's arms, an enormous gold-framed mirror in fragments about us as the whole house rocked back and forth while a sound like thunder or the atomic bomb deafened us and put out all the lights.

They picked a fine moment to bomb Washington was my first conscious thought. My second thought was to check myself in the dark for broken bones. I was all in one piece, I decided, though my cheek was bleeding . . . from the broken glass. Then the shouts and shrieks began. I heard Mr. Hollister cursing in the dark near me, heard the tinkle of glass as he got to his feet and brushed himself off. Then, from all directions, candles appeared, held by servants, by Mrs. Rhodes, by Miss Pruitt, who was standing in the corridor with the Pomeroys. No one knew what had happened. Not until an hour later did we find out, when a police official addressed us in the drawing room.

It was a curious scene.

A dozen candelabras cast a cool yellow light over the room, making long shadows on the floor. The house party and the servants, in various states of dress and undress, sat in a circle about the police lieutenant, a young man named Winters who stood sternly between two uniformed policemen and surveyed his audience.

"In the first place," he said, glaring for some inexplicable reason at Verbena Pruitt, "Senator Rhodes is dead." Mrs. Rhodes, who had already been informed, sat very straight in her chair, her face expressionless. Ellen sat beside her, her eyes shut. The others looked stunned by what had happened. And what *had* happened?

"Some time between nine o'clock yesterday morning and one-thirty-six this morning, a small container of a special new explosive, Pomeroy 5X, was hidden behind some logs in the fireplace of the Senator's study." There was a gasp. Ellen opened her eyes very wide. Mr. Pomeroy stirred uneasily; his wife chewed her lip nervously. Verbena Pruitt was nearly as impassive as Mrs. Rhodes: she had been through too many political battles to be unnerved by such a small thing as murder, and it *was* murder in the eyes of Lieutenant Winters.

"It is our belief that someone who was closely acquainted with the Senator's habits knew that he usually went to his study alone after dinner to work, and that he always lit his own fire on cold nights. In fact, according to Mrs. Rhodes and the butler here, he was very particular about this fire, insisting that it be made like an Indian tepee of ash logs and strips of pine kindling. It was never lighted by anyone except himself and, in the morning, the coals were always taken out by one of the maids. Yesterday morning they were removed at nine o'clock by . . ." Lieutenant Winters squinted in the candlelight at a sheet of paper he was holding in his hand, "by Madge Peabody, a maid. Fifteen minutes later the butler, Herman Howells, laid the fire. From that moment until Senator Rhodes retired to his study the library was visited by no one . . . except the murderer." Lieutenant Winters paused dramatically and peered through the gloom of candles at his captive audience, unconscious of his errors. I wondered if he'd ever thought of television for a career; with that handsome dull profile, that hypnotic voice he could write his own ticket. I was suddenly very tired; I wanted to go to bed.

Mr. Hollister provided a mild diversion. "And myself," he said calmly. "I was in the study shortly before dinner, at the Senator's request." I held *my* fire.

"I will get your testimony later," said the Lieutenant, a little sharply I thought. His great moment robbed of some of its drama. He then told us that we were, none of us, to leave the house without police permission. Then, beginning with the ladies, the interviews began. They were held in the dining room. The rest of us remained in the drawing room, talking in hushed voices of what had happened, and drinking nervously. Mrs. Rhodes was the first to be interviewed; which was fortunate since her presence embarrassed us all. When she was gone, I was surprised at how calmly the guests took this sudden, extraordinary turn in their affairs . . . especially Ellen who was the coolest of the lot.

"Do fix me a Scotch," she said, while I was standing by the bar getting more brandy for Miss Pruitt. When I had finished my bar duties, I sat beside Ellen on an uncomfortable love seat. Across the room Miss Pruitt and Mr. Hollister were talking animatedly to Walter Langdon. Close to the fire the Pomeroys, man and wife, conferred in low voices while the servants hovered on the outskirts, silent in the shadows.

"This is awful," I said inadequately, conventionally.

"I should hope to hell it is," said Ellen, guzzling Scotch like a baby at its mother's breast. "It's going to tie us all in knots for the next few months."

This was cold-blooded but I saw her point and, after all, it was her honesty which has always appealed to me. She had obviously not liked her father and I was oddly pleased that she had not, despite the crisis, acted out of character. It would have been such a temptation to weep and carry on. "What a funny way to kill someone," I said, not knowing quite what to say.

"Dynamite in the fireplace!" Ellen shook her head; then she put her drink down and looked at me. "It's the most impossible thing I've ever heard of."

"How do you feel?" I asked, suddenly solicitous.

"Numb," she said softly, shaking her head. "Did you ever find yourself not knowing what to think? Well, that's the way I am now. I keep waiting for an alarm or something to go off inside me and show me how to act, what to feel."

"Your mother's taking it pretty well," I said.

"She's numb, too."

"Where were you when it happened?"

Ellen chuckled; for a moment she was like her old self. "That would be telling!"

"With that boy?" I motioned to Langdon who was still talking to the politicos.

Ellen nodded, with a wicked smile. "We were just talking, in *his* room. He wanted to hear some stories . . . you know, life with father kind of things. . . ."

"I can imagine what you told him."

"Well, we really hardly had time. He had just told me he was being divorced from his wife, a Bennington girl, when the lights went out and . . ." She stopped abruptly, took a long drink; then: "Did you ever know any girls from Bennington? They're so terribly earnest. They *know* everything. I pity a boy like that being married to one of them."

"I suppose your compassion will very soon take a more positive turn," I said pompously; it was unseemly, I felt, to be talking about Ellen's sex life when her father, at this moment, lay dead in his study, guarded by the police, a blanket hung over the doorway to keep the cold air out of the rest of the house: part of one wall had been blown off while the furniture and the door, as well as the Senator, had all been shattered in the explosion.

"Oh, who cares," she said, without much interest. "How long do you think they'll take to figure all this out?"

"Who? The police? I haven't any idea."

"Well, I hope they're quick about it. It shouldn't take long, God knows."

"You sound as though you know who killed him?"

The blue eyes flickered almost humorously in the wavering candlelight. "Of course I know, darling . . . but, for one reason and another, I'm not opening my mouth . . . wouldn't interfere for the world."

I felt very cold then . . . as though a blast of December air from that ruined study had penetrated the drawing room and chilled me to the bone.

II

I was interviewed at 4:27 in the morning by the Police Lieutenant who seemed nearly as weary as the rest of us.

"Full name," he mumbled mechanically. A plain-clothes man took down my testimony. The three of us sat at one end of the dining-room table by the light of two candelabras: the candles were half-burned away.

"Peter Cutler Sargeant II."

"Age?"

"Twenty-nine."

"Occupation?"

"Public relations."

"By whom employed."

"Myself."

"Residence?"

"120 Christopher Street, New York City."

"How long have you known Senator Rhodes?"

"About one day."

"How did you happen to know him?"

"I was hired to handle his publicity. I only got here today . . . yesterday morning."

"What time did you come to the house?"

"About four-thirty in the afternoon."

"Did you go to the study at any time?"

"Not until after dinner, when the Senator asked me to join him there."

The Lieutenant opened his eyes and looked interested. His voice lost its official mechanical tone. "What time did you leave?"

"Around one-thirty, I guess . . . just before he was killed."

"Where were you when he was killed?"

"I went back downstairs . . . for a drink. I ran into Miss Pruitt and we talked for a bit . . . she had left her cigarettes or something in the living room . . . then I went upstairs. I was on the first landing when it happened; I was talking to Mr. Hollister."

"About what?"

"About what? oh . . . well, I don't remember. I think I'd just met him when it happened. We were both knocked down, and the lights went out."

"How did the Senator seem when you were with him?"

"I'm afraid I didn't know him well enough to say . . . I mean I don't know what he was like ordinarily. I got the impression that he was worried about something. I presumed it had to do with his announcement on Friday."

"At the Margarine Council?"

I nodded. The Lieutenant lit a cigarette. What a wonderful break it was for him, I thought. This was going to be one of the most publicized cases in years. As a matter of fact, I was already trying to figure out some angle on how I might be able to cash in on it since my big job had been, to employ an apt phrase, blown to bits at the same time as my client. I was aware that I could get quite a price from my old newspaper and the *New York Globe* if I could do a series of pieces on the murder, the inside story. I should have to cultivate the police, though.

"The Senator had many enemies," I volunteered.

"How do you know?" The Lieutenant was properly skeptical. "I thought you only met him yesterday."

"That's true but from what he told me just before he was murdered, I should say that almost any one of a million people might have killed him."

"Why?"

"He was going to run for President."

"So?"

"He was being backed by some very shady characters."

"Names and addresses," the Lieutenant was obviously missing the point.

"I'm afraid it's not that simple," I said coolly. "I don't want to tangle with them and I don't expect you do either. Besides, I'm sure they didn't have anything to do with this murder . . . directly at least. The point is that *their* enemies might have wanted to do away with the Senator for the good of the country."

"I don't follow you. If we don't know who they are then how are we going to know who *their* enemies are, the ones who might want to kill Senator Rhodes?" The Lieutenant was not taking me very seriously, I decided, and I took this as a tribute to the stability of our country . . . the whole idea of a political murder, an assassination on ideological grounds, seemed like complete nonsense to him. The Presidents who had been killed in the past were all victims of crackpots, not of political plots. I decided to hold back my theories on political murder until I had a contract from the *Globe* safely in my pocket. In the meantime I had to be plausible.

"Let's put it this way," I said, speaking earnestly, as glibly as possible. "A lot of people didn't like the idea of a man like Rhodes becoming President. One of them, a crackpot maybe, might have got an idea that the best way to handle the situation would be to kill the Senator before the convention. For instance, right now, in this house, I should say there are four out-and-out political enemies of the Senator."

This had some effect. The Lieutenant stifled a yawn and sat up very straight. "Who are they?"

"Langdon, the newspaperman . . . he's a young fellow, very liberal, he was sent here to write an attack on Rhodes for the *Advanceguard Magazine*. He couldn't have been more anti-Rhodes; and if he'd found out half as much as I did this evening he might have, for patriotic reasons, eased the Senator across the shining river."

"Across where?"

"Killed him. Then Miss Pruitt, though she's an old friend, was opposed to his running for President. Pomeroy, I gather, was a political enemy of Rhodes back in Talisman City and, finally, after my little talk with Rhodes this morning I was tempted to do him in myself."

"That's all very interesting," said the Lieutenant mildly. "But since you refuse to tell us who the Senator's supporters were, I'm afraid you aren't much help to this investigation. Please don't leave the house until further notice." And I was dismissed.

In the drawing room I found Walter Langdon and the servants. All the others had been interviewed and had gone to bed. He looked haggard and pale and I felt a little guilty as I said good night, recalling the dark hints I had made to the Lieutenant . . . but they had been necessary. I was sure of that. This was not an ordinary murder . . . presuming that any murder could be called ordinary. I was both excited and frightened by the possibilities. Just as I got to the first landing, the lights came on again and, thinking of Rufus Hollister, I went to my room.

2

I was called for lunch at noon by the butler who volunteered the information that no one had got up for breakfast except Mrs. Rhodes who was now making arrangements for the Senator's burial at Arlington. I was also informed that the police were still in the house and that the street was crowded with newspapermen and sightseers.

Ellen greeted me cheerily in the drawing room. Wan winter sunlight shone in the room. All the ladies except Miss Pruitt, brave in rose, wore black. Everyone looked grim.

"Come join the wake," said Ellen in a low voice, pulling me over to one of the French windows.

"Has anything happened?" I asked, looking about the room for Mrs. Rhodes. She had not returned.

"Among other things, this," and Ellen gestured at the crowd of newspapermen in the street below. Several police stood guard.

"Where is your mother?" I asked, as we stepped back out of the window; I had caught a glimpse of a camera being trained on us.

"She's still with the undertaker, I think. She should be here for lunch. There's to be a service tomorrow morning at the Cathedral; then to Arlington." She was excited I could see . . . I looked for some trace of sorrow in her face but there was none: only excitement, and perhaps unease . . . a lot of skeletons were going to be rattled in several closets before this case was done. I picked up a newspaper and read, on the front page, how "Statesman Meets Violent End," complete with a photograph of the late politico and an inset of the house with a gaping hole in it where the library had been. "I had no idea it made such a hole," I said, handing Ellen the paper. She put it back on the table: everyone had read it, I gathered.

"Nobody's been allowed to go in the study yet . . . not even Mother or me. Rufus is raising hell because he says there are important papers there."

Exactly on cue, Rufus appeared in the doorway, his owl face peevish and his tweed suit looking as though he'd slept in it. He went straight to Ellen. "Have you any idea when your mother will be back?"

"I thought she'd be here by lunchtime. She said she would be finished in a few hours with the people at the Cathedral."

"We must do something about the files," said Rufus, looking at me nervously, as though unwilling to be more explicit.

"Files?" said the statesman's daughter; in political matters she was even more at sea than usual. Only one or two things really interested her . . . affairs of state left her cool and confused.

"Yes, yes," said Rufus impatiently. "All your father's supporters are listed in the secret files . . . along with their contributions: not that there is anything illegal going on," he chuckled weakly, "but if those names fell into the hands of our political enemies. . . ." He moaned softly; then the doors to the dining room were thrown open and we went in to lunch.

I was surprised, as we took our seats, to find that Lieutenant Winters was also at the table. Needless to say, his presence threw something of a pall over what was, to begin with, a very gloomy group. The Lieutenant seemed calm, however, and I wondered whether or not it was usual for a police officer to dine with suspects. The fact that he was sitting next to Ellen I had duly noted and registered: he was no fool. She was susceptible and she was indiscreet. If he managed everything properly, he would know all he needed to know about the house of Rhodes in a few hours, pleasant hours.

"I can hardly believe this terrible thing has happened," said a rather nasal voice in my ear. I turned and saw for the first time that Mrs. Pomeroy was seated on my left. Her eyes were red and puffy and, from the sound of her voice, she had either been weeping or else she was catching a bad cold. As it turned out she had a touch of the grippe.

"Our room was next to the Senator's study," she said, sniffing dolefully, her red eyes turned on me for sympathy. "Well, after this *terrible* thing went off the whole second floor was *freezing* cold, especially our room. I had had a slight cold when we left Talisman City . . . well, after last night's *terrible* event I *now* have the grippe. My temperature just before lunch was a hundred point three."

I suggested that she drink lemon juice in a glass of hot water and go to bed until the fever was over, but she wasn't much interested in my homely remedies. "It has been," she said in a low voice, "a *shattering* experience."

Especially for the Senator, I wanted to add but decided not to. Across the table Ellen was deep in conversation with Lieutenant Winters. Walter Langdon, her next fiancé (or so I had thought), seemed forgotten; he was talking to Verbena Pruitt.

"You must have been very fond of Senator Rhodes," I said.

Mrs. Pomeroy nodded. "Oh, there were some *little* frictions between him and my husband . . . you know how men are, so *touchy*, concerned with trifles . . . but my own friendship with the Senator was, well, very real . . . and for many, *many* years." Something in her voice made me not only believe everything she was saying but, more important, suggested a sudden, unexpected possibility. I looked at her curiously.

"How long had you known the Senator?" I asked gently.

"All my life," she said. "I was born in Talisman City, you know; Roger of course only moved there from Michigan about fifteen years ago."

"And you were married fifteen years ago?"

She giggled; then she sniffled and sneezed. I looked away until she had pulled herself together. "Not *quite* fifteen years ago," she said archly.

"You should do something about that cold."

"I'm taking pills . . . except for occasional political differences our families have been very *very* close all these years."

"What were those differences?"

"Oh, one thing and another. . . ." She gestured vaguely. "Political. My husband was for Roosevelt . . . that makes *quite* a difference, you know, out where we come from, that is. *I* was always for Dewey . . . so distinguished-looking, and so young. I think we need a young President, don't you?" I said that I hadn't given the question much thought. I was growing more and more suspicious, however; yet there seemed no way to find out what I wanted to know . . . unless Ellen knew, which was not likely. If Mrs. Pomeroy had been the Senator's mistress years ago, the fact would probably not have been well known by the Senator's family. I would have to find out, though. Mrs. Pomeroy despite her red eyes and silly manner was a very good-looking woman. If a man like Pomeroy should have a jealous nature. . . . An elaborate plot began to unwind in my head.

"Did you and Mr. Pomeroy visit here often?" I asked, the roast beef on my plate getting cold as I conducted my investigation.

She shook her head. "As a matter of fact we usually stay at the Mayflower and the Senator joins us for lunch over there."

"This is the first time you've stayed here in the house then?"

She nodded; for a moment her serene features seemed agitated, as though she suspected that I was questioning her for other than polite reasons. Quickly I began to gabble about sure-fire cures for head colds and the crisis passed.

We were given a little speech over the fingerbowls by Lieutenant Winters. He was as unlike a policeman as any man I've ever known and he was obviously delighted with the whole business . . . no matter what happened he was going to get a good deal of publicity; he was also going to meet a number of very important people who might do him some good one day. The murder of the Senator involved, in a sense, everyone in Washington political life, from the White House down to the most confused officeholder. He addressed us quietly, as though he were a fellow guest, anxious to make a good impression.

"I may as well admit quite frankly, ladies and gentlemen, that we are baffled. We haven't the slightest idea who murdered Senator Rhodes." This unusual admission on the part of someone in authority made a considerable impression. I almost expected a polite round of applause . . . only the presence of death in the house prevented his audience from showing their pleasure at his originality.

"We are fairly confident that the murderer or murderers are, if you will pardon me, in the house at this time . . . but even of that we're not entirely sure. We *do* know that only someone who knew the Senator's habits fairly well could have contrived the . . . trap which worked so successfully. It would also seem that whoever did the murder could not have planned it too far in advance because the 5-X explosive was brought to the house only yesterday by Mr. Pomeroy. Four paper cartons of 5-X were kept in Mr. Pomeroy's room. Mr. Pomeroy discussed the new explosive with the Senator yesterday morning at the Senate Office Building in the presence of Mr. Hollister. He then joined Mrs. Pomeroy, Mr. Langdon, Miss Pruitt, Mrs. Rhodes and Miss Rhodes here in the house and there was, I am told, more talk of the new explosive. In short, all the guests, with the exception of Mr. Sargeant, knew about the 5-X, knew that Mr. Pomeroy had four cartons of it in his room, cartons which were to have been turned over to the army this afternoon with Senator Rhodes' recommendation. The cartons were kept in a special fireproof bag which was locked. Some time between four in the afternoon, when Mr. Pomeroy placed the bag in his closet, and one-thirty-six the next morning when Senator Rhodes lit the fire in his study, the murderer went to Mr. Pomeroy's room, broke the lock on the bag and took out a single container which he then placed in the fireplace of the study. I believe that whoever did this must have known something about explosives because, had he taken all four and put them in the fireplace, the house would have been wrecked and the murderer killed along with everyone else." The Lieutenant paused. All eyes were upon him. The room was silent except for the rather heavy breathing of Mrs. Pomeroy beside me, struggling with her cold.

"Now," said the Lieutenant, with a juvenile actor's smile, "I realize that you people are very busy. Your affairs are very important to the country and the Department wants to do everything in its power to make this investigation as easy as possible for you. Unfortunately, until we have a clearer idea of what we're up against, you will have to be inconvenienced to the extent of remaining in this house for at least a week." There was an indignant murmur; the official soft soap forgotten.

"Do you realize, young man," said Miss Pruitt, "that a national election is coming up? that I have a million things to do in the next few weeks?"

"I certainly do, Miss Pruitt. Everyone knows how important your work is but we're all caught in the law. The Department, however, has agreed to allow you ladies and gentlemen to leave the house on urgent business, on condition that we always know where you are. Mrs. Rhodes has kindly consented to let us keep you here in the house for the next few days so that you'll be available for questioning. I realize how inconvenient this must be but those are my orders." And the law took command. There were a few more complaints but the comparative freedom allowed us put everyone in a better mood. The Lieutenant then permitted a recess until five o'clock, at which time there would be more questioning. Like children we trooped out of the dining room.

Verbena Pruitt was the first to leave and, from the grim look on her face, I was quite sure that she would be in touch with the White House before many minutes had passed: after all she was, in a sense, The American Woman. Mr. Pomeroy murmured something to his wife and also left. Walter Langdon went upstairs and Rufus Hollister tangled with the Lieutenant in my presence.

"Lieutenant, you must let me get certain papers out of the Senator's file. It's extremely urgent, as I've said before."

"I'm sorry, Mr. Hollister, but those papers are all being gone over by the Department. There's nothing I can do about it."

"I don't think you realize how serious this is, Lieutenant," said Hollister, flushing angrily. "The papers I want have nothing to do with the murder . . . I swear to you they don't. They involve, however, certain people of the greatest importance—the leaders of this country —and they were meant only for the Senator's eyes."

"We're not politicians," said the Lieutenant quietly . . . a little inaccurately, I thought. "We're not interested in the political implications of all this. Those papers are being gone over by men who are looking for only one thing: clues to the murder of Senator Rhodes. I don't need to tell you that they are discreet men. In any case, all the papers will be returned to your office in a day or two."

"You don't understand," said Rufus furiously, but there was very little he could say: the Lieutenant's attitude was perfectly reasonable, and legal. "I shall talk to the District Commissioners about this," he said, finally; then he was gone. The Lieutenant sighed. I looked about me and saw that we were the only two left in the room. Ellen had quietly vanished . . . in pursuit of Walter Langdon, I presumed. The other policemen were all upstairs in the study. In the dining room behind us, the servants were cleaning up.

"You've got your work cut out for you," I said sympathetically.

He nodded. "It's like doing a tightrope act. Do you realize the influence this gang has? I don't dare offend any of them."

"Or dare make a mistake."

"We don't make mistakes," said the Lieutenant, suddenly stuffy, a policeman after all in spite of his college manners and Grecian profile.

"I might be able to help you," I said, going off on another tack: one which would interest him. He didn't react quite the way I would have liked, though.

"Why do you want to do that?" He was suspicious. It gave me quite a turn to realize that this man regarded me as a possible murderer.

"Money," I said callously. Self-interest makes beasts of us all . . . and all men understand self-interest: it is the most plausible of motives, the one which is seldom ever questioned.

"What do you mean?"

"I mean that I would like very much to be the first to know who did the murder because I could then get quite a large sum of money from my old newspaper the *New York Globe* for an exclusive story on the murder."

"I thought you were in public relations."

"Before that I was assistant drama critic on the *Globe*. You may recall I was the one who did the story on the murder of Ella Sutton, the ballerina, last year. I made a good deal out of that particular story."

"I remember." I couldn't tell how he was reacting. Then: "Just how do you think you can help us?"

"Through the family," I said glibly. "Through Ellen Rhodes. You see we used to be engaged. I can find out quickly a lot of things you people might never know."

"Such as?"

"What's really going on. What the Senator's true relationships were with this gang. By an odd coincidence almost everyone here disliked him, or had reason to."

"Except you?"

I was getting nowhere; I was also getting rather put out with this decorative arm of the law. "Except me. No, I didn't murder the old goat so that I could marry his daughter and get all his money. Having sat next to her at lunch you are probably quite aware of Miss Rhodes' true nature."

Against his will, the Lieutenant grinned. I had made a chink in the official mask. I charged ahead. "We're old friends, that's all, Ellen and I. I have a hunch she knows a good deal about this and I can find out what she knows, quickly."

"All just for a newspaper story?"

"Just!" I was genuinely outraged. "Yes," I said, more calmly, "just for a newspaper story, for the money and the publicity."

"We're not supposed to work with the press . . . not like this, at this stage of an investigation."

"On the other hand, I'm not just the press either."

"I'll say you're not. You're a murder suspect."

This was putting it too coldly, I thought. I shrugged and turned away, "In that case, you'll get no cooperation from me, Lieutenant. What I do know I'll keep to myself."

"What's the deal?" He was abrupt.

"I want to know what's going on. In exchange I'll find out things for you . . . family skeletons. On top of that, remember the pieces I'll do for the *Globe* 'll be widely reprinted and you, Lieutenant Winters, will be getting a good deal of attention."

"What do you know?" I had won the first round.

"Pomeroy," I said. There was no need to explain further: we understand each other.

"Why Pomeroy?"

"Old enemy. The Senator was blackmailing him over that 5-X . . . at least that's my guess. Rhodes wanted to be paid off either in cash or votes, probably the last. Pomeroy's a big gun in their state."

"How did you find this out?"

"I know a little about politics," I said quietly; as a matter of fact I had figured out the whole plot at lunch. I didn't care to admit, at this point however, that I was relying rather heavily on intuition and a few chance remarks dropped my way the day before by Rufus Hollister.

The Lieutenant extended to me his first confidence. "That's one way of looking at it," he said. "But the fact is the Senator refused yesterday to recommend Pomeroy to the Defense Department . . . Pomeroy admitted as much."

"I wonder, though, why the Senator's recommendation should be so important?" I asked, a little puzzled.

"Pomeroy was in bad with the Defense Department. They canceled his contract last month."

I nodded as if I knew all this; actually it was a surprise; the first real lead. "I knew," I lied, "that he hoped his 5-X would put him back into business again."

"It's not very clear, though," said the Lieutenant sadly, moving over to the window which overlooked the street. Several newspapermen were trying to get past the guards. Most of the crowd, however, had gone on about their business. "Why would Pomeroy want to kill the one man who could help him get his contract?"

"Isn't revenge one of the usual motives? Along with greed and lust?"

"It's a little extreme . . . and obvious, too obvious." It was the first time that I had ever heard a member of any police department maintain that anything was too obvious: as a rule they jump wildly, and often safely, to the first solution that offers itself. This was a bright boy, I decided; I would have to handle myself very carefully around him.

"One other thing," I said, playing my only card.

"What's that?"

"Mrs. Pomeroy. I have an idea, a hunch."

"That what?"

"That she and the old boy were carrying on, a long time ago. It would complete the revenge motive wouldn't it? Not only was Pomeroy angry about losing his contract but he also had an old grudge against the Senator because of something which had happened even before Pomeroy ever met his wife."

"Where'd you find all this out?"

"Deduction, I'm afraid. No evidence. At lunch today she made several remarks which started me thinking, that's all. I found out that she'd known the Senator all her life, that she was very fond of him ... really so ... that Pomeroy, as we know, was not; that Pomeroy came to the state only about fifteen years ago from Michigan and about the same time married the Senator's old friend, Mrs. P."

"It'll take a good deal of investigating to check on this."

"I know some short cuts."

"We could use them."

"You *do* think Pomeroy killed the Senator, don't you?"

The Lieutenant nodded, "I think he did."

3

After my session with Winters, I went upstairs and telephoned my office in New York. My secretary, a noble woman in middle life named Miss Flynn, admitted that she had been concerned about me. She gave me a quick report on the progress of my other clients: a hat company, three television actresses of the second rank, a comedian of the first rank, a society lady of mysterious origin but well-charted future, and a small but rich dog-food concern. All of my clients seemed reasonably pleased and the few problems which had arisen in my absence were settled over the phone with Miss Flynn. "I trust you will soon return to New York now that your client Senator Rhodes has been Gathered Up," said Miss Flynn ceremoniously.

"As soon as the police let us go," I said. "We're all in quite a spot."

"Washington!" said Miss Flynn with a note of disgust: next to Hollywood she regarded it as the end, the absolute moral end of a country which was rapidly degenerating into something Roman and horrid.

After I had finished with Miss Flynn, I called my old editor at the *Globe* and I managed to extort a considerable sum for a series of articles on the death of Senator Rhodes. I need not now recall the details of this transaction; enough to say that I did pretty well, considering the depressed state of the dollar.

My business over, I strolled downstairs to the second floor. At one end of the corridor, on the left, was the blanketed and guarded entrance to the study. Three bedrooms opened off that corridor. The one nearest the study was occupied by the Pomeroys. Across from it was Walter Langdon's and, next to his, was Rufus Hollister's room. To the right of the landing was another hall with four bedrooms opening off it. They were the rooms, I knew, of Senator Rhodes, of Mrs. Rhodes, of Ellen and Miss Pruitt. My room on the third floor was definitely in the outfield, up where the servants lived. On an impulse I went to Ellen's room and opened the door, without knocking.

Had I been half an hour later, I should probably have witnessed as fine a display of carnality as our Puritan country has to offer; happily, for my own modesty, I found Walter Langdon and Ellen still clothed in spite of a steaming embrace on the bed which broke abruptly when they heard me. Langdon leaped to his feet like a track star warming up for the high hurdles; Ellen, an old hand at this sort of discovery, sat up more slowly and straightened her hair. "A pin just stabbed me in the back of the neck," she announced irritably, rubbing her neck. "Why the hell don't you knock?" Then, before I could answer she turned to Langdon angrily and said, "I thought you said you locked the door?"

"I . . . I thought I did. I guess I turned the key over in the lock." He was blushing furiously and I could see that my ex-fiancé had aroused him. Embarrassed he trotted into the bathroom and slammed the door behind him.

"A cooling-off period at this point in an affair is often considered very sound," I said smoothly. "It gives both parties an opportunity to determine whether or not their needs can be served only through sin."

"Oh, shut up! Where do you think you are? in a railroad station? We were just talking, that's all . . . and now look what you've done."

"What have I done?"

"Embarrassed the poor little thing to death. It may take me days to get him back to where I had him before you came in."

"He's not that much of a baby," I said. "And your methods are foolproof anyway."

"Hell!" said Ellen, in a mood of complete disgust and dejection.

"Anyway I want to talk to you."

"What about?"

Before I could answer, Langdon came back into the bedroom noticeably soothed. "I'll see you later," he said calmly and left the room.

"*Now* look what you've done!"

"You can finish your dirty work tonight," I said. "I want to talk to you about the murder."

"Well, what about it?" She was still angry. She went over to her dressing table and sat down, repairing her blurred make-up. I ambled about the room, looking at the bookcase full of girls' stories and passionate adult novels, at the rather unfeminine décor.

"Was this always your room?"

She nodded. "Up until I got married it was."

"Where did you go after the marriage was annulled?"

"To a finishing school in New York. When I was thrown out of that, I stayed in New York. . . ."

"On a liberal allowance."

"Depends on your idea of liberal; now what about the murder?"

"They think, the police think, Pomeroy did it?"

"So?"

"Did he?"

"How should I know. Why don't you ask him?"

"I thought you said you knew who did it."

She laughed, "Did I say that? I must've been lit . . . or maybe *you* were lit . . . which reminds me will you push that bell over there. It's getting near teatime and I'm developing that funny parched feeling."

I pushed the mother-of-pearl button.

"Who do you think did it?"

"My darling Peter, I'm not sure that even if I did know I would tell you. I realize that's an unnatural way to feel about the murderer of your own father but I'm not a very natural girl, as you well know . . . or maybe *too* natural, which is about the same thing. If somebody disliked Father enough to kill him I'm not at all sure that I would interfere. I have no feeling at all about him, about my father I mean. I never forgave him for that annulment . . . not that I was so much in love, though I thought I was, being young and silly, but rather because he had tried to interfere with me and that's one thing I can't stand. Anyway he was not very lovable, as you probably gathered, and when I could get away from home I did. I still don't know what on earth prompted me to come down here with you. I guess I was awfully high at Cambridge and it seemed like a fun idea. I regretted the whole thing the second I woke up on that train but it was too late to go back." The butler interrupted the first serious talk I had ever had with Ellen and, by the time half a Scotch Mist had given her strength to face the afternoon, she was herself again and our serious moment was over.

"What do you know about the Pomeroys?" I asked when the butler had disappeared.

"What everybody knows. They're not that mysterious. He came to Talisman City in the late Thirties and set up a factory . . . I suppose he had some capital to start with . . . he manufactured explosives. When the war came along he made a lot of money and the factory grew very big and he grew with it, got to be quite a power politically. Then the war ended, business fell off and he lost his contract with the government, or so I was told yesterday."

"By whom?"

"By my father." She paused thoughtfully; then she swallowed the rest of the Scotch.

"Did he . . . did your father seem nervous to you?"

"You know, Peter, you're beginning to sound like that police Lieutenant . . . only not as pretty."

"I've got a job to do," I said, and I explained to her about the *Globe*, told her that she had to help me, that I needed someone who could give me the necessary facts about the people involved.

"You're an awfully fast operator," she said.

"That makes two of us."

She laughed; then she sat down beside me on the couch. "I'm afraid I've been away too long to be much help . . . besides, you know what I think or rather what I *don't* think about politics."

"I have a hunch that the murder doesn't have anything to do with politics."

"Your guess is as good as anybody's," said Ellen and she helped herself to another drink.

"What about Mrs. Pomeroy?"

"What about her?"

"What's her relationship to your family . . . I gather she knew the Senator before she married Pomeroy."

"That's right. I remember her as a child . . . when *I* was a child, that is. She's about twenty years older than I am, though I'm sure she'd never admit that, even to her plastic surgeon."

"Plastic surgeon?"

"Yes, darling; she's had her face lifted . . . don't you know about those things? There are two little scars near her ears, under the hair. . . ."

"How was I supposed to see those?"

"*I* noticed them; I know all about those things. But that's beside the point. She's been around ever since I can remember. Her family were very close to ours . . . used to live right down the street, as a matter of fact: she was always coming over for dinner and things like that . . . usually alone. Her father was an undertaker and not very agreeable. Her mother didn't get on very well with my mother so we seldom saw much of her . . ."

"Just the daughter?"

"Yes, just Camilla. She was always organizing the Young People's Voter Association for Father, things like that. She used to be quite a bug on politics, until she married Roger. After that we saw less of her . . . I suppose because Roger didn't get on with Father."

"I've got a theory that Mrs. Pomeroy and the Senator were having an affair."

Ellen looked quite startled; then she laughed. "Well, I'll be damned," she said. "Now that *is* an idea."

"Well, what's wrong with it?" I don't like my intuitions to be discredited so scornfully.

"Well, I don't know . . . it just seems terribly unlikely. Father was never interested in women . . . as far as I know. *She* might have had a crush on him: that often happened when he was younger. There was always some dedicated young woman around the house doing odd jobs, but I'm sure nothing ever happened. Mother always kept a sharp eye on Father."

"I still think something might have happened."

"Well, what if it did?"

"It would give Pomeroy another reason for wanting to kill your father."

"So, after fifteen years, he decides to be a jealous husband because of something which happened before he met Camilla? Not very likely, darling. Besides, he had just about all the motive he needed without dragging that sheep in. You know, Peter, I think you're probably very romantic at heart: you think love is at the root of everything."

"Go shove it," I said lapsing into military talk; I was very put out with her . . . also with myself: the Pomeroy business didn't make sense . . . it almost did but not quite. There was something a little off. The motive was there but the situation itself was all wrong. You just don't kill a man in his own house with your own weapon right after having a perfectly open quarrel with him over business matters. I was sure that Mrs. Pomeroy was involved but, for the life of me, I couldn't fit her in. I began, rather reluctantly, to consider other possibilities, other suspects.

"But I love it," said Ellen cozily. "It shows the side of you I like the best." And we tussled for a few minutes; then, recalling that in the next few hours I would have to have some sort of a story for the *Globe*, I disentangled myself and left Ellen to her Scotch.

As I walked down the hall, the door to Langdon's room opened and he motioned for me to come in. The presence of the plain-clothes man at the other end of the hall, guarding the study, made me nervous: he could see everything that happened on the second floor.

Langdon's room was like my own, only larger, American maple and chintz, that sort of thing. On the desk his typewriter was open and crumpled pieces of paper littered the floor about it: he had been composing, not too successfully.

"Say, I hope I didn't bother you . . . my being in Miss Rhodes' room like that." He was very nervous.

"Bother me?" I laughed. "Why should it?"

"Well, your being engaged to her and all that."

"I'm no more engaged to her than you are. She's engaged to the whole male sex."

"Oh." He looked surprised; I decided he wasn't a very worldly young man . . . I knew the type: serious, earnest, idealistic . . . the sort who have wonderful memories and who pass college examinations with great ease.

"No, I should probably apologize to you for barging in like that just as you were getting along so nicely." He blushed. I pointed to the typewriter, to change the subject. "Are you writing your piece?"

"Well, yes and no," he sighed. "I called New York this morning and asked them what they wanted me to do now: they sounded awfully indefinite, I mean, we never write about murders . . . that's hardly our line. On the other hand, there is probably some political significance in this, maybe a great deal, and it would be quite a break for me if I could do something about it . . . a Huey Long kind of thing."

"I used to work on the *Globe*," I said helpfully. "But of course we handled crime differently. You're right, I suspect, about the political angle but it won't be easy to track down."

"I'm sure of it," said Langdon with sudden vehemence. "He was a dangerous man."

"How long did it take you to figure that out?"

"One day, exactly. I've been here four days now . . . in that time I've found out things which, if you'd told me about them, I would never have believed possible, in this country anyway."

"Such as?"

"Did you see the names of some of those people supporting Rhodes for President? Every fascist in the country was on that list . . . every witch hunter in public life was backing his candidacy."

"You must have suspected all that when you came down here."

Langdon sat down on the bed and lit a cigarette; I sat opposite him, at his desk. "Well, naturally, we were on to him in a way. He was a buffoon . . . you know what I mean: an old-fashioned, narrow-minded demagogue always talking about Americanism. . . . Now our specialty is doing satirical articles about reactionaries . . . the sort of piece that isn't openly hostile, that allows the subject to hang himself in his own words. You have no idea how easy it is. Those people are usually well-protected, by secretaries . . . even by the press . . . people who straighten their grammar and their facts, make them seem more rational than they really are. So what I do is take down a verbatim account of some great man's conversation, selected of course, and publish it with all the bad grammar and so on. I thought that's what I'd be doing here but I soon found that Rhodes wasn't really a windbag, after all. He was a clever man and hard to trap."

"Then you found out all about his candidacy?"

"It wasn't hard."

"Where did you see those names? the names of the supporters?" The memory of the indignant Rufus Hollister browbeating Lieutenant Winters was still fresh in my memory.

Langdon looked embarrassed. "I . . . happened to find them, see them, I mean . . . in the Senator's study."

"When he wasn't there?"

"You make it sound dishonest. No, he asked me to meet him there day before yesterday; I got there before he did and I, well . . ."

"Looked around."

"I was pretty shocked."

"It's all over now."

He mashed his cigarette out nervously. "Yes, and I might as well admit that I'm glad. He could never have been elected in a straight election but you can never tell what might happen in a crisis."

"You think that gang might have invented a crisis and tried to take over the country?"

He nodded, looking me straight in the eye. "That's just what I mean. I know it sounds very strange and all that, like a South American republic, but it *could* happen here . . ."

"As Sinclair Lewis once said." I glanced at the sheet of paper in the typewriter. A single sentence had been written across the top: *"And therefore think him as a serpent's egg, Which, hatch'd, would as his kind grow mischievous, And kill him in the shell."* Langdon was suddenly embarrassed, aware that I was reading what he had written. "Don't look at that!" He came over quickly, pulled the sheet of paper out of the typewriter. "I was just fooling around," he said, crumpling the sheet into a tight ball and tossing it onto the wastebasket.

"A quotation?" I asked.

He nodded and changed the subject. "Do you think Pomeroy did it?"

"Killed Rhodes? I suppose so. Yet if he was going to kill the Senator why would he have used his own 5-X, throwing suspicion on himself immediately?"

"Anybody could have got at the 5-X."

"Yes but . . ." A new idea occurred to me, "Only Pomeroy knew how powerful one of those cartons of dynamite would be. Anybody else would be afraid of using something like that, if only because they might get blown up along with the Senator."

Langdon frowned. "It's a good point but . . ."

"But what?"

"But I'm not so sure that Pomeroy didn't explain to us that afternoon about the 5-X, about the cartons."

I groaned. "Are you sure he did?"

"No, not entirely . . . I *think* he did, though."

"Yet isn't *that* peculiar?" I was off on another tack. "Just why should he want to talk about his stuff in such detail?"

We talked for nearly an hour about the murder, about Ellen, about politics. . . . I found Langdon to be agreeable but elusive; there was something which I didn't quite understand . . . he suggested an iceberg: he concealed more than he revealed and he was a very cool number besides. At last, when I had set his mind at ease about Ellen, I left him and went downstairs.

In the living room I found Ellen and Mrs. Rhodes, pale but calm; they were talking to a mountainous, craggy man who was, it turned out, Johnson Ledbetter, the Governor of Senator Rhodes' home state.

"I flew here as quick as possible, Miss Grace," he said with Midwestern warmth, taking Mrs. Rhodes' hands in his, a look of dog-like devotion in his eyes.

"Lee would have appreciated it," said Mrs. Rhodes, equal to the occasion. "You'll say a few words at the funeral tomorrow?"

"Indeed I will, Miss Grace. This has shocked me more than I can say. The flag on the State Capitol back home is at half-mast," he added.

As the others wandered into the room, Ellen got me aside; she was excited and her face glowed. "They're going to read the will tomorrow, after the funeral."

"Looks like you're going to be a rich girl," I said, drying my sleeve with a handkerchief . . . in her excitement she had slopped some of her Scotch Mist on me. "I wonder if the police have taken a look at it yet."

She looked puzzled. "Why should they?"

"Well, darling, there's a theory going around that people occasionally get removed from this vale of tears by over-anxious heirs."

"Don't be silly. Anyway tomorrow is the big day. That's why the Governor's here."

"To read the will?"

"Yes, he's the family lawyer. Father made him Governor a couple of years ago. I forget just why . . . you know how politicians are."

"I'm beginning to find out. By the way, have you gotten into that Langdon boy yet?"

"What an ugly question!" she beamed; then she shook her head. "I haven't had time. Last night would have been unseemly . . . I mean after the murder. This afternoon I was interrupted."

"I think he's much too innocent for the likes of you."

"Stop it . . . you don't know about these things. He's rather tense, I'll admit, but they're much the best fun . . . the tense ones."

"What a bore *I* must've been."

"As a matter of fact, you were; now that you mention it." She chuckled; then she paused, looking at someone who had just come in. I looked over my shoulder and saw the Pomeroys in the doorway. He looked pale and weary; she, on the other hand, was quite lovely, her attack of grippe under control. The Governor greeted them cordially. Ellen left me for Walter Langdon. I joined the Governor's group by the fireplace. For awhile I just listened.

"Camilla, you grow younger every year!" intoned the Governor.

Mrs. Pomeroy gestured coquettishly. "You just want my vote, Johnson."

"How long are you going to be with us, Governor?" asked Pomeroy. If he was alarmed by the mess he was in, he didn't show it; except for his pallor, he seemed much as ever.

Mrs. Rhodes excused herself and went into the dining room. The Governor remarked that he would stay in town through the funeral and the reading of the will; that he was flying back to Talisman City immediately afterwards: "Got that damned legislature on my hands," he boomed. "Don't know what they'll do next." He looked about him to make sure that no members of the deceased's family were nearby; then he asked: "How did your session with the Defense Department go?"

Pomeroy shrugged. "I was at the Pentagon most of the day . . . I'm afraid the only thing they wanted to talk about was the . . . accident."

"A tragical happening, tragical," declared the Governor, shaking his head like some vast moth-eaten buffalo.

Pomeroy sighed: "It doesn't do my product much good," he said. "Not of course that I'm not very sad about this, for Mrs. Rhodes' sake, but after all, I've got a factory back home which has got to get some business or else."

"How well I know, Roger," said the Governor with a bit more emphasis than the situation seemed to call for. I wondered if there was any business connection between the two. "We don't want to swell the ranks of the unemployed, do we?"

"Especially not if *I* happen to be one of the unemployed," said Roger Pomeroy dryly.

"I always felt," said his wife who had been standing close to the Governor, listening, "that Lee's attitude was terribly unreasonable. He should've done *everything* in his power to help us."

"What do you mean?" asked the Governor.

Pomeroy spoke first, quickly, before his wife could elaborate. "Lee didn't push the 5-X as vigorously as I thought he should, that's all . . . that was one of the reasons I came to Washington on this trip . . . poor Lee."

"Poor Lee," repeated Mrs. Pomeroy, with real sincerity.

"A great statesman has fallen," said the Governor, obviously rehearsing his funeral oration. "Like some great oak he leaves an empty place against the sky in our hearts."

Overwhelmed by the majesty of this image, I missed Pomeroy's eulogy; the next remark I heard woke me up, though. "Have you seen the will yet?" asked Mrs. Pomeroy, blowing her nose emotionally.

The Governor nodded gravely. "Indeed I have, Camilla. I drew it up for Lee."

"I wonder . . ." she began, but then she was interrupted by the appearance of Lieutenant Winters who joined us at the fireplace, bowed to the Governor and then, politely but firmly, led Mr. Pomeroy into the dining room. Interviews, I gathered, had been going on for some time. The Governor detached himself from Camilla Pomeroy and joined Miss Pruitt on the couch and, considering the "tragical" nature of the occasion, both were quite boisterous, talking politics eagerly.

My own interview with the Lieutenant took place right after he had finished with Pomeroy. I sat down beside him in the dining room; the table was brilliantly set for dinner, massive Georgian silver gleaming in the dim light. Through the pantry door I could hear the servants bustling about. The usual plain-clothes man was on hand, taking notes. He sat behind Winters.

It took me several minutes to work my way past the Lieutenant's official manner; when I finally did, I found him troubled. "It won't come out right," he said plaintively. "There just isn't any evidence of any kind."

"Outside of the explosive."

"Which doesn't mean a thing since anybody in this house, except possibly you, could have got to it."

"Then you don't think Pomeroy was responsible?"

Winters played with a fork thoughtfully. "Yes, I think he probably was but there's no evidence. He had no motive . . . or rather he had no more motive than several others."

"Like who?"

A direct question was a mistake I could see; he shook his head, "Can't tell you."

"I'm beginning to find out anyway," I said. I made a guess: "Rufus Hollister," and I paused significantly.

"What do you know about him?" Winters was inscrutable; yet I had a feeling that I was on the right track.

"It seems awfully suspicious his wanting to get into the Senator's office. I have a feeling there's something in there he doesn't want you to find."

Winters stared at me a moment, a little absent-mindedly. "Obviously," he said at last. "I wish I knew, though, what it was." This was frank. "We're still reading documents and letters. It'll take us a week to get through everything."

"I have a hunch you'll find your evidence among those papers."

"I hope so."

"None of the press has been let in on this yet, have they?"

Winters shook his head. "Nothing beyond the original facts. But there's a lot of pressure being brought to bear on us, from all over."

I was suddenly sorry for him: there were a good many disadvantages to being mixed up in a political murder in a city like Washington. "That Pruitt woman, for instance . . . she was in touch with the White House today, trying to get out of being investigated."

"Did it work?"

"Hell no! There are times when the law is sacred. This is one of them."

"What about the will?" I changed *that* subject.

"I haven't seen a copy of it yet. The Governor won't let us look at it until tomorrow . . . says he 'can't break faith with the dead.'"

"You may find out something from that, from the will."

"I doubt it." The Lieutenant was gloomy. "Well, that's all for now," he said at last. "The minute you turn up anything let me know . . . try and find out as much as you can about the family from Miss Rhodes: it'd be a great help to us and might speed things up."

"I will," I said. "I've already got a couple of ideas about Hollister . . . but I'll tell you about them later."

"Good." We both stood up. "Be careful, by the way."

"Careful?"

He nodded grimly. "If the murderer should discover that you were on his tail we might have a double killing to investigate."

"Thanks for the advice."

"Think nothing of it." On a rather airy note, I went back to the company in the drawing room. My mind was crowded with theories and suspicions . . . at that moment they all looked like potential murderers to me. Suddenly, just before I joined Ellen and Walter Langdon, I thought of that quotation I had found in his room, the one he had snatched away from me. I also remembered where it came from: my unconscious had been worrying it for several hours and now, out of the dim past, out of my prep school days, came the answer: William Shakespeare . . . the play: *Julius Caesar* . . . the speaker: Brutus . . . the serpent in the egg: Caesar. There was no doubt about it. Brutus murdered the tyrant Caesar. It was like a problem in algebra: Senator Rhodes equals Julius Caesar; X equals Brutus. X is the murderer. Was Walter Langdon X?

III

I went to bed early that night. At dinner I drank too much wine and, as always, I felt bloated and sleepy. Everyone was in rather a grim mood so I excused myself at ten o'clock and went off to bed. I would have no visitors, I decided: Ellen was at work again on young Langdon and I was quite sure that they would be together, finishing what I had interrupted that afternoon.

I awakened with a start. For a moment I thought there was someone in the room and by the dim light of a street lamp I was positive that a figure was standing near the window. My heart racing, a chill sweat starting out on my spine, I made a quick lunge for the lamp beside my bed; it fell to the floor. Positive that I was alone in the room with a murderer, I jumped out of bed and ran to the door and flicked on the overhead light.

The room was empty and the figure by the window turned out to be my clothes arranged over an armchair.

Feeling rather shaky, even a little bit unwell, I went into the bathroom and took some aspirin. I wondered if I had caught Camilla Pomeroy's grippe; I decided that the wine had made me sick and I thought longingly of soda water, my usual remedy for a hangover. It was too late to ring for the butler. According to my watch it was a little after one o'clock, getting near the hour of the Senator's death, I thought as I put on my dressing gown, ready now to go downstairs in search of soda.

I remember thinking how dark the stairway seemed. There was one dim light burning on the third-floor landing and, from the bottom of the stair well, there was a faint light. The second landing was completely dark, however. Barely able to see, I moved slowly down the stairs, my hand on the banister. I was creeping slowly across the second landing, fumbling in my pocket for matches which were not there, when I suddenly found myself flying through space.

I landed with a crash on the carpeted stairs, stumbled forward, unable to stop my momentum; and, finally, bumped all the way downstairs like a comedian doing pratfalls, landing at the feet of Lieutenant Winters.

"What in Christ's name happened?" he asked, picking me up and helping me into the drawing room where the lights were still on.

It took me several minutes to get myself straightened out. I had twisted my left leg badly and one shoulder felt as though it had been dislocated. He brought me a shot of brandy which I gulped; it made a difference . . . I was able to bring him and the room into focus, my aches and pains a little less overpowering.

"They should install elevators," I said weakly.

"What happened?"

"Someone shoved me."

"Did you see who it was?"

"No . . . too dark. The lights were out on the second landing."

"What were you doing up?"

"I wanted to get some soda . . . upset stomach." I stretched my arms carefully; my shoulder throbbed. Nothing was broken, though.

"I wonder. . . ." Then the Lieutenant was gone in a flash, running up the stairs two at a time. I followed him as fast as possible. When I reached the second landing, I was almost bowled over again by a gust of ice-cold air from the end of the hall. Then the lights came on and I saw Winters standing in front of the wrecked study; he was bending over the unconscious figure of a plain-clothes man. The blanket which had been hung over the study door was gone. I shivered in the cold.

"Is he dead?" I asked.

Winters shook his head. "Help me get him downstairs." Together we carried the man down to the drawing room and stretched him out on a couch. Then Winters went to the front door and called one of the guards in and told him to look after his fallen comrade, to bring him to. "Somebody hit him," said the Lieutenant, pointing to a dark red lump over one temple. The man stirred and groaned. The other plain-clothes man went for water while Winters and I went back upstairs again.

It was the first time I had been in the study since my interview with the Senator. The lights were still out of order in this room. Winters pulled out a small pocket flashlight and trained the white beam of light on the room. There was a gaping hole in the wall where the fireplace had been. All the ruined furniture had been pushed to the far end of the room, away from the hole. The various filing cabinets were open, and empty.

"You mean to say somebody got in here and took all the papers just now?" I was amazed.

Winters grunted, flashing his light over the shelves of books, over the photographs which hung crazily on the walls. "*We* took them," he said. "They're all down at headquarters. I wonder if our prowler knew that."

"A wasted trip then," I said, stepping back into the warm corridor, out of the cold room. Winters joined me a moment later. "Nothing's been touched as far as I can tell," he said. "We'll have the fingerprint squad go over the place tomorrow . . . not that I expect they'll find anything," he sounded discouraged.

"Maybe the guard will know something," I suggested cheerfully.

But the guard remembered nothing. He rubbed his head sheepishly and said: "I was sitting in front of that blanket when all of a sudden the lights went out and then I stood up and the next thing I knew *I* went out."

"Where's the light switch?" asked Winters.

"At the head of the stairs," said the man unhappily. "Right by the door to Mr. Hollister's room, in the center of the landing."

"How could somebody turn off those lights without your seeing them?"

"I . . . I was reading." He looked away miserably.

Winters was angry. "Your job was to watch that corridor, to make sure that nothing happened, to protect these people as well as to guard the study."

"Yes sir."

"What were you reading?" I asked, interested as always in the trivial detail.

"A comic book, sir." And this was the master race!

Winters ordered the other plain-clothes man upstairs to take prints of the light switch. Then we went upstairs again and the Lieutenant proceeded to wake up everyone in the house for questioning. It was another late night for all of us and the discomfited politicos complained long and loudly but it did no good . . . it also did the law no good as far as I could tell. No one had heard my fall downstairs or the clubbing of the policeman; everyone had been asleep; no one knew anything about anything, and, worst of all, as far as the police could tell, nothing had been taken from the study.

2

I shall draw a veil of silence over the Governor's funeral oration: suffice it to say it was heroically phrased. The occasion, however, was hectic.

It was the first time I had been out of the house since the murder. I had no business in Washington and since my main interest was the murder I had spent most of the time talking to the suspects, calling various newspaper people I knew to check certain facts. Consequently, it was something of a relief to get out of the house, even on such an errand.

We were herded into several limousines and driven downtown, through a miserably gray sleet, to the National Cathedral, a vast Gothic building only half completed. A crowd was waiting for us outside one of the side doors. Flash bulbs went off as Mrs. Rhodes and Ellen, both in heavy black veils, made a dash through the sleet from their car to the chapel door.

We were led by a pair of ushers down into a stone-smelling crypt, massive and frightening: then along a low-ceilinged corridor to the chapel, brilliant with candles and banked with flowers: the odor of lilies and tuberoses was stifling.

Several hundred people were already there . . . including the police, I noticed. I recognized a number of celebrated political faces: Senators, members of the House, two Cabinet officers and a sprinkling of high military brass. I wondered how many of them were there out of sympathy and how many out of morbid curiosity, to survey the murder suspects of whom I was one. I was very conscious of this, as I followed Mrs. Rhodes and the Governor down the aisle to the front row. When we sat down the service began.

It was very solemn. I sat between Mr. Hollister and Mrs. Pomeroy, both of whom seemed much affected. It wasn't until the service was nearly over that I was aware of a slight pressure against my left knee.

I glanced out of the corner of my eye at Mrs. Pomeroy but her head was bowed devoutly and her eyes were shut as though she was praying. I thought it must be my imagination. But then, imperceptibly, the pressure increased: there could be no doubt about it, I was getting the oldest of signals in a most unlikely place. I did nothing.

At the cemetery, the service was even quicker because of the sleet which had now turned to snow. There were no tourists: only our party and a few cameramen. I thought it remarkable the Senator's wife and daughter could behave so coolly . . . for some reason only Rufus Hollister seemed genuinely moved.

When the last bit of hard black earth had been thrown onto the expensive metal casket, we got into the limousines again and drove back across the Potomac River to Washington and Massachusetts Avenue. It was a very depressing day.

The drawing room, however, was cheerful by contrast. The fire was burning brightly in the fireplace and tea had been prepared. Mrs. Rhodes, a model of serenity, poured. Everyone cheered up a good bit, glad to be out of the black December day.

Ellen had thrown off her veil; she looked fine in her basic black dress. "I loathe tea," she said to me in a low voice as we sat together on a Heppelwhite couch at the far end of the room, close to the windows. The others were buzzing about the room in a dignified manner.

"Good for the nerves," I said; as a matter of fact tea was exactly what I wanted at the moment. "What's next on the agenda?"

"Reading the will, I suppose."

"Your mother seems to be holding up awfully well."

"She's pretty tough."

"Was she very fond of your father?"

Ellen chuckled. "Now that's a leading question . . . as far as I know she was, but you never can tell. They used to be very close but then I've been away such a long time that I've rather lost touch with what's been going on." Across the room the Governor was talking gravely to Mrs. Rhodes who looked pale but controlled.

Then I told Ellen about Mrs. Pomeroy.

She laughed out loud; she stopped when she saw Verbena Pruitt looking at us with disapproval. "I didn't know Camilla had it in her," she said with admiration.

"I only hope you're not jealous," I teased her.

"Jealous? Of Camilla?" Ellen was amused. "I wish the poor dear luck. I hope she has a good time . . . you will give her one?"

"I haven't thought that far ahead," I said loftily, wondering myself what I should do about this situation. I wasn't much attracted; on the other hand if her husband was the murderer I should, perhaps, devote a little time to her. "By the way," I asked, "how is the *affaire* Langdon coming?"

Ellen scowled. "It's not coming at all. Every time something is about to happen the lights go out or someone gets murdered. At this present rate it will be weeks before anything happens."

"Were you with him last night?"

She smiled slyly.

"I don't think it would be very easy: with that guard watching the corridor all the time."

"He looks the other way. Besides, our rooms are on the same side and at the other end of the landing. He can't tell whether I'm going into my room or the one next to it."

"I see you've figured it all out."

"Don't forget that where the guard sits used to be my father's study and that once upon a time Father used to work in there with the door open, keeping an eye on the hall and me, especially when we had young men staying in the house."

"Jezebel!"

"There are times when I think I may be a little abnormal," said Ellen calmly. Then, at a signal from the Governor, she got up and followed him into the dining room: the room of all work. In a few minutes only Verbena Pruitt, Langdon and Mr. Pomeroy were left in the room. The four of us sat cozily about the fire. Pomeroy mixed drinks. From the other room came the monotonous, indistinct sound of the Governor's voice.

"I hope they'll be finished with us soon," said the great lady of American politics, scratching the point where her girdle stopped and her own firm flowing flesh began. She was in black now but her hat was trimmed with quantities of imitation cherries.

"So do I," said Langdon gloomily, cracking his knuckles. "I have to get back to New York. The magazine is bothering the life out of me."

"I should think they'd be delighted to have one of their people in this house," I said reasonably, remembering my own newspaper days. Mr. Pomeroy handed me a Scotch and soda.

"I guess they think they have the wrong person here," said Langdon truthfully.

"Nonsense, my boy. It's all in your head. You can do anything you want to," Miss Pruitt fired her wisdom over a jigger of straight rye.

"But remember, Verbena, a murder story without a murderer isn't the most interesting thing in the world," Mr. Pomeroy said quietly, shocking the rest of us a little since we all believed, deep down, that he *was* the murderer. If he was aware of our suspicions, he didn't show it. He went right on talking about the murder, in a tired voice. "It's one of those odd cases where no one is really involved, as far as we know . . . on the surface. I gather from the papers that some people think that because of the weapon used and because of my own troubles with Lee that I killed him . . . but, aside from the fact I *didn't* kill him, doesn't it seem illogical that I would use my own 5-X, immediately after a quarrel, to blow him up? It's possible, certainly, but too obvious, and I will tell you one thing: considering the people involved in this affair nothing, I repeat *nothing*, is going to be simple or obvious." There was an embarrassed silence after this.

"You *know* none of us think you did it," said Verbena Pruitt with a good imitation of sincerity. "Personally, I think one of those servants did it . . . that butler. I never have approved of this habit of leaving money to servants, to people who work for you every day . . . it's too great a temptation for them."

I tried to recall who the butler was; I couldn't, only a vague blur, a thin man with a New England accent.

"I don't see why they think one of *us* had to do it," said Langdon petulantly. "Anybody could have got in this house that day and planted the stuff in the fireplace. According to the butler, two plumbers were on the second floor all that afternoon and nobody paid any attention to them."

This was something new. I wondered if Winters knew this. "Perhaps the plumbers didn't have any motive?" I suggested.

"Perhaps they weren't plumbers," said Pomeroy, even more interested than I in this bit of information.

"Hired assassins?" This was too much I thought . . . still it happened quite often in the underworld . . . and the political world of Lee Rhodes had, in more than one place, crossed the world of crime.

"Why not?" said Pomeroy.

"But the reason the police think someone on the inside did it was because only a person who knew the Senator's habits well could have figured out how to kill him that way, with the stuff in the fireplace." I was sure of this: for once the official view seemed to me to be right.

Langdon dissented, to my surprise. "You're going under the assumption that the only people in the world who knew the Senator's habits were in this house as guests that night. You forget that a good many other people knew him even better than most of us did . . . people who would have been just as capable of blowing him up . . ."

"Perhaps," I said, noncommittally. I made a mental note to call Miss Flynn in New York and have her check up on the past of Walter Langdon. I didn't quite dig him, as the jazz people say.

Suddenly there was an unexpected sound from the dining room . . . a little like a shriek, only not so loud or so uncontrolled: an exclamation . . . a woman's voice. Then the double doors were flung open and Mrs. Rhodes, white-faced, rushed through the room to the hall, not stopping to acknowledge our presence. She was followed by Ellen, also pale and odd-looking, and by Mrs. Pomeroy who was in tears. Outside, the Governor and Rufus Hollister were deep in an argument while, behind them, several servants, minor beneficiaries, trooped back to the kitchen.

Mrs. Pomeroy, without speaking even to her husband, left the room close on the heels of Mrs. Rhodes. Pomeroy, startled, followed her.

It was Ellen who told me what had happened, told me that Camilla Pomeroy, born Wentworth, was the illegitimate daughter of Leander Rhodes and a principal heir to his estate.

3

"Who would have thought it," was Ellen's attitude when we got away from the others after dinner; we pretended to play backgammon at the far end of the drawing room. Everyone had been shocked by the revelation. Winters was having a field day and Mrs. Rhodes was hiding in her room.

"Rufus is trying to keep it out of the papers but the Governor says that it's impossible, that under the circumstances the will would have to be made public because of the murder. It's going to kill Mother."

"Did you ever suspect anything like this?"

She shook her head. "Not in a hundred years. I knew Camilla adored Father but I think I've already told you there was almost always some goose girl around making eyes at him and getting in Mother's hair."

"Did she know?"

"Mother? I don't think so. You never can tell, though. She's just about the most close-mouthed person in the world . . . has to be in politics. She *seemed* awfully shocked."

"I'm not surprised . . . it must have been awful for her, hearing it like that . . . in front of everyone."

Ellen grimaced. "Awful for everybody."

"I wonder why he'd admit something like that . . . even in his will."

"I suppose he never thought he'd die this soon . . . besides, it could have been kept quiet if there hadn't been a murder to complicate things."

"How much does she get?"

"A little over a million dollars," said Ellen without batting an eye.

I whistled. "How much of the estate is that?"

"Around a third. Mother and I each get a third . . . and then the servants get a little and Rufus gets all the law books, and so on."

"This changes everything."

"I don't know."

"Do you still think you know who killed your father?"

She looked at me vaguely. "Darling, I haven't the faintest idea what you mean."

"You did a couple of days ago."

"Now I'm not so sure." She was obviously not listening to me. She kept rolling the dice onto the backgammon board, again and again without looking at the numbers.

"What made you say you thought you knew?"

"I've forgotten." She seemed irritated. "Besides, why is it so important to you?"

"I have to do a story."

"Then write about something else."

"Don't be silly. Anyway, even if I didn't have to worry about the *New York Globe* I'd be worried on my own account . . . being shut up like this with a murderer . . . in the same house."

"Oh, stop being so melodramatic! You haven't the faintest connection, as far as I can see, with all this . . . why should *you* be in danger?"

"Because of my theories," I said a little pompously . . . as a matter of fact I was still completely at sea.

Ellen said a short four-letter word which communicated her opinion of my detective abilities with Saxon simplicity.

"Tell me, then," I said coolly, "why I should be shoved downstairs in the dark with such force that I could've broken my neck . . ."

"If your head hadn't been so solid," said the insensitive Ellen, rolling snake eyes. "By the way did you get a look at whoever it was who pushed you?"

"How could I? I told you it was dark on the landing."

"I must say all that's very exciting . . . it's the one really interesting thing that's happened since the murder."

What a cold-blooded piece she was, I thought. She acted as though she were in a theater watching a play, interested only in being shocked or amused. I wondered if *she* might not have been the illegitimate daughter after all . . . no Electra she, as *Time* magazine would say. "It would be a lot more interesting if they could find out what the murderer wanted in that room."

"Why? Did he take anything?"

"Not as far as the police could tell. There weren't any papers there anyway . . . everything had been taken down to headquarters."

"Poor Rufus."

"Why do you say that?"

"He's terrified all his political shenanigans will be found out . . . he and Father were awfully close, you know . . . I suspect they were involved in all sorts of deals which might not bear investigating."

"Well, if there was anything shady the police haven't found it," I said with more authority than I actually had: I was not naive enough to think Lieutenant Winters had confided all he knew to me, "I wonder if Rufus could have been the one who knocked the guard out last night, and pushed me downstairs."

"I wouldn't be at all surprised."

"I doubt if there was anything in there the murderer could have wanted . . . if there had been he would have got it the night of the murder, *before* the murder . . . unless he left something by mistake."

"Which the police would have found by now."

There were so few real leads, I thought sadly. Pomeroy's feud over the 5-X; Langdon's strange quotation and highly political attitude . . . very much the fanatic type; Rufus Hollister's terror of certain documents falling into the hands of the police; Camilla Pomeroy's unexpected relationship to the Senator . . . her large inheritance which provided both her and her husband with ample motive for murder. But had they known she was included in the will? Had Pomeroy known that his wife was the Senator's daughter? This was a question which should be cleared up soon: it would make a great deal of difference.

Across the room I saw Langdon excuse himself and go upstairs; a moment later Ellen gave a vast stage yawn and said, "I'm worn out darling. I think I'll go up now."

"And get a little shut-eye?" I mocked.

"Don't be a cad," she said grandly and swept out of the room.

I found Winters in the dining room going over what looked like a carbon copy of the will. He looked up when I came in; his ever-present plain-clothes man made a move to bar my way but Winters wearily waved him aside. "Come on in."

I sat beside him at the table. I asked the important question first.

He nodded in answer. "Yes, Pomeroy knew who his wife's father was. It seems she told him last year . . . at the height of his quarrel with the Senator . . . she thought it would make him more reasonable."

"Did it?"

Winters sighed. "The big question."

"There's a bigger question . . . did either of them know about the will?"

"It'll be a long time before we figure that one out," said the Lieutenant grimly. "Both deny having known anything about it. But . . ."

"But you think they did."

He nodded. "The Governor drew up the will . . . he's also Pomeroy's lawyer, and an old friend."

"Can't very well grill a Governor."

"Not directly."

Remembering the pressure on my knee at the Cathedral, I had an idea. "I think I can find out something about the will, from Mrs. Pomeroy." I told him about the knee-pressing episode. He was interested.

"It would be a great help. It'd just about wind up the case we're making against Pomeroy: double motive, the weapon, the opportunity . . ."

"Two more suspects, though."

"Who?"

"Hollister . . . he and the Senator were obviously involved in some illegal activities. And Langdon who's something of a fanatic." I related the business about the quotation but it was much too tenuous for the official mind. As for Hollister, we both agreed that he was an unlikely murderer since, had he done away with the Senator, he would have taken care to have got all the incriminating papers out of the study first. With a promise to do my best with Mrs. Pomeroy, I left Winters to his bleak study of the will.

I was staring at my typewriter with a feeling of great frustration, when there was a rap on my door. "Come in," I said.

Rufus Hollister put his head inside the door, tentatively, like one of those clowns at a carnival who make targets of their heads for customers with beanbags. "May I come in?"

"Sure." I motioned to the armchair opposite me. He sat down with a moan, crumpled I should say. I sat very straight at my desk, the light behind my head, ready to yell if he pulled a gun on me.

But if Rufus was the murderer, he was not in a murdering mood. In fact he was hardly coherent. "Just wandering by," he mumbled.

"If I had a drink I'd offer it to you."

"Quite all right. I've had a few already . . . maybe too many." He sighed again, deeply; then he took off his thick spectacles and rubbed his owl eyes . . . they were rather tiny I noticed . . . quite different without the magnifying glasses.

"Do the papers know yet?" I asked, recalling that I was, after all, in the public relations business.

"Know?" He blinked at me.

"About the will? About Mrs. Pomeroy?"

"Not yet. I suppose they will be told tomorrow."

"Has Mrs. Rhodes tried to do anything to keep the news out of the papers?"

"You know as well as I do there isn't any way of keeping something like that secret."

"I know. I just wondered if she had tried to keep it quiet."

Rufus shrugged. "I haven't seen her since the will was read." There was a long pause. I wondered when he would come to the point; he obviously had some reason for wanting to see me. But he said nothing. He stared blankly at the floor; he seemed a little drunk.

Growing nervous, I said, "Is there anything in particular you think I should do for the family . . . in the way of public relations?"

"What? Oh . . . oh, no. It's out of our hands now, I'm afraid." He put his glasses on again and looked at me; with an effort he pulled himself together. "You're doing a story about all this, aren't you?"

I nodded. "For the *Globe.*"

"I wish you'd check with me before you send them anything."

"Certainly . . . if I can ever find out anything to write for them."

"You will," he said ominously. "Soon, very soon."

I waited for more, but he had drifted off again. "Tell me," I asked, "did the Pomeroys come here much in the old days?"

He shook his head. "Pomeroy himself seldom came to the house. Mrs. Pomeroy did . . . fairly often."

This was unexpected. "I seem to remember her telling me . . . or somebody telling me that they never came here, either of them."

"She was here often."

"And she knew the Senator's habits well?"

He nodded; he knew what I was getting at but he refused to volunteer anything. He changed the subject. "You and Ellen are old friends aren't you?"

I said that we were.

"She made her father unhappy, very unhappy," said Mr. Hollister rubbing his palms together. It was my turn to wonder what *he* was getting at. "Her life has not been exemplary."

"You're not kidding!"

"At one time he even threatened to cut her off without a cent."

"You mean when she married?"

"Later . . . last year when she was making a scandal of herself in New York."

"I can't exactly blame him."

"Poor man . . . he had so many terrible things to bear during his life."

"Why didn't he cut her off?"

"Ah! You know her. She came down from New York last month and they had a terrible scene. I suppose she threatened to disgrace him once and for all if he didn't give her the money she needed . . ."

"That sounds like Ellen."

"What could he do? She was his own flesh and blood . . ."

"And he was about to run for President . . ."

"Exactly. She got her way . . . we always supposed that she had left for good until she came back with you this week. Why?"

"Why what?"

"Why did she come back?"

"I haven't the faintest idea. It seemed like a good idea, I suppose. We had both been drinking."

"*That* explains it then?"

"She drinks a lot," I added, but this wasn't necessary . . . and still Mr. Hollister hadn't come to the point.

"By the way," he asked suddenly, "did you have any idea who pushed you last night?"

I shook my head; then I had an idea . . . a daring one. "I didn't see who it was," I said; then I added, slowly, looking straight at him, "But I have a very good idea who it was."

I wasn't able to interpret his reaction; he turned pale but I couldn't tell if it was from guilt or astonishment. "Did you see *anything?*" he asked.

"A glimpse, that was all. I couldn't say for sure who it was but I have a good idea."

"Who . . . who do you think it was?" He sat on the edge of his chair, his breath coming in quick gasps.

"I can't tell you," I said, waiting for some sign . . . but there was none, other than this excitement.

"Be careful," he said at last. "Be careful what you say to the police. The repercussions might be serious."

"I know what I'm doing," I said quietly, never more confused.

"I hope so. By the way, did the Senator talk to you at all about family matters?"

"No, not much . . . a little about Ellen since he thought I was going to marry her, but I straightened all that out."

"And the campaign . . . did he talk about that? About those close to him in it?"

"Not a word . . . just general talk."

"That was a pity," he said cryptically; then he rose to go. I stopped him momentarily with a direct question.

"Who killed him?" I asked.

"Pomeroy," said Rufus Hollister; then he said good night and left me.

4

I undressed slowly, thinking of what had been said. Hollister made me uneasy . . . I couldn't tell just why but I had more than a faint suspicion that he might have been the murderer after all. It was evident that he had visited me to try and find out whether or not I had recognized whoever it was who'd shoved me down the stairs and it was possible that he was the one who had done the shoving . . . the murder, too? It was perplexing. I locked the door, leaving the key in the lock. I was nervous.

Then, dressed in pajamas, I sat down at the desk again and began to type idly. Pomeroy, Langdon, Hollister, Miss Pruitt, Mrs. Rhodes, Ellen, Mrs. Pomeroy. There was a knock on the door. I flipped on the overhead light (if I was to be shot I preferred a great deal of light); then I unlocked the door and slowly opened it. To my surprise Camilla Pomeroy, wearing a pale blue silk negligee, stood in the doorway.

"May I come in?" she asked in a low voice.

Startled, I said, "Yes." I locked the door behind her. She stood in the center of the room as though unsure of herself, not certain what to do next. "Sit down," I said, trying to be as casual as I could under the circumstances. Uncertainly, she went over to the armchair recently vacated by Rufus Hollister. She sat down; I sat opposite her. She was nearly as embarrassed as I.

"I . . . couldn't sleep," she said at last with a nervous laugh.

"Neither could I." We looked at one another stupidly. I noticed with surprise how lovely she was . . . noticed also that she had not yet been to bed: her make-up was perfect and her hair was carefully arranged.

"You must think it awful of me coming in here like this in the middle of the night." This came out in a rush.

"Why no . . . not at all."

"I had to talk to someone." She *did* sound desperate, I thought. I wondered whether or not I should suggest that her husband might be the man to talk to at this time of night. She guessed what I was thinking, though. *"He's* asleep. He takes sleeping pills . . . very strong ones, since . . . it happened." She almost sobbed. I wondered if I should get her a Kleenex. But she got a hold of herself. "Do turn that light out," she motioned to the bright one overhead. "A woman doesn't like too direct a light when she's been crying." Her attempt at frivolity was pretty ghastly but I turned out the light. She looked even better in the warm glow of a single lamp . . . and of course her looking better hardly helped the cause.

"Thank you," she murmured. She pulled the negligee tight about her throat, emphasizing the full curve of her breasts. I wondered if she intended this.

"I had to talk to someone," she repeated. I looked at her brightly, like one of those doctors in an advertisement: ready to make some comment about halitosis or life insurance.

"About . . . everything," she said.

"About the will?"

"Yes." She looked at me gratefully; glad that I was coming around. "Tomorrow all the world will know," she said with a certain insincere overstatement which made me think that for a million dollars she didn't give a damn *what* the world knew.

"There's nothing you can do about it now," I said soothingly.

"If only there were!" She still held one hand close to her throat, the way bad actresses do in moments of crisis on stage.

"People forget so quickly," I said.

"Not in Talisman City," she snapped. Then, recollecting herself, she added more softly, "the world is so unkind."

I allowed that, all things considered, this was so.

"It was unfair of Lee . . . of my father to act the way he did."

"You mean in . . . *being* your father?" I was dense.

"No, I mean in declaring to all the world my . . . shame."

To which I replied, "Ah."

"I can't think why he chose to do it like this, so publicly."

"Probably because there wasn't any other way of leaving you his money."

There was no real answer to this so she exclaimed again how terrible it all was.

"What does your husband think about it?"

She sighed.

"Did he know all along that . . . about the Senator and you?"

"Oh yes. He's known for a year."

"And the will . . . did he know about that, too?"

She closed her eyes, as though in pain. "Yes," she said softly, "I think he knew about the will, too. I think the Governor told him."

"But they never told you?"

She hesitated. "No," she said. "Not exactly. I suppose I knew, in a way, but they never actually told me." This was a bit of news, I thought. The outline of a plot suggested itself to me. "My husband never liked to talk about it . . . neither did I. It was just one of those things. What was that?" She started, and looked toward the door.

Nervously, expecting an angry husband, I opened the door and looked out. The hall was empty. "It was the wind," I said, turning around. She was standing directly behind me . . . I could smell the musk and rose of her perfume.

"I'm frightened," she said and this time she was not play-acting. I moved back into the room, expecting her to move too but she did not. Then I had my arms around her and we edged toward the bed. She wore nothing under the blue silk negligee and her body was voluptuous and had a young feel to it, smooth and taut with wide firm hips and her nipples pressed hard against my chest, burning through the pajama top. We kissed. She was no novice at this sort of thing, I thought as she gave the cord of my pajama trousers a deft tug and they fell to the floor beside her crumpled dressing gown. She pulled me against her violently and for a moment we stood swaying back and forth in one another's arms. Then we fell across the bed.

An hour passed.

I sat up and looked down at her white body sprawled upon the bed;

the eyes shut and her breathing regular and deep. "It's late," I said in a low voice.

She smiled drowsily and opened her eyes. "I haven't been so relaxed in a long time," she said.

"Neither have I," I lied nervously; I didn't like the idea of being treated like some kind of sedative.

She sat up on one elbow and pushed her hair back out of her eyes. She was obviously proud of her body; she arranged it to look like the Duchess of Alba. "What on earth would my husband say?"

"I hope I never know," I said devoutly.

She smiled languorously. "He'll never know."

"Great thing, sleeping pills."

"I don't make a habit of this," she said sharply.

"I didn't say you did."

"I mean . . . well, I'm not promiscuous, that's all . . . not the way Ellen is."

I was a little irritated by this. Somehow, I felt she had no business talking about Ellen like that since, for all she knew, we might really have been engaged. "Ellen's not that bad," I said pulling on my pajamas. Then I handed her her negligee. "You don't want that cold to get worse, do you?"

Reluctantly she snaked into the blue silk. "I'm very very fond of Ellen," she said with a brilliant insincere smile. "But you have to admit she's a law unto herself."

I was about to make some crack about their being sisters under the skin when it occurred to me that this might be tactless since, as a matter of fact, they *were* sisters in a way.

She asked for a cigarette and I gave her one. "Tell me," she said, exhaling blue smoke, "how long do you think it'll be before the police end this case?"

"I haven't any idea."

"But you *are* working with Lieutenant Winters, aren't you?"

This was shrewd. "How did you know?"

"It wasn't hard to guess. As a matter of fact I caught the tail end of a telephone conversation you were having with some newspaper in New York." She said this calmly.

"An eavesdropper!"

She chuckled. "No, it wasn't on purpose, believe me; I was trying to call a lawyer I know in the District . . . you were on this extension, that's all."

"I haven't any idea," I said. "About the murder . . . about how long it'll be before the police make an arrest."

"I hope it's soon," she said with sudden vehemence.

"So do all of us."

She was about to say something . . . then she stopped herself. Instead she asked me about the affair on the landing and I told her that I had seen no one. She looked disappointed. "I suppose it was too dark."

I nodded. "Much too dark."

She stood up then and arranged her hair in a mirror. I stood beside her, pretending to comb my own hair. I was aware of her reflection in the glass, very pale, with the dark eyes large and strange, staring at me. I shuddered. I thought of those stories about vampires which I had read as a child.

She turned around suddenly; her face close to mine . . . her eyes glittering in the light. "You must help me," she said and her voice was strained.

"Help?"

"He'll try to kill me . . . I'm sure of it. Just the way he killed my father."

"Who? Who killed your father? Who'll try to kill you?"

"My husband," she whispered. Then she was gone.

IV

Before breakfast, I composed a communiqué for the readers of the *New York Globe;* then, just as the morning light began to stream lemon yellow across the room, I telephoned it to New York, consciencelessly allowing the Rhodes family to pay for it; I was aware that my conversation was being listened to by a plain-clothes man on an extension wire: I could hear his heavy breathing.

My story was hardly revelatory but it would, I knew, keep me in business awhile longer, and it would also give the readers of the *Globe* the only inside account of how the bereaved family was taking their loss: "Mrs. Rhodes, pale but calm, was supported by her beautiful daughter Ellen Rhodes yesterday at the National Cathedral while thousands. . . ." It was the sort of thing which some people can turn out by the yard but which I find a little difficult to manage; a mastery of newspaper jargon is not easily come by: you have to have an instinct for the ready phrase, the familiar reference. But I managed to vibrate a little as I discussed, inaccurately, the behavior of the suspects at the funeral.

I smiled as I hung up the phone and put my notes in the night table drawer; I had thought of a fine sentence: "While your correspondent was attending the funeral services for the late U. S. Senator Leander Rhodes at the Washington Cathedral yesterday morning, a knee belonging to the attractive Camilla Pomeroy of Talisman City, wife of

Roger Pomeroy, the munitions maker, was pressed against your correspondent's knee . . ."

I lit a cigarette and thought idly of my session with Mrs. Pomeroy the night before. There had been a faint air of the preposterous about everything she'd said, if not done. The one thing she could do well was hardly preposterous: she was even better geared, as they say, than her half-sister . . . though Ellen would have been furious to know this. Ellen, like all ladies of love, thought there was something terribly special about her performances when, in fact, they were just about par. But I am not faintly interested in such things early in the morning and despite the vividness of Camilla's production I was more concerned, at eight in the morning, with what she had said.

I have a theory that I think best shortly after I wake up in the morning. Since no very remarkable idea has ever come to me at *any* time, to prove or disprove my theory, I can happily believe that this is so and my usual plodding seems almost inspired to me in these hours between waking and the clutter and confusion of lunchtime.

I had a lot to think about. Lying on the bed in my bathrobe, arms crossed on my chest like a monument, I meditated. Camilla Pomeroy is the daughter of Leander Rhodes. She has inherited a million dollars from her father, despite the bar sinister. She married a man who disliked Rhodes. Rhodes disliked *him* . . . why? (The first new question that had occurred to me; jealous of his daughter? Not likely. Why then did Rhodes dislike his son-in-law to such an extent he would queer his chances of staying in business? Today's problem.) And why did Pomeroy not like Rhodes? Political enemies . . . Senator uncoöperative about business matters . . . a deal, somewhere? a deal which fell through? Someone crossed up someone else? A profitable line of inquiry.

And Camilla Pomeroy? What was she trying to do? There was no doubt that she genuinely believed her husband killed her father, but why then had she come to me instead of to the police? Well, that was easily answered. She knew that I was in touch with Winters. That I was writing about the case for the *Globe* . . . anything she planted with me would get to the attention of the police, not to mention the public, very quickly. But she had asked me to help her. How? Help her do what? Now, there was a puzzle. The thought that she might not like her husband, might in fact like to see him come to grief for the murder of her father, occurred to me forcibly. If she did not care for Pomeroy and *had* cared for her father; if she believed Pomeroy killed the Senator, then the plot became crystal clear. She could not testify against her husband, either legally or morally (socially, that is), but she could take care of him in another way. She could spill the beans to someone who would then spill them to the police, saving her the humiliation and danger of going to the police herself. That was it, I decided.

Of course she could have killed her father to get the money and then, in an excess of Renaissance high spirits, implicated her husband. But that was too much like grand opera. I preferred not to become enmeshed in any new theory. I was perfectly willing to follow the party line that Pomeroy did it. After all, what I had learned from Camilla corroborated what everyone suspected. Yet why had absolutely no evidence turned up to cinch the case?

I was the first down to breakfast. Even before the ill-starred house party the family evidently breakfasted when they felt like it, not depressing one another with their early-morning faces.

I whistled cheerily as I entered the dining room. Through the window I could just glimpse a plain-clothes man at the door. "An armed camp," I murmured to myself, in Bold Roman. The butler, hearing my whistled version of "Cry" complete with a special cadenza guaranteed to make even the heartiest stomach uneasy, took my order for breakfast, placed a newspaper in front of me and stated the hope, somewhat formally, that the morning would be good for one and all.

The murder was on page two, moving slowly backwards until a *Sudden Revelation* or *Murder Suspect Indicated* brought it back to its proper place between the Korean war and the steel strike. There was a blurred photograph of the widow and daughter in their weeds at the cemetery . . . also a few hints that an arrest would presently be made. As yet there was no mention of the will . . . that would be the plum for the afternoon papers, and my own *New York Globe* would have the fullest story of them all ("pale but unshaken Camilla Pomeroy heard the extraordinary news in the dining room. . . ."). I was disagreeably struck, as I often am, with my elected role in life: official liar to our society. My lifework is making people who are one thing seem like something very different . . . manufacturers are jailed for adulterating products but press agents make fortunes doing the same thing to public characters. Then, to add to all this infamy, I was now using for my own advantage a number of people I knew more or less well . . . all for a story for the *New York Globe*, for money, for publicity. *Mea Culpa!*

Fortunately what promised to be an orgy of guilt and self-loathing was cut short by the arrival of ham, eggs, coffee and Ellen, dashing in black.

"Oh, how good it smells! I could eat the whole hog," said that dainty girl, dropping into the chair opposite me. She looked as though she could, too, ruddy and well-rested.

"Did you sleep well?" I asked maliciously.

"Don't be a pry," said Ellen, giving her order to the butler and grabbing the newspaper from me at the same time. I noticed with amusement that she only glanced at the story of the murder, that she quickly turned to society gossip and began to read, drinking coffee slowly, her eyes myopically narrowed. She would never wear glasses. "Oh, there's going to be a big party tonight at Chevy Chase . . . for . . . oh, for Heaven's sake, for Alma Edderdale! I wonder what *she's* doing in Washington."

I said that I didn't know, adding, however, that whenever there was a great party Alma, Lady Edderdale—the meat-king's daughter and a one-time Marchioness—was sure to be on hand. I had been to several of her parties in New York the preceding season, and very grand they were, too.

"Let's go," said Ellen suddenly.

"Go where?"

"To Chevy Chase, tonight."

"If I remember my English literature Chevy Chase was the title of a celebrated poem by . . ."

"The Chevy Chase *Club,*" said Ellen, picking up the paper again and studying the Edderdale item. "Everyone goes there . . . ah, Mrs. Goldmountain is giving the party. We must go."

"But we can't."

"And why not?" She arranged the newspaper on a silver rack to the right of her plate. "You know perfectly well why not." I was irritated, not by her lack of feeling but by her want of good sense. "It would be a real scandal . . . murdered Senator's daughter attends party."

"Oh, I doubt that. Besides, people don't go into mourning like they used to. Anyway *I'm* going." And that was that. I agreed finally to escort her, *if* she wore black and didn't make herself conspicuous. She promised.

Just as I was having my second cup of coffee, Walter Langdon appeared in the dining room, wearing a blazer and uncreased flannels, giving one the impression that he was very gently born . . . some time during the last century. His freckled face and red hair slicked down with water, provided an American country-boy look, however.

"Hi," said the journalist of the Left Wing, taking his place beside

Ellen. She smiled at him seraphically . . . how well I knew that expression: *you* are the one. Despite all the others, experienced and cynical as I am, my pilgrim soul has been touched at last . . . lover come back to me . . . this is it. That look which had appeared over more breakfast tables after more premières than I or any decent man could calculate. *It,* as Ellen euphemistically would say, had happened.

"Anything in the press?" said the Left Wing, glancing shyly at his seductress.

"A wonderful party, dear . . . we're going . . . you and I and Peter. Mrs. Goldmountain is giving it for darling Alma Edderdale . . . you know, the meatpacker bag who married old Edderdale."

"But. . . ." Walter Langdon, like the well-brought-up youth he was, went through the same maze of demurs as had I, with the same result. He too would join us at the Chevy Chase Club that night . . . and Ellen would wear black, she vowed. She surrendered the paper to Langdon who read about the murder eagerly.

Ellen reminisced somewhat bawdily on the career of Alma Edderdale while I pretended to listen, my thoughts elsewhere, in the coffin there with Caesar . . . and I recalled again Walter Langdon's quotation about the serpent's egg. Could Walter Langdom have killed the Senator? Unlikely, yet stranger things had happened. He was very earnest, one might even say dedicated. He had had the opportunity . . . but then everyone had had an opportunity. This was not going to be a case of *how* but of *why,* and except for Pomeroy there weren't too many strong *whys* around. I decided that during the day I would concentrate on motives.

The Pomeroys arrived for breakfast and I avoided Mr. Pomeroy's gaze somewhat guiltily, expecting to see the cuckold's horns, like the noble antlers of some aboriginal moose, sprouting from his brow. But if he had any suspicions he did not show them, while she was a model for the adulterous wife: calm, casual, competent for any crisis . . . the four Cs. I decided that it was time someone wrote a handbook for adulterers, a nicely printed brochure containing the names of roadhouses and hotels catering to illegal vice, as well as the names of those elusive figures who specialize in operations of a crucial and private nature . . . operations known as appendectomies in Hollywood and café society. I remembered the time one of the great ladies of the Silver Screen was rushed to the hospital with what an inept member of my profession, her press agent, called a ruptured appendix, unaware that his predecessor of six months before had also announced the removal of her appendix . . . there were repercussions all the way from Chasen's to "21": and of course the lady was in even greater demand afterwards, such being the love of romance in our seedy world.

While I pondered these serious topics, there was a good deal of desultory talk at the table on sleep: who had slept how well the preceding night, and why. It seemed that Mr. Pomeroy always slept like a top, in his own words, because of a special brew of warm milk, malt and phenobarbital.

"I'm so lucky," said Camilla, "I don't need a thing to make me sleep." Nothing but a good hot . . . water bottle, I murmured to myself, behind my coffee cup. Verbena Pruitt swung into the room like a sailboat coming about in a regatta. She boomed heartily at us. "Clear morning, clear as a bell," she tolled, taking her place at the head of the table where the Senator had always sat. Cross-conversations began and before I knew it I found myself staring into the dark dreamy eyes of Camilla Pomeroy. We talked quietly to one another, unnoticed by all the others . . . except Ellen who noticed everything and smirked broadly at me.

"I . . . I'm so sorry," said Camilla, looking down at her plate shyly . . . as though expecting to find two-fifty there.

"Sorry?" I made a number of barking noises, very manly and gallant.

"About last night. I don't know *what* came over me." She glanced sharply across the table to see if her husband was listening; he was engrossed in an argument with Verbena Pruitt about the coming Nominating Conventions. "I've never done anything like that before," she said softly, spacing the words with care so that I would get the full impact. I thought for some reason of a marvelous army expression; it was like undressing in a warm room. I was in a ribald mood, considering the earliness of the hour.

"I guess," I whispered, "that it was just one of those things."

"You see I'm *not* like that really."

I barked encouragingly.

"It's this *tension*," she said, and the dark eyes grew wide. "This *horrible* tension. First, Lee's death . . . then the will, that *dreadful* will." She shut her eyes a moment as though trying to forget a million dollars . . . since this is not easily done, she opened them again. "There . . . there's nothing in the papers about it, is there?"

"Not yet. This afternoon."

"I don't know how I shall live through it. I didn't tell you last night but the reporters have been after me . . . I don't know *how* they find out about such things, but they knew immediately. This morning one of them actually got through to me on the phone and asked for an interview, on how it felt to be . . . in a position like this." She was obviously excited by all the attention; at the same time, under the mechanical expressions of woe, I sensed a real disturbance: if ever a woman was near hysteria it was Camilla Pomeroy, but why?

I told her that the next few days would have to be lived through, the sort of reassurance which irritates me but seems to do other people good, especially those who do not listen to what you say . . . and she never listened to anyone.

"I also wish," she said slowly, "that you would forget everything I said last night."

Before I could comment on this unusual turn of affairs, Mrs. Rhodes, a sad figure in black, entered the room and we all rose respectfully until she was seated. Conversation became general and very formal.

When breakfast was over, I went into the drawing room to see if I had any mail. The mail was always placed on a silver tray near the fireplace . . . a good place for it: you could toss the bills directly on the fire without opening them. Needless to say, there was a pile of letters: the guests were all busy people involved in busy affairs. I glanced at all the letters, from force of habit: condolences seemed the order of the day for Mrs. Rhodes. There were no letters for Ellen, or Miss Pruitt whose office was at Party Headquarters.

There were a half-dozen letters for me, three of which went into the fireplace unopened. Of the others, one was from Miss Flynn, suggesting that my presence in New York at my office would be advisable considering the fact that the dog I had produced for my dog-food concern had been sick on television while being interviewed and it looked as if I would lose the account. This was serious but at the moment there was nothing I could do about it.

The other letter was a chatty one from the editor at the *Globe*, commenting on the two pieces I had done for them and suggesting that I jazz my pieces up a little, that unless I produced some leads, the public would cease to read the *Globe* for news of this particular murder, in which case, I might not get the handsome sum we had decided upon earlier for my services. This was not good news at all. Somehow or other we would have to keep the case on fire, and there was no fire: a lot of smoke and a real blaze hidden somewhere, but where? Three days had passed. Pomeroy was thought to be the murderer yet the police were unable to arrest him. There was no evidence. Despite the hints by several columnists, the public was in the dark about everything and, not wanting to risk a libel suit, I could hardly take the plunge and inform the constituents of the *Globe* that Pomeroy was the likeliest candidate for the electric chair.

Worried, exasperated, I opened the third letter.

"Boom! Rufus Hollister. Another boom? Maybe not. Maybe so. Repeat, Rufus Hollister. Paper chase leads to him. Who's got the papers?" The note was unsigned. It was printed in red pencil on a sheet of typewriter paper. The letters slanted oddly from left to right, as though someone had deliberately tried to disguise his handwriting. I sat down by the fire, stunned.

"What's the matter, Peter?" asked Ellen, coming into view, "Camilla hurt your feelings?"

"Nothing's the matter," I said, folding the letter: I had decided, in a flash, to tell no one about it, not even Winter. If someone wanted to give me a lead I wasn't the man to share it, "if it be a sin to covet honor" and all that.

"Well, I'm off, with Walter. We're going to see the Senate in session . . . God knows why. We'll pick you up after dinner tonight. I've told Mother a number of white lies to explain our absence."

"What about Winters? Did you get his permission?"

"Didn't you hear? He's not going to be around at all today. Somebody called up from the police department and said he was busy. But he'll be with us again tomorrow. Walter, get my coat, will you, like a dear? It's in the hall closet." And talking of this and that, she left, the obedient Walter knotted loosely around her neck.

I was about to go upstairs and get my own overcoat, when Mrs. Rhodes suddenly appeared from the dining room. It was her first visit to the drawing room since the reading of the will; she had kept hidden, since then, except for meals. I felt very sorry for her.

"Ah, Mr. Sargeant," she smiled wanly. "Don't get up." She sat down opposite me. The fire burned merrily. The butler moved silently about the room; except for him, we were alone: our fellow suspects had all gone on about their business.

"I suspect this is more than you bargained for," she said, almost apologetically. The old diamonds gleamed against her mourning.

"It's been a shock," I said . . . it was the phrase we all used to discuss what had happened.

"We must all bear it as best we can. I . . ." she paused as though uncertain whether or not she could go on; she was a most reserved lady, lacking in that camaraderie so many politicians' wives assume. "I was not prepared for the will. I don't understand how Lee could . . . have made it." This was odd; she was not concerned at his having had an illegitimate child, only that he had allowed the world to know it.

"I don't suppose he expected to . . . die so soon," I said.

"Even so there was Ellen to think of, and his good name, his posterity . . . and me. Though I never expected to outlive him." She played with her rings; then she looked up at me sharply, "Will you write about the will?"

I hadn't expected a question so blunt; until now my dual role as suspect and journalist had not been referred to by anyone but Camilla even though all of them knew by now that I was covering the case for the *Globe*. "I suppose I'll have to," I said unhappily. I decided not to mention that I had already written about it in some detail, that my somewhat lurid version would be on the streets of New York in a few hours.

She nodded. "I realize you have a job too," she said, charitably. I felt like a villain, living in her house and exposing her private life to the world, but it couldn't be helped. If I didn't do the dirty work someone else would. As a matter of fact others *were* doing it, their inaccurate reports delighting tabloid readers all over the country. She understood all this perfectly: she hadn't spent a life in the limelight for nothing.

"And since you must write about these things, I think I should tell you that Camilla, though born out of wedlock, was, in a sense, legitimate. Her mother was my husband's common-law wife . . . a well-kept secret, considering the publicness of our lives. When he went into politics he married me, leaving Camilla's mother—leaving her pregnant as he learned later—only it was too late of course to do anything about that after *we* were married. Happily, the unfortunate woman, taking a sensible view of the whole business, got herself a husband as quickly as possible, an undertaker named Wentworth. She died a few years later and the story, we thought, was finished."

"But didn't Camilla know who her father was?"

"Not for many years. Wentworth suspected the truth, however; he approached my husband . . . now, what I am telling you is in absolute confidence: some of it you can use. I'll tell you later what I want told to the public . . . Wentworth tried to blackmail my husband, in a cautious way. First, this favor; then, that favor. We sent his nephews to West Point. We got his brother-in-law a post office . . . the usual favors. Then his demands became unreasonable and my husband refused to fulfill them. Wentworth came to me and told me the story of Camilla which is how *I* learned the truth. He threatened to tell everyone, but by then Lee would not be budged; he was like a rock when his mind was made up. Wentworth told Camilla the truth and she left him, left his house and went to work; she supported herself until she married Roger."

"Did Wentworth spread the word after that?"

"He did, but it was useless. Those things have a habit of backfiring, you know. Most of the newspapers back home were for Lee and they wouldn't print Wentworth's rumors, and since there was no proof of any sort, it was his word against Lee's. In one of the campaigns the story of Camilla was used to smear us but the other party got nowhere with it. When one of our papers came to us and asked what they should do about these rumors, Lee said: 'Print the truth.' I think his stand won him the election." She was very proud of that frightful husband of hers. In a way, I couldn't blame her. He *had* been like a rock, very strong and proud.

"I want you," she said, firmly, "to print the truth: that Camilla was his daughter by a common-law wife and that, considering the circumstances, he was in every way a good father, even to remembering her equally in his will with our daughter and with me."

"I'll do that," I said humbly, hardly able to contain my excitement at this coup. So far no journalist had bothered to check the Senator's early years.

"I will appreciate it," she said gravely.

"Tell me," I said, suddenly brave, "who killed the Senator?"

"If only I knew." She looked bleakly into the fire. "I have no idea. I don't dare think . . . it's all so like *a paper chase.*"

2

The idea was outrageous, but who else? A paper chase. She was trying to give me a signal of some kind, a desperate attempt at communication because . . . because she was terrified . . . of the murderer? I wondered, though, why, if she *had* written me the note, she had not admitted it outright instead of referring so obliquely to it. A paper chase: that was exactly it. I was suddenly very tired. If only one person would stop playing his game long enough to tell the truth, I might be able to unravel the whole business to the delight of the *Globe* and the police.

That she had written to me, I was sure. But for some reason she didn't wish to be more explicit. Well, I would have to continue in the dark awhile longer. In any case, I was better off than I had been. I knew a good deal more about the Senator's youthful indiscretions than anyone else and I had been warned about Rufus Hollister.

After my talk with Mrs. Rhodes, I put on my overcoat and left the house. The day was bright and cold and a sharp wet wind blew down Massachusetts Avenue, making my ears ache.

The plain-clothes man at the door looked at me gloomily as I went out, his nose nearly as red from the cold as his earmuffs. I saluted him airily and headed down the avenue as though I knew in which direction I was going.

Just as I was about to hail a taxi, a young man stepped from behind a tree and said, with a big smile, "I'm from the Global News-service and I wonder. . . ."

"I'm from the *New York Globe*," I said solemnly. This brought him to a full stop. He was about to walk off. Then he changed his mind.

"How come you were inside there if you're on the *Globe?* They haven't let any reporters in since the old bastard was blown up."

I explained to him.

"Oh, I know about you," he said. "You're one of the suspects. The Senator's public relations man."

I said that I had been the latter, that I doubted if I was the former.

"Well, anyway, the big arrest is going to take place soon." He sounded very confident.

"Is that so?"

"So we were tipped off . . . sometime in the next twenty-four hours Winters is going to arrest the murderer. That's why I'm hanging around . . . deathwatch."

"Did they tell you who he was going to arrest?" (I would rather say "whom" but my countrymen dislike such fine points of grammar.)

"Damned if I know. Pomeroy, I suppose. Say, I wonder if you could do me a favor. You see. . . ." I took care of him and his favor in a few well-chosen words. Then I caught a taxicab and rode down to the Senate Office Building.

This was my second visit to the Senator's office; it was very unlike the first. Large wooden crates filled with excelsior were placed everywhere on the floor. Two gray little women were busy packing them with the contents of the filing cabinets. I asked for Mr. Hollister and was shown into the Senator's old office. He was seated at the desk studying some documents. When I entered he looked up so suddenly that his glasses fell off.

"Ah," he sounded relieved. He retrieved his glasses and waved me to a chair beside his own. "A sad business," he said, patting the papers on the desk. "The effects," he added. There was a long pause. "You wanted to see me?" he said at last.

I nodded. I was playing the game with great care. "I thought I'd drop by and see you while I was downtown . . . to say good-by, in a way."

"Good-by?" The owl-eyes grew round.

"Yes, I expect I'll be going back to New York tomorrow . . . and since there'll probably be quite a bit of commotion tonight we might not have a chance to talk before then."

"I'm afraid. . . ."

"They are going to make the arrest tonight." I looked at him directly. His face did not change expression but his hands suddenly stopped their patting of the papers; he made two fists; the knuckles whitened. I watched everything.

"I assume you know whom they will arrest?"

"Don't you?"

"I do not."

"Pomeroy." I wondered whether or not I had ruined the game; it was hard to tell.

He smiled suddenly, his cheeks rosy and dimpled. "Do they have all the evidence they need?"

"It would seem so."

"I hope they do because they will be terribly embarrassed if they're not able to make it stick. I'm a lawyer, you know, and a very thorough one, if I say so myself. I would *never* go into court without ultimate proof, no sirree, I wouldn't. I hope that Lieutenant is not being rash."

"You don't think Pomeroy did it, do you?"

"I didn't say that." He spoke too quickly; then, more slowly, "I mean, it would be unfortunate if they were unprepared; the murderer might get away entirely, if that was the case."

"And you wouldn't like to see that?"

"Would you?" He was very bland. "You forget, Mr. Sargeant, that it is not pleasant for any of us to be suspected of murder. Even *you* are suspected, in theory at least. I am, certainly, and all the family is, too. None of us like it. We would all like to see the case done with, but if it isn't taken care of properly then we are worse off than before. Frankly, something like this can do us all great harm, Mr. Sargeant."

"I'm sure of that." I sat back in my chair and looked at the bare patch on the wall over the mantelpiece where the cartoon had been. Then I fired my last salvo: "Where are those papers you took from the study the other night? The night you shoved me downstairs?"

Hollister gasped faintly; he adjusted his glasses as though steadying them after an earthquake. "Papers?"

"Yes, the ones you were looking for. I assume you found them."

"I think your attempt at humor is not very successful, Mr. Sargeant." His composure was beginning to return and my shock-treatment had, to all intents and purposes, failed. I looked at him coolly, however, and waited. "I did *not* take the papers," he said, smiling. "I admit that I should have liked to but someone else got them."

"You are sure of that?"

Hollister chuckled but his eyes were round and hard despite his smiling mouth. "Perfectly sure." At that moment the telephone rang; he picked it up and talked to some newspaperman, very sharply, I thought, for someone in public life, but then his public life was over, at least as far as the Senate was concerned. "Wolves!" he groaned, hanging up.

"Closing in for the kill."

"Closing in for what?"

"The arrest . . . tonight, I am told."

Hollister shook his head gloomily. "Poor man. I can't think why he did it; but then he has a most vindictive nature, and a terrible temper. He depended a great deal on the Senator's backing in Washington. It was probably too much for him to bear, being turned down like that."

"I have a hunch that there will be a good deal of singing, though, as the gangsters say." I was beginning to talk out of the side of my mouth, the way private eyes are meant to talk. I caught myself in time: this was, as far as I could recall, the first time in my life I had used the word "singing" in its underworld sense.

Mr. Hollister looked properly bewildered. "I mean," I said, "that in the course of the trial a lot of very dirty linen is going to be displayed. I mean, Mr. Hollister, that all your political dealings with the Senator will become known." This was wild; I forged ahead in the dark. "The papers you wanted and which you say someone else got will be very embarrassing for all concerned." I was proud of my emphatic vagueness; also of the effect I was making.

"What are you trying to tell me, Sargeant?" The soft-soap political manner was succeeded by an unsuspected brusqueness. He was near the end of the line.

"That Pomeroy is going to tear you to pieces."

Hollister half-rose in his chair; before he could speak, the telephone rang again. He picked it up impatiently; then his manner changed. He was suddenly mild. "Yes, yes. I certainly will. Anything you say. Yes. Midnight? Fine. Yes. . . ." His voice trailed off into a series of "yeses" accompanied by little smiles, lost on his caller. When he hung up, he changed moods again. "I'm sorry, Mr. Sargeant, but I have a great deal of work to do, packing up the Senator's papers and all. I don't know if you've heard the news but Governor Ledbetter has just appointed himself to succeed to the Senator's unfilled term and we're expecting him tomorrow. Good afternoon."

3

The Chevy Chase Club is a large old-fashioned building outside Washington, in Maryland. There is a swimming pool, a fine golf course, lawns, big trees, a lovely vista complete with fireflies in the early evening, in season; but we were not in season and my information as to the fireflies and so on was provided by Ellen as we taxied from Washington to the Club. She waxed nostalgic, relating episodes from her youth: in the pool, on the courts, on the course, even on the grass among the trees, though the presence of the innocent Langdon spared us a number of unsavory details.

We had had no trouble getting away that evening, to my surprise. Mrs. Rhodes was properly hoodwinked and the Lieutenant, when we called him to ask permission to go off for the evening, gave it easily. The arrest was going to be made after all, I decided. I wondered if I should leave the dance early so that I could be on hand for the big event. Langdon and Ellen would doubtless be so absorbed in one another that my early departure would not be noticed.

Ellen looked almost regal in her black evening gown. I had never seen her in a black evening dress before, and she was a most striking figure. Her tawny hair pulled straight back from her face like a Roman matron's and her pale shoulders bare beneath a sable stole. Langdon wore a blue suit and I wore a tuxedo; I had arrived in Washington all prepared for a real social whirl.

The Club was a handsome building with high ceilings and great expanses of polished floor. It had a summery atmosphere even though snow was on the ground outside and the night was bitter cold.

The gathering looked very distinguished . . . half a thousand guests at least, in full evening dress. Poor Langdon blushed and mumbled about his blue serge suit but Ellen swept us into the heart of the party without a moment's hesitation.

Mrs. Goldmountain was a small woman of automatic vivacity, very dark, ageless, with exquisite skin carefully painted and preserved. I recognized her from afar: her picture was always in the magazines smiling up into the President's face or the Vice-President's face or into her dog's face, a celebrated white poodle which was served its meals at its own table beside hers on all state occasions: "Because Hermione loves interesting people," so the newspapers had quoted her as saying. Whether Hermoine Poodle liked famous people or not, we shall never know; that Mrs. Goldmountain did, however, is one of the essential facts about Washington, and famous people certainly liked *her* because she made a fuss over them, gave rich parties where they met other celebrities. One of the laws of nature is that celebrities adore one another . . . are, in fact, more impressed by the idea of celebrity than the average indifferent citizen who never sees a movie star and seldom bothers to see his Congressman, presuming he knows what a Congressman is. I looked about me for the poodle but she was nowhere in sight: the dream no doubt of a press agent. Mrs. Goldmountain retained several.

"Ellen Rhodes! Ah, poor darling!" Mrs. Goldmountain embraced her greedily, her little black eyes glistening with interest: this was a coup for her. We were presented and each received a blinding smile, the dentures nearly as bright as the famous Goldmountain emeralds which gleamed at her throat like a chain of "Go" lights. Mr. Goldmountain had been very rich; he had, also, been gathered up some years ago . . . or ridden on ahead, as my Miss Flynn would also say . . . leaving his fortune to his bride.

"I am so touched, poor angel," said Mrs. G., holding both of Ellen's hands tight in hers and looking intently into her face. "I know how much you cared for your poor father."

"I wanted to see you," said Ellen simply, the lie springing naturally to her coral lips.

"Your mother? Shattered?"

"Utterly . . . we all are."

"Oh, it's too horrible."

"Too."

"And the Chief Justice told me only yesterday that he might well have got the nomination."

"Ah!"

"What a President he would have been. . . . How we shall miss him! all of us. I wanted terribly to get to the funeral but the Marchioness of Edderdale and the Elector of Saxe-Weimar were both visiting me and we could hardly get away. I sent flowers."

"Mother was so grateful."

"Darling, I couldn't be more upset and you *are* an angel to come. . . ." Then she began to speak very rapidly, looking over our shoulders at an Ambassador who was arriving with his retinue, their ribbons and orders gleaming discreetly. Before we knew it we were cut adrift as the high enthusiastic voice of our hostess fired a volley of compliments and greetings at the Ambassador and his outriders.

"*That* is over," said Ellen, in a cool competent voice and she led us to the bar; the guests parted before our determined way. Those who recognized her looked surprised and murmured condolences and greetings; then, mild complaints at her lack of rectitude when we had passed on. I caught only a few words, here and there: mostly disparaging.

The bar was a paneled room, a little less crowded than the main hall. From the ballroom could be heard the sound of a very smooth orchestra playing something with a lot of strings.

"Now isn't this better than being cooped up in that awful house?" said Ellen blithely, clutching a Scotch in her strong predatory fingers.

"Of course it is," I said. "But . . ." And mechanically I reminded her that she was making an unfavorable impression.

"Who cares? Besides, I always do and everyone adores it: gives them something to talk about." She smoothed her hair back, though not a strand was out of place. She was easily the best-looking woman in the room and there were, for some reason, more women in the bar than men, Washington women being, perhaps, a trifle more addicted to the grape than their menfolk: the result of the tedium of their lives, no doubt, the dreary round of protocol-ridden days.

Walter Langdon then wanted to know who was who and while Ellen explained to him, I wandered off to the ballroom.

Beneath tall paintings of old gentlemen in hunting costume, the politicos danced. I recognized the Marchioness of Edderdale, a Chicago meat-man's girl who had bought a number of husbands, one of whom was the ill-starred Marquis of Edderdale who had got caught in the rigging of his schooner during a regatta some years ago and was hanged, in the presence of royalty, too. The Marchioness whose present name no one bothered with, the title being so much more interesting, stood vaguely smiling at the guests who were presented to her and to the Vice-President of the United States who was drinking champagne beside her and telling, no doubt, one of his celebrated stories. I made my way over to her and presented my compliments.

"Ah, Mr. . . ." She gestured handsomely.

"Sargeant," I said, and quickly I reminded her of my last visit to her house. She recalled it, too.

"I hope you will come see me soon," she said. "Mr. Sargeant, this is . . ." And she paused; she had forgotten the Vice-President's name. I quickly shook his hand murmuring how honored I was, saving the dignity of the nation. It occurred to me that she might not have known who he was either: her world after all was New York and the south of France, Capri, and London in the month of June not Washington and the unimportant world of politics.

The Vice-President began a story and, by the time he had got to the end of it, a large group of politicians and climbers had surrounded us and I was able to creep away, my brush with history ended. Just as I reached the outskirts of the party, a familiar figure crossed my line of vision, heading toward the great man. The familiar figure stopped when he saw me and a wide smile broke his florid hearty face. It was Elmer Bush, renowned commentator and columnist ("This is Elmer Bush, bringing you news while it's news."). We had been on the *Globe* together; or at least he had been a star columnist when I was the assistant drama critic. In the ballet murder case I had managed completely to undo his foul machinations. He had been of the opinion that my young woman of the time, a dancer, was the killer and he had presented her to the public as such. I scooped him, in every sense, and as a result we had not seen each other, by design, since.

Bygones were now allowed to be bygones, however.

"Peter Sargeant, well, isn't this a surprise?" My hand was gripped firmly, the sunlamp-tanned face broke into a number of genial triangles; the bloodshot blue eyes gleamed with whiskey and insincere goodfellowship. I loathe Elmer Bush.

"How are you, Elmer," I said quietly, undoing my hand from his.

"Top of the world. Looks like us country boys are traveling in real society, doesn't it?" Which meant of course: what the hell are you doing here, you little squirt?

"Always go first class," I mumbled, wondering what he had in mind, why he was in Washington.

"You talking to the Vice-President?"

I nodded casually. "He was telling a story. It seems there was a farmer who . . ."

Elmer laughed loudly. "Know it well," he said, before I could get started. I had intended to bore the life out of him with it. "Marvelous old devil, marvelous. Say, I saw your by-line the other day."

I nodded gravely.

"Didn't know you were still in the game. Thought you were mostly involved in publicity."

"I am," I said. "This was just one of those things."

"Rhodes hired you, didn't he?"

"Couple of days before he died."

"I may drop by and see you . . . living in the house, aren't you?" I nodded. "Terrible tragedy," he said thoughtfully, the Vice-President still in focus in the background, me slightly out of focus in the foreground since the eyes can't look two places at once. "I thought I might do a program about the case. You might like to be on it. I'm on television now, coast to coast."

I said that I knew all about this, that I probably wouldn't be able to go on television and that he probably would not be allowed to visit the house since all newspaper people were rigidly excluded. I was on to him: he was ready to move in, positive that for a half hour's display of my pretty face to the television audience of America, I would give him the beat on the murder. Not a chance in the world, Brother Bush, I vowed.

"Mrs. Rhodes is an old friend of mine," said Elmer with a hurt expression. "The Senator and I were very close, very. Well, I suspect young Winters will be able to fix it for me, unless he's too busy with the arrest."

This was unexpected, but then Elmer Bush was no fool; he was still a first-rate newspaperman despite his sickening homespun television manner. He had already closed in on Winters who was doubtless giving him all the information he needed. All he needed me for was to get to know the family, and to get me sidetracked along the way.

"Arrest?" I looked surprised.

"Pomeroy . . . tonight . . . that's the word. Matter of fact I plan to get down to the police station about one o'clock to see him booked." Then Elmer was gone to join the group around the Vice-President.

This gave me pause. Thoughtfully I made my way to the men's room, a large locker room, as it turned out. I was meditating on what to do next when I noticed that Walter Langdon was standing beside me.

"Nice party?" I asked.

He beamed foolishly. "Just fine," he said. He sounded a little drunk.

"Ellen having a good time?"

"Doesn't she always? She's dancing with some Ambassador or other now."

"Jilted you already?"

"Oh no." He missed the humor of my remark. "She's just having a good time."

"I suppose you'll be publishing the banns soon."

"How did you know?" He turned very red and I felt like kicking him for being such a baby. Instead I arranged my garments and departed, leaving him to his dreams among the tile and enamel.

I glanced at my watch. It was eleven-forty. At twelve I would go back to the house, alone. Langdon could manage Ellen by himself; if he couldn't, well, it was his business now.

I danced a few times with various ladies, all belonging to the embassies of South American powers, dark vital girls devoted to dancing.

I saw Ellen only once, whirling by in the arms of a sturdy Marine officer. She gave me her devil-leer, over his bulging arm. That might very well be the end of little Walter. I thought, extricating myself from the last Latin girl under pretext of having to join my wife.

Shortly before midnight, Hermione, a large precious-looking white poodle, made her appearance. After being introduced to the more interesting people, she sang, rather badly while the orchestra played what accompaniment it could. There was a great deal of applause when she finished and Hermione was given a sherry flip. Thinking of the decline of Rome, I left the club, bowing first to Mrs. Goldmountain who, under the impression that I was a new Congressman, said she would see me at the House Office one day soon when she paid the Speaker a call.

Since neither Ellen nor Langdon was in sight, I left without telling them of my plans. Actually, I preferred to be alone at this stage of the game. We were approaching a climacteric, as Mr. Churchill would say, and I was becoming tense. I took one of the fleet of taxis in front of the club, and set out for Washington.

For some reason I expected to find the house blazing with light and crowded with television cameras while Pomeroy, shrieking vengeance, handcuffed to Lieutenant Winters, awaited the Black Maria.

Instead everything was as usual. The plain-clothes man still stood guard and no more lights were on than usual.

In the drawing room, I found Mrs. Rhodes and Verbena Pruitt. Both looked quite shaken.

"Has it happened?"

Miss Pruitt nodded, her chin vanishing into its larger fellows. "They took Roger away half an hour ago."

I sat down heavily opposite them. "Roger!" said Mrs. Rhodes, but I could not tell whether or not she spoke with sorrow or anger or fright. I fixed myself a drink.

"Where is Mrs. Pomeroy?" I asked.

"She's gone to the police station with him. Brave girl. But then it's a woman's place to be beside her mate when dark days come," announced Miss Pruitt in a voice not unlike her usual political manner. She talked for several minutes about the ideal relationship between man and wife, not in the least embarrassed by her own maidenhood.

"Then it's all over?" I asked.

Mrs. Rhodes closed her eyes. "I hope so," she murmured.

Miss Pruitt shook her head vigorously; hairpins flew dangerously across the room. "They have to *prove* it," she said. "Until then we *all* have to be on hand. God knows how long it will take."

"We won't have to stay here during the trial?" I was becoming alarmed.

"No, just the preliminaries . . . Grand Jury . . . indictment. Then we can go. Even so it means the rest of the week is shot."

"I always liked Roger," said Mrs. Rhodes thoughtfully, looking into the fire.

"The whole thing is a bad dream," said Miss Pruitt with finality.

"I'm sure he would never have done such a thing."

"Then who *would've* done it? Not I, nor you, nor this boy, nor Ellen . . . and I doubt if that newspaper boy or Rufus or Camilla would have done it. Of course I will admit that *I* suspect the servants, especially that butler. Oh, I know how fond you are of him and how devoted he is *supposed* to be to you but let me tell you that on more than one occasion domestics of unimpeachable character have been found to be murderers, and why? because of this habit of leaving them money. Think how many old ladies are undoubtedly murdered by their beloved companions for money, for a small inheritance. An everyday occurrence, believe you me." Verbena Pruitt rattled on; Mrs. Rhodes stared at the fire. Neither asked me what I was doing in evening clothes. Ellen had not been missed either, or if she had neither mentioned it.

Soon they left the drawing room and went to bed. The moment I was alone, I telephoned Winters. To my surprise I was put through to him. He sounded very lively.

"I suppose it's all over?" For some reason my voice had a most lugubrious ring.

"That's right. We've arrested Pomeroy."

"Has he confessed?"

"No, and doesn't seem to have any intention of confessing. Won't make any difference, though."

"Then I can say that Lieutenant Winters has sufficient evidence on hand to justify his dramatic arrest of the chief suspect?"

"That's right." Winters sounded very happy about the whole thing. I contributed to his happiness by indicating that as a reward for giving me the news first, I would see that he was liberally rewarded with space and applause in the *Globe*. He assured me that no other journalist had been informed as yet: a number of newspaper people had collected at the police station but so far he had made no statement; I was getting the news first, for which I thanked him although the *Globe* is an afternoon paper and would, if the morning papers were sufficiently alert, be scooped. Still, I had the whole story.

"By the way, what are you building your case on?" This seemed like a fair question; one which would doubtless be evaded.

It was. "I can't say yet. There's enough circumstantial evidence, though, to make the story. Just say the police have the affair in hand."

"Is Mrs. Pomeroy at the station?"

"Yes. She's talking to her husband; they're waiting for their lawyer to arrive."

"Is she pale but dry-eyed?"

"I haven't looked."

"Who, by the way, is the lawyer?"

"The new Senator . . . the Governor. He just got in from Talisman City."

"Is *he* going to handle the case?" I was surprised. Senators did not, as far as I knew, handle criminal cases.

"No, he's going to direct the legal operations, though. We're not worried." And on a note of confidence, our interview closed.

Now all that was left was to write the story. I picked up a pad of paper with the legend "U.S. Senate" across the top and then, with a pencil, I began to sketch out my story for the *Globe*. I had a lot to record. The story Mrs. Rhodes had told me about the childhood of Camilla Pomeroy; a description of the relations between the Senator and the accused; a perfervid account of the arrest and Pomeroy, pale but dry-eyed, being led away by the police, protesting his innocence.

As I took notes, however, I was aware that the case was not solved. I am not sure now, when I look back on these events, *why* I should have doubted that the most likely man to do the murder had done the murder. I am not one of these devious-minded souls who feel that the most obvious culprit is never the one who did the dirty work. My respect for human ingenuity is not that great. In most cases involving violence, the guilty party is also the most obvious one . . . the professional writers of mystery novels to the contrary. But Pomeroy just did not strike me as the murdering type.

Halfway through my notetaking, I stopped and looked about the room, brilliantly lit and empty. The fire burned cozily; from far away I could hear the wind. The phrase "a paper chase" kept going through my head. Someone in the house knew who the murderer was, or suspected. Someone had tried to give me a lead about some papers, about Rufus Hollister. The someone, I was fairly certain, was Mrs. Rhodes, a woman far less simple and direct than she appeared to be . . . a frightened woman, too. Yet the note didn't imply that Rufus was the murderer, only that he held the key to the murder, perhaps without knowing it. Papers. I frowned, but even this solemn expression did not help me much. Every time I tried to unravel the puzzle, my mind would become completely unfocused and frivolous, all sorts of irrelevancies floating about in it. There was really nothing to go on, no real facts, no clues other than the letter, only my intuition which is, according to my friends, somewhat below-average and my knowledge of the characters involved which was slight, to say the least.

Yet Rufus had been up to some skulduggery with the Senator. He had, I was almost certain, made a raid on the study in the hopes of finding papers there, documents so hidden that not even the police would have been able to find them. Since it was generally known that Winters had removed all the files from the study only someone intimately connected with the Senator's affairs would have known where to find papers hidden so well the police had not seen them. Who knew his affairs the best? Hollister and Mrs. Rhodes and, of the suspects at least, that was all. Hollister wanted something; Hollister knew where to find it; Hollister had taken a big chance and, probably, got what he wanted and cleared himself.

Cleared himself of what?

I decided to embark upon the chase. I stuffed my notes into my pocket. I wouldn't have to telephone my story in to the *Globe* until dawn. By which time I might have some real news.

I went upstairs to Rufus Hollister's room. The blanket still hung at the end of the corridor although the door behind it had been repaired and bolted shut, no longer requiring the presence of a plain-clothes man.

I knocked on Hollister's door, very softly. There was no answer. Not wanting to disturb the other sleepers, I turned the knob and pushed the door open.

Hollister was seated at his desk, apparently hard at work.

I shut the door softly behind me; then, since he had made no move, I walked over to his desk and said, "I wonder if . . ." But the sight of blood stopped me.

Great quantities of blood covered his face, his shirt, the desk in front of him; only the typewriter was relatively clear of it.

He was dead, of course, shot through the right temple. The gun, a tiny pearl-handled affair, lay on the floor beside his right hand; it gleamed dully in the lamplight.

My first impulse was to run as far as I could from this room. My second impulse was to shout for the plain-clothes man out front. My third impulse, and the one which I followed, was to make a search of the room.

I was surprised at my own calm as I touched his hand to see if rigor mortis had set in: it had not. He was only recently dead. I looked at my watch to check on the time: 1:19. I looked at *his* watch, recalling how watches were supposed to stop magically when the wearer died . . . this watch was ticking merrily: about five minutes fast, too.

I don't know why it took me so long to notice the confession which was still in the typewriter.

"I killed Senator Rhodes on Wednesday the 13th by placing a package of explosive in his fireplace shortly after we returned from the Senate Office Building Tuesday afternoon. Rather than see an innocent man be condemned for my crime, I herewith make this confession. As to my reason for killing the Senator, I prefer not to say, since a complete confession would implicate others. I will say though that we were involved in an illegal business operation which failed. Because of the coming election, the Senator saw fit to make me the victim of that failure . . . which would have involved a jail sentence for me and the ruin of my reputation. Rather than suffer this, I took the occasion of Pomeroy's visit to Washington to kill the Senator, throwing guilt on

Pomeroy. Unfortunately I was not able to discover the documents pertaining to our business venture. They are either in the hands of the police or shortly will be. I have no choice but to take this way out, since I prefer dying to a jail sentence and the ruin of my career. I feel no remorse, however. I killed in self-defense. Rufus Hollister." The name was typewritten but not signed; as though immediately after typing this confession he had shot himself, without even pulling the paper out of the typewriter.

Well, this was more than I had bargained for. The paper chase had led me to a corpse, and to the answer.

Methodically, I searched the room. As far as I could tell there was nothing else to add or subtract from what had happened. The case, it would seem, was closed. With a handkerchief I carefully wiped any prints I might have made on the watch and wrist of the corpse (I had touched nothing else); then I went downstairs and telephoned Lieutenant Winters. It was now 1:36, the anniversary of the Senator's death.

V

It was another all-night session.

Winters nearly had a nervous breakdown that night and the rest of us were far from being serene. We were interviewed one after the other in the dining room, just like the first night but under more distracting circumstances, for police photographers and investigators were all over the place and there was talk that Winters would soon be succeeded by another, presumably more canny, official.

The Pomeroys returned, looking no worse than the rest of us that grisly dawn. The newspaper people were at every window until they were finally given a somewhat muffled and confused statement by Winters. He made no mention of the arrest of Pomeroy, an arrest which had not been legally completed, I gathered, since Mr. Pomeroy was now among us.

I sat beside Ellen in the drawing room. The others, the ones who were not being interviewed, talked quietly to one another or else dozed like Verbena Pruitt in her chair, her mouth open and snoring softly, her hair in curlers and her majestic corse damascened in an intimate garment of the night.

Ellen for once looked tired. Langdon sat some distance away, staring at the coals in the fireplace, wondering no doubt how on earth he was to get a story for *Advanceguard* out of all this confusion.

"Why," said Ellen irritably, "do they keep us up like this if Rufus did the murder? Why all this damned questioning? Why don't they go home?"

"They have to find out where we all were," I said, reasonably ... but I wondered too why the confusion since the police had not only a confession but the confessor's corpse, the ideal combination from the official point of view: no expensive investigation, no long-drawn-out trial, no angry press demanding a solution and a conviction.

Through the crack between the curtains, I saw the gray dawn and heard the noise of morning traffic in the streets. My eyes twitched with fatigue.

Ellen yawned. "In a few minutes I'm going to go to bed whether they like it or not."

"Why don't you? They've already got your testimony." There was a commotion in the hall. We both looked and saw Rufus Hollister departing by stretcher, a sheet of canvas over him. As the front door opened, there was a roar of triumph from the waiting photographers; flash bulbs went off. The door was slammed loudly and Rufus Hollister's earthly remains were gone to their reward: the morgue and, finally, the tomb.

"Disgusting!" said Ellen, using for the first time in my experience that censorious word. Then, without permission, she went to bed.

After the body was gone, a strange peace fell over the house. The policemen and photographers and investigators all stole quietly away, leaving the witnesses alone in the house with Winters and a guard.

At five o'clock I was admitted to the dining room.

Winters sat with bloodshot eyes and tousled hair looking at a vast pile of testimony, all in shorthand, the work of his secretary who sat a few feet down the table with a pad and pencil.

He grunted when I said hello; I sat down.

He asked me at what time I had found the body. I told him.

"Did you touch anything in the room?"

"Only the corpse's hand, his wrist, to see how long he was dead, or *if* he was dead."

"Was the body in the same position when we arrived that it was in when you found it?"

"Yes."

"What were you doing in Hollister's room at that time of night?" The voice, though tired, was sharp and impersonal.

"I wanted to ask him something."

"What did you want to ask him?"

"About a note I received this morning."

Winters looked at me, surprised. "A note? What note?"

I handed it to him. He read it quickly. "When did this arrive?" His voice was cold.

"This morning at breakfast . . . or rather yesterday morning."

"Why didn't you tell me about it?"

"Because I thought it was a hoax. I figured there was plenty of time to give it to you. I had no idea you were planning to arrest Pomeroy so quickly." This was a well-directed jab at the groin. Winters scowled.

"You realize that there is a penalty for withholding vital evidence?"

"I didn't withhold it. I just gave it to you."

A four-letter word of exasperation and anger burst from his classic mouth. We were both silent for a moment. He studied the letter. "What," he said in a less official voice, "do you think this means?"

"I thought it meant that Hollister was the one who broke into the library that night and got some incriminating documents, or tried to find some."

"Obviously he didn't find them."

"Did *you* find them."

The law shook its head. "If we did we aren't aware of their significance," he said candidly. "We've checked and double-checked all the secret files and, as far as I can tell, there isn't anything in any of them which would send Hollister to jail, or even the Senator . . . a lot of fast political deals but nothing illegal."

"Do you think the Senator might have kept his business transactions somewhere else?" I recalled those mysterious safety deposit boxes belonging to pillars of the Congress which revealed, when opened posthumously, mysterious quantities of currency, received for services rendered.

"I think we'd have found it by now."

"Maybe the Governor might be able to tell you. He was the Senator's lawyer."

Winters sighed and looked discouraged. "I can't get a word out of him. All he does is harangue me about our heritage of civil liberty."

"Maybe you can track down who wrote that note and ask them."

Winters looked at me vindictively. "You picked a fine time to let me know, right after I almost made a false arrest. What was the big idea?"

"Remember that I didn't see you all day. I got the note in the morning. I went to see Hollister to question him . . ."

"Then you *did* talk to him about the papers?"

"I certainly did."

Winters was interested. "What did you get out of him? How did he seem?"

"I got nothing out of him and, for a man who planned to commit suicide in the next few hours, he was remarkably calm."

"No hint at all? What exactly happened? Word for word."

I tried to recall as exactly as possible my conversation, making my bluffs sound, in the telling, more insidiously clever than they were. My testimony was recorded by the silent clerk.

When I finished the Lieutenant was no wiser. "Was anyone else there? Did he mention anyone else's name?"

"Not that I remember. We were alone. Some newspaper people tried to get him on the phone and . . ." A light was turned on in my head, without warning. "What time did Hollister die?"

"What time . . ." Winters was too weary to react quickly.

"The coroner, what time did he fix his death?"

"Oh, about twelve. They'll know exactly when the autopsy is made."

"Hollister was murdered," I said with a studious avoidance of melodrama, so studiously did I avoid the dramatic that Winters did not understand me. I was forced to repeat myself, my announcement losing much of its inherent grandeur with repetition.

"No," said Lieutenant Winters, beginning to weave in his chair, "he was the murderer. We have his confession."

"Which was typed by the murderer after he was shot."

"Go to bed."

"I plan to, in a few minutes. Before I go I want to make sure that you plan to keep a heavy guard in this house. I have no intention of being the next ox slaughtered."

"Why," said Winters with a mock-show of patience, "do you think Hollister was murdered?"

"Because when I was in his office yesterday morning he got a telephone call from an unknown party who made a date to see him last night at midnight, at twelve o'clock, at the hour of his death. From what he said over the phone I could tell it was someone he was very anxious to please . . . someone he had every intention of meeting."

"Perhaps he saw them and then killed himself."

"Not likely. Not in the house. He was home all evening, I gather. He had made no plan to go out. Therefore his guest was coming to see him here. But no one entered or left the house, as far as we knew . . . no *stranger* that is. Whoever he was supposed to meet was already in the house, one of the suspects . . . the murderer, in fact."

While I had been talking Winters sat straighter and straighter in his chair. When I paused for breath, he said, "I don't want you to say anything about this to anyone. Understand?"

"I do."

"Not only because you may be right and the murderer would be warned but because if you are right and the murderer does think you're on his trail we will have a third victim."

I said that I had no desire to make the front pages as a corpse.

"There's a chance you're right," he said thoughtfully. "I wish to hell you'd used your head and got that anonymous letter to me earlier. We could have tested it for prints, checked the handwriting and the paper . . . now it'll take us several days to get a report on it. In the meantime, keep your mouth shut. Pretend the case is finished, which is what we're going to do. We'll keep the house party together for a few days longer, as long as we can. We'll have to act quickly."

"I know," I said, feeling a little chilly and strange. "By the way whose pistol was it that did the murder?"

"Mrs. Rhodes'."

2

I was most reluctant to meet the light the next morning, as the Roman poets would say, or rather the afternoon of the same day. I probably would have slept until evening if the telephone beside my bed hadn't rung. I picked up the receiver, eyes still closed, positive that I could continue sleeping while conducting a lively conversation on the phone.

For several moments I mumbled confidently into the receiver, aware of a faraway buzz. Then I opened one eye and saw that I was talking into the wrong end. Correcting this, completely awake, I listened to Miss Flynn's gentle reproaches.

"A number of things have Come-up," she said. "Which require your *personal* Supervision."

I explained to her that a Number of things had Come-up here, too, that I couldn't get away for several days.

"We were of the opinion that the case had been concluded in Washington and that the recent Suicidalist was, *ipso facto*, the Murderer of the Statesman."

"Are the papers out?" I had not realized it was so late, that the afternoon papers were already on the street.

"Indeed they are. With a Prominent Display in the *Globe* bearing your Signature."

I had pulled out all the stops in that article, just before going to bed. I had used more colors than the rainbow contains in my description of finding the body, of the case's conclusion, for that was how Winters and I wanted it to sound. The editor had been most pleased and it took considerable strength on my part not to tell him there would be yet another story.

I stalled Miss Flynn as, unhappily, she outlined the various troubles which had befallen my clients. Most of the complications were easily handled over the phone. The dog food concern offered a serious crisis, however; fortunately, I was visited with one of my early morning revelations. I told Miss Flynn to tell those shyster purveyors of horsemeat that in twenty-four hours I would have a remarkable scheme for them. She was not enthusiastic but then enthusiasm would ill become her natural pomp.

After our conversation, I telephoned Mrs. Goldmountain and, rather to my surprise, got her. We made an appointment to meet later that afternoon.

Then I bathed, dressed and, prepared for almost anything, went downstairs. I was a little surprised to find life proceeding so calmly. Lunch was just over and the guests were sitting about in the drawing room. The law was nowhere in sight.

If anyone had noticed my absence during the day, it was not mentioned when I joined them.

I told the butler I wanted only coffee, which I would have in the drawing room. Then I joined Ellen and Langdon by the window. The shades were drawn, indicating either a bad day or the presence of police and newspaper people outside.

"Ah!" said Ellen, at my approach. She looked, of them all, the freshest. Langdon was rather gray and puffy.

"Ah, yourself." I sat down across from them. Coffee was brought me. I took a long swallow and the world at last fell into a proper perspective.

"The case," I said in Holmesian accents, "is closed."

"Not quite," said Ellen, looking at me with eyes as clear as quartz, despite the debauchery and tension of the night before. "It seems there is another day or two of questioning ahead of us, lucky creatures that we are. I've done everything except offer Winters my person to be allowed to go back to New York."

I didn't say the obvious; instead I asked her why she wanted to go back. "Tonight is Bess Pringle's party, that's why. It's going to be *the* party of the season and I want to go."

"Why does he want us to stay here?" I pretended innocence.

"God only knows. Red tape of some kind."

"I've thought of one approach to the murder," said Langdon suddenly, emerging from a gray study.

"And that?" I tried to look interested.

"The red tape aspects. You know, the complications which a murder sets in motion, all the automatic and pointless things which must be done, the . . ." His voice began to trail off as our lack of interest became apparent. I did see how the *Advanceguard* was able to keep its circulation down to the distinguished and essential few.

Before Ellen could begin her laments about Bess Pringle or Langdon could discuss the case with me, I asked about the party, explaining my early return to the house with some ready lie.

"We didn't get back until two," said Langdon gloomily.

"And I wouldn't have come back at all if I had known what had happened," said Ellen sharply.

"Did I miss anything?"

"A member of the Cabinet played a harmonica," said Langdon coldly.

"He played a medley from Stephen Foster," said Ellen.

"I thought you were with that Marine when the concert was given," Langdon was catching on to our Ellen with considerable speed, considering his youth and idealism.

"Ah," said Ellen and closed her eyes.

I left them and went over to the table by the fireplace where the mail was kept. There was only one letter for me, a thick one addressed in red pencil, the handwriting slanting backwards. My hands shook as I opened it.

Out fell a sheaf of legal documents. I looked through them rapidly, trying to find some explanation; there was none, no covering letter: nothing but a pile of legal documents which, without examining them, I knew concerned the business affairs of Hollister and the Senator, the papers for want of which he had apparently killed himself.

Before I could examine them further, Camilla Pomeroy came over to me, smiling gently. "How wonderful to be out of all this!" she exclaimed, looking deep into my eyes.

"You'll be going back to Talisman City soon, won't you?"

"As soon as possible," she said.

"You must be relieved," I said, trying to tell from her expression what she was actually thinking; but I could not: her face was as controlled as a bad actress'.

"Oh, terribly. Roger is like a new man."

"He was in a tough spot."

"Very!" She was not at all like the woman who had come to my room the other night with every intention not only of forbidden pleasure but of incriminating her husband. She was again the loyal wife, incapable of treachery. What was she all about?

"I . . . I want you to know that I wasn't myself the night we had our *talk*. I was close to a breakdown and I'm afraid I didn't know what I was doing, or saying. You *will* forgive me, won't you?"

"There's nothing to forgive," I said gallantly, knowing perfectly well she was afraid I might let her husband know in some fashion about her betrayal, her double treachery.

"I hope you really feel that," she said softly. Then, since there was nothing else to say, I excused myself; I asked the guard at the door where Winters might be found. He gave me the address of the police headquarters and so, without further ado, I took a taxi downtown.

I was escorted to Winter's office, an old-fashioned affair with one tall window full of dirty glass. He sat at a functional desk surrounded by filing cabinets. He was studying some papers when I entered.

"What news?" I asked.

He waved me to a chair. "No news," he said tossing the papers aside. "A report on your note from Mr. Anonymous. The handwriting isn't identifiable, even though we have compared it to everyone's in the house . . . the paper is perfectly ordinary and like none in the house, a popular bond sold everywhere, the red pencil is an ordinary red pencil like perhaps a dozen found scattered around the house, the fingerprints on the letter are all yours . . ."

"I didn't rub off someone else's, did I?"

"There were none to rub off. I think sometimes that it should be made illegal for movies and television to discuss fingerprinting . . . since fingerprinting came into fashion, practically every criminal now wears gloves, and all because they go to movies." He swore sadly to himself.

"Well, you got a good press," I said cheerfully.

"It won't be so good when it develops that someone murdered Hollister, *if* someone did."

"You don't have any doubts, do you?"

"When it comes to this case my mind is filled with doubts about everything."

"Well, here's a bit of news." I handed him the documents.

We spent an hour going over them; neither of us was much good at reading corporation papers but we got the general drift: a company had been formed to exploit certain oil lands in the Senator's state. Stock had been floated; the company had been dissolved at considerable profit to the original investors; it had been reformed under another name but with the same directors, more stock had been issued; it had been merged with a dummy company belonging to the Governor of the state. The investors took a beating and only Rufus Hollister, the Governor and the late Senator profited by these elaborate goings-on. Needless to say the whole subject was infinitely more complicated and *The New York Times'* subsequent account of the deals gives a far more coherent account than I can. It was also clear that the Senator had fixed it so that he was in the clear should all this come to light and that Rufus Hollister was responsible, on paper at least, for everything: the Governor seemed in the clear, too.

Winters called in his fingerprint people, also a lawyer; the papers were handed over to them for joint investigation.

"It waxes strange," I said.

"Why," said Winters, "would Mr. X want to send you these papers? And the earlier lead, if it was the same person who sent you both?"

"I suppose because he thinks I will use them properly."

"Then why not send them to the police?"

"Maybe he doesn't like policemen."

"Yet why, of all the people in the house, send it to you?" He looked at me suspiciously.

"The only reason I can think of, outside of my enormous charm and intelligence, is that I am writing all this up for the *Globe* ... maybe the murderer is interested in a good press. I think maybe that's the reason; then, perhaps, it doesn't make too much difference to him who gets the information since he knows it will come to the police in the end anyway ... it might have been just a whim ... you have to admit the style of the first note was pretty damned whimsical."

Winters grunted and looked at the ceiling.

"A number of people have seen fit to confide in me because of my position with the Fourth Estate. I may as well tell you that Camilla Pomeroy came to me the other night with the information that her husband was the Senator's murderer; then, the next morning, Mrs. Rhodes gave me some exclusive information about the common-law marriage of Mr. Rhodes some years ago ... you probably read all about it in my *Globe* piece."

"And wondered where you'd got it, too. What did Mrs. Pomeroy tell you exactly?"

I repeated her warnings, omitting our tender dalliance as irrelevant.

"I don't understand," sighed Winters.

"The only thought which occurs to me is that they are *both* beneficiaries. I've thought all along that we should be real old-fashioned and examine the relations of the three beneficiaries of the late Senator." I had not of course thought of this until now; it seemed suddenly significant, though.

"We do that continually," said Winters.

"It's possible one of them killed him for the inheritance."

"Quite possible."

"On the other hand he might have been killed for political reasons."

"Also possible."

"Then again he might have been killed for reasons of revenge."

"Very likely."

"In other words, Lieutenant Winters, you haven't the foggiest notion why he was killed or who killed him."

"That's very blunt, but that's about it." Winters seemed not at all disturbed.

I had a sudden suspicion. "You wouldn't by any chance be thinking of allowing this case to go unsolved, would you? Stopping it right here, with a confession and a corpse who, presumably, made the confession before committing suicide."

"What ever made you think that?" said Winters blandly, and I knew then that that was exactly what he had in mind. I couldn't blame him; by admitting that Hollister had been killed and the confession faked, he put himself squarely behind the eight ball, a position which the servants of the public like even less than we civilians do. Though he might have proven to all and sundry that he was a pretty sharp character to guess that Hollister was killed, he would also be running the risk of never finding the murderer, which would mean that public confidence in the police would be shaken, in which event he himself would be shaken back to a beat in Georgetown. I could hardly blame him for this indifference to the true cause of justice. After all who really cared if the Senator and Hollister had been murdered? No one mourned the passage of either to the grave. For a moment love of law and sense of right wavered, but then I recalled myself to stern duty (the fact that I would have the success of the year if I could unearth the murderer after the case had been nominally shut by the police affected my right action somewhat).

"How long will you hold the crew together?" I asked, writing Winters off as an ally.

"Another day or so, until all the evidence is double-checked . . . the autopsy and so on completed."

"We will then be free to go?"

"Unless something unforeseen happens."

"Like another murder?"

"There won't be another murder," he said confidently and I wondered if he might have some evidence which I didn't have. After all it was just possible that Hollister *had* committed suicide . . . driven to it by Mr. X, the possessor of the documents, a whimsical cuss who was obviously enjoying himself immensely.

"What about the gun?"

"Well, what about it? It belonged to Mrs. Rhodes, didn't it?"

"That's right . . . no prints on it except Hollister's. Mrs. Rhodes kept the gun in the table beside her bed. She hadn't looked at it in over a month. Anyone could have gone in there and taken it."

"But how many people in the house would have known there was a gun in that night-table?"

"I haven't any idea. Hollister knew, though." He smiled contentedly. "He knew where everything was."

"Except the papers which the Senator had hidden in the study, which someone else found first."

"But who?"

"The murderer."

"I see no evidence."

"The evidence is in front of you or rather in the other room being gone over by your lawyer. How does this Mr. X know so much about the case? How did he know where to find the papers? Why did he send them to me at all since Hollister's death was intended to finish the case?"

"It may be," said Lieutenant Winters in the voice of innumerable Mary Roberts Rinehart heroines, "that we shall never know."

"Go to hell," I said.

He frowned. "Why don't you stop fussing around, Sargeant? This is none of your business, we all have a perfect out. Let's take it. I am as dedicated to duty as anyone and I don't intend to drop the case, really; but I'm not going to beat my brains out over it and I *am* going to pretend it's all finished. I suggest you do the same." This was a threat, nicely phrased.

"I will," I said. "But I'm not going to let it go unsolved if I can help it." We sat staring hostilely at one another . . . conscious of the righteousness of my tone, I was almost ready to recite the Wet Nurses' Creed in a voice choked with emotion. But I let it ride.

"Well, I better be going," I said, standing up.

"Thanks for letting me have the papers."

"Think nothing of it." Full of wrath, I departed.

3

Mrs. Goldmountain lived in a large house of yellow stone, mellowed with age, in Georgetown, the ancient part of the city where, in remade slums of Federal vintage, the more fashionable Washingtonians dwell. Her house, however, was larger than all the others, the former residence of some historic personage.

I was shown to an upstairs sitting room, hung in yellow silk, all very Directoire. After a moment's wait, Mrs. Goldmountain appeared, neat in black and hung with diamonds. "Mr. Sargeant, isn't this nice? I was so happy you could come to the party last night with darling Ellen . . . poor shatteed lamb!" I could see now why I had been admitted so quickly, without hesitation: I was straight from the Senator's house and would know, presumably, all about the murders. I had every intention of indulging La Goldmountain.

"She's taking it very well," I said, which was putting it as nicely as possible.

"She was devoted to Lee Rhodes. Of course they never saw much of each other but everyone knew of their devotion. They were so alike."

I failed to see any resemblance but that was beside the point. I mumbled something about "like father like daughter."

"Of course some people were shocked by her going out so soon after his death but *I* said after all she is young and high-spirited and there is nothing, simply nothing she can do about his being dead. I love tradition, you know, but I see no reason for being a slave to it, do you? Of course not. They must all be relieved that that horrible man who killed himself confessed."

"Yes, we were pretty happy about that: I mean, justice being done and all that."

"Of course. Is it true that poor Roger Pomeroy was nearly arrested?"

I said that it was true.

"How frightful if the wrong man had been convicted! I have always liked Roger Pomeroy, not that our paths have crossed very often, just official places, that's all, especially during the war when he was here on one of those committees. I never took to *her* I'm afraid; I always thought her rather common, never having the *slightest* notion that she was really Lee's daughter, like *that!* What a cross it must have been for her to bear: it could explain everything. My analyst, who studied with Dr. Freud in Vienna, always said that whatever happens to you in the first nine months before you're born determines everything. Well, I mean if the poor little thing *knew* before she was born that she was illegitimate (and they've practically proved that we *do* know such things . . . we later forget them during the trauma of birth, like amnesia) it would certainly have given her a complex and explained why I always thought her just a little bit common."

I stopped the flow gradually. I diffidently explained my proposition to her.

"For some time now my clients, the Heigh-Ho Dogfood Company, have wanted an outstanding public relations campaign. I've tried any number of ideas on them but none was exactly right. The campaign we had in mind must have dignity as well as public appeal and, you will admit, those two things aren't easy to find together. The long and the short of it, Mrs. Goldmountain, is that I think we could make a dandy campaign out of Hermione."

"Oh, but I could never consent . . ." She began, but I knew my Goldmountain.

"We would arrange . . . Heigh-Ho would arrange . . . for her to give a recital at Town Hall. As a result of all that publicity she would appear on television, on radio and perhaps even a movie contract might be forthcoming. You, as her owner, would of course lend considerable dignity to all of this and though the publicity might be distasteful . . ."

That did it. Any mention of publicity made Mrs. Goldmountain vibrate with lust.

"If I were to accept such a proposal, I would insist on supervising Hermione's activities myself."

"I think that is a fair request . . . I'm sure Heigh-Ho would consult you on everything."

"I would also insist on having final say about her program at Town Hall. I know what her capacities are and I know the things she can do.

I would never permit her to sing any of these modern songs, only the classics and of course the National Anthem."

"You will be allowed to choose the repertoire of course. Also the voice coach."

"You feel she *needs* a coach?" I had made a blunder.

"All the stars at the Metropolitan have voice coaches," I said quickly. "To keep their voices limbered up."

"In that case, I would be advised by you," said Mrs. Goldmountain graciously, her eyes narrowing as she saw the spread in *Life* as well as the image of Hermione and herself flickering grayly on the little screen in millions of homes.

"What songs does she do best?" I asked, closing in.

"German *Lieder*, and Italian opera. If you like we can hear her now."

"Oh, no," I said quickly, "not now, some other time. I know her genius already. All Washington does and, soon, the whole world will know."

"You may tell Heigh-Ho, that I shall seriously entertain any offer they wish to make." And so our treaty was fashioned. I asked permission to telephone the Vice-President of Heigh-Ho in New York. It was granted. The official was delighted with my plan and made an appointment to meet Mrs. Goldmountain the next afternoon, in Washington.

Everyone was happy and my firm was again on solid footing. Mrs. Goldmountain invited me to take tea with her and a few guests who were at this moment arriving. One of them turned out to be the new Senator, former Governor Johnson Ledbetter.

"Remember you well!" he boomed, pumping my hand. "A much less unhappy occasion I am glad to say." He beamed vaguely and accepted a drink from the butler. I took tea, as did our hostess and the two other guests; one a political commentator of great seriousness, the other Elmer Bush who had arrived while I was greeting the Senator. Elmer was every bit as cordial as the old political ham, both slices off the same haunch, as it were.

"Well, it looks like you're innocent," said Elmer toothily as we stepped back out of the main line of chatter which circulated around the new Senator and Mrs. Goldmountain.

"It certainly does, Elmer."

"I suppose you'll be going to New York?"

"Very soon."

"Winters, I gather, is very pleased about the way the case shaped up, very pleased."

"I should think so."

"Quite a trick of his, pretending to arrest Pomeroy while really making a trap for Hollister."

"Trap?"

"Isn't that what happened? Wasn't Hollister driven to commit suicide by the police? Naturally, they wouldn't admit anything like that but it *seems* clear: they pretended to have evidence which they didn't have, forced him to confess and then to kill himself, an ingenious, a masterful display of policemanship."

Elmer Bush never joked so I assumed that he was serious and left him rigorously alone.

"I've already discussed it on my show. You probably saw it night before last, got a good response too. The public seems unusually interested in this affair, something out of the ordinary, Senator being murdered and all that, very different. I thought I might drop by and take a few shots of the house on film to be used in my next program . . ." And he tantalized me with promises of glory if I would help him get in to see the house and Mrs. Rhodes. I told him I would do what I could.

Across the room the Senator-designate was booming.

"Dear lady, I will be saddened indeed if you don't attend the swearing in tomorrow at the Capitol. The Vice-President is going to do it, in his office, just a few friends will be there, very cozy, and the press. Say the word, and I shall have my secretary send you a ticket."

"It will be a moment to be cherished," said our hostess, looking up into his full-blown face like a gardener examining a favorite rose for beetles.

"I am only saddened that my appearance in the halls of Congress should have been like this . . . in the place of an old and treasured friend. How tragical!"

A murmur of sympathy eddied about him. "Lee was a man to be remembered," said the statesman.

His oration was shorter than I had suspected; when it was over he and Elmer Bush fell into conversation about the coming convention while I chatted with Mrs. Goldmountain.

"You're going to be in Washington a little while longer?"

"Two days at least . . . so the police say."

"Why on earth do they want you now that it's all over?"

"Red tape. You know how they are."

"Well, give my love to darling Ellen and tell her to come see me before she goes back."

"I certainly will."

"And also to Mrs. Rhodes." She paused and sipped some tea, her black eyes dreamy. "She must be relieved."

"That the case is finally over?"

"In *every* sense," said Mrs. Goldmountain significantly.

"What do you mean?"

"Only what everyone in Washington knows and has always known, that she hated Lee Rhodes, that she tried, on at least two occasions, to divorce him and that he somehow managed to talk her out of it. I'm quite sure it was a relief to her when he was killed, by someone else. That awful Hollister really *did* do it, didn't he?"

4

I returned to the house shortly after five, and went straight to my room. As I bathed and dressed for dinner, I had a vague feeling that a pattern was beginning to evolve but precisely what I could not tell. It was definite that there were a number of charades being performed by a number of people for a number of reasons . . . figure out the meanings of the charades and the identity of the murderer would become clear.

I combed my hair and began to construct a plan of attack. First, the Pomeroys. It was necessary that I discover what her game was, why she had come to me with that story about her husband. I should also find out why he had been, all in all, so calm about his arrest: had he been so sure of vindication? And, if he had, why?

Second, I should like to investigate Mrs. Rhodes' whole mysterious performance, her reference to the paper chase, her possible authorship of the anonymous letters, the fact of her revolver's use as a murder weapon. What had her relationship been, truly, to Senator Rhodes? I found Mrs. Goldmountain's assertion difficult to believe. Yet she had, Heaven knew, no reason to be dishonest and if Mrs. Rhodes *had* detested her husband. . . . I thought of that firm old mouth, the controlled voice and gestures: I could imagine her quite easily killing her husband. But how could I find out? Ellen was much too casual about her family to know. Verbena Pruitt seemed the likeliest source, the old family friend . . . except it would not be easy to get anything out of her; she was too used to the world of politics, of secrecy and deals to be caught in an indiscretion. Still I decided to give her a try that evening.

The third charade concerned my erstwhile ally Lieutenant Winters; as a matter of curiosity I wanted to know just what game *he* was playing, what was the reason for his apparent desertion of the case.

And, finally, there was always Langdon; the idea that he might have committed a political murder appealed to me enormously: it was all very romantic and Graustarkian . . . unfortunately he hardly seemed the type to do in poor Hollister, but then murder knoweth no types as the Detectives' Hand Manual would say, if there was such a thing.

Verbena Pruitt could undoubtedly have done the murders, but there was no motive as far as I could tell. Ellen was quite capable of murdering her father, me, Langdon and the President of the United States, but she had been at the Chevy Chase Club when Hollister was murdered, as had Langdon, ruling them both out.

This left Verbena Pruitt and Mrs. Rhodes as the only two who were in the house at the time of Hollister's death (the Pomeroys had been at the police station). The murderer then, barring the intervention of an outsider, was either Verbena or Mrs. Rhodes and, of the two, only Mrs. Rhodes had had the motive.

The result of all this deductive reasoning left me a little cold. I sat down heavily on the bed, hairbrush in hand and wondered why I hadn't worked all this out before. My next thought concerned Winters. He had obviously worked it out for himself. He must've known for some hours what the situation was; he had studied all the statements, had known where each of us was. He must know then that Mrs. Rhodes was, very likely, the murderer and yet he had seemed ready to give up the case. Why? Had he been bought off? This was altogether too possible, knowing the ways of the police, in my own city of New York anyway. Or had he, out of a sense of chivalry, not chosen to arrest her, preferring to rest on the laurels provided him by Hollister's apparent suicide?

I began to think that it might be a good idea if I forgot about the whole thing. I had no desire to see justice done, either in the abstract or in this particular case. Let the tyrants go to their graves unavenged, such was my poetical thought.

The telephone by my bed rang. I answered it. Ellen was on the line. "Come to my room like a good boy," she commanded. "We can have a drink before dinner."

She was already dressed for dinner when I opened the door; she was buffing her nails at her dressing table. "There's a drink over there on the table, by the bed." And sure enough there was a martini waiting for me. I saluted her and drank; then I sat in a chintzy chair, looking at her. I have always enjoyed watching women make themselves up, the one occupation to which they bring utter sincerity and complete dedication. Ellen was no exception.

"When are you going back?" she asked, examining her nails in the light, a critical, distracted expression on her face.

"I hope tomorrow," I said. "It depends on Winters."

"I'm going to go tomorrow, too," she said flatly. "I'm tired of all this. I'm sick of the reporters and the police, even though that Winters is something of a dear . . . and on top of all that I have, ever since I can remember, loathed Washington. I wonder if we could get out of here tonight?" She put down her piece of chamois or whatever it was she was polishing her nails with and looked at me.

"I doubt it," I said. "For one thing Winters will be here."

"Oh damn!"

"And for another thing I don't think those detectives would let us go without permission from him."

"We could duck them; there's a side door off the small drawing room nobody ever uses. We could get out there; there's no guard on that side of the house . . ." As she spoke she sounded, for the first time since I'd known her, nervous and upset.

"Why do you want to leave so badly?"

"Peter, I'm scared to death." And she was, too; her face was drawn beneath the skillful make-up and her hands shook as she drank her martini.

"Why? There's nothing to be afraid of, is there?"

"I . . ." Then she stopped, as though changing her mind about something. "Peter, let's go back tonight, after Winters leaves."

"It wouldn't look right; on top of that we might be in contempt of court or something." I was very curious, but it was up to her to tell me why she wanted, so suddenly, to get out of Washington.

She lit her cigarette with that abrupt masculine gesture of hers, quite unlike any other girls I had known. This seemed to soothe her. "I suppose I'm just getting jittery, that's all, delayed reaction."

"I *will* say you've been unnaturally calm through everything; in fact I've never seen anything like the way you and your mother both managed to be so clear-headed and unemotional about everything." This was a direct shot and it hit home; a flicker of emotion went across her face, like a bird's shadow in the sun. But she told me nothing.

"We're a cold-blooded family, I guess."

"I can understand *you*," I said. "I mean you'd lived away from home so long and you didn't care much about your father, but Mrs. Rhodes . . . well, it's quite something the way she's taken all this."

"Ah," said Ellen distractedly. She stood up. "I think I'll go mix us another martini. I keep the stuff in the bathroom . . . force of habit. In the old days I always had a mouthwash bottle full of gin." She disappeared. I stood up and stretched. I could hear Ellen rattling around in the bathroom . . . somewhere in the house a door slammed, a toilet was flushed: life went on, regardless of crisis. In a pleasantly elegiac mood, brought on by the first martini and increased by the knowledge that soon there would be a second, I wandered about the room, examining the girlhood books of my one-time fiancée. It was an odd group. The Bobbsie Twins were next to *Fanny Hill* and *Lady Chatterley* nestled up to the *Rover Boys*, as she might well have done in life. It was obvious that Ellen's girlhood interests had changed abruptly with puberty. Only a bound volume of the *Congressional Record* attested to her birth and position in life, and *it* looked unopened.

"Here you are, love." She looked somewhat rosier and I decided that she had very likely had herself a large dividend, if not a capital gain, while she was preparing my drink. I toasted her again and we discussed the merits of *Fanny Hill* until dinnertime.

For the first time since I had arrived in Washington nearly a week before, the company at table could have been described as hearty. It was not clever nor amusing, the guests were too solid for that, but it was at least not gloomy and everyone drank Burgundy with the roast and even Mrs. Rhodes smiled over her black lace and jet, like the moon in its last quarter.

I watched her carefully for some sign of guilt, some bloody ensign like Lady Macbeth's spotted hand, but she was as serene as ever and if she were a murderess she wore her crimes with an easy air.

I sat beside Roger Pomeroy and we talked to one another for the first time in some days; he was most cheery. "Had a most profitable visit with the Defense Department today," he said, drying his lips after a mouthful of wine, staining the napkin dark red . . . I was full of blood-images that night.

"About your new explosive?"

"That's right. I gather it's been checked out favorably by their engineers and chemists and it looks as though they'll be placing an order with us soon."

"All this *without* the Senator's help?"

Pomeroy smiled grimly. "There's a new Senator . . . as of tomorrow anyway. We made it very clear that Talisman City was a pretty important place come next November and that the Administration would do well to keep us happy."

"And it worked?"

"Seems to've. Tomorrow Cam and I are flying back home. I'll be glad to get out of this goddamned town, you may be sure."

"Do you think they'd really have been able to convict you?" It was the first time I had ever mentioned the murder directly to him, out of sympathy for a "murderer's" feelings.

"Hell no!" He set his glass down with a thump. "In the first place that young fool Winters went off half-cocked. He assumed that since the explosive was mine and I was angry at Lee for his behavior about the new contract and I knew that my wife stood to inherit a lot of money, that I went ahead and killed him. How dumb can you get? I was perfectly willing to kill Lee if I'd thought I could get away with it. But not in his own house and under suspicious circumstances; besides, in business you never kill anybody, as much as you'd like to." He chuckled.

"Even so, they felt they had enough evidence to convict you with."

"All circumstantial . . . every last bit of it."

"How did you plan to get out of it, though? A lot of people have been ruined on much less evidence than Winters had on you."

"Oh, I had a way." He grinned craftily. He was a little tight and in an expansive mood.

"An alibi?"

"In a way." He paused. "Now this is in absolute confidence . . . if you repeat it I'll call you a liar." He beamed at me, full of self-esteem. "I didn't need Lee. Before I even got to Washington I had contacted someone else, someone very highly placed who promised to help me get the contract. That person was able to do it . . . had, in fact, told me that the contract would be forthcoming in the next ten days, told me in a letter sent the day before Lee was killed, special delivery, too, which I am pleased to say would have proven that I knew before I talked to Lee that the contract was set."

"Why *did* you talk to him then?"

Pomeroy frowned. "Because Lee and I had been involved in a number of other deals before we quarreled. He was a vindictive man, like a devil when he thought that he was right about something, or rather that something was right for *him* . . . a bit of a difference, if you get what I mean. He was the boss of the state and it's a good idea to clear anything which has to do with patronage and government contracts with the boss . . . that's a simple rule of politics."

"Then you had to have his O.K.?"

"No, but it would have helped. I was angry with him but that was all. I was a long way from being the 'desperate and ruined man' which the papers and the police thought I was."

"Why didn't you tell the police right off that you had already got the contract and that consequently there was no real motive for killing Lee Rhodes?"

Pomeroy smiled at me pityingly, as though unaware anyone could have reached the age of twenty-nine in a state of ignorance of business and politics comparable to my own. He spoke slowly, as though to a child. "If I had told the police that I had already fixed the contract, they would have asked for proof. I would have had to show them the letter. They would have got in touch with the author of the letter who would have been embarrassed and possibly ruined by the publicity. This country is run on one set of principles while pretending to another. Contracts are *supposed* to go to the best and the most economical company. Pomeroy, Inc. is a perfectly good company but so are a hundred others; to get a contract I must use influence . . . if I had exposed my benefactor I would have lost the contract, the friendship of a powerful person, my business . . ."

"But you would have saved your life."

"My life was never in any danger. If things had got bad I would have told the whole story but I knew damn well they wouldn't be able to indict me . . . though I suppose they came pretty close."

One thing still bothered me. "Why did you and the Senator fall out in the first place? Why wouldn't he back you up with the Defense Department?"

Pomeroy chuckled. "Lee always got the best price possible for his services. I was outbid, after ten years. A rival company bought him and he stayed bought, like they say. A big outfit from the North which has been expanding all over the country started up in Talisman City a year ago and since they're real professionals they went to Lee right off and underwrote his campaign for the nomination. You probably know who I mean if you were handling his publicity."

I knew indeed . . . one of the biggest cartels in the country. I had known they were contributors; I had no idea they were buyers as well.

"There wasn't much I could do against them. Lee wanted to help me, you know, but he couldn't. At least not until after the nominating convention was over, by which time I'd have been out of business. So I managed the deal without him. I only came to see him to find out about the future, to find out how long they had him tied up. I never *did* find that out. Lee was a devil, never think he wasn't. He was cold and shrewd and he would've sacrificed his own mother for his career. He didn't care about anybody except my wife. I don't know why, but Cam and he were awfully close and he liked her better than Ellen, better than his wife, too. If only because of that, we could've proven that I'd not've been likely to kill him . . . in spite of the inheritance. He never liked me much but he would never have hurt her if he could have helped it. In time he would've made it up to us. I'm sure of that. Anyway, I was never in much danger."

The pieces fell gradually into place. It was like a picture puzzle. I was now at the point where I had filled in the sky, got the frame of the picture all put together: now all that I had to do was fit the central pieces in, numerous tiny pieces, many of them the color of blood.

Winters had attended the dinner but not once did he speak to me or look in my direction. He spoke mostly to Camilla Pomeroy and Walter Langdon. After dinner we went into the drawing room. By the time I was seated, coffee in hand, the minion of the law had disappeared. His departure was noticed by no one, as far as I could tell.

I tried to maneuver toward Mrs. Rhodes but she, as though divining my plot, excused herself and went off to bed.

Langdon and Ellen played backgammon at the far end of the room; I noticed they no longer seemed to enjoy one another's company as much as formerly and it looked as though Ellen would soon be in the market again for another fiancé. This shouldn't be difficult, I thought, recalling that not only was she a handsome uninhibited piece but that she was now worth close to a million dollars, before taxes.

The Pomeroys conversed contentedly by the fire and Verbena Pruitt and I, the couple left over, fell into conversation.

"You have had quite an introduction to Washington," said the lady of state, her face creasing amiably.

"It's not what I'd expected."

"I should think not. It's lucky for all of us that everything worked out as neatly as it did. It could've been one of those cases where nothing was ever proved and everyone would have remained under suspicion for years . . . and that, young man, is *grist* for political enemies."

"Grist," I repeated sagely.

"Rufus didn't use his head," said Miss Pruitt thoughtfully, fondling a cluster of wax red cherries which a malicious dress designer had sewed in strategic places to her coffee-colored gown. "If I'd been he I wouldn't have given up that easy. Suppose those papers *had* come to light and he *was* involved in a business scandal . . . who could have proven that he killed Lee? The worst that would've happened was a jail sentence for larceny, or whatever the crime was. Besides, how did he know that all this was going to come to light anyway?"

"I suppose that someone had threatened to expose him . . . someone who knew about the plot, the business deals, and also knew about the murder . . ." Miss Pruitt had obviously thought about this more carefully than one might have suspected.

"Piffle!" said Miss Pruitt in a voice which made the others start. Then, lowering her voice and looking at me significantly, she said, "Why would anyone want to do that?"

"Revenge?"

"Not very likely . . . to avenge Lee? Perhaps, but it seems far-fetched."

"On the other hand, assuming Hollister was murdered by the Senator's murderer, that would make no sense either since Pomeroy was obviously going to be indicated for the murder and since *he* was to take the rap there was hardly any reason to confuse matters further by killing Hollister and making *him* seem like the murderer."

"I have not of course allowed myself to think that Rufus was killed. Yet, if he had been it might've been by someone who wanted to get Pomeroy off."

"The only two people who were interested in that were both at the police station when Rufus was shot."

"Who can tell?" said Miss Pruitt mysteriously, detaching a wax cherry by mistake; she looked at it unhappily for a moment; then she plunged it between her melonish breasts.

"It could be," I said, trying to divert my morbid attention from her well-packed bodice, "that we are being much too subtle about all this. Hollister might have been remorseful; he might have known that his business dealings were going to be found out anyway and he might've thought: what the hell, I'm going to jail anyway, I might as well confess, save Pomeroy and get out of this mess 'with a bare bodkin.' "

" 'For who would fardels bear. . . .' " boomed Miss Pruitt, recognizing my allusion to him whom they call "the bard" in political circles.

She fardeled on for a moment or two; then, her soliloquy done, "It's possible you're right," she said. "Since it is the police view I am perfectly willing to subscribe to it. I will follow them down the line *one hundred* per cent."

It took me several moments to get her off the subject of Rufus Hollister and onto Mrs. Rhodes. The closer I got to what interested me, though, the more reticent the stateswoman became.

"Yes, she is taking all this bravely, isn't she? Of course she has character. Women of our generation do have character though I am some years younger than she. Of course living with Lee was not the easiest experience. He was a difficult man; that type is. I think to be the wife of a politician is the worst fate in the world, and I should know because I'm both a woman *and* a politician."

"But they were fond of each other?"

She paused just long enough to confirm my suspicions. "They were very close," she said, without conviction.

"Did she have much to do with his official life . . . elections and all that?"

"Not much. She handled the finances, though. I believe they owned everything jointly. I think she wanted him to retire this year but then all political wives are the same: she opposed his going after the nomination, which was good sense because he had no chance of getting it." She looked craftily into the middle distance, implying that she knew who would be the peerless standard-bearer.

"Would you say that she had a vindictive nature?"

If I had slapped the great woman, I could not've got a more startled reaction. "What makes you ask that?" she blustered.

"Oh, I don't know. It had occurred to me that she might have been the one who threatened Rufus, forced him to confess."

"Nonsense!" Alarm ripped through the Pruitt, like a revolution of an African anthill; her face turned dark and I was afraid she might have a stroke; but then the odd convulsions ceased and she added, quietly, "Charity could be her middle name. Her life has been one long martyrdom, endured without complaint. She hated politics; she hated the idea of Camilla Pomeroy . . . as well she might; she almost died when Ellen ran off with a gymnast and the marriage had to be annulled . . ."

"I thought she married him in a church, properly." I recalled the photograph of Ellen in wedding veil which the Senator kept in his study.

"No, she was supposed to marry an eligible young man, a fine upstanding lad who might have made something out of her. Two days before the wedding, a wedding which her parents approved of even though she was only seventeen, she ran off with this muscular animal. Her father caught her in Elkton, Maryland and the marriage was duly annulled. Yet in spite of the scandal, her mother took her back without a reproach. Her father . . ." The butler crept into the room to inform Miss Pruitt that there was a telephone call for her.

She disappeared into the hall. I sat drowsily by the fire. A moment later, she appeared, very pale, and asked me for brandy. I got some for her.

She gulped it sloppily, spilling half of it on her majestic front. I looked about the room to see if the others had noticed anything; they had not; they were deep in their own problems.

"Has anything happened?" I asked.

She dabbed at her dress with a piece of Kleenex; she was, for her, pale . . . her face mottled pink-gray. "That was Governor Ledbetter. It seems that the papers have got hold of some business deal he and Lee were involved in; something which involved Rufus: the thing he referred to in that confession. A terrible scandal. . . ."

VI

"Moral turpitude," said the Senate and they refused to seat the Senator-Designate until a committee had checked him out.

The morning was full of meetings and reports in the house. Mrs. Rhodes and Miss Pruitt were especially upset. Langdon was remarkably interested (at last having found a suitable theme for his magazine) and even the Pomeroys delayed their trip back to Talisman City to find out what would happen. To what extent Pomeroy himself was involved in the Senator's numerous deals, I did not know. As far as I could tell, not at all: in this one at least.

After breakfast, I conferred with Winters who, under the ruse of taking some last photographs of the Senator's study and of Rufus Hollister's bedroom had returned to the house where he was largely ignored, in marked contrast to his earlier visits.

I found him alone in the study. The wall which had been blown away was now repaired, as far as the brick went. The plastering had not been done, however, so the room had a raw look to it: half paneled and half new-laid brick.

Winters was glancing idly at some of the scrapbooks when I came in.

"Oh, it's you." He sounded neutral, to say the least. He looked calmer and happier than usual . . . with good reason considering that he was now off the hot seat, his case successfully concluded.

"Did you ever go through these?" I asked, looking over his shoulder at a yellowed clipping, dated 1927: a photograph of the Senator shaking hands with a slim woman in a cloche hat.

"Oh yes."

I tried to read the caption of the picture, Winters tried to turn the page; I deliberately lifted his hand off the page and read the caption: "Senator Rhodes being congratulated on his recent victory in the primaries by Verbena Pruitt, National Committeewoman."

"Who would've thought she ever looked like that?" I was impressed. It was impossible to tell what her face was like in this old picture . . . but she had a good figure.

"I don't think she was ever much," said Winters; if he was irritated with the abrupt way I had pushed him aside, he didn't show it.

"What do you think about this new development?"

"What new development?" He looked at me blandly.

"You know what I mean. The business which Hollister was to take the rap for, it's come out in the papers."

"The case is finished," said Winters, opening the 1936 scrapbook.

"Who got the word to the papers?"

"I haven't any idea."

"According to the *Times* the Government has been investigating the Senator's company for two years."

"I think that's right." Winters sounded bored.

"According to the papers this morning the Senator was just as much implicated as Hollister."

"Yes?"

"In other words, it doesn't look as if Hollister was to have taken the rap for the Senator's misdeeds . . . in other words, the confession was a phony."

"Very logical," said Winters, admiring a Berryman cartoon of Lee Rhodes in the *Washington Star*.

"I'll say it's logical." I was growing irritated. "Is there any real evidence that Hollister was to take the rap for the Governor and Rhodes? According to the newspaper account, they were all in it equally."

"What about the papers you got in the mail from your anonymous admirer? What about them? They proved that the Senator had fixed it for Hollister to be the front man. Hollister killed him before he could finish the arrangements . . . that's simple enough, isn't it?"

"You don't really believe that?"

"Why not?" And that was the most that I could get out of Winters. The thought that someone might have bought *him* occurred to me again with some force. More than ever I was determined to meddle in this affair.

While he looked at the old clippings, I wandered about the study, looking at the bomb-scarred desk, the books on the shelves. Then, aware that I was going to get no satisfaction out of Winters, I left the study, without a word of farewell. I had about twenty-four hours, I knew, in which to produce the murderer and since I had almost nothing to go on it was a little difficult to determine what to do next. I had several ideas, none very good.

It occurred to me, being of a logical disposition, that I might come to a solution more quickly than not if I were to proceed in an orderly way to examine each of the suspects and then, by collating their stories, arrive at a solution. It sounded remarkably easy; in fact, just the thought of being logical so delighted me that for several minutes I enjoyed the sensation of having solved the murder successfully.

I had taken care of Pomeroy. I knew, very likely, more about his relations with the Senator than the police did, thanks to Mrs. Rhodes' excellent Burgundy of the night before.

I still had certain doubts about Camilla. She was the next logical person to eliminate. Why, I wondered, had she tried to make me think her husband was the murderer? It was an important point, all the more so since she was a beneficiary in the old man's will, and had known it, too.

I found her off by herself in a corner of the drawing room, studying the latest issue of *Harper's Bazaar.* She was reading the thin ribbon of text which accompanies the advertisements; this thin ribbon was, I could see, the work of the latest young novelist; it concerned a young boy in Montgomery, Alabama, who killed nine flies in as many minutes on the eve of the Fourth of July . . . I had read it earlier, being of a literary turn (though I belong to the older literary generation of Carson McCullers and have never quite absorbed the newcomers even though they take mighty nice photographs).

"I just love it," said Camilla, without enthusiasm, closing the magazine; she was dressed in a very businesslike suit, as though ready for traveling.

"We were going to take the noon train, Roger and I, but since poor Johnson got involved in this terrible mess Roger thought, out of loyalty, we should stay and see him through."

"I think that's swell," I said earnestly.

"Yes," she said brightly. We stood looking at one another awkwardly for perhaps a minute. Even in this age of jet-planes and chromium plate, there are certain proprieties which those who occupy the upper echelon of our society insist upon maintaining, regardless of their true feelings. It is usually agreed upon in these circles that when a man has gone to bed with a gentlewoman he has become, up to a point, her *cavaliere servente,* as they used to say in Venice . . . the Venetians used to say, that is.

It was apparent to both of us that a certain dignity was lacking in our relationship; neither had spoken of love or duty, and both, in fact, had acted subsequently as though nothing had happened, depriving man's greatest emotion and most sacred moment of its true splendor; in fact there has been the faintest note of the barnyard in our coupling which, doubtless, worried the hen though the rooster, if I can call myself one even in this analogy, was not much concerned. But there was a game to be played . . . two games, even . . . and I had very little time.

"Camilla," the name sounded rich and husky on my lips.

"Yes?" Her voice squeaked just a little as she turned two dark bright eyes up at me.

"I . . . I wonder if you'd have lunch with me."

"Oh, but . . ." She "butted" for a few moments and then, aware that her position as a lady was at stake, she agreed to a brief lunch at the Mayflower where the food was good in the cocktail lounge and there was a string quartet.

The Mayflower was very grand; I had been there only once before, in the main dining room. This time we went to the cocktail lounge, a dim, marbleized, ferny place full of people dining in the gloom to the sound of soft music; it was a perfect place for an assignation. Unfortunately the customers were mainly ladies who had dropped in after a hard morning of shopping, or five-percenters discussing deals with prospective clients . . . the Congressional and political figures did not, presumably, lunch here though they could be found, often, in this room at five o'clock.

We were led to a corner table by a distinguished-looking headwaiter who resembled a Bavarian Foreign Minister.

"Here we are," said Camilla and a high mouse-giggle escaped from behind her ruddy lips; she was very nervous. I could not imagine that this great plain fool was the same woman who had only a few nights before come to my room like a winged furnace, like Lady Potiphar at the end of the first month. Dressed and full of rectitude, she seemed what she was: an ordinary girl from Talisman City.

We ordered corn, Virginia ham and mint juleps. I have always hated mint juleps and I don't think she cared for them either but somehow our proximity to the Old Dominion made us reckless; outside snow was wetly falling.

"I suppose you look forward to getting back home?" I began formally.

"I certainly look forward to leaving this horrid city," she said sincerely, biting off a piece of mint.

"It hasn't been a very nice time for any of us," I said.

"We have aged, Roger and I, a hundred years," she said looking deep into my eyes. Unfortunately the stately gloom of the place prevented me from experiencing the full power of those shining dark eyes.

"It looks as though his contract is all set, doesn't it?"

She nodded. "I'm told the first orders are being made up now. We couldn't be more thrilled."

"I should think so. Do you think you'll start back tonight?"

She shook her head. "No, not now. Of course it may not be as nice as I think."

"What may not be?"

"Home. My friends. What on earth will they think when they know? And of course they know now; *everyone* does."

"Knows what?"

"That I am Lee's daughter. I hardly dare face them at the club, assuming we'll be allowed to keep our membership." We were approaching by a circuitous route the true soul of Camilla Pomeroy: the club and all that the club meant.

"At least your mother was his common-law wife." This didn't sound too good but my intention was kindly.

"As if that will make any difference to *them*. No, I must face this thing through." She set her jaw, a sprig of mint clenched between her teeth.

"It's hardly your fault, your birth."

"You don't understand Talisman City." she said grimly, "The people there live by the book . . ."

"And have not charity . . ."

"What?"

"And are difficult," I said. I have always regarded as a stroke of good fortune that I was not born or brought up in a small American town; they may be the backbone of the nation but they are also the backbone of ignorance, bigotry, and boredom, all in vast quantities. I remember one brief stay in a little upstate New York village where I was referred to, behind my back, as "the Jew from New York City," despite the presence of a Sargeant at that very moment in the Episcopal Church of Bishops . . . such is the generous feeling of our American peasants for strangers; I didn't envy Mrs. Pomeroy's return to her native heath.

"Oh, very. But then we *have* to have standards after all," she said, showing she was one of them, fallen or not.

While we lunched, we talked about her early days, about the Senator. "We were very close even though I never dreamed the truth. Mother would never say anything except that she was glad I was seeing him because he was such a distinguished man. She was especially pleased when I organized a platoon of Girl Scouts to work for him on one of his campaigns. Father, that is her husband, hated Lee and used to make very uncivil remarks whenever I came home from one of my visits to the Rhodes' house but Mother always made him keep still."

"It must've been quite a shock, when you found out."

She rolled her eyes briefly to heaven. "I'll say it was. I thought seriously of killing myself, being young and dramatic but then after awhile I got used to the idea . . . and Lee was marvelous with me, called me 'his own girl.' " She seemed, suddenly, very moved, for the first time since the trouble began.

"He must have been very fond of you. He would have to have been to include you in his will, knowing everything would come to light, embarrassing his family."

"Much he cared about them!" This came out like a small explosion.

"You mean . . ."

"He hated both of them. Mrs. Rhodes was an ice-cold woman who married him because he was a young man who was going to make his mark, because *she* was ambitious. He went into politics and ruined his health and got mixed up with all sorts of terrible people and finally was killed by one of them just because she wanted to be a Senator's wife, a President's wife. How he used to complain to me about her! And his daughter: well, he understood her altogether too well . . . everyone did, what she was and is. Of course, he stopped her that once, when she ran off with a weight lifter on the eve of her wedding to Verbena Pruitt's nephew . . ."

"She was supposed to marry Verbena's nephew?" I had not heard this before.

"That was the plan, only at the last minute, after the wedding dress was made and the reception already planned, she left home with this man. Lee brought her back and annulled the marriage but that didn't change *her.*" I was rather proud of Ellen's character; she would not be controlled by anyone.

"How did Verbena's nephew turn out?"

Camilla frowned. "He became an alcoholic and later died in an accident. Even so, he was the catch of the season and everyone thought he had a great future ahead of him. He was rich and in the Foreign Service, his father had been Ambassador to Italy and what with Verbena's influence and so on he could have risen to great heights."

"But he *did* take to drink."

"Even so, no one knew it at the time. Ellen had no business walking out."

"Perhaps she suspected what his future might be; it looks as though she had better sense than her father."

Camilla shook her head stubbornly; then, with woman's logic, "Besides, he might not have been an alcoholic if she had married him. Well, her parents never forgave her for that particular scandal and then after she began to have men friends of all sorts they sent her away to New York where that sort of thing isn't so noticeable." Talisman City suddenly showed its bleak intolerant head, besprinkled with hayseed and moral rectitude. I saw no reason to defend Ellen who is a bit of a madwoman about sex; on the other hand, Camilla's high and mighty line did not accord with her own behavior. It was obvious she hated Ellen and would use any stick to beat her with and Ellen always proffered a formidable mace for this purpose to anyone hostilely minded.

"Tell me," I said, a little maliciously, "why do you think Rufus killed your father?"

She was startled. "Why Rufus . . . but obviously because of that business deal, the one Johnson's involved in, too. At least that's what Winters said. Rufus was to cover up for the others; he was to take the blame."

"But now it's all in the newspapers and Rufus is *not* taking the blame."

"Then why did he say he was going to in his confession?"

"Perhaps because someone else wrote it for him, after killing him."

Her eyes grew round. "You're not suggesting that Rufus was killed, too?"

"It's possible."

"But who would want to kill him?"

"The same man who murdered your father."

"But that man was Rufus."

"There was a time when you weren't so sure."

Even in the gloom, I could see her flush. "That's not fair," she said in a small voice.

"Why did you think your husband killed the Senator?" I closed in, aware of my advantage.

"I told you. I was upset, hysterical. . . ."

"Why did you think he did it?"

"For . . . for the same reason everyone else did, because of the contracts running out, because Lee wouldn't help him."

"Yet you knew that the contract had already been secured through someone else."

"Verbena told you that, didn't she?" Out it shot, before she could stop herself. She bit her lip.

I was slowly getting the picture, all the background was in at last: now for the foreground, to fill in the shadowy outline at the puzzle's center, to construct the murderer. I was growing nervous with excitement.

I controlled my voice, though, sounded offhand. "Yes, as a matter of fact Verbena did mention to me that she had helped Pomeroy get his government contract before he came to Washington to see Lee. . . ."

"That wasn't wise of her at all. These things are so delicate; it could affect our whole business. That was why Roger said nothing about it even after they arrested him."

"If you knew that he had no real quarrel with the Senator, that he wasn't ruined, why did you tell me that night that he was the murderer?"

"Because," she had regained control of herself now, "because I didn't know until the next day that his contract *was* set. He told me when it looked as if he might be arrested any minute. He knew that I adored my father more than anyone else in the world. He knew that I had lost my head when he was murdered and I think he knew, also, though he never mentioned it, that I suspected him of the murder, to get even with Lee, to get my inheritance . . . so he broke an old rule of his and told me about his business, about how he had gone to Verbena and she had helped him, despite the Senator. Then I knew how absurd the whole case against him really was. . . ."

"But you had come to me and told me you thought he was the murderer."

"I thought he was, yes. I thought he'd gone mad. I thought he'd kill *me* next to get the inheritance. I thought he was desperate and so I went off my head for twenty-four hours. It was just too much, having everybody know I was Lee's daughter; everything was so awful that I . . . I came to your room. I don't know why but I did. For some reason I was afraid Roger might kill me that night. I . . . was terribly ashamed afterwards."

There seemed nothing more to clear up here. Her story was accurate, as far as I could tell. It was also revelatory. Verbena Pruitt began to loom large in the background. What was her role in all this? I had never suspected that she would ever seem mysterious to me. I had underestimated her.

I was ready now to end the session with Camilla Pomeroy; unfortunately we had to go through a number of gyrations which propriety, at least in Talisman City, demands of those who have known one another's bodies.

I told her that knowing her had been one of the most wonderful events of my life and that I hoped we should meet again, soon.

She told me that I had helped her more than she could say, at a desperate moment. She asked me to forgive her for what she had done. Not entirely sure of which of her treacheries she desired forgiveness, I delivered myself of a blanket absolution. Then, our love affair put on ice as it were, each with a beautiful memory, she pressed my hand and left me to pay the check.

When I got to the lobby she was gone. I was about to call a cab when I saw two familiar figures in serious talk, half-hidden by a potted tree. I went over and said hello to Elmer Bush and Johnson Ledbetter, the Senator-Designate and perhaps never-to-be.

They both looked as though I was the last person in the world they wanted to see at this moment. The falling statesman looked puffy-eyed and tired. The journalist looked eager, like an opportunistic tiger courting a lost sheep. They were cooking up some scheme.

"How are you today, 'Senator'?" I said brightly; even the falling statesman gets the quotes.

"Very well, Sargeant." I was surprised he remembered my name.

"This is a grave crisis," said Elmer Bush in his best doom-voice.

"A misunderstanding," said Ledbetter in a strangled voice.

"We hope, however, to have the truth before the public tonight, on my program," said Elmer tightly.

"I hope, sir, that you will be vindicated."

"Thank you, my boy," said Ledbetter in a husky voice. At that moment the famous newspaperman's cry, "There he is!" was heard in the lobby, somewhat muffled out of deference to the Mayflower's dignity; and a journalist and photographer came pounding toward us, their rimless spectacles gleaming, their faces red from cold and pleasure as they cornered the falling star.

"It has all been," intoned Johnson Ledbetter, "a fantastic mistake."

2

Fantastic mistake or not, it was the main conversation in Washington these days and, to read the newspapers, everywhere else, too. Corruption, when it stains senatorial togas, always ceases to become squalid and becomes tragical, as Mr. Ledbetter would say.

After leaving the Mayflower, I went to the house of Mrs. Goldmountain, knowing that she was to be at home this afternoon. She was, I had discovered, a good source of information, having spent the better part of her fifty years climbing upwards socially; along the way she had investigated nearly every eminent closet in Washington society, she was also proving to be a source of revenue to me as far as the Heigh-Ho Dogfood Company went.

I was led to the yellow room where I found her in deep conversation with that Vice-President of Heigh-Ho to whom I had spoken the day before.

As I entered, she was saying, "Hermione has a range of four octaves, of which three are usable."

"But that's marvelous," said the official, a doggish-looking man, constructed on the order of a chow.

"Mr. Sargeant, I'm so happy you came by, and just at this moment, too. I'm sure your ears must've been burning."

"Pete, here, knows what we think of him at Heigh-Ho," said the chow, beaming, handing me his damp squashy paw to shake; I shook it quickly and let it drop. I bowed a moment over Mrs. G's hand, the way diplomats are supposed to do.

"In many ways," said the chow, "this will be the most novel public relations stunt of the age. You realize that?"

"That's what I'm paid for," I said modestly, making a mental note to arrange to take a percentage of the gross on Hermione's various activities; I was wondering whether an agent's fee, as well, would be too exorbitant, when Mrs. Goldmountain recalled me from my greed.

"Although I am, in principle, opposed to Self-Exploitation, I couldn't, in all conscience, allow my girl not to take advantage of this wonderful opportunity, nor could I be so cruel as to keep her talent under a bushel."

I refrained from commenting that that was probably just where it belonged, under the biggest heaviest bushel there was.

"You've taken the right line," said the official gravely impressed by Mrs. Goldmountain's wealth and hard-earned social position, *and* excellent press relations; all that glitters is not a gold-mountain, I felt like telling him, but then it was to my interest to keep the farce going.

"Have you made arrangements about engaging Town Hall?"

He nodded. "It's all being prepared now. I'm lining up the press. We'll have a full coverage."

"I can do all that," I said quickly. "That's my job, after all."

"There'll be a lot for you to do; don't worry. Heigh-Ho, however, is getting behind this campaign with everything it's got. We may even take radio time." The noise of money coming my way, lulled me for a moment, like the sirens singing; but then, before I knew it, Hermione and not the sirens was singing.

She had been brought into the large drawing room next to the yellow room and her accompanist had begun to play.

A long yowl chilled my blood, more chilling was the fact that, despite the unmistakable canine quality of the voice, Hermione had perfect pitch. She was not, however, a trained musician.

Mrs. Goldmountain looked dreamily toward the open door through which floated, or rather raced, the poodle's voice. "She practices every day . . . not too long, though. I don't want her to strain her voice."

"Maybe we ought to insure it," said the dog-food purveyor anxiously, "wouldn't want anything to happen to her. Lloyd's would be only too glad to oblige us."

"If you like . . . though I'm sure nothing will happen; she is always under the closest supervision."

Hermione screamed her way through the "Bell Song" from *Lakmé* and, my nerves in tatters, my ears vibrating like beaten drums, I applauded loudly, along with the official from Heigh-Ho. Mrs. Goldmountain only smiled.

Then, after several points of business had been cleared up, Mrs. Goldmountain and I were left alone: the official gone back to New York to make an announcement to the news services, Hermione gone back to her quarters and the tin of foie gras to which she was often treated after singing.

It took me some time to get the subject off Hermione and back to the Rhodes family or rather to Ledbetter who now occupied my hostess's thoughts.

"Johnson called me on the phone this morning (we're very close, you know); he sounded simply awful."

"I know, I saw him at the Mayflower this afternoon. He was with Elmer Bush."

"At least Elmer will stand by him through thick and thin. Johnson will need friends." I allowed that this was probably the case.

"This morning I telephoned the Vice-President to tell him that I was confident Johnson had done nothing wrong."

"What did the Vice-President say?"

"Oh, he was on the floor. I didn't get him but his secretary said she would give him my message."

"Well, according to all accounts he seems guilty of fraud, along with the other two."

"I doubt it but then I must confess I never read the newspapers . . . at least the political sections; those people are always writing lies about personal friends of mine, and then they never know what's going on until it's already happened." She smiled sphinx-like, implying she *did* know; and perhaps she did.

"In any case, he probably won't be allowed to take his seat."

"I'm sure they'll be able to arrange it," she said confidently. "They need him, you know."

I didn't pursue this point.

"I blame that dreadful little man, the secretary, the one who killed himself, for everything. I'm sure he did it deliberately . . . made up all sorts of documents just to implicate Johnson. He was a nasty creature, I always thought, killing Lee like that and then purposely framing poor Johnson." This was a novel twist.

"Did you know him at all?"

"Who? The secretary? Hardly, but I never liked his looks those few times I saw him. Johnson is building his case on the little man's dishonesty, however. He swears to me that it's a deliberate plot and I believe him. He quarreled with him the night he died."

"Who quarreled with whom?"

"Johnson and that little man, you know, Hollister."

"How do you know?"

"Johnson told me. He tells me everything, not that it's any particular secret; soon everyone will know it."

"But where did this take place?" Veils were trembling before my eyes; the figure at the puzzle's center grew more distinct.

"Johnson spent the evening at the Rhodes', with Mrs. Rhodes, the evening Hollister killed himself. Didn't you see him? But of course not, you were at my party and Johnson should have been there, too, except he rightly decided that his first evening in Washington as a Senator should be spent with his predecessor's widow, a very, very nice thing to do, but then Johnson is a nice man."

"You mean he was in the house when Hollister died?"

"But of course and he had, he tells me, a private conversation with Hollister of the most unpleasant kind."

"Without witnesses?"

"There would hardly be witnesses if the conversation was private."

"I wonder why the papers didn't mention that he was in the house when the murder took place."

"Perhaps no one thought to tell them . . . they never know anything."

3

For awhile I entertained the mad fantasy that Verbena Pruitt, Mrs. Rhodes and the Senator-Designate (the only three in the house at the time, other than servants) might have got together and killed Rufus on their own. Each had a motive, except perhaps Verbena. The vision, however, of these three elderly political figures tiptoeing upstairs to shoot Rufus Hollister was much too ludicrous.

I arrived at the house shortly before dinner. It was already dark outside and the curtains were drawn against the night. The plainclothes man who usually stood guard was nowhere in sight.

In the drawing room I found Mrs. Rhodes, quite alone, playing solitaire at a tiny Queen Anne desk. She greeted me with her usual neutrality.

"I suppose," I said, "you'll be glad to see the last of us."

"The last of you under these circumstances," she replied courteously, motioning me to sit beside her.

"What do you plan to do when all this is over, when the estate is settled and everything is taken care of?"

"Do?" she looked at me blankly for a moment, as though she had not, until now, conceived there would be a future.

"I mean do you intend to go back to Talisman City, or live here?"

She gave me a long look, as though I had asked her a nearly impossible question. Finally she said, "I shall stay here of course. All my friends are here," she added mechanically.

"Like Mrs. Goldmountain?"

She smiled suddenly, for the first time since I met her, like sun on the snow. "No, not like Mrs. Goldmountain. Others . . . my old friends from the early days. We had no very close friends back home, the old ones died off and we made no new ones, except politically. I haven't lived there since we came to Washington."

"I saw Mrs. Goldmountain today."

"Yes?" She was clearly not interested.

"I understand she's a great friend of Governor Ledbetter's."

"I believe so."

"She is certainly taking his side in this business."

"As she should. I'm sure that Johnson did nothing dishonest, nor did Lee." But this came out automatically; she seemed to be making a series of prepared responses, her mind on something else.

"I didn't know the Governor was here the night Rufus died."

"Oh yes, we had a nice chat. He is a good friend, you know, as well as our lawyer."

"He told Mrs. Goldmountain that he and Rufus quarreled that night, about the business of those companies."

Mrs. Rhodes frowned, "Ida Goldmountain should show better sense," she said sharply. "Yes, they had a disagreement. Over what I don't know; it took place upstairs, in Rufus's room."

"Did the police know this?"

"That Johnson was here? Oh yes, both Verbena and I told them when we were questioned as to who was in the house."

"Did they know that the Governor went upstairs to talk to Rufus, alone? That they quarreled?"

She looked at me coldly, with sudden dislike. "Why, I don't know," she said. "The police didn't ask me and I don't remember having volunteered any information. I am so used to having things misunderstood," she said and her voice was hard.

"I'm sure they must know," I said thoughtfully, trying to figure out

Winters: why had he kept this piece of information secret? Not only from me but from the official report given to the newspapers.

"Besides," she said, "the case ended when Rufus killed himself. There was no need to involve one's friends any more than was necessary. I appreciated Johnson's kindness in coming to see me his first night in Washington, before he was to take his seat. If I were you," and she looked at me with her clear onyx eyes, unmarked by age or disaster, "I would say nothing about Johnson's exchange with Rufus."

"I'll have no occasion to, yet," I said, quite as cool as the old lady. "In any case, I'm not the person to silence. Mrs. Goldmountain is. She's the informer."

"That fool!" Mrs. Rhodes exploded.

"Fool or not, she's given us a new angle on the case."

"Case? What case?"

"On who killed your husband, Mrs. Rhodes, and who killed Rufus Hollister."

She sat back in her chair, "You're mad," she said in a low voice. "It's all over. The police are satisfied. *Leave it alone,*" her voice was harshly urgent.

"But the police aren't satisfied," I said, and this was a big and dangerous guess. "They know as well as you and I that Rufus was killed; they are waiting for the real murderer to make some move. So am I."

"I don't believe you."

"But it's true."

"Even if all you say is true why do you involve yourself in it? Why not go back to New York? Why involve yourself in a world which has nothing to do with yours?"

"Because, Mrs. Rhodes, I'm already involved, because I'm in danger no matter where I go."

"Danger? Why?"

"Because I know who the murderer is and the murderer knows that I know." This was a crashing lie but there was no help for it.

She pushed her chair back and stood up, as though prepared to run from the room; her face was ash-gray. "You're lying," she said at last.

I stood up, too. From the hall I could hear a door shut and the sound of someone running upstairs. We stood looking at one another like two graven images, like gargoyles on a mediaeval tower.

Then she recovered her composure and gave a strange little laugh. "You are trying to confuse me," she said, attempting lightness. "We all know that Rufus was the murderer and that he killed himself.

Whatever argument Johnson had with him was perfectly innocent ... as far as the main thing goes. Certainly the thought that Johnson killed Rufus is a ridiculous one, quite unimaginable."

"Then why did *you* imagine it, Mrs. Rhodes? It never occurred to me that he did."

She flushed, confused. "I . . . I was mistaken then. I was under the impression you thought Johnson was in some way involved."

I was conscious that she had betrayed something of enormous value to me, but what I could not tell. "No," I said. "I never thought the Governor killed Rufus but I am curious about their conversation."

"I suspect that it is none of your business, in any case, Mr. Sargeant," Mrs. Rhodes was herself again.

"As I pointed out, it *is* my business if it concerns the murder." I could be quite as cold as she.

"And you think there is some connection?"

"Certainly. The collapse of this company has a great deal to do with the case . . . not only with your husband's death but with the career of Governor Ledbetter."

She gathered up her purse, a handkerchief, prepared to go. "I assume then you will be staying with us for quite some time, after the others leave tomorrow?" This was insulting.

"No, Mrs. Rhodes," I said looking her straight in the eye, "I will deliver the murderer tomorrow."

She looked at me for one long moment, quite expressionless; then in a low voice, intensely, she said, "You meddlesome fool!" and she swept out of the room.

Feeling somewhat shaken, and a little silly, I went out into the hall. A familiar perfume was in the air as I walked slowly up the stairs, wondering what to do next. There was very little chance that I would be able to unmask the murderer, much less be able to collect sufficient evidence to assure conviction.

I was tempted to forget about the whole thing.

I was surprised, when I opened the door to my room, to find Walter Langdon leaning over my desk in a most incriminating fashion. He gave a jump when he saw me.

"Oh! I . . . I'm awfully sorry. I came in here just a minute ago, looking for you. I wanted to borrow some typewriter paper."

At least it could have been a match, or wanting to know the time. "There's some in the top drawer," I said.

He opened it and, with shaking hands, took out a few sheets. "Thanks a lot."

"Perfectly all right."

"Hope I can do the same for you one day."

"Never can tell." The sort of dialogue which insures, or used to insure, any number of Hollywood scriptwriters a secure and large income.

"Sit down," I said.

"I really better get ready for dinner."

"You look just fine." He sat down in the chair at the desk; I sat on the foot of the bed, legs crossed in a most nonchalant fashion. "Are you satisfied with the way things turned out?"

He looked puzzled. "You mean the murders?"

I caught that. "So you think Rufus was murdered too?"

"No, he killed himself, didn't he? That's what the police seem to think."

"Why did you say 'murders'?"

"A slip of the tongue. Two deaths is what I meant." He was perfectly calm.

"But I take it you think Rufus was murdered?"

"You take it wrong, Sargeant," said Langdon. "I see no reason to think Rufus might have been killed. It makes perfect sense the way it is. I think you should leave it alone." The second time I had been advised, in exactly those words, to keep my nose clean. I was beginning to feel that a monstrous cabal had been formed to misguide me.

"You don't have much of the newspaperman in you, Langdon," I said in the hearty tone of a stock company actor in *The Front Page*.

"I'm not really one," said Langdon with a touch of frost in his voice. "I just do occasional articles. I'm mainly interested in the novel."

I have all the pseudo-intellectual's loathing of those who have dedicated themselves, no matter how sincerely and competently, to art . . . a form of envy, I suppose, which becomes contempt if they fail. Langdon had all the earmarks of a potential disaster.

"Even so you should be more interested in this sort of thing. Have you decided what you're going to write about for your magazine?"

He nodded. "I'm working on it now, that's why I needed the paper. I want to have a first draft ready by the time I get back to the office, tomorrow afternoon."

"What line are you taking?"

"Oh, the implications of a political murder . . . I use the Rhodes thing as a point of departure, if you know what I mean."

I knew only too well: the Dichotomy of Murder or The Theology of Crisis in Reaction. It would be great fun to read, I decided grimly.

"Then you'll be taking the noon train with Ellen?" This was a guess, but perfectly logical.

"Yes, as a matter of fact, we *are* going back together."

"She's quite something isn't she?"

Langdon nodded seriously. "She certainly is."

"Are you still engaged to her?"

"Oh, it wasn't a formal engagement."

"I'm sure of that; they never are."

Langdon blushed. "She . . . she's very promiscuous, isn't she?"

"Yes, Walter, she is," I said in the tone of a Scoutmaster explaining to a new tenderfoot the parts of the body and their uses.

"I didn't think it was so bad until we went out to Chevy Chase and she ducked off with a Marine . . ."

"She's been known to complete a seduction in ten minutes."

"Well, this took a lot longer. I was mad as hell at her but she told me it was none of my business, that she thought the Marine much too nice-looking to let go; it was then I caught on."

"You didn't really care about her that much, did you?" I was curious; both Ellen and I had thought him a fool.

He scratched his sandy hair in a bumpkin manner. "Not really. I never ran into anything quite like her before and I guess I was taken in for a little bit."

"The fact she now has a million dollars, as well as an uninhibited technique, might make her irresistible to an American boy."

"Not this boy." But I detected a wistful note; she had used him up, as it were. I wondered what would become of her now that she was rich; there were bound to be operators cleverer than she in the world, and what a ride they could take her for. Well, it was no business of mine.

"Let me see what you write for the *Advanceguard*, if you don't mind."

"Not at all. I'd like your advice." Then he left the room.

I puttered about the room, getting ready for dinner, the last dinner in this house. I packed my bag, slowly, reluctantly, aware that the puzzle was incomplete and would doubtless remain so now, forever. I cursed my ill luck, my slow brain, the craft of my opponent: for some time now I had regarded the killer as a malicious personal opponent whose delight it was to torment me.

I opened my desk to see if there were any letters or old socks in the drawers. There was nothing. Only a few sheets of typewriter paper. On one of them I had made some elaborate doodles; at the center of the largest decoration I had written "paper chase" in old English type.

Paper chase. I thought of Mrs. Rhodes. Something I had heard that day came back to me; something I had known all along appeared in a new way. Unexpectedly every piece fell into place.

And I knew who had killed Senator Rhodes, and Rufus Hollister.

4

It was evident from the happy faces at table that night that this was to be our last supper together. No one was sorry that the ghastly time was finally over. I was giddy with triumph and I had a difficult time not showing it. My exuberance was doubtless attributed to our coming freedom. We were like prisoners on the eve of parole.

I took great care not to betray myself. I made no reference all that evening to the case; I indicated in no way that I had completed the picture puzzle. I even refrained from staring too long at the killer, who was most serene, doubtless confident that the whole desperate gamble had been won at last.

Winters was noticeable by his absence. There had been some talk that he would come by to say farewell but he did not, out of shame at facing me, I decided, complacent in my victory, keyed up to an extraordinary pitch both by my discovery and by the danger which attended it.

I lacked evidence, of course, but when one knows a problem's answer its component parts can be deduced *and* proved, by working backwards. I had, I was sure, the means of proving what I knew.

After dinner, we were joined in the drawing room by Johnson Ledbetter and Elmer Bush. They came in out of the black winter night, their faces red from cold, bringing cold air with them.

Their entrance depressed, somewhat, the gala mood of the guests.

Mrs. Rhodes poured us coffee. Cups were handed about. The discredited statesman took bourbon. His journalistic ally did the same. They sat talking by the fire to Mrs. Rhodes, Roger Pomeroy and Verbena Pruitt, leaving the women and children to amuse themselves. We amused ourselves, even though I was anxious to join the circle by the fire.

Ellen and Camilla fell to wrangling in a most sisterly fashion while Langdon and I exchanged weighty opinions on the state of contemporary letters ("decadent").

After an hour of this, everyone shifted positions, as often happens with a group in civilized society: a spontaneous rearrangement of the elements to distribute the boredom more democratically.

I ended up with Ledbetter and Elmer and Verbena Pruitt at the fireplace.

"It has become," said Ledbetter slowly, "A Party Issue."

"In which case you're bound to win," said Verbena comfortably. "I have word that the White House intends to intervene."

"But when? When?" His voice rose querulously.

"*His* hands are tied. You know how *he* feels about interfering in legislative problems. Yet I have it on the highest, the very highest, authority that *he* intends to act before the week is over. One word from *him* and the Party will support you."

"Meanwhile I undergo martyrdom."

"It may turn out to be political Capital," said Elmer Bush, nodding happily, pleased to be involved in such high and dirty politics.

The Senator-Designate snorted. He looked at the end of his rope; he was also getting tight. "What a mess it is, Grace," he said, turning with a sigh to Mrs. Rhodes. She smiled and patted his hand.

"It won't last much longer," she said softly.

"I hope you're right." I was surprised by this sudden gentle exchange; could they have been . . . but it was too far-fetched.

I was suddenly tempted to drop the whole thing; to retire from the scene with the secret satisfaction of having solved a case which, all things considered, had proven to be damned near insoluble.

I looked at the murderer thoughtfully, aware, disagreeably, of my own power. I have few sadistic impulses and I had no chivalrous love for any of the dead. I resolved at that moment to keep my information to myself.

"The point I have been making continually," said Ledbetter, turning on the professional political voice which became him so well, if you happen to like politicians of the old school, "is that my connection with the company was perfectly legal, that Rufus and Lee between them ran it and that all I did was have my office occasionally handle their legal work for them. I had no other connection with it."

"But why, Senator, if you had so little to do with the companies, did you have an equal share with Mr. Rhodes?" I was surprised at my own boldness; hostile eyes were turned upon me.

"I left all that to them, young man. Instead of paying me a legal fee, they gave me stock. I paid very little attention to what they were doing.

I will not say that I was used by Lee, my oldest and dearest friend, but I *will* say that Rufus Hollister was a most sinister figure. I am now engaged in investigating, at considerable expense, his business dealing for the past fifteen years, since he came to Washington. It will make unsavory reading, sir, most unsavory."

Elmer Bush nodded. "There is already enough proof at hand to show that Hollister was involved, on his own, in a number of rackets which would completely discredit him."

"While my own record is . . ." An open book, I murmured to myself, "an open book," said Johnson Ledbetter, scowling honestly, "I was used by him. I am being used now by politicians in an effort to discredit not only me but the Party. We will win, though," he added, his voice solemn, like a keynoter at a convention.

"You should've shown more sense," said Verbena sharply. Mrs. Rhodes excused herself aware, doubtless, that her husband's memory might be impugned. It was. "Lee was always getting involved in some get-rich-quick scheme and though he was perfectly honest he couldn't resist a deal, no matter how shady, if it looked like a million dollars might be made. The fact that he never made a cent on these things is proof enough that he was a dupe himself, though he thought he was a financial genius."

"Where did he make that three and a half million he left in his will?" I asked, always practical.

"Inherited," said Verbena crisply.

This was interesting; I wondered why I had never thought before to inquire into the source of the Rhodes fortune. "One thing that puzzles me, though," I said, in a very humble way, "is why, if Senator Rhodes was perfectly innocent in this deal, did he go out of his way to arrange it so that Rufus Hollister would be solely responsible for the company's illegality?"

"How," said Ledbetter, "do we know that Lee did? We have only Hollister's word for it, in that farewell note of his."

"We have also those documents which were sent to me anonymously."

"Had they been executed?"

"No, sir, they had not, but the fact that they had been drawn up indicated that someone expected to use them in case the various deals were ever made public; the papers provided a perfect out for Rhodes." And for you, I added to myself.

"But there is no proof that either Lee or myself drew up those documents, remember that," said Ledbetter, and I saw quite clearly the direction his defense would take.

"By the way," I asked, "what was his attitude the other night when you talked to him, before he died?"

The Senator-Designate was startled.

Verbena snorted angrily. "How did you know Johnson was here?"

"It's no secret, is it?"

"At the moment, yes," said Verbena and she looked like an angry mountain before an eruption.

"You will do me a great favor by saying nothing about that visit in the press, my boy," said Ledbetter with an attempt at good-fellowship.

"I'm sure Pete wouldn't think of it," said Elmer, warningly: reminding me that he was still author of the *Globe's* main feature: "America's New York," and of considerable influence with the editor.

"I have no intention of printing any of this, Senator," I said earnestly. "My only interest was in the murder. Politics is out of my line. I was only curious, that's all. I mean you *were* the last person to see Rufus alive."

"This is, then off the record," said Ledbetter heavily. "Rufus Hollister threatened me, threatened to blackmail me. I told him to do his worst. He said he would, that he would cause a scandal even if it would involve him. I am afraid that we parted enemies, never to meet again in this world." There was a long silence.

I was suddenly weary of the whole business, sleepy, too.

Mrs. Rhodes returned and the company rearranged itself like musical chairs. I refused a drink, was given coffee, but it did not wake me up. Yawning widely behind my hand, I excused myself and went up to bed.

The case was solved and I had the satisfaction not only of having solved it but also of denying myself the glory of announcing my solution to the world, to the accompaniment of fame and glory. I was quite pleased with myself.

When I got to my room, I went straight to the bathroom to brush my teeth. I was so exhausted that I had trouble keeping awake. When I finished I sat down for a moment on the toilet seat to rest. I awoke suddenly to find that my head had fallen with a crack against the washbasin. I had gone to sleep.

Rubbing my eyes, I got to my feet and went into the bedroom. Each step I took fatigued me. I wondered if I might be ill, if I'd caught Camilla Pomeroy's virus. I fell across the bed. I was ill. I tried to sit up but the effort was too great. My hands and feet were ice-cold and I felt chill waves engulf my body.

Clouded as my brain was, on the verge of unconsciousness, I realized that I had been poisoned. I was just able to knock the telephone off its hook before I passed out.

VII

"Is he dead?" asked Lieutenant Winters, his voice coming to me from behind some dark green clouds through which a light shone fitfully.

"Not yet," said a voice and I slipped away, discouraged.

My next attempt at consciousness occurred when a great many yards of tubing were withdrawn from my insides. I opened my eyes, saw a pair of hands above me, felt the tube being withdrawn, felt hideously sick and passed out again. The next day, however, I was sitting up in bed ready to receive callers. My head ached terribly and I was extremely weak. Otherwise my mind, such as it is, was functioning smoothly.

A trained nurse was the first person I saw on my return to the vale of tears. She smiled cheerfully. "They took out two quarts," she said.

I moaned.

"Now it's not as bad as all that."

I said that it was as bad as all that. I asked her what time it was. "Eleven forty-seven. You can have milk toast now if you want it."

I said that it was unlikely I should ever want milk toast at any time; in fact, the whole idea of food, despite the complete vacuum in my stomach, was sickening. I asked if it was day or night.

"Daytime, silly."

"How long have I been unconscious?"

"About ten hours, since last night. You came to once or twice while Doctor was pumping your stomach; you made things very difficult for Doctor."

"For Nurse, too, I'll bet," I said, remembering my hospital-talk from an appendectomy of some years before.

"I'm used to difficult cases," she said with some pride. "We had a very difficult case, Doctor and I, a week ago. It involved a total castration and my gracious . . ."

"Send for Lieutenant Winters," I said weakly, putting a halt to these dreadful reminiscences.

"Well, I'm not sure that . . ."

"I will get up and go to him myself," I said, sitting up with a great effort.

She grew alarmed. "You stay right there, dear, and I'll go get him. Now don't you move." I couldn't have moved if I wanted to.

A moment later she returned with Winters. He looked upset; as well he should have been. He motioned for the angel of mercy to leave the room.

When we were alone, he said, "Why did you do it?"

"Why did I do what?"

"Take all those sleeping tablets. According to the doctor you took over a dozen, of the strongest type. If you hadn't knocked the receiver off the hook and the butler heard the phone ring in the pantry, you would've been dead now which, I suppose, is what you intended to do."

"Winters," I said softly, "when I go you go with me."

He looked alarmed. "What do you mean?"

"Only that I did not take any sleeping tablets, that I was deliberately poisoned."

"Are you sure of this?"

I called him several insulting names. He took them gravely, as though trying to determine whether or not they suited him.

"Who do you think gave them to you, and how?"

"They were given me by the killer you failed to apprehend, and, as for the how, they were slipped rather cleverly into the coffee I drank after dinner. Mrs. Rhodes serves something which tastes not unlike Turkish mud, very expensive and heavy, so heavy that it's impossible to taste whether it's been tampered with or not."

"Why do you think you were poisoned?"

"Because I know who did the murders."

"You do not." Winters sounded suddenly like an angry schoolboy trying to put a braggart in his place.

"I do, too," I said, mocking his tone. He blushed.

"I didn't mean it like that. I just don't see how you happen to know who did the murder from the information available."

"It may be that I have a better mind than yours."

It was his turn to attribute rude characteristics to me. I smiled seraphically all through his insults. When he finished, I suggested that this was hardly the way to speak to a man who has only recently returned from the other side. Then, all passion spent, I spoke to him reasonably. "As soon as I have enough evidence I'll let you know."

"When will that be?"

"Tonight at dinner," I said gaily, not at all sure that I could produce enough evidence but undisturbed by any thought of failure: so great is the love of life. I had recovered; I was not to die just yet. It is a feeling common to soldiers and those who survive operations and accidents of a serious nature.

"I insist you tell me now." Winters became suddenly official.

"Not a chance in the world, friend," I said, pulling myself up in bed. My head still ached but I was no longer dizzy. "Now you tell the doctor to give me a shot of something to put a little life back into me and then, like Dr. Holmes, full of morphine or whatever it was he took, I shall proceed to arrange the evidence in such a manner that not even the police will be confused."

"You're out of your mind."

"Will you do as I tell you?"

"No. If someone did try to kill you, and I have only your word that they did, the police would never allow you to be without protection."

"You may protect me as much as you like."

"Damn it, man, you're withholding evidence from the proper authorities, do you realize that? Will you stop playing detective long enough to allow us to do our job properly?"

I was irritated by this. "If you'd done your job properly Rufus Hollister would not be dead and I would be feeling much more fit than I do. Since you can't be trusted to do it on your own, I prefer to do it myself."

Winters bit his lower lip furiously. It took him a second to regain control of his temper. His voice shook when at last he spoke. "I have my own methods, Sargeant. I know what I'm doing. I was perfectly aware that there was a good chance Hollister had been murdered. But we must be thorough. We can't go off after every harebrained theory which occurs to us, even if it happens to be the right one. We have to build slowly and carefully. It happens that at this moment we are on the verge of some new evidence which may bring us closer to the murderer, assuming Hollister was not a suicide. Amateur help is not much use because amateurs usually end up dead. We were fortunate, I suppose, that we could save *you.*" This was a good point and I softened considerably.

"I am," I said, "very moved by your rhetoric. The fact that you people saved my life is one point in your favor. So we'll make a bargain. I will get up today. I will collect what evidence I need and contrive, if possible, a trap . . . one which will be sprung tonight. I will then, if successful, give Lieutenant Winters full credit for the amazing apprehension of a clever killer. Does that satisfy you?"

It did not satisfy him. We fought for half an hour; finally he agreed, but only after I told him that even if he arrested me I would never reveal what I knew in any way except my own. Reluctantly, he consented. He insisted on following me about all day and I said that he could.

He then called in the nurse who called the doctor who gave me several shots; the nurse then brought me bread and milk which she insisted I eat. Winters excused himself. He would, he said, join me when I was dressed.

"Come on, dear, finish the nice bread." Nurse did everything but stuff the concoction down my throat. I found to my surprise that I liked it, that it restored the lining to my stomach. The return of bulk made me gurgle pleasantly; it was nice to have the body functioning again and my head felt less sore.

"Now, you rest there like a good boy for twenty minutes before you get up. Doctor's orders. Shots must have time to take effect." With that she was gone. As she went out the door, I saw that a plain-clothes man was standing guard over me. I closed my eyes and breathed deeply, preparing myself for the battle ahead. It was going to be a full day.

There was a sudden commotion outside the door and I heard Ellen's clear commanding voice ring out over the gruff tones of the law: "I insist on seeing him. He happens to be my fiancé."

"Let her in!" I shouted; the door was opened and Ellen swept in.

"Bloody oaf," she said, plumping down in the chair beside the bed. Her voice softened. "Poor darling! You tried to kill yourself for love of me, didn't you?"

"I couldn't bear the thought of you and Walter Langdon living together in Garden City with a dog and little ones."

"I should've known that I wasn't the cause of your suicide. I never am. No man ever seems to want to kill himself on my account."

"Someone tried to kill *me*, though, on general principle, I suspect."

Ellen frowned suddenly and looked nervously at the door, as though expecting a gunman to be lurking there. Then: "Rufus was killed, wasn't he?"

I nodded.

"And the same person who killed him killed my father and tried to poison you?" I nodded again. She looked thoughtful. "I figured that out some time ago. I didn't believe the story that you tried to kill yourself."

"Was that what the police said?" I was incredulous.

"Of course . . . they'd hardly admit their case wasn't closed."

I whistled. "Winters is pretty smart. If I had died he would have said I was a suicide and that would've been the end of the case . . . everything would be just ducky."

"They're so corrupt," said Ellen, betraying more feeling for me than I had thought possible.

"I wonder why Winters didn't let me quietly drift off to a better world."

"Because, my darling, I for one raised such a fuss and summoned the doctor. It was completely a matter of self-esteem. I couldn't take the chance of your killing yourself for me (as Verbena Pruitt maintained you had, out of jealousy over Walter) and then having you actually die and there be some doubt. I insisted you be saved so that the world could hear from your own foam-flecked lips that it was because of me you wanted to end it all. How in demand I should've been!" She chuckled; then, seriously, slowly, "Peter, do be careful. Of all my fiancés I am fondest of you, at this moment anyway. For God's sake be careful."

"I will, dear. I have no intention of letting myself get killed."

"You haven't done so well so far," she said. She paused; when finally she spoke, her voice trembled and for the first time since I'd known her she was no longer in control. "I'm terrified," she whispered. "There's something I should've told you when Father was killed. You remember I said then I knew who did it? Well, in a way, I did. When Mother . . ."

But she wasn't allowed to continue. At that moment the door opened and Mrs. Rhodes entered. "Ah, Ellen, I didn't know you were here." She seemed disagreeably surprised. But quickly she became all sympathy, brushing past her daughter to me. "Mr. Sargeant, I do hope you're better; I tried to see you earlier but you were still unconscious."

"It looks as if I'll be all right, Mrs. Rhodes," I said with a gallant smile.

"I'm glad. One more tragedy would have been too horrible to bear."

"It seems," said Ellen, "that he did not kill himself for love of me."

"I never thought he had," said Mrs. Rhodes with a certain sharpness. "Verbena is the romantic one . . ."

"Well, *if* I had tried to kill myself, Mrs. Rhodes, it would have been for your daughter's sake."

"A pretty speech," said Ellen; she looked drawn and tired.

"Are you getting up now?" asked Mrs. Rhodes.

"Yes, I have an appointment downtown. I'll be back in time for dinner; you must be so sick of your boarders by now."

"Not at all. In any event, when you come back from your appointment I should like to talk to you." Over her mother's shoulder Ellen shook her head suddenly, warningly.

I told Mrs. Rhodes that I would be glad to see her later in the afternoon, if we had time. Mother and daughter withdrew.

Carefully I sat up in bed and swung my legs over the edge of the bed. Some fairly discreet fireworks went off in my head. I was weak but not ill. Slowly I dressed. I was tying my tie when Miss Flynn rang me from New York.

Her usual composure had obviously suffered a shock. "You are well?" was her first majestic misuse of an adverb. I told her I had survived, that the report she had read in the newspaper about attempted suicide was not true. I assured her that I would see her the next morning at my office in New York. She was very much relieved. I asked her for news and she told me that all Gotham was Agog at the thought of Hermione's recital. It was generally considered that I had pulled off the public relations stunt of the minute. I told her to contact the editor of the *Globe* and tell him that I should have another article for him on the Rhodes murder case and that, since it would be the eyewitness account of the murderer's arrest, I would expect X number of dollars for this unique bit of coverage. Miss Flynn agreed to Talk Turkey with the *Globe*. "I trust, however, you will be very careful in the course of this most Crucial Day." I said that I would. I then asked her to check, if possible, some records and to call me back at five o'clock. She said that neither rain nor sleet . . . or so many other words, equally prolix . . . would keep her from finding out what I wanted to know.

2

The day went smoothly.

Winters went everywhere I did but, perversely, I kept throwing him off the track, to his fury. He could say nothing, though, for it was part of his official pose that he knew already, on his own, who the murderer was. I am fairly certain that he did not figure it out until the business was finished.

Before I left, I requested that Johnson Ledbetter be asked to dinner that night, *without* Elmer Bush.

On our way downtown, I read the afternoon paper. My attempted suicide appeared on page ten, with very little tie-up to the Rhodes affair. The Ledbetter affair occupied the front page, however. He was quoted at length to the effect he had been smeared by the opposition. There was even an editorial on the subject of morality in politics. Everyone was having a good time with all this and none of the papers seemed aware that either the Governor's fiasco or my own misadventure was in any way connected with the recently "solved" murder. All this was to the good, I thought, with some satisfaction. It would make the beat all the more exciting.

"What's our first stop?" asked Winters.

"Our first stop is the Party Headquarters and the office of one Verbena Pruitt."

"But . . ."

"There will be neither 'buts' nor outcries. You will in fact have to wait outside in the anteroom while I speak to her." There was considerable outcry at this but I won my point.

Verbena's office was large and comfortable. Its position on the second-floor corner, southern exposure, indicated her importance in the Party. I was allowed to come in right away. Winters waited outside in the hall, trying, no doubt, to listen through the door.

"Come sit over here, beside me," boomed the second or third lady of the land from behind a dainty knee-hole desk which looked as if it might crumple at any moment beneath the weight of her huge arms.

I sat down and she swiveled around in her chair and fixed me with her level agate-gaze. "You look green," she said at last.

"I don't feel so good," I admitted.

"Love!" she snorted. "Root of all evil if you ask me . . . *money* certainly isn't. I'm all for money . . . it's pure; it's useful; you can measure it . . . or at least you could before they started monkeying with the gold standard."

"I didn't kill myself for love, Miss Pruitt."

She brightened. "Money worries? Career on the downgrade?"

"Just the opposite. I was doing too well and someone decided to kill me."

"You're a very daring young man," said Miss Pruitt enigmatically.

"I suppose so. I wish you'd help me, though. There's a lot at stake."

She smiled. "How do you know that *I* may not be 'at stake'?"

"I'm fairly sure. I don't know everything of course; that's why I want you to help me."

To my surprise she said nothing to show that she was surprised by this turn of affairs, that the murderer of Lee Rhodes was still free and dangerous. Instead she said: "Ask me what you like and I'll answer what I like."

"How long did you know Lee Rhodes?"

"Twenty-five years or so."

"Were you in love with him?"

This was daring. She sat back in her swivel chair; I was afraid that it might give way under her, tipping the great lady on her head, but she knew what she was doing. "You're awfully fresh, young man," she said.

"I was curious."

"Then to satisfy your curiosity, yes, we were very close at one time. Shortly after Ellen was born, Lee wanted to divorce Grace and marry me. I may say with some pride that I talked him out of it. We were fond of each other but I was almost as fond of Grace. I didn't want to wreck her life; though, since, I've sometimes wondered if it was the right thing."

"You mean not separating them?"

She nodded, her eyes focused on the far wall, her voice dreamy. "They never got on of course. Grace would've been so much happier with another man, I'm sure of that, but the opportunity never arose again and they settled down with one another, neither contented."

"You went on seeing a great deal of both?"

"Oh yes. I saw them through a hundred crises. When Ellen was supposed to marry that nephew of mine, it was I she came to after her father annulled the marriage. I was the one who reconciled them . . . though not for long since she went away as soon as she was of age. I practically brought her up. They were the most helpless family you ever saw when it came to managing their private affairs."

"Mrs. Rhodes disliked Camilla, didn't she?"

"Not really. She hated the *idea* of her, naturally, when she found out. Grace is a woman of high principles, you know, and it was a devastating blow for her, finding out Lee had had a by-blow, as they say back home. I think she was quite indifferent to Camilla one way or the other, as a person."

"You obtained the contract for Roger Pomeroy before he came to Washington, didn't you?"

She looked startled. "You're very well informed," she said coldly. "Yes, as a matter of fact I did."

"You must've known all along that he had a pretty good alibi in case of arrest."

"I did. As a matter of fact Grace and Ellen and I discussed the whole thing the morning of the day Pomeroy was to be arrested. I had discovered that that young fool of a policeman was going to arrest Roger and I talked it over with the family: should I or should I not let the police know that I had helped Roger get his contract before he came to see Lee. Roger himself begged me not to. I must say I didn't want to: I would've found myself in a very uncomfortable position. On the other hand, we didn't want Roger arrested. I will tell you, frankly, that none of us knew what to do until Rufus saw fit to kill himself and Roger was released, ending, I may add, one of the worst days of my life."

"Do you think Rufus killed himself?"

"You should know," she said, slowly, looking at me speculatively.

"*I* should know."

"Did you take sleeping pills?"

"Certainly not."

"Then it would seem Rufus was killed, and the confession was a fake."

"That's how I see it."

"Why would the murderer want to kill you, though?"

"Because I knew everything. I've been poking around, you know, out of curiosity; while nosing about I figured out who did it."

Verbena Pruitt's face was a mask: a vast roseate larger-than-life-size mask. "I can see then why you were poisoned. Now I will give you some advice: leave Washington. I can promise you that the police will forget the whole thing. There will be no more trouble for any of us. The dead are dead and can't be recalled. The rest of us are well out of it. *You* get out of it, too."

"No."

She was suddenly angry. "What then *do* you want? What's your price?" This was ugly indeed.

"I'm not for sale," I said, becoming indignant although my sense of reality didn't entirely desert me even in this heroic moment. "At least, not now, to you. I'll tell you one thing, though. I was ready to drop the whole thing last night. I decided it was, as you say, none of my business. I didn't want to upset everyone again. I saw no reason to interfere in an affair which did not, really, concern me at all. But then the murderer tried to kill me and that, for reasons which will become more apparent, was more than I could take. I now intend to turn the killer over to the police."

"When?"

"Tonight."

There was nothing more to say; we were through with one another. I had learned what I needed to know already, earlier in the conversation, and so, very politely, I excused myself and left her office. She did not speak.

"Well?" said Winters, joining me in the corridor.

"Well, yourself, my fine minion of the law."

"Don't be cute."

"It's my nature," I said, feeling blithe.

In the entrance hall we ran into Johnson Ledbetter. He looked more than ever like an harassed buffalo at the end of the trail. He greeted me with hollow vigor. I detached myself from Winters and moved off into a corner with him. Politicos wandering in and out of headquarters quickly averted their gaze when they saw him: he was a fallen star and no one wanted to catch the infection of failure which, as all professionals know, is remarkably contagious.

"We'll be seeing you tonight, won't we, Senator?"

"Yes, of course I'll be there. What's going to happen?"

"We're going to unveil the murderer of Rufus Hollister and Leander Rhodes."

Ledbetter's gray face looked set. "I hope you know what you're doing."

"I do. There's one thing I would like to know, if I may: what *did* happen when you talked to Rufus, before he was shot?"

"That's private."

"You will be forced to tell it to the court, Senator." I was reckless.

"I don't see that it has any bearing on the murders," he said weakly.

"I'm sure Winters can keep you off the witness stand if we know just what happened." I was quite willing to commit Winters to anything at this point.

"We discussed the business of the two companies, all of which you have no doubt read about in the papers."

"What did he have to say?"

"He said we were in danger of being exposed, that a Federal Commission was ready to publish its findings and begin legal proceedings. I said that I, of course, had no connection with any of this, even though my name appeared as a director and there was some stock issued in my name."

"Did Hollister say anything about being exposed?"

"That's all he talked about."

"I mean being exposed by some malicious party, by the murderer?"

Ledbetter paused for one long moment; then he shook his head. "No, he didn't mention anything like that."

"Why did you quarrel?"

"Because he wanted me to accept equal blame with him; since I was not guilty I saw no reason to associate myself with him." This canard was uttered with pious sincerity. "He thought I could get the Party to hush the whole thing up, or at least blame it on Lee. Unfortunately, I couldn't." Ledbetter betrayed himself in a most un-lawyerlike fashion; I wondered how on earth a man of his limited intelligence had managed to become the Governor of a state.

"What time did you go upstairs to talk to him?"

"About eleven-thirty."

"How long were you there?"

"Twenty minutes, I should say."

"Did he act as though he had another appointment?"

Ledbetter's eyes grew wide. "How did you know? Yes, as a matter of fact he did say he was to meet someone at twelve."

"In his room or somewhere else?"

"I assumed some other place since only Verbena, Grace and I were in the house."

"Did you notice anything unusual on your way downstairs?"

He shook his head thoughtfully. "No, I was too angry to pay much attention. It is not a pleasant thing, young man, for a political figure to have his honor impugned and his integrity questioned. I may add that it looks as if I shall soon be vindicated. The Senate committee has already informed me, unofficially, that according to the documentation sent you by the unknown party, I was, along with Lee, the innocent dupe of Rufus Hollister."

"Isn't the committee at all interested in discovering who sent me those papers?"

"I don't think the question arose." I trembled for the safety of our country: these were the elders who framed our laws!

"Have you ever wondered who might have sent me those very convenient documents?"

"I'm afraid I've been much too busy to give the matter much thought."

"Well, it was obviously someone who had your interest at heart, as well as a considerable stake in the business of the murders."

"I always assumed that it was sent by a well-wisher who wanted to see justice done."

"A well-wisher who had access to Senator Rhodes' library, who knew where the papers were hidden, who implicated Rufus Hollister, who murdered Rufus Hollister, who mailed the papers to me in a very whimsical fashion, a well-wisher who . . ."

Ledbetter frowned menacingly, "Leave her out of this, hear me? If you drag her into this I'll . . ." But there was no reason to continue our talk and so I excused myself and joined Winters at the door.

"What in the name of God did you tell him? He looked like he was going to kill you."

"Everyone wants to kill me today," I said, not inaccurately.

"You can say that again," muttered Winters as we walked out into the bright winter noon.

I had one more errand to do, one which particularly mystified Winters; then we drove back to the house.

No one was in sight when we got there and I was suddenly afraid that the whole lot had fled; the presence of four detectives in gray business suits reassured me; the situation was under control.

Winters and I sat in the drawing room drinking martinis; at least I drank several and he tasted one. I found I was still groggy from the sleeping pills and needed the stimulant or depressant of alcohol, whichever it is. I also needed a bit of courage for the evening ahead. I was like an actor preparing for a crucial first night. I couldn't afford to muff a line.

We chatted about one thing and the other, both growing more excited by the minute . . . he against his will, too, since he disapproved of what I was doing and would have, if it had been possible, stopped me right then and there and concluded the case on his own more pedestrian lines.

At five o'clock Miss Flynn called with the information I had requested. I thanked her profusely; she had, in that inexorable way of hers, found out more than I should have thought possible. "Nevertheless, Mr. Sargeant, bearing in mind these Revelations, I would conduct myself with Extreme Caution." I assured her that I would.

"All the evidence is now at hand, buddy," I said, patting Winters on the back, feeling very content and a little drunk.

"It had better be," said the policeman solemnly, eating the onion which I had put in his martini.

3

There was no doubt in anyone's mind that evening that something extraordinary was going to happen.

Everyone was studiedly casual at table. Ledbetter told a few old-time political stories and there was a great deal of merry laughter. I sat next to Walter Langdon and we discussed politics and journalism.

"The theme of the demagogue," I said, weightily, "seems particularly fascinating to American writers. I suppose because we have so few of them in this country."

"You mean so few *effective* ones." Of them all, Langdon was perhaps the most relaxed, in appearance.

"Well, yes. The great modern example was Huey Long. I suspect a hundred novels and plays will be written about him before the century's over."

"Penn Warren did a pretty thorough job," said Langdon.

"I always liked the book Dos Passos wrote better. You remember? It was called *Number One.*"

Langdon nodded. "I read it. I think I've read everything about Long ever written."

"I've been told he had a good chance of becoming President."

"A lot of people thought it might happen, God help us. Fortunately God did and he was assassinated."

" 'Killed in the shell,' as it were."

Langdon looked startled; he smiled. "Yes, that's one way of putting it."

"Your way, or rather Shakespeare's."

"The theme of my piece for the *Advanceguard,* too."

"I thought you were going to show it to me."

"You can see it any time you like. I'm taking it back with me tomorrow. I got it all done, first draft, that is . . . thanks to your typewriter paper."

"Think nothing of it. Is it thus always with tyrants?"

"Not always . . . if only it were."

"We should have a much better world, I suspect."

Langdon nodded, his eyes suddenly bright. "If only people would act in time they could save the world so much pain. But they're weak, afraid to take the life of one man for fear of losing their own."

"But you would risk yours, wouldn't you?"

"Oh yes," said Langdon quietly, "I would."

When dinner was over we went into the drawing room, as was the custom of the house, for coffee. Winters kept trying to catch my eye for some sign but I gave him none. I was in no hurry. Timing was important at this stage.

I was standing off at one end of the room observing the dinner guests and witness-to-be when Roger Pomeroy came over and said, "I'm afraid I was very indiscreet the other night . . . must've been tight . . . didn't realize I'd told you all I had."

"It's perfectly all right," I said.

"Do wish you would keep what I said in strictest confidence, no matter what happens. Verbena was furious with me for telling you about that contract she arranged. She's afraid you're going to write it up in the papers."

"Not a chance," I said amiably. "I don't even think it'll come out at the trial."

"Trial?"

"Tell her I'm not really a newspaperman, that I'm not down here to try and ferret out scandals for the delight of the people. All I'm interested in is the murders."

"Oh." Pomeroy looked at me blankly. "Well, don't get me in Dutch with her, will you? That contract could be misunderstood, you know. Perfectly legal and all that but you know what a stink those people like Pearson make when they find out that a friend has done another friend a good turn, all perfectly on the up and up."

I allowed that I knew just how it was. I could see he was uneasy but I gave him no more assurances. Then I strolled over to Mrs. Rhodes. She was sitting by the silver coffeepot, pouring, as she had done the night before and every night, doubtless, for many years. I sat down beside her.

"It is very hard," I said.

She looked away, her face set. "Will you have more coffee?" she asked mechanically.

"No thank you." The thought of coffee made me ill. I had tasted it all day: the result of that stomach pump.

"You are going to go through with this?" She did not look at me as she spoke; her hand toyed with the silver sugar tongs.

"I must."

Before she could speak, Camilla Pomeroy was upon us. "I couldn't've been more horrified!" she said, her eyes wide. "I just found out from Mr. Winters what really happened . . . and with *my* sleeping pills, too, or rather Roger's only we keep them in my vanity case. Someone came in yesterday and took the whole bottle. They must've emptied it all in your cup last night. Though how, I don't know, since Mrs. Rhodes was the one who poured." Then, as though alarmed at the implications of what she had said, she began to talk very fast. "Thank heavens, though, you're all right today. A third tragedy would have been more than flesh could bear."

"Well, I have a strong stomach."

"You must have. Of course I've always hated the idea of having sleeping pills around, especially those strong ones Roger takes. They could knock out an elephant in no time at all. I think they're an absolute menace."

"A menace," repeated Mrs. Rhodes absently.

Across the room Ellen signaled to me. I excused myself and joined her at the backgammon table.

"Are you really going to be a sleuth?" she asked, setting up the board.

"I suppose so."

"What fun! You take the greens; I'll take the whites."

"For chastity?"

"Don't be rude." We set up our board. I watched Mrs. Rhodes across the room; she seemed distracted. Her hands nervously touched objects: silver, china, the jewels at her throat, as though she were trying to satisfy herself that the world was real, that this was not all a dream.

Langdon sat talking quietly to Ledbetter, discussing politics, no doubt. Every now and then Langdon looked over at us, at me; if he was anxious he did not betray it. Verbena Pruitt sat like a colossus between the Pomeroys who chattered loudly across her, talking of Talisman City. She ignored them, as though they were chattering birds come to rest upon her monumental self. Her eyes had a vacant, faraway look. Soon. Soon. Soon.

Ellen was off to a good start with double sixes.

We played in silence for several minutes. I watched the room, aware that Winters had a man at each door and another out on the street by the windows. Winters himself pretended to read a magazine.

"Well, it'll soon be over," said Ellen, shaking her dice.

"Will you be glad?"

"Lord yes! Though I've missed Bess Pringle's party because of your silly sleeping pills."

"Bess Pringle gives a lot of parties."

"I know but I wanted particularly to go to this one."

I picked up one of her men. She swore softly. She rolled but couldn't come in. "Peter dear, who did it? Tell me. I'm dying to know."

"You did, my love."

She rolled her dice and came in on a four and picked up my man. Her face had not changed expression. "What a horrid thing to say, even as a joke."

"What a horrid thing to do, even as a joke. It's all right with me if you want to kill your father and Rufus but I think it ever so unfriendly to try and knock off your fiancé. It shows a lack of sensitivity."

Ellen smiled, her old dazzling smile. "You're going to have a hard time proving it, my lamb," she said, her voice pitched so that only I could hear.

"It's already proven. I spent the day getting evidence."

"And?"

All my men were in homeplace; I began to take them off. "When you were a small and wicked girl you were engaged to be married to Verbena's nephew. At the last minute that passion of yours for forbidden vice made you run off with a gymnast. Your father caught you and brought you back home. He had the marriage annulled and you hated him for it. When you were old enough, you left home for good."

"Ancient history," said Ellen, unperturbed.

"Ancient, yes, but we must construct a motive carefully. There is a great deal of proof that you hated your father for other reasons; this particular interference is good enough for a start. About a year ago he tried to get you to go into a sanitarium for observation. When you refused, he reduced your allowance; he also threatened to have you committed. You came down here a month ago to talk to him about it. While you were here you learned, probably by accident, about his business dealings with Hollister. The first thought which went through your head was to blackmail your father into giving you more money. It is possible that you *did* get something out of him . . . we'll find that out by checking your bank. In any case, you were aware of the papers that he had drawn up, implicating Rufus in the company scandal and clearing himself . . ."

"There's an awful lot of guesswork in this," said Ellen.

"There has to be when it comes to a complicated motive. Fortunately, there is no guesswork in what happened afterwards. On the spur of the moment you came to Washington, full of a desperate plan. I'm sure that you didn't arrive with any intention of killing your father: talk, however, of the new Pomeroy explosive did the trick. It looked like a perfect setup: your father is killed and his enemy Pomeroy is suspected, all very convenient.

"The first part worked beautifully but then the complications began, proving no doubt that murders should not be committed on such short notice. Verbena Pruitt told you and your mother that Pomeroy had a perfect alibi, that he could be proven motiveless at a moment's notice. So you had to act quickly. Rufus Hollister seemed like the next best possibility. You had access to the papers which implicated him in the business tangle; all you had to do was, strategically and while the heat was still on Pomeroy, direct suspicion toward Rufus . . . and it was here that your troubles really began. In the last few hours I have tried to figure how you might have done it differently; you will be pleased to know that your method was about the best I could think of, though of course it wasn't good enough."

"I think I'd like a drink," she said, thoughtfully, rolling two and one.

"Later. You wrote me a very whimsical note which, if I'd been quicker, I should have spotted as being vintage Ellen. You directed my attention to Rufus Hollister, knowing that I would follow the lead, that I would also pass it on to the police. You were also in possession of the papers, having the night before assaulted a plain-clothes man, looted the library and sent me, on the return visit to your room, hurtling through space, a bit of predatory behavior I find in the worst taste."

"I'll have Scotch," said Ellen.

"You are deliberately trying to diminish my one great moment," I said irritably.

"Well, if this proves to be your one great moment all I can say is . . ."

"Shut up. You went, the night before I got the letter, to the study and took down a copy of the *Congressional Record* in which you, or perhaps your father in your presence, had hidden documents which, if certain affairs came to light, would be executed, absolving the Senator of guilt. You then made a mistake. You left the copy of the *Record* in your bedroom where I saw it and, though I must admit I didn't quite get the point the first time I saw it, I realized later that it could only have come from your father's study and since you had not the faintest interest in politics and since all the papers had been cleared out of the study, this volume must, in some way then, be connected with the Hollister papers."

She grunted; she kept on playing, though, rolling the dice and moving her men mechanically. I continued to take mine off as I talked.

"So, then, you had the papers and suspicion was cast, rather cleverly, on Rufus even before the Pomeroy alibi was known to either me or the police. I suggest if you had left it at that, you might have got off. I suppose you lost your head. The case against Pomeroy was due to fall apart any minute. Even though you had cast suspicion on Hollister, you weren't satisfied that that would be enough. So, instead of letting me chase the papers you sent the papers to chase me . . . and, incidentally, it was that phrase which first set me moving in the right direction. Do you know why?"

"No, and I don't want to hear."

"I shall tell you anyway," I said serenely. "Your mother, by accident, used it to me a few minutes after I had got the letter, making me think *she* had written the letter. Later, when I was fairly sure she had not written it, it occurred to me in a flash of purest inspiration that a paper chase was an old children's game which she had doubtless played and which she had taught her daughter. In other words, it was a family reference so immediate as to be common to you both."

"Oh, for Christ's sake!" she exploded scornfully. "I can't bear this on an empty stomach. Get me a drink or I'll get it myself."

"Not yet. But that will not be a part of the case . . . I just thought you might be interested in how a superior mind can proceed through semantic association to a correct deduction." I paused for some outcry but she went on playing, scornfully. "Now the plot moves quickly. You decide Hollister must commit suicide. You toy with the idea of forcing him into it by threatening him with exposure. But this won't work. You telephone him at the office while I am there and make a date to meet at midnight, in his room, implying no doubt that you have the papers, knowing he is terrified they may fall into the hands of the police. You keep that date collecting en route your mother's pistol you used to play with as a girl, shooting targets in the backyard."

"I thought we were all at the Chevy Chase Club that night?"

"All but you; from eleven-thirty to twelve-thirty you were occupied not with that muscular Marine officer but with the murder of Rufus Hollister. You took a taxi home. You slipped in that unguarded side entrance which you unwisely told me about later. You waited, no doubt in the hall, until Ledbetter stormed out of Hollister's room and then you marched in, shot him with that remarkably quiet pistol, typed a confession at great speed, left the house by the same way you entered, hailed a cab and rejoined Langdon at the Club. Total time elapsed: one hour."

"Very fanciful."

"This afternoon I paid a visit to the taxicab company where, I am happy to say, you were identified after three hours of rather discouraging confusion."

Only a sharp intake of breath indicated I had scored at last.

"Yesterday, when I had my talk with Mrs. Rhodes and announced (inaccurately you will be sad to hear) that I knew who the murderer was, you were listening in the hall. In that direct way of yours you determined that *my* suicide was definitely in order, the sooner the better."

"Prove I was in the hall."

"Just a bit of circumstantial evidence. I heard someone run up the stairs. A few minutes later I went up myself; I got a strong whiff of your perfume."

She chuckled softly. "Sherlock Holmes by a nose. I'd like to hear *that* in a court."

"You won't, though you'll hear other things. I am merely trying to give you an intimate view of the way my mind works. You will have to listen to so much dull evidence that I thought I would treat you to those fine little points . . ."

She told me what I could do with those fine little points as I rolled doubles and took my last three men off the board. The game was over.

"Fortunately, you will not be executed, for which I am thankful despite the heartless way you tried to murder me. You will be removed to a private institution where you will spend the remainder of your life weaving baskets and causing no end of trouble for the other inmates."

"What do you mean?" Her lips had tightened in a thin red line; her eyes were large and dangerously bright.

"I mean, Ellen, that after the court consults with that middle-aged analyst of yours, Dr. Breitbach, whom you only partly conquered, you will be declared criminally insane, which you are, and committed for the rest of your unnatural days."

"You son of a bitch," said Ellen Rhodes, throwing her dice in my face.

4

The story was all mine and I made the most of it.

The Pomeroys returned to Talisman City, and, I assume, barring an occasional excursion on Camilla's part into extramarital situations, lived a contented and exemplary life, manufacturing munitions.

Verbena Pruitt, untouched by scandal, proceeded to deliver the women's vote to a successful candidate for President for which she was rewarded with the Bureau of Fisheries and a private car and chauffeur.

Johnson Ledbetter was allowed to take his seat in the Senate though everyone deplored the necessity of seating him for several days. But now his pronouncements on the economic structure of the nation are taken with great seriousness; he is already on the Committee of Spoils and Patronage. His nephew is employed as his private secretary while his niece draws a considerable salary as a typist in his office, a task for which she has demonstrated a remarkable skill since she lives in Talisman City, her salary being collected *in absentia* by the Senator.

Mrs. Rhodes conducted herself with great dignity during the trial, which was mercifully short. No family skeletons were rattled in public and the court speedily brought in a decision that the defendant was indeed paranoiac, placing her for life in a shady institution in Maryland where she would receive the best of care.

I did not appear in court. My testimony was handled by the prosecutor and though I should have liked the glory it was wisest, all things considered, to let it fall upon the sturdy shoulders of Lieutenant Winters whose photograph appeared in the papers many times during the week, giving him an illusion of celebrity which the passage of time, I knew, would dispel. He had had his moment, though.

I had mine when the *Globe* hit the street the following afternoon with the exclusive story. We had beaten every paper in town and my intimate descriptions of the murderess at bay were very fine. The sort of thing which ordinarily would have broken Ellen up with laughter.

Walter Langdon and I went back on the train to New York together and he allowed me to read the first draft of his study in political murder. I thought it very fine and suggested he make an epic poem of it. He did not take this kindly, but I was quite serious: there hasn't been a decent narrative poet since Byron.

I had moments of remorse when I thought of Ellen in that insane asylum. It had been, after all, no business of mine. I would have dropped the whole thing if she hadn't tried to kill me which, I thought, had been carrying her role as the Lucrezia Borgia of Massachusetts Avenue too far. We had been, after all, fond of each other.

Two weeks later, just before the poodle's recital at Town Hall, I met Mrs. Goldmountain backstage. It was the first time I had seen her since Washington, since the trial.

She rushed up to me. She was magnificently dressed, with a diamond butterfly in her hair and gold dust sprinkled over her eyelids.

"I couldn't be more nervous!" she said, clutching my hands.

"There's no cause for alarm," I said calmly. "We've got the whole show under control. I've been in consultation with Heigh-Ho all week. We have television cameras in the lobby to televise the celebrities, *Look* to take photographs, and all the news services are represented; nothing can go wrong."

"I hope not. Hermione had been practicing like mad these last two weeks. Oh, we *can't* let her down."

She twisted a bit of black lace nervously between her fingers. "Alma Edderdale is here and I asked Margaret Truman especially to come. There's to be a whole trainload of Washington people." Photographers, newsmen, officials of Heigh-Ho pushed by us. There was a great racket. From where we stood in the wings we could see the stage and part of the house: it was nearly filled already.

"Oh, by the way, how clever you were about the Ellen Rhodes thing. Who would have thought it? And according to everyone *you* worked it all out."

"Just luck," I said, quietly.

"I'm sure it was more than that. You know I went over to Maryland to see her yesterday."

"Who? Ellen?"

"Certainly. I was always very fond of her. I thought I'd go and console her . . . nasty girl."

"What did she do?"

"Do! She barked at me and pretended she was a dog!" Ellen Victrix, I thought . . . the ending was not so unhappy after all. I pitied the younger doctors.

But then Hermione, wearing a black velvet bow decorated with seed pearls, was led past us. Mrs. Goldmountain gave her a parting hug.

There was loud applause when she appeared on stage with her accompanist.

A moment later the piano broke into one of the very grandest arias from *Norma* and Hermione's voice, unearthly and loud, floated in the air.

Her subsequent stardom in nine movies is known to all; after the ninth she lost her voice and was forced to make personal appearances until the grim reaper laid her low. Her Town Hall debut was a public relations success though artistically her press was mixed. Virgil Thomson in the *Herald Tribune* summed up the general view when he said that her voice was a small one and not well trained; nevertheless, despite her unreadiness, he found her stage presence utterly beguiling and her graciousness, especially during the curtain calls, remarkable.

DEATH LIKES IT HOT

I

The death of Peaches Sandoe, the midget, at the hands, or rather feet, of a maddened elephant in the sideshow of the circus at Madison Square Garden was at first thought to be an accident, the sort of tragedy you're bound to run into from time to time if you run a circus with both elephants and midgets in it. A few days later, though, there was talk of foul play.

I read with a good deal of interest the *Daily News'* account. A threatening conversation had been overheard; someone (unrevealed) had gone to the police with a startling story (unrevealed) and an accusation against an unnamed party. It was very peculiar.

Miss Flynn, my conscience and secretary, elderly, firm, intolerant, ruthless but pleasingly gray, looked over my shoulder as was her wont. "You will not, I presume—"

"Get involved in this grisly affair? No. Or at least not until I'm asked which is unlikely since the circus has its own public relations setup . . ."

"It's possible that some member of the circus, however, knowing your propensity for Shady Personages and Crime, might engage your services . . ."

"They'll have to catch me first. Miss Flynn, I'm gone." I stood up abruptly; she looked bewildered . . . wondering if perhaps I had gone over to the world of bebop: Miss Flynn is a student of argot, though her own conversation is very courtly—cool, in fact.

"I'm gone for a week," I explained.

She nodded, understanding at last. "You'll accept Mrs. Veering's invitation to partake of the sun at her palatial estate on Long Island?"

"Just this moment decided. No reason to hang around here. August is a dead month. We haven't any business you can't handle better than I." She inclined her head in agreement. "So I'll go out to East Hampton and see what it is she wants me to do."

"Social Position has never been Mrs. Veering's aim." Miss Flynn is a resolute snob and follows with a grim fascination Cholly Knickerbocker's rich accounts of the rich.

"Well, she won't be the first dowager we put over on an unsuspecting public."

Miss Flynn scowled. Next to my affinity for Shady Personages and Crime she dislikes nearly all the clients of my public relations firm: ambitious, well-heeled characters trying to exploit products or themselves in the press. With the exception of a singing dog who lost her voice, my record has been pretty good in this crooked profession. Recently business had slowed down. In August, New York dies and everybody tries to get out of the heat. Mrs. Veering's mysterious summons had come at exactly the right time.

"Alma Edderdale, I know, is a friend of yours . . . and a dear friend of mine . . . it was at the advice of a friend of hers that I got your name. I do wish you could come and see me here Friday to spend the weekend and talk over with me a little project close to my heart. Let me know soon. Trusting you won't let me down, I am, sincerely yours, Rose Clayton Veering." That was the message on thick expensive note paper with the discreet legend at the top: "The North Dunes, East Hampton, Long Island, N.Y." No hint of what she wanted. My first impulse had been to write and tell her that I'd have to have a clear idea before I came of what she wanted. But the heat of August relaxed my professionalism. A weekend in East Hampton in a big house . . .

I dictated an acceptance telegram to Miss Flynn, who snorted from time to time but otherwise said nothing.

I then fired a number of instructions in my best business-executive voice, knowing that in my absence Miss Flynn would do exactly as she pleased, anyway. Then we gravely shook hands and I left the office: two small rooms with two desks and a filing cabinet in East Fifty-fifth Street (good address, small office, high rent) and headed down Park Avenue through the sullen heat to my apartment on Forty-ninth Street (big rooms, bad address, low rent).

2

The Long Island Cannon Ball Express pulled away from the station and there was every indication that it would be able to make Montauk before nightfall; if not . . . well, those who travel that railroad are living dangerously and they know it. Cinders blew in my face from an open window. The seat sharply cut off the circulation in my legs. The hot sun shone brazenly in my face . . . it was like the days of my childhood fifteen years (well, maybe twenty years) before, when I used to visit relatives in Southampton. Everything had changed since then except the Long Island Railroad and the Atlantic Ocean.

The *Journal American* was full of the Peaches Sandoe murder case, even though there were no facts out of which to make a story. This doesn't bother newspapers, however, and there were some fine pictures of naked girls wearing sequins and plumes. Peaches Sandoe herself was, in life, a rather dowdy-looking, middle-aged midget with a 1920s bob.

I was well into the *New York Globe*'s account, written by my old friend and rival Elmer Bush, when a fragrant thigh struck mine and a soft female voice said, "Excuse me . . . why, if it isn't Peter Sargeant!"

"Liz Bessemer!" We stared at one another in amazement, though why either should have been particularly surprised I don't know since we see each other at least once a month at one party or another and I have, on several occasions, tried to get a date out of her without success since I'm shy and she is usually engaged to some young blade around town. Though it was perfectly logical that we both find ourselves on a Friday heading for a weekend on Long Island by Cannon Ball Express, we professed amazement at seeing each other.

Amazement turned to excitement, at least on my part, when I found she was visiting an aunt and uncle in East Hampton. "I just had to get out of the city and since Mummy is out in Las Vegas getting a divorce" (Liz, though a big girl of twenty-five with blue eyes and dark-brown hair and a figure shaped like a Maidenform Bra ad, still refers to her progenitress as "Mummy," which is significant, I think), "and I wasn't invited any place this weekend, I just thought I'd go out and stay with my aunt who's been after me all summer to visit her. So you're going to be there too?'

I nodded and we kicked that ball around a bit. She knew of Mrs. Veering, even knew her place which, it seemed, was about half a mile down the road from where *she* would be staying. I experienced lust, mild but persistent. Mentally, I caressed the generous arm of coincidence.

"I hope you're not a friend of Mrs. Veering's . . . I mean, she's perfectly nice but, well, you know . . ."

"Kind of on the make?"

"That's putting it gently." Liz made a face; I noticed she was wearing nothing under her simple worth-its-weight-in-gold cotton dress; absolutely nothing, at least from the waist up. I felt very good about this for some reason and decided Christian Dior was a regular fellow, after all.

"Well, it's only a job," I said vaguely, as we rattled desperately through Jamaica. "She got some project or other she wants me to look into for her. So, what the hell . . . it's a living and I get out of town for the week-end . . . maybe longer," I added softly, but Liz, according to legend at least, is the least romantic girl in New York, and though she's gone around with some sharp boys in her time and no doubt given them a certain satisfaction, she has never been the type to hold hands in the moonlight or exchange radiant myopic glances across crowded rooms. She's very matter-of-fact, which I like, in spite of the "Mummy" business.

"That's right." She looked at me coolly, at least as coolly as it's possible to look with the cinders flying about your head and the heat one hundred degrees Fahrenheit in the car. "You have your own firm, don't you?"

I nodded. "Ever since I left the *Globe*."

"It must be awfully interesting," she said in the vague tone of Bryn Mawr. "I'm at *Harper's Bazaar* now."

I said I didn't know she worked.

"Oh yes . . . every now and then."

"What do you do there?"

"Oh . . . well, you know: that sort of thing."

I knew indeed. All New York is the richer for these vague elegant girls with some money, a set of Tecla pearls and a number of basic black dresses who, while marking time between college and their first marriage, work for the fashion magazines. They are charming and they love art like nobody's business . . . zooming around the galleries on Fifty-seventh Street to look at pictures and around Second Avenue to various "fun apartments" where High Bohemia gives cocktail parties for Edith Sitwell and worries about Marlon Brando.

Liz was a member in good standing of this community, but she was also careful not to get typed: she was not one of the fashionable *ugly* girls who end up making a career out of that kind of thing; she kept the lines of communication open with the young Wall Street set, the Newport gang, the Palm Beach crew and even the night club bachelors who think that Fifty-seventh Street is just something you pass on your way from the Plaza to the St. Regis.

We talked about mutual acquaintances. I haven't the time to circulate much in her world, but I know it well enough since it's made up of old school friends of mine as well as those professional zombies that you're bound to meet sooner or later if you live in New York and go out at all.

It wasn't until we had stopped for water, or whatever it is the train stops for besides passengers at Speonk, that I asked her what she knew about Mrs. Veering.

"I don't think I know anything about her except what everybody does. You see her around, that's all. She comes from somewhere out West and she has a lot of money from a husband who's dead, I guess. I suppose she's out to make the grade as a dowager."

This was as much as *I* knew about my hostess-to-be, so we talked of other things, agreeing to meet Saturday night at the Ladyrock Yacht Club, where a big dance was being held. It was assumed I'd come as the guest of Mrs. Veering, but just in case she didn't go, I said I'd sneak over somehow. Liz thought this was a fine idea.

Then we read our tabloids while the train passed millions of white ducks and potatoes, the principal crop of this green island.

Shortly before we arrived at East Hampton, we both agreed that someone had undoubtedly pushed Peaches Sandoe in the way of that elephant. But who?

3

The North Dunes is a large gray clapboard house sitting high on a dune to the north of the Ladyrock Yacht Club which, in turn, is north of the village.

I was met by a slovenly fellow in a chauffeur's hat and overalls who spotted me right off and said Mrs. Veering had sent him to fetch me. I climbed in the station wagon, which was parked with all the others beside the railroad, waved to Liz, who was getting into a similar station wagon, and sat back as I was driven in silence through the handsome village with its huge elm trees and silver pond and the house where somebody did not write *Home Sweet Home,* but was perhaps thinking about it when he did write the song.

On the oceanfront, one vast gloomy house after another sat among the treeless dunes where clumps of sword grass waved, dark upon the white sand. The lush green-gold course of the Maidstone provided a neat, well-ordered touch to the road which runs north of the village toward Montauk Point, a road off which, to left and right at this point, are the big houses and the cottages of the summer residents.

The North Dunes was one of the largest and gloomiest. A screened-in porch ran halfway round the house on the oceanside and, from the outside, the place looked like nothing so much as a palace of bleached driftwood.

Inside it was better.

A lean butler took my suitcase and showed me into the sunroom: a big chintzy place on the south side of the house with a fine view of the golf course and ocean; high trees screened the village from view.

Mrs. Veering greeted me, rising from the chair where she'd been seated beside the empty fireplace.

"I couldn't be more delighted, Mr. Sargeant, to have you here on such short notice." She shook my hand warmly; she was a big competent woman with a mass of blue hair and a pale skin from which two small blue eyes stared at the world expressionlessly. She was in her fifties, with a bosom like a sandbag and a clear voice which was neither Western nor Colony Restaurant–New York, but something in between. "Come sit over here and have a little drink. I'll ring for . . . unless you'd rather mix your own . . . it's over there. I'll have a dash of Dubonnet. I never have anything else; just a bit before dinner is nice, don't you think?"

She gabbled away and I made all the expected answers as I mixed myself a Scotch and soda and poured her some Dubonnet over ice. Then I sat down in the fat chair opposite her and waited.

Mrs. Veering was in no hurry to get to the point.

"Alma Edderdale is coming next week, Monday, did you know that? I love her. She's staying at the Sea Spray . . . she's an old friend of yours, isn't she? Yes? I'll want to see her, of course. I would've asked her here but she likes to be alone and besides I have a house full of friends this weekend." She finished the Dubonnet in one lightning gulp. "Friends and acquaintances," she added vaguely, looking out of the window at the golf course, golden in the afternoon sun.

"I wonder . . ." I began, wanting to get to business right away.

"Will I have another? Yes, I think I might. It does me good, the doctor says: 'Just a touch of Dubonnet, Rose, before dinner to warm the blood.' "

I poured a highball glass of the stuff, which should, I thought, be enough to bring her blood to the boil. Two ladylike sips got her to the bottom of the glass and I could see what one of her problems undoubtedly was. Anyway, the drink seemed to do her good, and her eyes glistened as she put the glass down and said, "I like a mixture, don't you?"

"A mixture of what, Mrs. Veering?" I had a feeling we were operating on two different frequencies.

"People. What else?" She smiled a dazzling smile, her dentures brilliant and expensive. "Now, this weekend I've tried to bring together *interesting* people . . . not just social . . . though they all are, of course. Brexton is here." She paused, letting this sink in.

I was reasonably impressed . . . or maybe surprised is a better word. My interest in modern painting ranges somewhere between zero and minus ten; nevertheless, having batted around New York in pretentious circles, I've picked up a smattering and I can tell Motherwell from Stuempfig with a canny eye. Brexton is one of the current heroes of Fifty-seventh Street. He's in all the museums. Every year *Life* magazine devotedly takes its readers on a tour of his studio, receiving for their pains a ton of mail saying they ought to know better than waste space on a guy whose pictures aren't any better than the stuff little Sue painted last year in fourth grade. But Brexton has hit the big time professionally and it was something of a surprise to hear that he was staying with Mrs. Veering. I found out why.

"His wife is my niece Mildred," she said, licking the ice daintily for one last drop of Dubonnet. "What a fuss there was in the family when she married him ten years ago! I mean, how could we know he was going to be famous?"

I allowed this was always a hazard.

"Anyway, it's terribly nice having them here. He isn't at all tiresome, though I must say I love art and artists and I don't really expect them to be like other people. I mean, they *are* different, aren't they? Not gross clay like ourselves."

Speak for yourself, hon, I said to myself while I nodded brightly. I wondered if the Brextons had anything to do with my being asked for the weekend: a big stunt of some kind to put him over maybe? I held my fire.

Mrs. Veering helped herself to another tumbler of Dubonnet. I noticed with admiration that her hand was steady. She chattered the whole time. "Then, the Claypooles are here. They're great fun . . . Newport, you know." She socked that one home; then she went back to her chair. "Brother and sister *and* utterly devoted, which is so rare. They've never married, either of them, though of course both are in great demand."

This sounded like one for Dr. Kinsey or maybe Dr. Freud, but I listened while Mrs. Veering told me what a nice couple they made and how they traveled together and were patrons of the arts together. I had heard of them dimly, but I had no idea of how old they were or what arts they patronized. Mrs. Veering assumed I knew everyone she did, so she didn't bother to fill me in on them . . . not that it made too much difference. I was assuming my duties would have nothing to do with this collection of guests.

She was just about to tell me all about the last guest—Mary Western Lung, the penwoman—when the butler crossed the room silently, swiftly, without warning, and whispered something in her ear. She nodded, then she motioned for him to leave, without instructions.

Whatever he had said to her had the effect of turning off the babble, to my relief. She was suddenly all business, in spite of the faintly alcoholic flush which burned now behind her white make-up.

"I'll come to the point, Mr. Sargeant. I need help. As to the main reason for my asking you here, I'll give you the general details right now. I plan to give a Labor Day party which I want to be the sensation of the Hamptons. It can't be cheap; it can't be obvious. I don't want anyone to know I've hired a press agent . . . assuming you will take the job. I'll expect full coverage, though, in the press."

"My fee—" I began; even as a boy scout of eleven I'd discovered that it's best to get that part of the business over with first.

"—will be met.' She was just as businesslike. "Write me a letter tonight saying how much you want, putting yourself on record, and I'll give you what you need." I was filled with admiration for her next few remarks, which had to do with hiring me and also with her purpose.

"The reason I've picked you is because it's possible for me to have you here as a guest without people asking questions." I was duly flattered and wished I'd worn my Brooks Brothers gabardine suit. "So don't say anything about your profession; just pretend you're a . . . writer." She finished brightly enough.

"I'll do my best."

"Tomorrow I'll go over the guest list with you. I think it's in good shape, but you might be able to advise me. Then we'll discuss what publicity would be wisest. I shall want a very great deal."

I stopped myself just in time from asking why. That's one question in my somewhat crooked business you never ask. Being a publicist is a little like being a lawyer: you take on a case without worrying too much about anything except putting it over. I figured Mrs. Veering would let me in on her game sooner or later. If not, considering the fee I was going to ask, it didn't make a bit of difference.

"Now you'll probably want to go to your room. We dine at eight-thirty." She paused; then: "I must ask a favor of you."

"What's that, Mrs. Veering?"

"Don't be disturbed by anything you might see or hear while you're in this house . . . and be discreet." Her rather silly face had grown solemn and pale while she spoke; I was alarmed by the expression in her eyes. It was almost as if she were frightened of something. I wondered what. I wondered if she might not be a little off her rocker.

"Of course I won't say anything, but—"

She looked about her suddenly, as though afraid of eavesdroppers. Then she gestured. "Do run along now, please." I could hear footsteps in the main hall, approaching us.

I was almost at the door of the drawing room when she said, in her usual voice, "Oh, Mr. Sargeant, may I call you Peter?"

"Sure . . ."

"*You* must call me Rose." It was like a command. Then I went out into the hall, almost bumping into a pale youngish woman who murmured something I didn't catch. She slipped into the drawing room while I went upstairs; a maid directed me to my room.

I was uneasy, to say the least. I wondered whether or not I should take my bag and head for one of the local inns, like the 1770 House. I didn't need the job that much and I did need a vacation which, under the circumstances, might not be in the cards. Mrs. Veering was a peculiar woman, an alcoholic. She was also nervous, frightened . . . but of what?

Out of curiosity more than anything else I decided to stay. It was one hell of a mistake.

4

At eight o'clock I went downstairs after a long bath and a slow ceremony of dressing while studying the faintly clammy but well-furnished room (all houses on dunes anywhere beside an ocean have the same musty smell) and reading the titles of the books on the night table: Agatha Christie, Marquand, the Grand Duchess Marie . . . I have a hunch those same books were beside every other guest bed in the Hamptons, except perhaps in Southampton they might have Nancy Mitford and maybe something off-color. I decided I would devote myself to Mrs. Christie in lieu of Miss Liz Bessemer, whom I'd probably not be able to see until Saturday, if then.

I found the other guests all milling around in the big room, which was now cheerful and full of light, the curtains drawn against the evening. Everyone was there except our hostess.

The woman I had bumped into earlier came to my rescue. She was slender, not much over thirty, with a pleasant muted face and dressed in gray, which made her seem somehow old-fashioned, not quite twentieth-century. "I'm Allie Claypoole," she said, smiling; we shook hands: "I think I ran into you—"

"In the hall, yes. I'm Peter Sargeant."

"Come and be introduced. I don't know what Rose is up to." She steered me around the room.

On a love seat for two, but just large enough for the one of her, sat Mary Western Lung, the noted penwoman; a fat dimpled creature with a peaches-and-cream-gone-faintly-sour complexion and her hair dyed a stunning silver-blond. The fact she was very fat made the scarlet slacks she was wearing seem even more remarkable than they were. I counted four folds in each leg from ankle to thigh, which made it seem as though she had four knees per leg instead of the regulation one.

Next stop was the other side of the room where Mrs. Brexton, a small dark-haired woman with china-blue eyes, was examining a pile of art books. I got a brisk nod from her.

Brexton, who was supervising the tray of whiskey, was more cordial. I recognized him from his pictures: a small stooped man of forty with a sandy mustache, a freckled bald pate, heavy glasses and regular, ordinary features, a bit like his few representational paintings.

"What can I do you for?" he asked, rattling ice around in a martini shaker. Next to "Long time no see," I hate "What can I do you for," but after his wife's chilly reception I fell in with him like a long-lost brother.

"I'll have a martini," I said. "Can I help?"

"No, not a thing. I'll have it in just a jiffy." I noticed how long his hands were as he manipulated the shaver: beautiful powerful hands, unlike the rest of him, which was nondescript. The fingernails were encrusted with paint . . . the mark of his trade.

Allie Claypoole then introduced me to her brother, who'd been in an alcove at the other end of the room, hidden from us. He was a good deal like her, a year or two older, perhaps: a handsome fellow, casual in tweed. "Glad to meet you, Sargeant. Just rummaging around among the books. Rose has got some fine ones; pity she's illiterate."

"Why don't you steal them?" Allie smiled at her brother.

"Maybe I will." They looked at each other in that quick secret way married people do, not at all like brother and sister; it was faintly disagreeable.

Then, armed with martinis, we joined the penwoman beside the fire. All of us sat down except Mrs. Brexton, who stood aloof at the far end of the room. Even without indulging in hindsight, there was a sense of expectancy in the air that night, a gray stillness, like that hush before a summer storm.

I talked to Mary Western Lung, who sat on my right in the love seat. I asked her how long she'd been in East Hampton while my eye traveled around the room, my ears alerted to other conversations. Superficially, everything was calm. The Claypooles were arguing with Brexton about painting. No one paid the slightest attention to Mrs. Brexton, her isolation officially unnoticed. Yet something was happening. I suppose I was aware of it only because of my cryptic conversation with Mrs. Veering; even so, without her warnings, I think I would have got the mood on my own.

Mary Western Lung was interminable; her voice was shrill and babyish but not loud; as a matter of fact, despite the size of her person, which could've easily supported a voice like a foghorn, it was very faint for all its shrillness and I found I had to bend very close to catch her words . . . which suited her just fine, for she was flirting like a mad reckless girl.

"Except now, with Eisenhower, it's all changed." What was all changed? I wondered, not having listened to the beginning of her remarks.

"Nothing stays the same," I said solemnly, hoping this would dovetail properly. It did.

"How clever of you!" She looked at me with faintly hyperthyroid eyes; her big baby's face as happy and smooth as another part of a baby's anatomy. "I've always said the same thing. This isn't your first visit to these parts, is it?"

I told her I'd spent a lot of childhood summers here.

"Then you're an old-timer!" This news gave her a great deal of inscrutable pleasure. She even managed to get her hand on my left knee for a quick warm squeeze which almost made me jump out of my skin; except under special circumstances, I hate being touched. Fortunately, she did not look at me when she administered her exploratory pinch, her attention addressed shyly to her own scarlet knees, or at least to a spot somewhere between two of the more likely creases.

I managed, after a few fairly hysterical remarks, to get to the console where the remains of the martinis were, promising I'd bring her back one. While I poured the watery remains from the shaker into my glass, Mrs. Brexton suddenly joined me. "Make me one too," she said in a low voice.

"Oh? Why, sure. You like yours dry?"

"Any way." She looked at her husband, who was seated with his back to us, gesticulating as he made some point. There was no expression on her face, but I could feel a certain coldness emanating from her, like that chill which comes from corpses after rigor has set in.

I made a slapdash martini for her, and another for Mary Western Lung. Without even a "Thank you" Mrs. Brexton joined the group by the fire, talking, I noticed, to Miss Claypoole only, ignoring the two men who were still arguing.

Since there was no place else to go, I had to rejoin Miss Lung, who sipped her martini with daintily pursed lips, on which sparkled a few long golden hairs.

"I never like anything but gin," she said, putting the drink down almost untouched. "I can even remember when my older brothers used to make it in bathtubs!" She roared with laughter at the thought of little-old-she being old enough to remember Prohibition.

I then found out why she was a noted penwoman. "I do a column called "Book Chat"; it's syndicated all over the United States and Canada. Oh, you've read it? Yes? Well, isn't that sweet of you to say so. I put a *great deal* of myself in it. Of course, I really don't have to make a living, but every bit counts these days and it's a lucky thing for me it's gone over so big—the column, that is. I've done it nine years."

I troweled some more praise her way, pretending I was a fan. Actually, I was fascinated, for some reason I couldn't define, by Mrs. Brexton and, as we talked, glanced at her from time to time out of the corner of my eyes; she was talking intently to Allie Claypoole, who listened to what she said, a serious, almost grim expression on her face; unfortunately their voices were too low for me to catch what they were saying. Whatever it was, I did not like the downward twist to Mrs. Brexton's thin mouth, the peevish scowl on her face.

"Rose tells me you're a writer, Mr. Sargeant."

Rose picked the wrong disguise, I thought to myself irritably; I could hardly hope to fool the authoress of "Book Chat." I stalled. I told part of the truth. "I used to be assistant drama critic on the *New York Globe* up until a few years ago when I quit . . . to write a novel."

"Oh? How exciting! Throwing everything to the wind like that! To live for your art! How I envy *and* admire you! Do let me be your first reader and critic."

I mumbled something about not being finished yet, but she was off, her great bosom heaving and rippling. "I did the same, too, years ago when I was at Radcliffe. I just left school one day and told my family I was going to become a Lady of Letters. And I did. My family were Boston . . . stuffy people, but they came around when I wrote *Little Biddy Bit* . . . you probably remember it. I believe it was considered the best child's book of the era . . . even today a brand-new generation of children thrills to it; their little letters to me are heart-warming."

Heart-burning seemed to me a more apt description. Then the career of Mary Western Lung was given me at incredible length. We had got her almost down to the present, when I asked what was keeping our hostess. This stopped her for a split second; then she said, "Rose is often late." She looked uncomfortable. "But then, you're a friend of hers . . . you probably know all about it."

I nodded, completely at sea. "Even so . . ."

"It's getting worse. I wish there was something we could do, but I'm afraid that, short of sending her to a sanatorium, *nothing* will do much good . . . and of course since she won't even *admit* it, there's really no way for those of us who are her oldest and most treasured friends to approach her. You know what her temper is!" Miss Lung shuddered.

"I thought she seemed a little, well, disturbed this evening. She . . ."

Miss Lung's hand descended with dramatic emphasis on my left thigh, where it remained some seconds like a weight of lead. "I'm afraid for her!" Her high voice grew mysterious and feeble. "She's heading for a breakdown. She now thinks someone is trying to kill her."

It was out at last and I was relieved to find that Mrs. Veering was only a mild psychotic and not, as I'd first thought, really in danger of her life. I relaxed considerably, prematurely. "Yes, she told me something like that."

"Poor Rose." Miss Lung shook her head and withdrew her hand from its somewhat sensitive resting place. "It all started a few years ago when she was not included in the New York Social Register. I suppose you weathered *that* with her like all the rest of us . . . what a time it was! It was about then that her"—Miss Lung looked about to make sure no one else could hear—"her *drinking* began. I remember telling Allie Claypoole (who's also from Boston, by the way) that if Rose didn't get a grip on herself she'd—"

But grip or no grip, our hostess appeared in a magenta dinner dress, looking handsome and steady, no worse for the gallon of Dubonnet she'd drunk before dinner.

"Come along, children!" she said, waving us all toward the dining room. I admired her steadiness. She obviously had the capacity of a camel. "I'm sorry I'm late, but I got held up. We have to go in now or the cook will make a scene."

It was while I accompanied Mrs. Brexton in to dinner I noticed, when she turned to speak to her husband, that across her neck, ordinarily covered by a long bob, was an ugly purple welt extending from under the ear down the side of her neck and disappearing into the high-necked dress she was wearing. It was a bruise, too, not a birthmark or a scar . . . it was a new bruise.

When she turned from her husband to speak to me, hair covered the discoloration. There was an odd look in her eyes, as though she could detect in my face what it was I'd seen, what I thought, for, as she made some remark about the dance to be held the next night at the Yacht Club, her hand strayed unconsciously to her neck.

5

Dinner went well enough. Mrs. Veering was in fine form, no trace of the earlier fear which had marred our first meeting. I studied her during dinner (I sat on her left; Brexton was on her right; Allie Claypoole was on *my* left). She was animated and probably quite drunk, though she didn't show it except, perhaps, in the feverish brightness of her eyes and in her conversation, which made no sense at all, though it sounded perfectly rational.

It was a queer crew, I decided. A hostess on the make socially in spite of her alcoholism and a big snub from the Social Register; a highbrow painter; his wife, whose blood could probably etch glass, with a bruise on her neck which looked as if somebody had tried to choke her to death and then decided what the hell and left the job half done. The somebody was probably her husband, whose hands looked strong enough to twist off a human head like a chicken's.

And the mysterious Claypooles, brother and sister and so in love, or something. He sat next to Mrs. Brexton at dinner and they talked together intently, ignoring the rest of the company, which seemed to irritate his sister. Brexton was oblivious of everyone, a good-humored, self-centered type who saw to it that the conversation never got too far away from him or from painting.

And of course my penwoman, a massive giggling friend to man . . . at least so she seemed underneath all the "Book Chat." Since her score was probably quite low, all things considered, her predatory instincts doubtless expressed themselves only in pats and pinches, at which she was pretty expert.

After dinner, a little high on white wine, we all went back to the drawing room, where a card table had been set up.

"Of course we're seven, but that doesn't mean four can't play bridge while the others are doing something more constructive." Mrs. Veering looked brightly around. At first everyone said they'd rather not play, but she apparently knew what she was up to and, finally, the bridge enthusiasts (I'm not one; poker's the only card game I ever learned) flocked to the table, leaving Mrs. Brexton, Allie Claypoole and myself in front of the fireplace.

It was obviously up to us to do something more constructive, but I couldn't think what. There's nothing worse than being at a formal house on a weekend with a group of people you don't know and who don't particularly appeal to you. There's always the problem of what to talk about which, in this case, was complicated by the sour behavior of Mrs. Brexton and the vagueness of Allie Claypoole, neither of whom seemed happy with the arrangements either.

"I suppose you and Fletcher will be going back to Boston after this." Mrs. Brexton snapped this out suddenly at Allie in a tone which, if it was meant to be pleasant, missed the mark wide. Fletcher, I gathered, was Claypoole's first name.

"Oh, yes . . . I think so. We're getting a smaller place in Cambridge, you know."

"I don't know why you won't live in New York. It's much more interesting. Boston is dead all year round." Mrs. Brexton was animated on the subject of Boston at least. This was the first conversation I'd heard out of her all evening.

"We like it."

"I suppose *you* would." The insult in this was so clear that I could hardly believe I'd got it right.

But Allie didn't seem particularly to mind. "People are different, Mildred," she said quietly. "I don't think either of us could take New York for very long."

"Speak for yourself. Fletcher likes the city and you know it. You're the one who keeps him in Boston."

Allie flushed at this. "He's always polite," she said.

"That's not what I mean." They faced each other, suddenly implacable enemies. What was going on?

A first-rate row was beginning. "What do you mean, Mildred?"

Mrs. Brexton laughed unpleasantly. "Don't play the fool with me, Allie, I'm one person who—"

"Partner, I *had* no hearts!" squealed Miss Lung from the table, followed by a groan from Mr. Brexton.

"For God's sake, shut up, Mildred." Allie said this under the squeal of Miss Lung, but I heard her if the others didn't.

"I've shut up too long." Mrs. Brexton seemed to subside, though; her spasm of anger replaced by her usual unpleasant expression. I noticed that her hands shook as she lighted a cigarette. Was she another alcoholic? One, of course, was par for any weekend. Two looked like a frame-up.

Miss Claypoole turned to me as though nothing unpleasant had been said. "I'm sure you'll have something good to say about Boston," she said, smiling. "I seem to be a minority here."

I told her I'd gone to Harvard and this forged a link between us so strong that, without another word, without even a "Good night" to her hostess, Mrs. Brexton left the room.

"Did I say something to upset her?" I asked innocently. I was curious to know what was going on.

Allie frowned slightly. "No, I don't think so." She glanced at the bridge table; the others were engrossed, paying no attention to us. "Mildred isn't well. She . . . well, she's just had a nervous breakdown."

So that was it. "What form did it take?"

She shrugged. "What form do they usually take? She went to bed for a month. Now she's up and around. She's really quite nice . . . don't get a wrong impression of her. Unfortunately, she makes almost no sense and you can see she's as nervous as a cat. We don't quarrel with her if we can help it. She doesn't mean to be as . . . as awful as she sounds."

"And she sounds pretty awful?"

"She's an old friend of mine," Allie said sharply.

"I'm sure she is," I said, not at all taken aback . . . if you're among eightballs, you have to be one yourself to survive, and I had two more days of this ahead of me and I didn't intend to be buffaloed at the beginning. Besides, I liked Allie. In her subdued way she was very good-looking and she had the sort of figure I like: slender and well-proportioned, no serious sags, and a lovely clear skin. I imagined her without any clothes on, then I quickly dressed her again in my mind; that wouldn't do at all, I decided. Besides, there was the luscious Liz Bessemer down the road waiting for me, or at least I hoped she was. One advantage of being an unmarried male in your early thirties is that most of your contemporaries are safely married and you have the field of single women to yourself—officially, that is.

Allie, unaware that she'd been brutally undressed and dressed again all in the space of a second, was talking about Mildred Brexton. "She's always been high-strung. That whole family is . . . even Rose." She nodded toward our hostess. "I suppose you know Rose is her aunt."

I said I did.

"We met them, Fletcher and I, about fifteen years ago when Rose came East and decided to do Newport, where we always go in the summers . . . at least we used to. Mildred's the same age as my brother and they were—are—great friends. In fact, people always thought they'd get married, but then she met Brexton and of course they've been very happy." I knew she was lying—if only because it seemed unlikely any man could get along with that disagreeable woman.

"I suppose you've known Rose a long time?" The question was abrupt.

"No, not very." I didn't know what to say, not knowing what Mrs. Veering had said.

She helped me out. "Oh, I thought Rose said you were an old friend, but then, she's so vague. I've seen her ask people here under the impression she's known them for years and it's turned out they're absolute strangers. That's one of the reasons her parties are so successful: everyone's treated like a long-lost cousin."

The butler slithered into the room at that moment and came, to my surprise, to me. "Mr. Sargeant, sir, you are wanted on the telephone." An honest-to-god English butler who said "telly-phone."

It was Liz. "Oh, hi, Peter. I wondered what you were doing."

"I've been wondering that myself."

"Dull?"

"Deadly. How's your place?"

"Not much better. Will you be at the dance tomorrow night?"

"I don't know. One of the guests mentioned it, so I figured we'll go; if not—"

"Come anyway. Say you're my guest. I'll leave a note at the door for you."

"I'll like that. It's a full moon, too."

"A full what?"

"Moon."

"Oh, I thought you said 'room.' Well, I'll be looking for you."

We hung up. I felt very much better. I had visions of the two of us rolling amorously in the deserted dunes while the moon turned the sea and the sand to silver. Maybe this job wasn't going to be as grim as I thought.

Around midnight, the bridge game broke up and everybody had a nightcap except our hostess, who had what could only be called an Indian war bonnet: a huge brandy glass half filled with enough cognac to float me straight out to sea.

"I hope we're not too dull for you," she said, just before we all parted for bed.

"I couldn't be having a better time," I lied.

"Tomorrow we'll do a little business and then of course we're going to the Yacht Club dance, where you can see some young people."

"And what's wrong with us?" asked Miss Lung roguishly.

I was not honor-bound to answer that and after a round of "Good nights," we all went upstairs. I followed Mary Western Lung, and the sight of those superb buttocks encased in red slacks would, I knew, haunt my dreams for ever.

To my dismay, I found her room was next to mine. "What a coincidence!" was her observation.

I smiled enigmatically, ducked into my room, locked the connecting door and then, just to be safe, moved a heavy bureau against the door. Only a maddened hippopotamus could break through that barricade; as far as I knew, Miss Lung was not yet maddened.

I slept uneasily until three-thirty when, right in the middle of a mild, fairly standard nightmare (falling off a cliff), I was awakened by three sharp screams, a woman's screams.

I sat bolt upright at the second scream; the third one got me out of bed; stumbling over a chair, I opened the door and looked out into the dimly lit hall. Other heads were appearing from doorways. I spotted both Claypooles, Miss Lung and, suddenly, Mrs. Veering, who appeared on the landing, in white, like Lady Macbeth.

"*Do* go back to sleep," she said in her usual voice. "It's nothing . . . nothing at all. A misunderstanding."

There was a bewildered murmur. The heads withdrew. I caught a glimpse of Miss Lung's intricate nightdress: pink decorated with little bows befitting the authoress of *Little Biddy Bit.* Puzzled, uneasy, I dropped off to sleep. The last thing I remember thinking was how strange it was that Mrs. Veering had made no explanation of those screams.

At breakfast there was a good deal of talk about the screams—that is, at first there was until it became quite clear that one of our company had been responsible for them; at which moment everybody shut up awkwardly and finished their beef-and-kidney pie, an English touch of Mrs. Veering's which went over very big.

I guessed, I don't know why, that Mrs. Brexton had been responsible; yet at breakfast she seemed much as ever, a little paler than I remembered, but then, I was seeing her for the first time in daylight.

We had coffee on the screened-in porch, which overlooked the ocean: startlingly blue this morning with a fair amount of surf. The sky was vivid with white gulls circling overhead. I amused myself by thinking it must really be a scorcher in the city.

After breakfast everybody got into their bathing suits except, fortunately, Mary Western Lung, who said the sun "simply poached her skin." She got herself up in poisonous-yellow slacks with harlequin dark glasses and a bandanna around her head.

Mrs. Veering was the only one who didn't change. Like all people who have houses by the sea, she wasn't one for sunbathing or swimming.

"Water's too cold for me," she said, beckoning me into the alcove off the drawing room.

She was all business. I thought longingly of the beach and the surf. I could hear the sound of the others splashing about.

"I hope you weren't disturbed last night," she said, sitting down at a handsome Queen Anne desk while I lounged in an armchair.

"It was unexpected," I admitted. "What happened?"

"Poor Mildred." She sighed. "I think she has persecution mania. It's been terrible this last year. *I* don't understand any of it. There's never been anything like it in our family, ever. Her mother, my sister, was the sanest woman that ever drew breath and her father was all right too. I suppose it's the result of marrying an artist. They *can* be a trial. They're different, you know, not like us."

She developed that theme a little; it was a favorite one with her. Then: "Ever since her breakdown last winter she's been positive her husband wants to kill her. A more *devoted* husband, by the way, you'll never find."

The memory of that ugly bruise crossed my mind uneasily. "Why doesn't she leave him?"

Mrs. Veering shrugged. "Where would she go? Besides, she's irrational now and I think she knows it. She apologized last night when . . . when it happened."

"What happened?"

"They had a row . . . just a married persons' quarrel, nothing serious. Then she started to scream and I went downstairs . . . their bedroom's on the first floor. She apologized immediately and so did he, but of course by then she'd managed to wake up the whole house."

"I should think her place was in a rest home or something."

Mrs. Veering sighed. "It may come to that. I pray not. But now here's the guest list for the party. I'll want you to make a press list for me and . . ."

Our business took about an hour; she had the situation well in hand and, though I didn't dare say so, she was quite capable of being her own press agent. She had a shrewd grip on all the problems of publicity. My job, I gathered, was to be her front. It was just as well. We decided then on my fee, which was large, and she typed out an agreement between us with the speed and finesse of an old-time stenographer. "I studied typing," she said simply, noticing my awe. "It was one of the ways I used to help my late husband. I did everything for him."

We each signed our copy of the agreement and I was dismissed to frolic on the beach; the last I saw of Mrs. Veering was her moving resolutely toward the console which held, in ever-readiness, ice and whiskey and glasses.

On the beach, the others were gathered.

The sun was fiercely white and the day was perfect with just enough breeze off the water to keep you cool.

I looked at my fellow houseguests with interest: it's always interesting to see people you know only dressed without any clothes on—or not much, that is.

Both Allie and Mrs. Brexton had good figures. Allie's especially; she looked just about the way she had the night before when I had mentally examined her . . . the only flaw perhaps was that she was a little short in the legs; otherwise, she was a good-looking woman, prettier in the sun wearing a two-piece bathing suit than in her usual dull clothes. She was stretched out on a blanket next to her brother, who was a solid-looking buck with a chest which had only just begun to settle around the pelvis.

Mrs. Brexton was sitting on the edge of a bright Navajo blanket in the center of which, holding a ridiculous parasol, was Miss Lung, sweating under all her clothes while Brexton, burlier than I'd thought, did handstands clumsily to show he was just as young as he felt, which apparently wasn't very young.

Miss Lung hailed me. "You must sit here!" she said, pounding the blanket beside her.

"That's O.K.," I said. "I don't want to crowd you." I sat down cross-legged on the sand between the blanket where she sat and the Claypooles. I was a good yard from her busy fingers.

"My, I've never seen such *athletic* men!" Behind her harlequin dark glasses, I could see I was being given the once-over.

At that moment Brexton fell flat on his face. Spluttering in the sand, he said, "Rock under my hand . . . sharp damn thing." He pretended his hand hurt while Allie and I exchanged amused glances.

"None of us is as young as we used to be," said her brother, chuckling, pulling himself up on his elbow. "You're getting more like Picasso every day."

"Damned fraud," said the painter irritably, rubbing the sand out of his face. "Nine tenths of what he's done I could do better . . . *anybody* could do better."

"And the other tenth?"

"Well, that . . ." He shrugged. I'd already found that Brexton, like most painters, hated all other living painters, especially the grand old men. He differed from most in that he was candid, having perhaps more confidence.

He harangued us a while in the brilliant light, I stretched out and shut my eyes, enjoying the warmth on my back. The others did the same, digesting breakfast.

Claypoole was the first to go in the water. Without warning, he leaped to his feet and dashed down to the ocean, diving flat and sharp into the first breaker. He was a powerful swimmer and it was a pleasure to watch him.

We all sat up. Then Mrs. Brexton walked slowly down to the water's edge, where she put on her bathing cap, standing, I could see, in such a way as to hide from us the long bruise on her neck.

She waded out. Brexton got to his feet and followed her. He stopped her for a moment and they talked; then he shrugged and she went on by him, diving awkwardly into the first wave. He stood watching her, his back to us, as she swam slowly out toward Claypoole.

Allie turned to me suddenly. "She's going too far. There's an awful undertow."

"She seems like a fair swimmer. Anyway, your brother's there."

"My!" exclaimed Miss Lung. "They swim like porpoises. How I envy them!"

Claypoole was now beyond the breakers, swimming easily with the undertow, which, apparently, was pulling south, for he was already some yards below where he'd gone into the water; he was heading diagonally for shore.

Mrs. Brexton was not yet beyond the breakers; I could see her white bathing cap bobbing against the blue.

Allie and I both got to our feet and joined Brexton at the water's edge. The water was cold as it eddied about our ankles.

"I don't think Mildred should go so far out," said Allie.

Brexton nodded, his eyes still on his wife. "I told her not to. Naturally, that was all she needed."

"It's quite an undertow," I said, remembering something about trajectory, about estimated speed: Claypoole was now sliding into shore on the breakers at least thirty feet below us.

As far as the eye could see to north and south the white beach, edged by grassy dunes, extended. People, little black dots, were clustered in front of each house. While, a mile or two down, there was a swarm of them in front of the club. The sky was cloudless; the sun white fire.

Then, without warning, Brexton rushed into the water. Half running, half swimming, he moved toward his wife.

She had made no sound but she was waving weakly on the line where the surf began. The undertow had got her.

I dived in too. Allie shouted to her brother, who was already on the beach. He joined us, half running, half swimming out to Mildred.

Salt water in my eyes, I cut through the surf, aware of Claypoole near me. I never got to Mildred, though. Instead, I found myself trying to support Brexton some feet away from his wife. He was gasping for air. "Cramp!" he shouted and began to double up, so I grabbed him while

Claypoole shot beyond me to Mildred. With some difficulty, I got Brexton back to shore. Claypoole floated Mildred in.

Exhausted, chilled from the water, I rolled Brexton on to the sand. He sat there for a moment trying to get his breath, holding his side with a look of pain. I was shaking all over from cold, from tension.

Then we both went up on the terrace where the others had gathered in a circle around the white still body of Mildred Brexton.

She lay on her stomach and Claypoole squatted over her, giving artificial respiration. I noticed with horrified fascination the iridescent bubbles which had formed upon her blue lips. As he desperately worked her arms, her lungs, the bubbles one by one burst.

For what seemed like a hundred years there was no sound but that of Claypoole's exhausted breathing as he worked in grim silence. It came like a shock to us when we heard his voice, the first voice to speak. He turned to his sister, not halting in his labor, and said, "Doctor . . . quick."

The sun was at fierce noon when the doctor came, in time to pronounce Mildred Brexton dead by drowning.

Bewildered, as shaky as a defeated boxer on the ropes, Claypoole stood swaying over the dead woman, his eyes on Brexton. He said only two words, said them softly, full of hate. "You devil!" They faced each other over the dead woman's body. There was nothing any of us could do.

II

Shortly before lunch, to everyone's surprise a policeman in plain clothes arrived. "Somebody sent for me," he announced gloomily. "Said somebody drowned." He was plainly bored. This kind of drowning apparently was a common occurrence in these parts.

"I can't think who sent for you," said Mrs. Veering quickly. "We have already notified the doctor, the funeral home . . ."

"*I* called the police," said Claypoole. Everyone looked at him, startled. But he didn't elaborate. We were all seated in the drawing room . . . all of us except Brexton, who had gone to his room after the drowning and stayed there.

The policeman was curt, wanting no nonsense. "How many you ladiesgemmen witness the accident?"

Those who had said so. Mrs. Veering, a tankard of Dubonnet in one hand and a handkerchief in the other, began to explain how she'd been in the house but if she'd only known that poor Mildred . . .

The policeman gave her one irritable look and she subsided. Her eyes were puffy and red and she seemed really upset by what had happened. The rest of us were surprisingly cool. Death, when it strikes so swiftly, unexpectedly, has an inexplicable rightness about it, like thunder or rain. Later grief, shock, remorse set in. For now we were all a little embarrassed that we weren't more distressed by the drowning of Mildred Brexton before our eyes.

"O.K." The policeman took out a notebook and a stub of pencil. "Give me names real slow and age and place of birth and occupation and relation to deceased and anything you remember about the accident."

There was an uneasy squeak from Mary Western Lung. "I can't see what our occupations and . . . and ages have to do with . . ."

The policeman sighed. "I take all you one by one and what you tell me is in strict confidence." He glanced at the alcove off the drawing room.

Mrs. Veering said, "By all means. You must interview us singly and I shall do everything in my power to . . ."

The policeman gestured to Miss Lung to follow him and they crossed the room together, disappearing into the alcove.

The rest of us began to talk uncomfortably. I turned to Allie Claypoole, who sat, pale and tense, beside me on the couch. "I didn't know it could happen like that . . . so fast," I said, inadequately.

She looked at me for one dazed moment; then, with an effort, brought me into focus. "Do give me a cigarette."

I gave her one; I lit it for her; her hands trembled so that I was afraid I might burn her. One long exhalation, however, relaxed her considerably. "It was that awful undertow. I never go out that far. I don't know why Mildred did . . . except that she is . . . she *was* a wonderful swimmer."

I was surprised, recalling the slow awkward strokes. "I thought she looked sort of weak . . . swimming, that is."

Across the room Mrs. Veering was crying softly into her Dubonnet while Fletcher Claypoole, calm now, his mysterious outburst still unexplained, tried to comfort her. From the alcove I heard a high shrill laugh from Mary Western Lung and I could almost see that greedy fat hand of hers descending in a lustful arc on the policeman's chaste knee.

"I suppose it was her illness," said Allie at last. "There's no other explanation. I'm afraid I didn't notice her go in. I wasn't aware of anything until Brexton started in after her."

"Do you think a nervous breakdown could affect the way somebody swam? Isn't swimming like riding a bicycle? You do it or you don't."

"What are you suggesting?" Her eyes, violet and lovely, were turned suddenly on mine.

"I don't know." I wondered why she was suddenly so sharp. "I only thought—"

"She was weakened, that's all. She's been through a great deal mentally and apparently it affected her physically. That's all."

"She might've had what they call the 'death wish.'"

"I doubt if Mildred wanted to die," said Allie, a little dryly. "She wasn't the suicide type . . . if there is such a thing."

"Well, it can be unconscious, can't it?" Like everyone else I am an expert in psychoanalysis: I can tell a trauma from a vitrine at twenty paces and I know all about Freud without ever having read a line he's written.

"I haven't any idea. Poor Brexton. I wonder what he'll do now."

"Was it that happy a marriage?" I was surprised, remembering the bruise on her neck, the screams the night before; "happy" didn't seem the right word for whatever it was their life had been together.

Allie shrugged. "I don't think there are any very happy marriages, at least in our world, but there are people who quarrel a lot and still can't live without each other."

"They were like that?"

"Very much so . . . especially when she began to crack up . . . he was wonderful with her, considering the fact he's got a terrible temper and thinks of no one but himself. He put up with things from her that . . . well, that you wouldn't believe if I told you. He was very patient."

"Was she always this way? I mean the way she seemed last night?"

Allie didn't answer immediately. Then she said, "Mildred was what people call difficult most of her life. She could charm anybody if she wanted to; if she didn't want to, she could be very disagreeable."

"And at the end she didn't want to?"

"That's about it."

Mary Western Lung in high good humor emerged, giggling, from the alcove. The policeman, red of face and clearly angry, said, "You next," nodding at Allie. Miss Lung took her place beside me.

"Oh, they're so wonderful, these police people! It's the first time I've ever talked to one that close and under such grim circumstances. He was simply wonderful with me and we had the nicest chat. I love the virile he-man type, don't you?"

I indicated that I could take he-men or leave them alone.

"But of course you're a man and wouldn't see what a woman sees in them." I resented faintly not being included among that rugged number; actually, our police friend could have been wrapped around the smallest finger of any athlete; however, Miss Lung saw only the glamour of the job . . . the subhuman gutturals of this employee of the local administration excited the authoress of "Book Chat." She scrounged her great soft pillow of a flank against mine and I was pinned between her and the arm of the couch.

I struck a serious note in self-defense. "Did he have anything interesting to say about the accident?"

The penwoman shook her head. I wondered wildly if there was a bone beneath that mass of fat which flowed like a Dali soft watch over my own thigh: she was more like a pulpy vegetable than a human being, a giant squash. "No, we talked mostly about books. He likes Mickey Spillane." She wrinkled her nose, which altered her whole soft face in a most surprising way; I was relieved when she unwrinkled it. "I told him I'd send him a copy of *Little Biddy Bit* for his children, but it seems he isn't married. So I told him he'd love reading it himself . . . so many adults do. I get letters all the time saying—"

I was called next, but not before I had heard yet another installment in the life of Mary Western Lung.

The policeman was trying to do his job as quickly as possible. He sat scribbling in his notebook; he didn't look up as I sat down in the chair beside the Queen Anne desk.

"Name?"

"Peter Cutler Sargeant Two."

"Two what?" He looked up.

"Two of the same name, I guess . . . the second. You make two vertical lines side by side."

He looked at me with real disgust. "Age . . . place of birth . . . present address."

"Thirty-one . . . Hartford, Connecticut . . . 280 East Forty-ninth Street."

"Occupation?"

I paused, remembering my promise to Mrs. Veering. I figured, however, the law was reasonably discreet. "Public relations. My own firm. Sargeant Incorporated: 60 East Fifty-fifth Street."

"How long know deceased?"

"About eighteen hours."

"That's all."

I started to go; the policeman stopped me, remembering he'd forgotten an important question. "Notice anything unusual at time of accident?"

I said I hadn't.

"Describe what happened in own words." I did exactly that briefly;

then I was dismissed. Now that I look back on it, it seems strange that no one, including myself, considered murder as a possibility.

2

Lunch was a subdued affair. Mrs. Veering had recovered from her first grief at the loss of a beloved niece and seemed in perfect control of herself or at least perfectly controlled by the alcohol she'd drunk which, in her case, was the same thing.

Brexton received a tray in his own room. The rest of us sat around awkwardly after lunch making conversation, trying not to mention what had happened and yet unable to think of anything else to talk about.

The second reaction had begun to set in and we were all shocked at last by what had happened, especially when Mrs. Veering found Mildred's scarf casually draped over the back of a chair, as though she were about to come back at any moment and claim it.

It had been originally planned that we go out to the Maidstone Club for cocktails, but at the last minute Mrs. Veering had canceled our engagement. The dance that night was still in doubt. I had made up my mind, however, that I'd go whether the others did or not. I hoped they wouldn't, as a matter of fact: I could operate better with Liz if I was on my own.

I had a chat with Mrs. Veering in the alcove while the others drifted around, going to their rooms, to the beach outside . . . in the house, out of the house, not quite knowing, any of them, how to behave under the circumstances. No one wanted to go in the water, including myself. The murderous ocean gleamed blue and bright in the afternoon.

"Well, do you think it will upset things?" Mrs. Veering looked at me shrewdly.

"Upset what?"

"The party . . . what else? This will mean publicity for me . . . the wrong kind."

I began to get her point. "We have a saying—"

"All publicity is good publicity." She snapped that out fast enough. "Socially, however, that isn't true. Get a certain kind of publicity and people will drop you flat."

"I can't see how having a guest drown accidentally should affect you one way or the other."

"If that's all there is to it, it won't." She paused significantly; I waited for more of the same, but she shifted her line of attack. "When the newspaper people come, I want you to act as my spokesman. One is on his way over here right now. But don't let on what your job really is. Just say you're a guest and that I'm upset by what's happened . . . as indeed I am . . . and that you've been authorized to speak for me.'

"What'll I say?"

"Nothing." She smiled. "What else can you say? That Mildred was my niece; that I was very fond of her; that she'd been ill (I think you'd better make some point of that) and her strength wasn't equal to the undertow."

"They've taken it . . . her, the body, I mean, to the morgue, haven't they?" The doctor and Brexton had carried her into the house and I hadn't seen the corpse again.

"I don't know. The doctor took it away in an ambulance. I've already made arrangements for the undertakers to look after everything . . . they're in touch with the doctor, who is an old friend of mine." She paused thoughtfully, fiddling with the pile of papers on her desk. I was surprised by the rapid change in her mood. I attributed this to her peculiar habits. Most alcoholics I knew were the same; gregarious, kindly, emotional people, quite irresponsible in every way and unpredictable. I had sat next to her at lunch and what had seemed to be a tumbler full of ice water was, I'd noticed on closer examination, a glass full of gin. At the end of lunch the glass was empty.

Then she said, "I would appreciate it, Peter, if nothing was said about the . . . the misunderstanding last night."

"You mean the screams?"

She nodded. "It could do me a great deal of harm socially if people were to get . . . well, the wrong idea about Brexton and Mildred. He was devoted to her and stayed at her side all through that terrible breakdown. I don't want there to be any misunderstandings about that."

"Are there apt to be any? The poor woman went swimming and drowned; we all saw it happen and that's that."

"I know. Even so, you know what gossips people are. I shouldn't like one of the newspapermen, one of those awful columnists, to start suggesting things."

"I'll see to it," I said with more authority than was strictly accurate under the circumstances.

340

"That's why I want you to handle the press for me. And another thing . . ." She paused; then, "Keep the others away from the newspapermen."

I was startled by this request. "Why? I mean what difference does it make? We all saw the same thing. The police have our testimonies."

"The police will keep their own counsel. Just do as I ask and I'll be very grateful to you."

I shrugged. "If I can, I will, but what's to stop one of your guests from talking to the press?"

"You, I hope." She changed the subject. "I've had the nicest chat with Alma Edderdale, who wishes to be remembered to you. She checked in at the Sea Spray this morning."

"That's nice."

' "I'd hoped to have her over tomorrow, but since this . . . well, I don't quite know how to act.'

"As usual, I'd say. It's a terrible tragedy, but—"

"But she was my niece and very close to me. It wasn't as if she were . . . well, only a guest." I realized that I was expendable. "Perhaps we can just have a few people over . . . friends of the family. I'm sure that'd be proper."

"I have an invitation," I said boldly, "to go to the Yacht Club dance tonight and I wondered, if you weren't going, whether I might . . ."

"Why, certainly, go by all means. But please, please don't talk to anyone about what has happened. I can't possibly go and I'm not sure the others would want to either, since they were all more or less connected with Mildred. You, of course, have no reason not to." And, feeling like a servant being given Thursday afternoon off, I was dismissed while Mrs. Veering took off for her bedroom and, no doubt, a jug of the stuff which banishes care.

An hour later I had the drawing room all to myself, which was fortunate because the butler advanced upon me with a member of the press, a chinless youth from one of the news services.

I waved him into a chair grandly.

"I want to speak with Mrs. Rose Clayton Veering and Mr. Paul Brexton," said the news hawk firmly, adenoidally.

"You must be satisfied with me."

"I came here to talk with Mrs. Rose . . ."

"And now you must talk to me," I said more sharply. "I am authorized to speak for Mrs. Veering."

"Who are you?"

"Peter Cutler Sargeant II."

He wrote this down slowly in what he pretended was shorthand but actually was, I could see, a sloppy form of longhand. "I'd still like to—" he began stubbornly, but I interrupted him. "They don't want to talk, Junior. You talk to me or get yourself out of here."

This impressed him. "Well, sir, I've been to see the police and they say Mrs. Brexton was drowned this morning at eleven-six. That right?"

I said it was. I fired all the facts there were at him and he recorded them.

"I'd like to get a human-interest angle," he said in the tone of one who has just graduated from a school of journalism with low marks.

"You got plenty. Brexton's a famous painter. Mrs. Veering's a social leader. Just rummage through your morgue and you'll find enough stuff to pad out a good feature."

He looked at me suspiciously. "You're not working for any paper, are you?"

I shook my head. "I saw a movie of *The Front Page* once . . . I know all about you fellows."

He looked at me with real dislike. "I'd like to see Mrs. Veering just to—"

"Mrs. Veering is quote prostrate with grief unquote. Paul Brexton quote world-famous modern painter refuses to make any comment holding himself incommunicado in his room unquote. There's your story."

"You're not being much help."

"It's more help than nothing. If I didn't talk, nobody would." I glanced anxiously around to make sure none of the other guests was apt to come strolling in. Fortunately, they were all out of sight.

"They're doing an autopsy on Mrs. Brexton and I wondered if—"

"An autopsy?" This was unusual.

"That's right. It's going on now. I just wondered if there was any hint—"

"Of foul play? No, there wasn't. We all witnessed her death. Nobody drowned her. Nobody made her swim out into the undertow. She'd had a nervous breakdown recently and there's no doubt but that had something to do with her death."

He brightened at this. I could almost read the headline: "Despondent Socialite Swims to Death at East Hampton." Well, I was following orders.

I finally got him out of the house and I told the butler, in Mrs.

Veering's name, to send any other newspaper people to me first. He seemed to understand perfectly.

Idly, wondering what to do next, I strolled out onto the porch and sat down in a big wicker armchair overlooking the sea. Walking alone beside the water was Allie Claypoole. She was frowning and picking up shells and stones and bits of seaweed and throwing them out onto the waves, like offerings. She was a lovely figure, silhouetted against the blue.

I picked up a copy of *Time* magazine to learn what new triumphs had been performed by "the team" in Washington. I was halfway through an account of the President's golf scores in the last month at Burning Tree when I heard voices from behind me.

I looked around and saw they were coming from a window a few feet to my left. The window, apparently, of Brexton's bedroom: it was, I recalled, the only downstairs bedroom. Two men were talking, Brexton and Claypole. I recognized their voices immediately.

"You made her do it. You knew she wasn't strong enough." It was Claypoole: tense, accusing.

Brexton's voice sounded tired and distant. I listened eagerly; the magazine slipped from my lap to the floor while I strained to hear. "Oh, shut up, Fletcher. You don't know what you're saying. You don't know anything about it."

"I know what she told me. She said—"

"Fletcher, she was damned near out of her mind these last few months and you know it as well as I do . . . better, because you're partly to blame."

"What do you mean by that crack?"

"Just what I say. Especially after Bermuda." There was a long pause. I wondered if perhaps they had left the room.

Then Claypoole spoke slowly. 'Think whatever you want to think. She wasn't happy with you, ever. You and your damned ego nearly ruined her . . . did ruin her."

"Well, I don't think you'll be able to blame her death on my ego . . ."

"No, because I'm going to blame it on you."

A cold shiver went down my spine. Brexton's voice was hard. "There's such a thing as criminal libel. Watch out."

"I expect to. I'm going to tell the whole story in court. I expect you thought I'd be too afraid of repercussions . . . well, I'm not. When I get through there won't be anybody who doesn't know."

Brexton laughed shortly. "In court? What makes you think there'll be a court?"

"Because I'm going to tell them you murdered her."

"You're out of your mind, Fletcher. You were there. How could I murder her? Even if I wanted to?"

"I think I know. Anyway, it'll be your word against mine as to what happened out there, when she was drowning."

"You forget that young fellow was there too. You've got his testimony to think about. He knows nothing funny happened."

"I was closer. I saw—"

"Nothing at all. Now get out of here."

"I warned you."

"Let me warn you then, Fletcher: if you circulate any of your wild stories, if you try to pin this . . . this accident on me, I'll drag Allie into the case."

Before I could hear anything more, the butler appeared with the news that a reporter from the local paper was waiting to see me. Cursing my bad luck, puzzled and appalled by what I had heard, I went into the drawing room and delivered my spiel on the accidental death of Mildred Brexton. Only, I wasn't too sure of the accident part by this time.

3

For some reason, the newspapers scented a scandal even before the police or the rest of us did. I suppose it was the combination of Mrs. Veering "Hostess" and Paul Brexton "Painter" that made the story smell like news way off.

I spent the rest of that afternoon handling telephone calls and interviewers. Mrs. Veering kept out of sight. Mary Western Lung proved to be a source of continual trouble, however, giving a series of eyewitness accounts of what had happened calculated to confuse an electric eye, much less a bewildered newspaperman.

"And so you see," she ended breathlessly to the local newspaperman, who sat watching her with round frightened eyes, "in the midst of life we are we know not where, ever. I comprehend full well now the meaning of that poor child's last words to me, 'I hope the water isn't cold.' *Think* what a world of meaning there was in that remark, now that we know what she intended to do."

"Are you suggesting Mrs. Brexton killed herself?" The member of the fourth estate was drooling with excitement.

I intervened quickly, pushing him to the door. "Of course not," I said rapidly. "There's no evidence at all that she wanted to do such a thing; as a matter of fact, she couldn't've been more cheerful this morning . . ."

"And I'll send you a copy of 'Book Chat,' the last one," Miss Lung shouted at the retiring interviewer's back. I told the butler to let no one else in for the day.

I turned to Miss Lung. "You know that Mrs. Veering asked me to look after the press, to keep them from doing anything sensational. Now you've gone and put it in their heads that she intended to commit suicide."

"*Did* commit suicide." Miss Lung smiled wisely at me over her necklace of chins.

"How do you know?"

"She was a marvelous athlete . . . a perfect swimmer. She deliberately drowned."

"In full view of all of us. Like that? Struggling? Why, I saw her wave for help."

Miss Lung shrugged. "She may have changed her mind at the last minute . . . anyway, you can't tell me she would've drowned like that if she hadn't wanted to."

"Well, as somebody who was a few feet from her when she was still alive I can tell you she was doing her best to remain in this vale of tears."

"What a happy phrase! Vale of tears indeed!"

"You said it." I was disgusted. "Did you tell the police you thought she intended to drown on purpose?"

"Why, certainly." Miss Lung was bland. I understood then the promptness of the autopsy. "It was my duty as a citizen and as a friend of poor Mildred to set the record straight."

"I hope you're right . . . I mean, in what you did."

"I'm sure I am. Didn't you think that man from the papers *awfully* distinguished-looking? Not at all my idea of the usual sort of newspaperman . . ."

A telephone call from Liz broke short this little chat. I took it in the hall.

"Peter?"

"That's right, Liz."

"What on earth is going on over there? Are you all right?"

"It didn't happen to me."

"Well, you should hear the stories going around. Just what did happen?"

"One of the guests, Mildred Brexton, drowned this morning."

"Oh, isn't that awful! And on a weekend too."

I thought this a strange distinction but let it go. "The place is a madhouse."

"She's not the painter's wife, is she?"

When I said she was, Liz whistled inelegantly into the phone, nearly puncturing my eardrum. People like Brexton are the fragile pillars on which the fashion world is built.

"That should make quite a splash."

I agreed. "Anyway, I'm coming to the dance tonight. The others are staying in, but I'm to be allowed out."

"Oh, good! I'll leave an invitation at the door for you. Isn't it terribly interesting?"

"You might call it that. See you later."

As I hung up, Mrs. Veering sailed slowly into view, gliding down the staircase with a priestess smile on her lips. She was loaded to the gills.

"Ah, there you are, Peter." For some reason her usually strong voice was pitched very low, gently hushed as though in a temple. "I understand we've been besieged by members of the press."

"Quite a few. More than you'd expect for a run-of-the-mill accident."

Mrs. Veering, catching a glimpse of Mary Western Lung in the drawing room, indicated for me to follow her out onto the porch, where we could be alone with the twilight. The beach looked lonely and strange in the light of early evening.

"Do you think I should give an exclusive interview to Cholly Knickerbocker or one of those people?" She looked at me questioningly; her face was very flushed and I wondered if she might not have high blood pressure as well as alcohol in her veins.

"Has he . . . or they asked you for one?"

"No, but I'm sure they will. We've been getting, as you say, an unusual amount of attention."

"I don't see it'd do any harm. I'd say that Knickerbocker would come under the heading of the right sort of publicity."

"So should I. My only fear is people will think me heartless in giving a Labor Day party so close to my niece's death."

"I wouldn't think so," I said soothingly; I had a pleasant week or two around East Hampton not to mention a salary to think of. I had no intention of letting Mrs. Veering give up her party at this stage of the game. "They'll all understand. Also, they'll be impressed by the publicity."

"Poor Mildred." With that eccentric shift of mood which I'd noticed earlier, Mrs. Veering had changed from calm rational matron to Niobe weeping over her children, if that's the one who wept over her children. She stood there beside me, quite erect, the tears streaming down her face. It was unnerving. Then, as suddenly as it'd started, her weeping ended and she wiped her eyes, blew her nose and in her usual voice said, "I think you're absolutely right. I'll have the invitations sent out Monday come hell or high water."

Considering the nature of her niece's death, I thought "high water" inept, but what the hell. "There's one thing I think I should tell you," I said, stopping her as she was about to go into the house.

"Yes?" She paused in the doorway.

"Your friend Miss Lung told the police she thought Mrs. Brexton drowned herself on purpose."

"Oh, no!" Mrs. Veering was shocked into some semblance of normality. "She didn't! She couldn't!"

"She did and she could. I found out when she cornered one of the newsmen a little while ago."

The angry alcoholic flush flickered in her cheeks, mottling them red and white. "How could she?" She stood weakly at the door.

I was soothing. "I don't suppose it'll do much harm. Nobody can prove it one way or the other unless of course there was a last message of some kind."

"But to have people say that . . . to say Mildred . . . oh, it's going to be awful." And Mrs. Veering, having said that mouthful, made straight for the drawing room and Miss Lung. I went upstairs to change for dinner.

4

I have my best ideas in the bathtub . . . at least those that don't come to me unheralded in another part of the bathroom where, enthroned, I am master of the universe.

As I crawled into the old-fashioned bathtub, a big porcelain job resembling an oversize Roman coffin, I thought seriously of what had happened, of the mystery which was beginning to cloud the air.

It's a temptation to say that, even then, I knew the answer to the puzzle, but honesty compels me to admit that I was way off in my calculations. Without going into hindsight too much, my impressions were roughly these: Mildred Brexton had had a nervous breakdown for reasons unknown (if any); there was some relationship between Claypoole and her which Brexton knew about and disliked; there were indications that Brexton might have wanted his wife dead; there was definite evidence he had attacked her recently, bruising her neck . . . all the relationships of course were a tangle, and no concern of mine. Yet the possibility that Mildred had been murdered was intriguing. I am curious by nature. Also I knew that if anything mysterious *had* happened, I would be able to get the beat on every newspaper in New York for the glory of the *New York Globe,* my old paper, and myself. I decided, all things considered, that I should do a bit of investigating. Justice didn't concern me much. But the puzzle, the danger, the excitement of following a killer's trails was all I needed to get involved. Better than big-game hunting, and much more profitable . . . if I didn't get killed myself in the process.

I made up my mind to get the story, whatever it was, before the weekend was over. I nearly did too.

I dressed and went downstairs.

Our doughty crew was gathered in the drawing room, absorbing gin.

To my surprise Brexton was on hand, looking no different than he had the night before when he made martinis. In fact, he was making them when I joined the party.

Everybody was on his best graveyard behavior. Gloom hovered in the air like a black cloud. I waded through it to the console where Brexton stood alone, the noise of the cocktail shaker in his hands the only sound in the room as the guests studiously avoided each other's gaze.

"What can I do you for?" were, I am afraid, the first words the bereaved husband said to me when I joined him. For a moment I had a feeling that this was where I came in: his tone was exactly the same as the night before.

"A martini," I said, reliving the earlier time. I half expected to see his wife examining art books on the table opposite, but tonight her absence was more noticeable than her presence had been the evening before. He poured me one with a steady hand. "I want to thank you," he said in a low voice, "for handling the press."

"I was glad to."

"I'm afraid I wasn't in any shape to talk to them. Were they pretty bad?"

I wondered what he meant by that, what he wanted to know. I shook my head. "Just routine questions."

"I hope there wasn't any talk of . . . of suicide." He looked at me sharply.

"No, it wasn't mentioned. They accepted the fact it was an accident." I paused; then I decided to let him in on Miss Lung's dereliction.

He nodded grimly when I told him what she'd said to the police. "I already know," he said quietly. "They asked me about it and I told them I sincerely doubted Mildred had any intention of killing herself. It's not a very sensible way, is it? Drowning in front of a half-dozen people, several of whom are good swimmers." I was surprised at his coolness. If he was upset by her death, he certainly didn't show it. A little chilled, I joined the others by the fireplace.

Dinner was not gala. Because Brexton was with us we didn't quite know what to talk about. Everybody was thinking about the same thing; yet it would've been bad form to talk about Mildred in front of her husband; he, of course, was the most relaxed of the lot.

It was interesting to note how the different guests reacted to the situation.

Mary Western Lung was deliberately cheery, full of "Book Chat," discussing at some length a visit she'd once paid Francine Karpin Lock, another noted penwoman, in the latter's New Orleans house. "The spirit of graciousness. And her table! Ah, what viands she offers the humblest guest!" This was followed by a close new-critical analysis of her works as compared to those of another great authoress, Taylor Caldwell. I gathered they were neck and neck—artistically speaking, that is.

Mrs. Veering spoke of the Hamptons, of local gossip, of who was leaving her husband for what other man: the sort of thing which, next to children and servant troubles, most occupies the conversation of East Hamptoners.

Fletcher Claypoole said not a word; he was pale and intense and I could see his sister was anxious. She watched him intently all through dinner and, though she and I and Brexton carried on a triangular conversation about painting, her attention was uneasily focused on her brother.

Out of deference to the situation, Mrs. Veering decided against bridge, though why, I'll never know. I should've thought any diversion would have been better than this glum company. I began to study the clock over the mantel. I decided that at exactly ten o'clock I'd excuse myself, go upstairs, change, sneak back down and walk the half-mile to the Club and Liz and a night of sexual bliss, as Marie C. Stopes would say.

My sexual bliss was postponed, however, by the rude arrival of the police.

The butler, quite shaken, ushered a sloppy little man, a detective Greaves, and two plain-clothes men into the drawing room.

Consternation would be a mild word to describe the effect they made.

"Mrs. Veering?" Greaves looked at Miss Lung.

"I am Rose Clayton Veering," said herself, rising shakily from an armchair and crossing the room with marvelous control. I'd counted her drinks that evening; she was not only loaded, but primed.

"I'm Detective Greaves, ma'am. Bureau of Criminal Investigation."

Miss Lung squeaked disconcertingly; it sounded like a mouse and startled us all. I glanced at Brexton and saw him shut his eyes with resignation.

"Pray follow me in here, Mr. Graves."

"Greaves." He followed her into the alcove; his two men withdrew to the hall. The guests, myself included, sat in a stunned circle. No one said anything. Claypoole poured himself a drink. Miss Lung looked as though she were strangling. Allie watched her brother as usual and Brexton remained motionless in his chair, his face without expression, his eyes still.

From the alcove there was a murmur of talk. I could hear Mrs. Veering's voice, indignant and emphatic, while the detective's voice was stern . . . what they said, though, we could not hear. We found out soon enough.

Mrs. Veering, her face flaming with rage, appeared in the door of the alcove accompanied by the policeman, who looked a bit sheepish. "Mr. Graves has something to say to us . . . something so ridiculous that—"

"Greaves, ma'am," he interrupted her pleasantly. "Please sit down," he said, indicating a chair. She did as he directed, controlling herself with some effort.

The detective looked at us thoughtfully. He was a sandy-haired little man with red-rimmed eyes and a pale putty face: he looked as though he never slept. But he seemed to have the situation, such as it was, well in hand.

"I hate to come barging in on you like this," he said softly, apologetically. 'I've got a list of names and I wish, as I read them off, you'd answer to your name so I'll know which is which." He ran through our names and we answered. Miss Lung startled us again with her shrill mouse-in-terrible-agony squeak.

"Thanks a lot," he said when he'd finished roll call. He was careful not to stare at any one of us too hard or too long. He kept his eyes for the most part on the doorway in the hall.

"Now, I won't keep you in the dark any longer. There is a chance that Mrs. Brexton was murdered this morning."

Not a sound greeted this news. We stared back at him, too stunned to comment.

He was disappointed not to have made a different effect. I could see he'd expected some kind of a rise, a significant outburst; instead he got deep silence. This gang was smarter than he'd thought, than I'd thought. I glanced rapidly at the faces but could see nothing more than intense interest in any of them.

When this had been allowed to sink in, he went on softly, "We're not sure, of course. It's a queer kind of case. This afternoon an autopsy was performed and it was discovered that the deceased died by drowning; there was no question of a heart attack or of any other physical failure. Her internal organs were sound and undiseased. She was apparently in good physical condition . . ."

"Then how could she've drowned like that, since she was a first-rate swimmer?" Claypoole's voice was tense with strain; it came surprisingly clear across the room.

Greaves looked at him with mild interest. "That's why we're here, Mr. . . . Claypoole. There was apparently *no* reason for her to drown so quickly so near shore, with three people attempting rescue . . ."

"Unless she wanted to." Miss Lung's voice was complacent; she was beginning to recover her usual composure and confidence.

"That is a possibility . . . I hope a probability. It is the alternative we'd like to accept. Otherwise, I'm afraid we're stuck with a murder by party or parties unknown."

There it was. Mrs. Veering rallied first. "Mr. Greaves, this is all supposition on your part, and very dangerous too. Regardless of what you might think, there is no evidence that my niece wanted to drown herself, nor is there the faintest possibility anybody murdered her. She was in a peculiar mental state as the result of a nervous breakdown ... I told you all that a few minutes ago ... In her condition she was quite apt to lose her head, to drown in that terrible undertow." I was surprised at Mrs. Veering's sharpness. She was completely sobered now and all her usual vagueness and nonsense had been replaced by a steely clarity, and anger.

"An intelligent analysis." Greaves nodded approvingly, as though a favorite pupil had come through. "That was our opinion, too, when the death was reported this morning. Almost every day there's something like this in these parts, a sudden drowning. Unfortunately, the autopsy revealed something odd. It seems that before going in swimming, immediately *after* breakfast, Mrs. Brexton took four sleeping pills ... or was given four sleeping pills."

This time the silence was complete. No one said anything. Mrs. Veering opened her mouth to speak, then shut it again, like a mackerel on dry land.

"With Mrs. Veering's permission, I'd like to have the house searched for the bottle which contained the pills."

Our hostess nodded, too dazed for words. Greaves poked his head into the hall and said, "O.K., boys." The boys started their search of the house.

"Meanwhile," continued the detective, "I'd appreciate it if everyone remained in this room while I interview you all, individually." He accepted our silence as agreement. To my surprise he motioned to me. "You'll be first, Mr. Sargeant," he said. I followed him into the alcove. Behind us the sudden buzz of talk, like a hive at swarming time, broke upon the drawing room: indignation, alarm, fear.

He asked me the routine questions and I gave him the routine answers.

Then he got down to the case in hand. At this point, I was still undecided as to what I wanted to do. My mind was working quickly. I've done a few pieces for the *New York Globe* since I left them and I knew that I could get a nice sum of money for any story I might do on the death of Mildred Brexton; at the same time, there was the problem of Mrs. Veering and my business loyalty to her. This was decidedly the kind of publicity which would be bad for her. I was split down the middle trying to figure out what angle to work. While answering his questions, I made an important decision: I decided to say nothing of the quarrel I'd overheard between Brexton and Claypoole.

This, I decided, would be my ace-in-the-hole if I should decide to get a beat on the other newspaper people. All in all, I made a mistake.

"Now, Mr. Sargeant, you have, I gather, no real connection with any of these people, is that right?"

I nodded. "Never saw any of them until last night."

"Your impression, then, should be useful, as an unprejudiced outsider . . . assuming you're telling us the truth." The detective smiled sadly at me.

"I understand all about perjury," I said stuffily.

"I'm very glad," said the officer of the law gently. "What, then, was your impression of Mrs. Brexton when you first saw her?"

"A fairly good-looking, disagreeable woman, very edgy."

"Was anything said about her nervous breakdown?"

I nodded. "Yes, it was mentioned, to explain her conduct, which was unsocial, to say the least."

"Who mentioned it to you?"

He was no clod; I began to have a certain respect for him. I could follow his thought; it made me think along lines that hadn't occurred to me before. "Mrs. Veering, for one, and Miss Claypoole for another and, I think, Miss Lung said something about it too."

"Before or after the . . . death?"

"Before, I think. I'm not sure. Anyway, I did get the impression pretty quick that she was in a bad way mentally and had to be catered to. It all came out in the open the night before she died, when there was some kind of scene between her and her husband." I told him about the screams, about Mrs. Veering's coming to us with soothing words. He took all this down without comment. I couldn't tell whether it was news to him or not. I assumed it was, since he hadn't interviewed any of the others yet. I figured I'd better tell him this, since he would hear about it soon enough from them. I was already beginning to think of him as a competitor. In the past I'd managed, largely by accident, to solve a couple of peculiar crimes. This one looked promising; it was certainly bewildering enough.

"No one actually *saw* Mrs. Brexton screaming?"

"We all heard her. I suppose her husband must've been with her and I think maybe Mrs. Veering was there too, though I don't know. She seemed to be coming from their bedroom, from downstairs, when she told us not to worry."

"I see. Now tell me about this morning."

I told him exactly what had happened: how Brexton got to Mildred first and then nearly drowned himself; how Claypoole pulled her to shore; how I rescued Brexton.

He took this down without comment. I could see he was wondering the same thing I'd begun to wonder: had Brexton had a chance to pull his wife under just before we got there? I couldn't be absolutely sure because the surf had been in my eyes most of the way out and I hadn't been able to see properly. I doubted it . . . if only because, when I reached them, Brexton was still several feet from his wife, who was already half dead. That Claypole might have drowned her on the long pull back to shore was an equal possibility, but I didn't mention it to Greaves, who didn't ask me either. He was only interested in getting the eyewitness part straight.

I asked a question then. "Just what effect would four sleeping pills have . . . four of the kind she took? Are they fatal?"

He looked at me thoughtfully, as though wondering whether to bother answering or not. Finally he said, "They weren't enough to kill her. Make her weak, though, groggy . . . they slowed down the beating of the heart."

"Well, that explains the funny way she swam. I thought the others were just sounding off when they said she was such a fine athlete. She almost fell on her face in the first dive into the surf, and her strokes were all off . . . even I could tell that, and I'm no coach."

"There's no doubt she died as a result of weakness. She wasn't strong enough to get out of the undertow. The question of course is why, if she'd taken the pills herself, would she've gone in the water instead of to bed, where she belonged?"

"To kill herself?" This was the puzzle, I knew.

"A possibility."

"But then, somebody might've slipped her those pills, knowing she would probably go swimming."

"Another possibility." Greaves was enigmatic.

"But how could anybody count on that happening? She wasn't feeling well . . . maybe she would've just stayed on the shore in the sun. From what I saw of her, that would've been *my* guess. I was even surprised, now that I look back, that she went in the ocean at all."

"The person who gave her the pills might have known her better than you. He might've known she would go in the water no matter what her condition." Greaves made notes while he talked.

"And the person who knew her best was, of course, her husband."

Greaves looked at me steadily. "I didn't say that."

"Who else? Even so, if I were Brexton and I wanted to kill my wife, I wouldn't do it like that, with everybody else around."

"Fortunately, you're not Brexton." The coldness in his voice gave me all the clue I needed. The police thought Brexton had killed his wife. I don't know why, but even then I didn't think he was responsible. I suppose because my mind dislikes the obvious, even though the obvious, as any detective will tell you, nine times out of ten provides the answer.

I threw one last doubt in his path. "Why, if somebody was going to give her pills, didn't they give her a fatal dose?"

"We must find that out." Greaves was reasonable, polite, bored with me.

Wanting to attract his attention for future need, I said coolly, "I'll be writing about all this for the *New York Globe.*"

This had the effect I intended. He winced visibly. "I thought you were in public relations, Mr. Sargeant."

"I used to be on the *Globe*. In the last few years I've done some features for them. I guess you remember that business a couple of years back when Senator Rhodes was murdered . . ."

Greaves looked at me with some interest. "You're *that* fellow? I remember the case."

"I was, if I may say so myself, of some use to the police."

"That wasn't the way I heard it."

This was irritating. "Well, no matter how you heard it, I intend to do a series on this case for the *Globe,* assuming there really was a murder done, which I doubt."

"Very interesting." Greaves looked at me calmly. At that moment one of the policemen came in and whispered something in his ear. Greaves nodded and the other handed him a handkerchief containing two small cylindrical objects. The policeman withdrew.

"Sleeping-pill containers?" I guessed that one right.

He nodded, carefully opening the handkerchief. "As a professional journalist and amateur sleuth, Mr. Sargeant, you should be interested to know that they were found in two places: one bottle in Mrs. Brexton's jewel box; the other in Fletcher Claypoole's bathroom. Both contain the same barbiturate found in Mrs. Brexton's system. Our problem is to determine, if possible, from which bottle the pills she took (or was given) came."

"Just like spin-the-bottle, isn't it?"

"That will be all, Mr. Sargeant."

I had one more shot to fire. I let him have it. "The bruise on Mrs. Brexton's neck was made *before* she went swimming. I noticed it last night at dinner."

"You're very observant, Mr. Sargeant. Thank you."

III

Shortly after one o'clock I sneaked down the back stairs of the house, across the deserted kitchen and out the back door. The policeman on guard was faced the other way, sprawled in a wicker armchair at the corner of the house. I ducked down behind the dunes, cursing the clear black night in which the white moon rode like a searchlight, casting dense shadows across the dunes, scattering silver light on the cold sea.

I made it to the road, however, without being observed. We'd all been told to remain in the house until further notice and I'd excused myself as soon as possible and gone up to bed, praying the dance wouldn't be over yet.

It wasn't.

East Hampton is a funny place with any number of sets, each mutually exclusive. The center of the village's summer life of course is the group of old-timers who belong to the Ladyrock Yacht Club, a rambling building with a long pier, situated a mile or so north of Mrs. Veering's house, on the road to Amagansett.

Members of the Club are well-to-do (but not wealthy) socially accepted (but not quite "prominent") of good-middle-class American stock (proud of their ancient lineage, which goes back usually to some eighteenth-century farmer). Their names are not known to the general public, yet they feel that America is a pyramid at the apex of which will be found themselves, a delusion nurtured by the fact that they are not accepted by the rich and the great, while they refuse to associate with those poorer than themselves. The favorite word, however, the highest praise, is "nice." You hear that word every few minutes in their company. So-and-so is nice, while somebody else isn't. They have divided the world neatly between the nice and the not-nice, and they're pretty happy with their side of the border.

Part of being nice means you belong to the Club and deplore the presence in the community of such un-nice elements as Jews, artists, fairies and celebrities, four groups which, given half a chance, will, they feel, sweep all that's nice right out to sea. Fortunately the other elements are not conscious of them; otherwise, there could be trouble in this divided village.

As it is, the painters and such-like mind their own business in the south end of the town, while their nicer neighbors live contentedly together in big houses and small cottages near the Ladyrock; they go to the John Drew Theatre in the town; they give parties for one another where at least half of the guests get drunk and the other half gets offended; they swap wives and husbands while their children coast around at great speed in new cars from Hampton to Hampton, wrapping themselves periodically around telephone poles. A typical resort community, and a nice one.

The clubhouse was lighted with Japanese lanterns. A good band was playing. College boys and girls were necking on the dark pier, which extended out into the sea. After a fumble with a pile of cards at the door, I was let in to join the nice people, who were, all in all, a fairly handsome crew, divided evenly between the well-fed middle-aged and the golden young on their summer vacation. The middle generation, mine, were all off working to make enough money to get a summer place out here and, at forty, to join the Ladyrock Yacht Club.

Liz found me at the bar, where I was ordering a Manhattan and hoping she'd come along and sign for it.

She was beautiful, in black and white with something or other shining in her hair: her eyes glittered and she was pleasantly high.

"Oh, it's wonderful you got away! I was afraid you wouldn't be able to." She signed for my drink like a good girl. "Come on, let's dance."

"Not until I've had this."

"Well, come out on the pier then. I want to talk to you." We made our way slowly across the dance floor. Young and old bucks pawed Liz, who apparently was the belle of this ball. Several old school friends of mine, bald and plump (guests like myself; not yet members) greeted me and I knew at least a dozen of the girls, which Liz didn't like.

"You're such a flirt," she said, once we were on the pier. The moon shone white upon our heads. The young lovers were farther out on the pier. A number of alcoholics reeled cheerfully along the boardwalk which separated the pier from the club itself.

"I've just been around a long time."

But she was more interested in the murder. And she knew it was murder. "It's all over town!" she said excitedly. "Everybody says Brexton drowned her."

"I wonder how that rumor started?" I hedged.

"Oh, *you* know and won't tell me." She looked at me accusingly. "I promise I won't breathe a word to anybody."

"On your honor as a Girl Guide?"

"Oh, Peter, tell me! You were there. You saw it happen, didn't you?"

"I saw it happen, all right." I put my empty glass down on the railing and put one arm around her; she shook away.

"You *have* to tell," she said.

"Don't I appeal to you?"

"Men don't appeal to women, as you well know," she said loftily. "We are only interested in homemaking and, on top of that, our sexual instinct does not fully develop until the late twenties. I'm too young to have any responses."

"But I'm too old. The male, as we all know, reaches his sexual peak at sixteen, after which he declines steadily into a messy old age. I am long past my prime . . . an erotic shell, capable of only a minor—"

"Oh, Peter, tell me or I'll scream!" Her curiosity brought an end to our Kinseyan dialogue. It has recently become the aim of our set to act entirely in accordance with the master's findings, and what the majority do and feel, we do and feel, more or less. But my companion, deeply interested in murder like any healthy young girl, had begun to scream.

"For God's sake, shut up!" I said nervously. Luckily only alcoholics were on the terrace . . . a trio of minor executives in minor banks applauded softly her first scream; the couples on the pier were all engaged in pre-marital petting (college-type) and chose not to hear.

"You'll tell me?" She took a deep breath, ready for a louder scream.

"There's nothing to tell. Mrs. Brexton took four sleeping pills, went in swimming and drowned before we could get to her."

"*Why* did she take four sleeping pills?"

"That is the question which hovers over all our heads like the sword of Themistocles."

"Damocles," said that classical scholar. "Somebody give her the pills?"

"Who knows?"

"She took them herself?"

"So I think, but the police have other ideas."

"Like Paul Brexton giving them to her secretly?"

"Or someone else . . . though why the non-fatal four, I'll never know. If he really wanted to do her in, I should think the usual dozen would have been in order."

"It's all a devious plot, Peter. Any fool can see it. She was going in swimming: what could be smarter than giving her something to make her groggy just as she got out in that awful undertow?"

"I can think of a lot of things which'd be smarter. Among them . . ." I slipped my arm around her again, but she was extremely unresponsive.

"On the other hand, I don't suppose there was any way of knowing for sure she would go in the water. Oh, isn't it terribly exciting? And happening to Brexton, too, of all people."

"It will cause unpleasant talk," I said, drawing her even closer to me; I smelled lilacs and the fresh warm odor of Liz.

"What on earth do you have in mind, Peter?"

"It's not in my mind . . ."

"Filthy, brutish creatures . . . all men are the same."

"If you'd rather, I'll get you a sixteen-year-old boy."

"And what on earth would I do with one of those?"

"Modesty impels me to draw a veil over—"

"It'll be in all the papers, won't it?"

"What? The sixteen-year—"

"No, you idiot. Mrs. Brexton's death."

"Well, of course . . ."

"Isn't that just wonderful for you? That's your job, isn't it?"

"I wasn't hired to handle Mrs. Brexton's murder." As I said this I was suddenly startled by the implications. It was too wild . . . yet mightn't Mrs. Veering have suspected there'd be trouble and hired me in advance, just in case? She was the kind to look ahead: a combination Hetty Green and lush. The possibility that *she* might have been the one to ease her niece into a more beautiful world occurred to me then. Motive was obscure, but then, I didn't know anybody's motive . . . they were all strangers to me. Even so, it was the kind of thing Mrs. Veering *might* do . . . she was both mad and methodical, an unusual combination. The thought was sobering.

Liz noticed my sudden thoughtfulness. "What're you thinking about?" she asked. "Are you considering ways of seducing me?"

I snorted. "What is more ignoble than a woman? You have not the slightest sensual interest in the male, even in such a perfect specimen as myself, yet at all hours of the day and night you think about seduction."

"And homemaking. A little two-room apartment in Peter Cooper Village. Birdseye products in the Frigidaire . . . Clapp's strained baby food on the shelf and a darling fat baby wetting itself periodically in a special fourteen ninety-five Baby Leroy crib from Macy's."

"My God, you *are* prepared for marriage!"

Liz smiled enigmatically. "We all are. Actually, I'm doing a piece on the young married couple in New York City for one of the magazines, not *Harper's Bazaar*. Something more middle-class. They want me to describe bliss on thirty-five dollars a week. You don't know what a good wife I'll make!"

"There's more to marriage than that."

"Than thirty-five dollars? I suppose there is. I think I'd like someone very rich. But seriously, Peter, you don't really believe Brexton killed his wife, do you? I mean it just isn't the kind of thing that happens."

"I don't know what to think." This was my clearest statement so far, and the most accurate. I then swore her to secrecy and we went back inside.

Everyone was fairly tight. The very nicest people had gone home. Only one stag had been knocked down in the john (you may recall what happened to the late Huey Long in a Long Island men's room some years ago); a husband and wife (another woman's husband, another man's wife) were locked tight together in a dim corner of the room. The college set, a particularly beautiful gang of sunburned animals, were singing songs and feeling each other happily while plotting their next move, which, from what I overheard, was an all-out attack on Southampton. Already I could hear the crash of cars into solid objects, the tinkling of broken glass: youth!

And youth, in the congenial form of Liz Bessemer, was all mine that night. Her uncle and aunt had gone home. The various bucks who had been competing for her favors had either gone off with whatever available girls were on hand or had quietly passed out among the parked convertibles.

"Let's go to Montauk!" This brilliant idea came to Liz as we moved slowly around the dance floor, waltzing to a fox trot . . . I have no sense of beat and, besides, only know how to waltz, which I do fairly well to any music.

"Walking?"

"I'll drive. I've got the car . . . at least I think I have. Aunt went home in our guest's car . . . I hope."

Aunt had indeed gone home in the houseguest's car, leaving us a fine Buick with its top down.

She leaped into the driver's seat and I relaxed beside her as we drove swiftly down the center of the long straight road which runs parallel to the dunes all the way to Montauk, Long Island's sandy terminus.

The moon almost blinded us; it shone directly in our eyes. We stopped a long way before Montauk. At my direction, we turned off the road and drove down a sandy trail which ended in the Atlantic Ocean. Between two dunes, a mile from the nearest darkened house, we made love.

I've never seen such a night as that one. The sky was filmed with all the stars available in that happy latitude while everywhere, in every part of the sky, meteors were falling.

When it was over, we lay side by side on the sand, which was still faintly warm from the sun, and we looked at the stars, the meteors and the moon. A salt breeze dried our naked bodies. She shivered and I put my arm under her and pulled her close . . . she was light in my arms.

"I ought to get back," she said, her voice small, no longer teasing.

"Almost day." We thought about that for a while. She pulled herself up on her elbow and looked at me curiously in the moonlight. "What are you thinking about?" she asked.

"Nothing."

"Tell me."

"Nothing . . . except maybe how pleasant it is on the beach like this and how much I'll hate having to get dressed again and go back to that house."

She sighed and stretched. "It *was* nice, wasn't it?"

I pulled her down on my chest and kissed her for answer; her small breasts tickled my skin. I was ready again, even though at my age I'm officially past the peak, but she sensed this and, instead, got to her feet and ran down to the water and dived in.

Remembering what had happened less than twenty-four hours before, I was scared to death. I leaped into the cold black water after her.

362

Fortunately, she was a good swimmer and we kept well within the surf line. It was strange, swimming in that black ocean under a black sky ... the moon and the beach white, and the tops of the waves bright with phosphorus.

Then, shivering and laughing, we ran back to the car and dried ourselves with her aunt's lap rug.

We both agreed that the other looked just fine with no clothes on and Liz admitted shyly to me that she got a minor thrill out of observing the male body in a state of nature if she liked the person who owned the body. I told her she was unnatural and might end up as a footnote in a textbook.

In a happy mood, we drove south and she let me off a few yards from the North Dunes just as daylight, gray and pink, smudged the east.

"Tomorrow?"

She nodded. "If I can manage it. I don't know what's on."

"I don't either, but I can sneak off."

"I can, too. I'll call you when I know."

We kissed long and blissfully; then she was gone in a screech of gears. She was one of the worst drivers I've ever known, but she was also a wonderful girl. I experienced an emotion which was something more than my usual athleticism; then I quickly put all romantic thoughts out of my head. She was a lovely girl; the night had been perfect; the moon bright; what should've happened did happen and that was that. I am not the serious kind in these matters, I said to myself sternly as I opened the back door quietly and stepped into the kitchen.

2

I came to in bed.

My head felt as if someone had whetted an ax on it and at first I suffered from double vision. Everything was blurred. Then, with an effort, I brought Mrs. Veering into focus.

She was standing over me with an anxious look on her face. Light streamed in the window.

"What time is it?" I asked.

"Ten o'clock. You certainly had us scared out of our wits! What on earth happened to you?"

I put my hand to my head where an enormous lump had formed. No skin had been broken and there was no bandage, only an aching head. "I haven't any idea. I got home about dawn and—"

Greaves appeared in the doorway. "Has he been conscious long, Mrs. Veering?"

"Just this moment. If you—"

"Could you leave us alone, please. I'd like to ask Mr. Sargeant a few questions."

"Certainly." With a reassuring pat Mrs. Veering trotted off, shutting the door behind her.

"Well?" The policeman looked at me, half smiling.

"Well what?" I felt awful. I noticed I was wearing only a shirt and shorts. I was suddenly very hot under the blanket. I threw it off and sat up dizzily, swinging my legs over the side of the bed.

"Were you trying to do our job for us, Mr. Sargeant?"

"Go away."

"I'm afraid you must answer my questions. You received a severe blow but, according to the doctor, there was no concussion and you'll be able to get up whenever you like."

"Would you do me the courtesy of going away and coming back when I feel better?" My head was pounding with pain as I moved shakily toward the bathroom. "I'm going to perform a natural function," I said sharply.

"I can wait."

I groaned and went into the bathroom, where I put my head under the cold-water tap; then I took two Empirin tablets, figuring if I wasn't supposed to take any, I'd have been warned. I was being treated too damn casually, I thought.

When I returned, Greaves was seated in the armchair by my bed, making marks in a small notebook.

"You still here?"

"What happened?" He looked at me expectantly.

"A woman dressed all in black and carrying what seemed to be calla lilies was crossing the kitchen when I entered. When I asked her if I might be of any assistance, she brought the lilies down on my head, shrieking, 'Thus to all members of the MacTavish clan!'"

Greaves looked faintly alarmed, as though not sure how serious the blow might have been. "Calla lilies?" he asked.

"Or something." I took my clothes off, hoping that would get rid of him, but he still regarded me with the same abstracted air while I got into a bathing suit.

"You didn't see her face?"

"I am making fun of you," I said, feeling light in the head as though I'd drunk too much too fast. I sat down weakly on the edge of the bed. "Didn't see anybody. Walked in the kitchen door and bang! that was the end until I just now opened my eyes."

"You were struck from the right side by a metal object held by a person as tall or a little taller than yourself."

"Or standing on a chair . . ."

"Or standing on something, yes. You were discovered at seven-thirty by the cook, who screamed for four minutes. One of my men brought you up here and a doctor was called."

"No clues?"

"We call them leads, Mr. Sargeant. The police department is not—"

"Then, were there any leads . . . like a strand of blond hair soaked in blood or maybe the old dandruff of a middle-aged murderer scattered beside my still form?"

"Nothing but your still form was found." He paused, indicating that for his money it wasn't still enough.

"Well, there's nothing more I can say."

"You were out. You left the house after I expressly asked everyone to stay in. You were dressed in a—"

"—tuxedo with a loose inner button. I went to the Ladyrock Yacht Club."

"After which you and a Miss Liz Bessemer drove north to Amagansett."

This stopped me. "What happened then, in Amagansett?"

"I don't know and I don't care. Miss Bessemer dropped you off here at five-twenty or thereabouts."

"I suppose your man saw all this? The one who was sound asleep when I came home."

"He *was* sound asleep and he's been replaced." Greaves was calm, implacable. "Sargeant, what do you know?"

He whipped this last out like a spray of cold water in my face. He was leaning forward now, intense, grimly serious.

"About what?" The Empirin hadn't begun to work yet and my head ached fiercely.

"You know something you haven't told us, something important . . . you know enough for the murderer to want to kill you."

This had occurred to me some minutes before when I came to, aware I'd been clubbed. I was in the dark, though. I was fairly certain neither

Brexton nor Claypoole knew I'd overheard their conversation. They were the likeliest pair.

Greaves was on a different tack, however. I found out soon enough what was on his mind. "What did you see out there in the water, when Mrs. Brexton was drowning? What did Brexton do exactly? What did Claypoole do? And the woman, did she speak? Did she call for help?"

"You think I saw something out there that somebody . . . the murderer, didn't want me to, is that it?"

"That's it."

I shook my head, which was beginning, slowly, to clear. "I've gone over the whole thing a dozen times in my mind since it happened, but I can't find anything unusual . . . anything you don't already know."

"How close was Brexton to his wife when you got to him?"

"About five feet, I'd say . . . not very close. He was gagging and getting blue in the face. I grabbed him while—"

"—Claypoole grabbed Mrs. Brexton."

"Yes. Then we came in to shore."

"Brexton never touched his wife, did he?"

I shook my head. "I don't think so. The spray was in my eyes. I was bucking surf all the way. When I got there, she was sinking, going down again and again, hardly struggling enough to get herself back up. She didn't make a sound."

"And Claypoole?"

"He was behind me all the way until we finally got out to them; then he spurted on ahead and grabbed Mrs. Brexton. I had my hands full with her husband."

"How did Claypoole handle her on the way in?"

"I wasn't watching. About the same way I managed Brexton . . . standard Junior Life Saver stuff."

Greaves lit a pipe thoughtfully. "He'll try it again."

"Who will try what?"

"The murderer will take another crack at you."

I chuckled, though I didn't feel any too merry. "I don't think that's why I was cracked over the head. After all, if somebody was interested in killing me, he wouldn't rely on one blow to do it. On top of that, how'd he know I was going to come creeping into the kitchen at five A.M.? And what was *he* doing there?"

"These are all questions we mean to consider," said Greaves with the slow ponderousness of a public servant out of his depth.

"Well, while you're considering them I'm going to get something to eat, and some sun. I ache all over."

"I'd be careful if I were you, Mr. Sargeant."

"I'll do my best. You might keep your boys on the alert, too."

"I intend to. There's a murderer in this house, Mr. Sargeant, and it's my opinion he's after you."

"You make me feel like a clay pigeon."

"I think 'bait' is a better word, don't you?" He was a cold bastard.

3

I got some breakfast on the porch where I held court, surrounded by the ladies of the party to whom I was something of a hero. Claypoole, it seemed, was in East Hampton and Brexton was in his room painting ... though where he'd get enough light I didn't know, glancing at the window near the chair where I sat with the ladies, aware that everything we said could be heard by anyone in that room.

It was Mary Western Lung who most appreciated my situation. She was in her yellow slacks; her harlequin glasses, adorned with rhinestones, glittered in the sun which streamed across the porch. "We all came running when the cook started carrying on. You never *saw* such a commotion . . . you looked so dead, there on the floor. *I* called for a doctor," she added, to show that hers was the clearest head.

"Did you get a glimpse of who did it?" Allie Claypoole was gratifyingly tense.

"No, nothing at all. When I opened the door to the kitchen somebody slugged me."

Mrs. Veering stirred her orange juice with her forefinger; I wondered what pale firewater it contained, probably gin, the breakfast drink. "The police requested us all to keep quiet about this," she said. "I can't think why. My theory is that we had a prowler . . . there's one loose in Southampton, you know. I think he stumbled in here; when he heard you he was frightened and—"

"—and tiptoed quietly home, past a sleeping policeman on the front porch?" I shook my head. "I don't think a run-of-the-mill burglar would go anywhere near a house with a policeman standing guard, even a sleeping one."

The others agreed. Mrs. Veering preferred her theory, though. The alternative made everybody nervous.

It was Miss Lung who said what we were thinking. "Somebody in this house wanted to . . . rub out Mr. Sargeant." She paused, eyes wide, obviously pleased with "rub out."

"The murderer," I said agreeably, "obviously thinks I know something." As I talked I was aware of that open window two yards away, of Brexton listening. "I don't, of course. The whole thing's—"

"—a nightmare!" Allie was suddenly vehement. "It *couldn't* be more awful, more pointless!"

"I think," said Mrs. Veering sternly, "that everybody tends to jump to conclusions. There's no proof that Mildred was murdered. *I* decline to think she was. Certainly no one here would do such a thing and as for Mr. Sargeant . . . well, there *are* other explanations." What they were, though, she didn't see fit to tell us. She turned accusingly to Mary Western Lung. "And I thought you *particularly* agreed with me that murder was out of the question."

Miss Lung gestured vaguely with her pincushion of a hand. "What happened to Mr. Sargeant changed my mind. As you know, I felt all along that poor Mildred had every intention of meeting her Maker when she stepped into that water yesterday. But now I'm not so sure."

They argued for some time about what had happened. There were no facts to go on other than my unexpected conjunction with a bit of metal. None of them had, until then, wanted to face the fact that Mildred was murdered. Their reasons were unknown to me . . . and their reasons, if ever I could understand them, would provide a key to the tangle. It was precisely at that moment, while drinking coffee and listening to the chatter of three women, that I made up my mind to go after the killer. The fact that he, or she, had gone after me first, of course, had something to do with my decision; I had no intention of dying in East Hampton that summer.

Mrs. Veering wanted to see me privately after breakfast, but I excused myself first to make some telephone calls. I cornered several newspapers and took them up to my room, which was now empty. I'm ashamed to confess I looked under the bed and in the closet before locking the door.

Then I read the papers quickly. No mention of murder yet. But the stories hinted at mysteries. The *Daily News* announced that the deceased had had a nervous breakdown, and indicated tactfully that suicide was a possibility. That seemed to be the general line in the press. There were some old pictures of Brexton about the time of their marriage, looking very Newport and not very Bohemian. Mrs. Veering was good for a picture in the *Journal* and the *Globe*. This was fine; she was still my client.

I telephoned Miss Flynn, wondering if anybody else was listening on the wire. House-party telephones are notorious; I suspect a great many divorces have occurred as a result of weekends at big houses with a lot of phones, all tuned in on one another.

Miss Flynn was cold. "I assume the late socialite wife of the well-known Modern Painter died a Natural Death?" The skepticism in her voice was heavy enough to cauterize the receiver.

"As far as we know," I said glibly. "Now, I may have to stay out here for a week. The police have asked—"

"I understand." She was a rock. She cut short any further explanations. "I will carry on at the office as best I can," she said. "I assume you will be in touch with the *Globe*."

"Well, come to think of it, I might give them a ring to find out if they'd like me to do—"

"—the Human Interest Angle, I know. I trust you will be cautious in your investigations."

I assured her that I would be. I told her then what I wanted done for our various clients during my absence.

Then I got the managing editor of the *New York Globe* at his home in Westport.

"Good to hear from you, boy. Not mixed up in another murder, are you?"

"Matter of fact, I am."

I could hear a quick intake of breath on the other end of the line; the managing editor was rapidly figuring how cheaply he could buy me. We had done business before. "What's the deal?" he asked, his voice carefully bored.

"Mildred Brexton."

"East Hampton? Are you out there now?"

"In Mrs. Veering's house. I suppose you've been following—"

"Thought it was an accident."

"Police think not. Now . . ." We haggled like gentlemen and I got my price. I also asked him to get me all the material he could on Mrs. Veering, the Claypooles, the Brextons and Mary Western Lung . . . they were all more or less public figures, either professionally or socially. He said he would and I told him I'd have a story for him in a couple of days, long before the other services had even got an interview out of the principals. I hung up . . . a second later I lifted the receiver and heard a click on the wire. Somebody had been listening.

The back of my head was beginning to feel more human, though it was still oddly shaped. I went back downstairs. On my way through the hall, Mrs. Veering beckoned to me from the door to the sunroom. I joined her in there. We were alone; the others were out on the beach. The police were nowhere in sight.

"Where's Greaves?" I asked.

"Gone . . . for the time being. We have a twenty-four-hour guard, though," she added dramatically. For once the inevitable tumbler of the waters of Lethe was not at hand. I wondered if she was sober; I wondered if there was any way of telling.

"I suppose he's investigating."

"Mr. Sergeant . . . Peter, I believe we are all in terrible danger."

I took this calmly enough . . . I could even go along with it. "Doesn't seem to be anything we can do about it," I said noncommittally.

"There must be!" She clasped and unclasped her hands nervously.

"I thought you felt it was an accident, that I was slugged by a prowler and—"

"I didn't want to upset the others. I didn't want them to know that I *knew.*" She looked at me darkly.

"Knew what?"

"That there is danger."

I decided she was off her rocker, or else *did* know something the rest of us didn't. "Have you told the police?"

"I can't tell them anything. It's only a . . . presentiment."

"Do you or don't you think Mrs. Brexton was murdered?"

She would not answer; instead she just sighed and looked out of the window at the velvety-green golf course, brilliant as a pool table in the light of noon. She changed the subject with that rapidity which I was finally getting used to; alcoholics find any train of thought too-long-sustained tiring. "I want you to mention my Labor Day party in your first dispatch to the *Globe.*" She smiled at me.

"You were listening on the phone?"

"Say that a little bird told me." She was coy.

"You don't mind my writing about the murder?"

"Of course I mind but, since everyone else will be writing about it in those *awful* tabloids, it'll be to my advantage to have you here in the house, a gentleman." Her realism always surprised me.

"I was afraid you might be upset."

"Not at all, but I'd like to see what you write from time to time. I may be able to help you."

"That'd be awfully nice of you."

"Not at all."

"Was your niece murdered?" I asked suddenly, trying to catch her off guard.

"You'll get no help from me there." And that was the end of that interview; I left her for the beach and the sun.

I found only Allie Claypoole on the beach.

She was lying on her back in a red two-piece bathing suit which was exciting to contemplate; I found her most attractive and, if it hadn't been for my fling with Liz the night before, and the peculiar discovery that despite a lifetime devoted to philandering I was unexpectedly held to the idea of Liz and didn't want anybody else, not even the slender Allie, who looked up at me with a smile and said, "Recovered?"

I sat down beside her on the sand. The sun was soothing. The sea sparkled. Just twenty-four hours before, it had happened. "I feel much better. Where's everybody?"

"Miss Lung has gone inside to write this week's 'Book Chat,' while my brother's in town. Brexton's in his room still. What on earth is going on?"

I gestured helplessly. "I haven't any idea. I never saw any of these people before Friday. *You* ought to know."

"I can't make any sense out of it." She rubbed oil on her brown arms.

"Mrs. Veering feels we are all in terrible danger."

Allie smiled wanly. "I'm afraid Rose always feels she's in great danger, especially when she's been drinking."

"She seemed quite sober this morning."

"You never can tell. I wouldn't take anything she says too seriously. It's all part of her own private madness."

"On the other hand, that knock on the head I got this morning was not just one of her hallucinations."

"No, that's more serious. Even so, I can't really believe anybody killed Mildred—not one of us, that is. This is the sort of thing which is supposed to happen to other people."

"What do *you* think happened?" I looked at her innocently; I had to pump these people, one by one. The best approach was bewildered stupidity.

"I believe what Paul says."

This was news; I hadn't known that Brexton had expressed himself yet on the murder, except perhaps to the police. "What does he say?"

"That Mildred was in the habit of taking sleeping pills at all hours of the day, to calm her nerves. That the ones she took the morning she died were a standard dose for her and that she went in swimming not realizing how tough the undertow was."

"Well, it sounds sensible."

"Except that my brother had a bottle of the same type pills . . ."

"You don't mean they suspect him?"

She shook her head, her face grim. "No, I don't think they do. He had no motive and, even if he did, there's no proof the pills came from him. Their idea seems to be that somebody might have had access to his bathroom who didn't have access to Mildred's pills, which were kept locked in her jewel box; she was the only one who knew the combination. Brexton swears *he* never knew it and couldn't have got the thing open if he wanted to."

"So either she got the pills herself or somebody went into your brother's bathroom and got some to put in her coffee or whatever it was she took them in?"

"That's the general line. If you hadn't been attacked last night, I'd have thought Mildred took the pills herself. Now I'm not sure."

"It looks like my adventure may have started the whole thing rolling."

She nodded. "I thought that awful man Graves, or whatever his name is, was just trying to scare us, to get himself attention. I still don't think he has the vaguest idea whether or not a murder was committed."

"He's fairly sure now. Are you?"

"I don't know what to think."

"What was between your brother and Mildred?" I asked this all in one breath, to take her by surprise; it did.

Her eyelids fluttered with alarm; she frowned, taken aback. "What . . . what makes you think anything . . .?"

"Mrs. Veering," I lied. "She told me that years ago—"

"That bloody fool!" She literally snarled, but then she was in control again. She even managed to laugh convincingly to cover up her sudden lapse. "I'm sorry," she said quickly. "It just seems so unnecessary, raking up family skeletons. The facts are simple enough: Mildred was engaged to marry my brother. Then she met Brexton and married him instead. That's all. My brother was devoted to her and not too friendly with Brexton, though they got on . . . that's all there is to it."

"Why didn't she marry your brother?"

She was evasive. "I suppose Brexton was more glamorous to her."

"Did *you* like the idea of his marrying her?"

"I can't think that that has anything to do with it, Mr. Sargeant." She looked at me coldly.

"I suppose it doesn't. I'm sorry. It's just that if I'm to be used as a punching bag by a murderer, I'd like to know a little something about what's going on."

"I'm sorry." She was quick to respond. "I didn't mean to be unpleasant. It's just that it's a sore subject with all of us. In fact, I didn't even want to come down here for the weekend, but Fletcher insisted. He was very fond of Mildred, always."

I was slowly getting an idea of the relationships involved, as much from what she didn't say as what she did.

The butler called me from the terrace. Liz was on the telephone. I answered it in the hall.

"Darling, are you all right?" Her voice was anxious.

"Don't tell me you heard . . ."

"Everything! My aunt told me this morning how, when you came home last night, you were *stabbed*. I've been trying to get you for two hours, but the line's been busy. Are you all right? Where . . ."

I told her what had happened, marveling at the speed with which news spread in that community. I supposed the servants had passed it on, since I knew that no one in the house, none of the guests, would have breathed a word of it.

She was relieved that I hadn't been stabbed. She was also alarmed. "I don't think you should stay another night in that awful place, Peter. No, I mean it, really. It's perfectly apparent that a criminal maniac is on the loose and . . ."

"And when do I see you?"

"Oh. Well, what about late tonight, around midnight? I'm tied up with the family till then, but afterward I'm invited to Evan Evan's house . . . the abstract sculptor. I could meet you there. It's open house." I took down the address and then, after promising her I wouldn't get in the way of any more metal objects, she rang off.

I wandered back to the beach. From upstairs I could hear the clatter of Mary Western Lung's feverish typewriter. The door to Brexton's room was shut. Mrs. Veering was writing letters in the sunroom.

Everything was peaceful. Allie Claypoole was talking to a stranger when I rejoined her on the beach. "Oh, Mr. Sargeant, I want you to meet Dick Randan . . . he's my nephew."

The nephew was a tall gangling youth of twenty-odd summers; he wore heavy spectacles and a seersucker suit which looked strangely out of place on that glaring beach. I made the expected comment about what a young aunt Allie was, and she agreed.

"Dick just drove down from Cambridge today . . ."

"Heard what had happened and came down to make sure everything was all right." His voice was as unprepossessing as the rest of him. He sat like a solemn owl on the sand, his arms clasping bony knees. "Just now got here . . . quite a row." He shook his head gloomily. "Bad form, this," he added with considerable understatement.

"Dick's taking his master's degree in history," said Allie, as though that explained everything. "You better run in the house, dear, and tell Rose you're here."

"Oh, I'll stay in the village," said the young historian.

"Well, go in and say hello anyway. I'm sure she'll ask you to dinner."

Wiping sand off his trousers, the nephew disappeared into the house. Allie sighed. "I should've known Dick would show up. He loves disaster. I suppose it's why he majored in history . . . all those awful wars and things."

"Maybe he'll cheer us up."

"It'll take more than Dick, I'm afraid."

"You're not much older than he, are you?"

She smiled. "Now that's what I call a nice thing to hear. Yes, I'm a good ten years older." Which made her thirty-one or -two, I figured with one of those rapid mental computations which earned me the reputation of a mathematical failure in school.

Then we went in swimming, keeping close to shore.

4

Miss Lung and I were the first to arrive for cocktails and I mixed us martinis. She was in an exotic Japanese kimono-type dress which made her look even more repellent than usual. She thought she was cute as a button, though.

"Well, looks like we're the first down. The vanguard." I gave her a drink and agreed. I sat down opposite her, though she'd done everything but pull me down beside her on the couch. I realize that, contrary to popular legend, old maids' traditional lechery is largely an invention of the male, but I can safely say that, in Miss Lung's case, masculine irreverence was justified.

She sipped her martini; then, after spilling half of it on the rug, put it down and said, "I hope you're recovered from your encounter with that unknown party."

I said I was.

"I could hardly keep my mind on 'Book Chat.' I was doing a piece on how strange it is that all the best penwomen with the possible exception of Taylor Caldwell possess three names."

I let the novelty of this pass. I was saved from any further observations by the appearance of Claypoole. He was pale and preoccupied. He looked as though he hadn't slept in a week.

He made conversation mechanically. "The whole town's buzzing," he said. "I was down at the theater seeing the pictures there . . . some good things, too, by the way, though of course Paul would say they're trash."

"What's trash? What would I call trash?" Brexton appeared in the doorway; he was even smiling, some of his old geniality returning. I wondered why. At the moment his neck was half inside a noose.

Claypoole looked at him bleakly. "I was talking about the pictures at the John Drew Theatre."

"Oh, they're trash, all right," said Brexton cheerfully, mixing himself a drink. "You're absolutely right, Fletcher."

"I liked them. I said you'd say they were—"

"—What they are. Well, here's to art!"

"Art? I love it!" Mrs. Veering and Dick Randan came in together; the former was her usual cheery self, high as a kite. She introduced the Claypoole connection to Miss Lung and Brexton, neither of whom knew him. The penwoman shifted her affections abruptly from me to the young historian. "So you're at Harvard?" she began to purr, and the youth was placed beside her on the couch. That was the end of him for that evening.

Allie was the last to join us. She sat by me. "Well, here we all are," she said irrelevantly.

The company was hectically gay that night. We were all infected by this general mood. Everyone drank too much. I was careful, though, to watch and listen, to observe. I knew that someone in that room had clubbed me with possible intent to kill. But who? And why?

I watched their faces. Brexton was unexpectedly cheerful. I wondered if he'd arranged himself an alibi that afternoon while locked in his room. On the other hand, Claypoole seemed to be suffering. He had taken the death of Mildred harder than anyone. Something about him bothered me. I didn't like him, but I didn't know why. Perhaps it was the strange relationship with his sister . . . but that was no business of mine.

Miss Lung responded to whatever was the mood of any group. Her giggles now rose like pale echoes of Valkyrie shrieks over the dinner table while Mrs. Veering, in a mellow state, nodded drunkenly from time to time. Randan stared about him with wide eyes, obviously trying to spot the murderer, uninfected by the maniac mood.

It was like the last night of the world.

Even I got a little drunk finally, although I'd intended to keep a clear head, to study everyone. Unfortunately I didn't know what to study.

We had coffee in the drawing room. While I was sitting there, talking absently to the nephew about Harvard, I saw Greaves tiptoe quietly across the hall. I wondered what he was up to.

"Did the murderer really slug you?" asked Randan suddenly, interrupting me in the middle of a tearful story about the old days when Theodore Spencer was alive and Delmore Schwartz and other giants brooded over the university.

"Yes." I was short with him; I was getting tired of describing what happened to me.

"Then you must possess some sort of information which he wishes to destroy."

"Me? Or the information?" Randan had expressed himself about as clearly as most history majors do.

"Both, presumably."

"Who knows?" I said. "Anyway, he's wasting his time, because I don't know a thing."

"It's really quite exciting." His eyes glittered back behind the heavy spectacles. "It presents a psychological problem too. The relationships involved are . . ." I got away as soon as was decently possible.

I told Mrs. Veering that I was tired and wanted to go to bed early; she agreed, adding it was a wonder I didn't feel worse, considering the blow I'd received.

In the hall I found Greaves. He was sitting in a small upright chair beside the telephone table, a piece of paper in one hand and a thoughtful expression on his face.

"Ready to make an arrest?" I said cheerfully.

"What? Oh, you plan to go out tonight again?"

"Yes, I was going to ask you if it was all right."

"I can't stop you," said Greaves sadly. "Do us a favor, though, and don't mention anything about what's been happening here."

"I can't see that it makes much difference. Papers are full of it."

"They're also full of something else. We have two men on duty tonight," he added.

"I hope that'll be enough."

"If you remember to lock your door."

"The murderer might have a key."

"One of the men will be on the landing. His job is to watch your room."

I chuckled. "You don't really think anything will happen with two policemen in the house, do you?"

"Never can tell."

"You don't have any evidence, do you?"

"Not really." The answer was surprisingly frank. "But we know what we're doing."

"As a bit of live bait and a correspondent for the *Globe, what* are you doing? When do you think you'll make an arrest? There'll be a grand jury soon, won't there?"

"Friday, yes. We hope to be ready . . . we call it Special Court, by the way."

"Already drawn up your indictment?"

"Could be. Tell me, Mr. Sargeant, you don't play with paper dolls, do you?"

This set me back on my heels. "Dolls?" I looked at him, at sea.

"Or keep a scrapbook?"

"My secretary keeps a scrapbook, a professional one . . . what're you talking about?"

"Then this should amuse you, in the light of our earlier discussions." He pushed the piece of paper at me.

It was an ordinary piece of typewriter paper on which had been glued a number of letters taken from headlines, they were all different sizes; they spelled out, "Brecston is Ciller."

"When did you get this?"

"I found it right here, this morning." Greaves indicated the telephone table. "It was under the book, turned face down. I don't know how I happened to turn it over . . . looked like scrap paper."

"Then it wasn't sent to you?"

"Nor to anybody. Just put on that table where anyone might find it. Very strange."

"Fingerprints?"

He looked at me pityingly. "Nobody's left a set of fingerprints since

Dillinger. Too many movies. Everybody wears gloves now."

"I wonder why the words are misspelled?"

"No X and not many K's in the headlines . . . these were all taken from headlines apparently. Haven't figured out which paper yet."

"Who do you think left it there?"

"You." He looked at me calmly.

I burst out laughing. "If I thought Brexton was the murderer, I'd tell you so."

Greaves shrugged. *"Don't* tell me. It's your neck, Mr. Sargeant."

"Just why would I want to keep anything like that a secret?"

"I don't know . . . yet."

I was irritated. "I don't know anything you don't know."

"That may be, but I'm convinced the murderer *thinks* you know something. He wants you out of the way. Now, before it's too late, tell me what you saw out there in the water."

"Nobody can say you aren't stubborn." I sighed. "I'll tell you again that I didn't see anything. I can also tell you that, since I didn't send you that note, somebody else must've . . . somebody who either does know what happened or else, for reasons of his or her own, wants to implicate Brexton anyway. If I were you, I'd go after the author of that note." A trail which, I was fairly certain, would lead, for better or worse, to the vindictive Claypoole.

Greaves was deep in some theory of his own. I had no idea what it was. But he did seem concerned for my safety and I was touched. "I must warn you, Mr. Sargeant, that if you don't tell me the whole truth, everything you know, I won't be responsible for what happens."

"My unexpected death?"

"Exactly." I had the sensation of being written off. It was disagreeable.

IV

At midnight I arrived at the party, which was taking place in a rundown gray clapboard cottage near the railroad station, some distance from the ocean. The Bohemian elements of East Hampton were assembled here: thirty men and women all more or less connected through sex and an interest in the arts.

Nobody paid any attention to me as I walked in the open front door. The only light came from stumps of candles stuck in bottles; the whole thing was quaint as hell.

In the living room somebody was playing a guitar, concert style, while everybody else sat on the floor talking, not listening. I found Liz in the dining room, helping herself to some dangerous-looking red wine.

She threw her arms about me dramatically. "I was so terrified!" I murmured soothing words to her while a bearded fat man drifted by playing with a Yo-Yo.

Then she looked at me carefully and I could see, under the playacting, that she was genuinely concerned. "You're sure you feel all right?" She felt my head; her eyes growing round when she touched the bump, which was now like a solid walnut.

"I feel just fine. Do you think you ought to drink that stuff?" I pointed to the wine, which had come from an unlabeled gallon jug, like cider.

"I don't drink it. I just hold it. Come on, let me introduce you to the host."

The host was a burly man with an Indonesian mistress who stood two paces behind him all evening, dressed in a sari, wedgies and a pink snood. She didn't know any English, which was probably just as well. Our host, a sculptor, insisted on showing me his latest work, which was out in a shed at the back of the house. With a storm lantern we surveyed his masterpiece in reverent silence: it was a lump of gray rock the size of a man with little places smoothed off, here and there.

"You get the feeling of the stone?" The sculptor looked at me eagerly; I wondered if Liz had told him I was an art critic.

"Very much so. Quite a bit of stone, too. Heavy."

"Exactly. You got it the first time. Not many people do. Heavy . . . the right word, though you can't describe sculpture in words . . . but it's the effect I was after: heavy, like stone . . . it *is* stone."

"*Heavy* stone," I said, rallying.

He was in an ecstasy at this. "You have it. He has it, Liz. *Heavy* stone . . . I may call it that."

"I thought you were calling it 'The Dichotomy of St. Anne'?"

"Always use a subtitle. By God, but that's good: heavy stone."

In a mood of complete agreement and mutual admiration, we rejoined the party.

Liz and I joined a group of young literary men, all very sensitive and tender with sibilants like cloth tearing; they sat and gossiped knowingly about dissident writers, actors, figures all of the new decline.

While they hissed sharply at one another, Liz and I discussed my problems or, rather, the problems at the North Dunes.

I told her what I really thought about the morning's adventure. "I don't think anybody was trying to kill me. I think somebody was up to something in the house and they didn't want to be observed. They saw me coming and they were afraid I might interfere so I was knocked over the head while they made their retreat. Anybody who wanted to kill me could've done so just as easy as not."

"It's awful! I never thought I'd know somebody mixed up in anything like this. How does it feel, living in a house with a murderer?"

"Uncomfortable . . . but kind of interesting."

"You should hear the talk at the Club!"

"What's the general theory?"

"That Brexton killed his wife. Everybody now claims to've been intimate friends of theirs and knew all along something horrible would happen."

"They may have a surprise ahead of them."

"You don't think he did it, do you?"

"No, I don't think so; he must've been tempted, though."

"Then what makes you think he *didn't* do it?"

"A hunch . . . and my hunches are usually wrong." I was getting tired of the whole subject. Every lead seemed to go nowhere and there weren't many leads to begin with.

We tried to figure on possible places to go later on that evening but, since I was tired and not feeling particularly hearty from my blow on the head, and, since we were both agreed that though sand was glamorous and all that for making love on in the moonlight, it was still scratchy and uncomfortable; several sensitive areas of my body were, I had noticed earlier that day, a little raw, as though caressed with sandpaper, so it seemed best to put off until the next night our return engagement. But though we were both fairly blithe about the whole thing, I found her even more desirable than before we'd made love, which is something that seldom happens to me. Usually, after the first excitement of a new body, I find myself drifting away; this time it looked as if it might be different. I vowed, though, that there would be no serious moments if I could help it.

Along about one o'clock somebody began to denounce T. S. Eliot and a thick blond girl took off most of her clothes to the evident boredom of the young men who were recalling happy days on Ischia while two intense contributors to the *Partisan Review* began to belt each other verbally for derelictions which no one else could follow; it was a perfect Village party moved out to the beach.

Liz and I lay side by side on the floor, talking softly about nothing at all, everything forgotten but the moment and each other.

I was interrupted by Dick Randan. "Didn't expect to find you here," he said, looking at us curiously.

"Oh . . . what?" I sat up and blinked at him stupidly. I'd been so carried away I'd lost all track of everything. He was the last person I'd expected to see in that place. I told him as much.

He sat down on the floor beside us, a little like a crane settling on a nest. "I'm an old friend of Evan's," he said, indicating our host, who was showing a sheaf of his drawings to the bearded man who'd put away his Yo-Yo and gone to sleep sitting bolt upright in the only armchair in the room.

"How were things back at the house?" I asked.

"All right, I guess. I left right after you did and went to the Club; there wasn't much on there so I came over here . . . took a chance Evan might still be up. I handled his Boston show, you know."

Then I introduced him to Liz. They nodded gravely at each other. Across the room the half-naked blond was sitting cross-legged like a yogi and making her heavy white breasts move alternately. This had its desired effect. Even the sensitive young men stopped their cobra-hissing long enough to watch with wonder.

"Nothing like this will ever happen at the Ladyrock Yacht Club," I said austerely.

"I'm not so sure," said Liz thoughtfully. "I wonder how she does that."

"Muscle control," said Randan.

"Somebody did something under the table once at the Club," said Liz. "But it was one of the terrace tables and there wasn't any light to speak of," she added, making it all right.

The blond ecdysiast then rose and removed the rest of her apparel and stood before us in all her mother-earth splendor.

The Indonesian mistress then decided that this was too much; she went out of the room, returning a moment later with a large pot of water which, with an apologetic oriental smile, she poured all over the exhibitionist, who began to shriek.

"It's time to go," said Liz.

A brawl had just begun when we slipped out a side door into the moonlight. Randan came with us, still exclaiming with awe over the blond's remarkable control. "People study for years to learn that," he said.

"It must be a great consolation on long winter evenings," I said. Then I discovered that Liz had no car tonight and, though I much preferred getting a taxi or even walking home, Randan insisted on driving us in his car.

I gave Liz a long good-night kiss at the door to her house while the collegian looked the other way. Then with all sorts of plans half projected, she went inside and Randan drove me back to the North Dunes.

He was more interesting than I'd thought, especially about the murder, which intrigued him greatly. "I've made a study of such things," he said gravely. "Once did a paper on the murder of Sir Thomas Overbury . . . fascinating case."

"Seventeenth century, wasn't it?" I can still recall a few things to confound undergraduates with.

"That's right. I hadn't planned to come down here, though Allie invited me. Then, when I heard about what happened, over the radio in Boston, I came on down. I used to know Mrs. Brexton slightly . . . when she was going around with my uncle."

"That was quite a while ago."

"Fifteen years, I guess. I remember it clearly, though. Everybody took it for granted they'd be married. I never understood why they didn't . . . next thing we knew she married Brexton."

"Your uncle and aunt seem awfully devoted to each other."

But he was too shrewd to rise to that bit of bait. "Yes, they are," he said flatly.

The North Dunes was black against the white beach. It looked suddenly scary, sinister, with no lights on . . . I wondered why they hadn't left a hall light for me.

We parked in the driveway. I couldn't see anybody on the darkened porch. I remembered only too well what had happened the last time I stepped into that gloomy house, late at night. "You staying here?" I asked, turning to Randan.

"No, I'm in the village. I don't want to get involved; lot of other people I want to see while I'm in East Hampton." He got out of the car. "I'll walk you to the house."

I was ashamed of my own sudden fear. I hoped Randan hadn't noticed it.

We skirted the front porch and approached the house from the oceanside.

He talked all the time about the murder, which didn't make me any too happy. For the first time since the trouble began, I was afraid, an icy, irrational fear. I wanted to ask him to go inside with me, but I didn't have the nerve, too ashamed to admit how shaky I was. Instead I filibustered, answering his questions at great length, putting off as long as possible my necessary entrance.

We sat down on a metal swing which stood near the steps to the porch, a little to one side of the several unfurled beach umbrellas, like black mushrooms in the night. Moonlight made the night luminous and clear.

We sat very still to keep the swing from creaking.

"I came down here," said Randan softly, "for a definite reason. I know Allie thinks I'm just morbid, but there's more to it than that. I'm very fond of her and my uncle. I was worried when I heard all this had happened."

"You mean that they might be . . . involved?"

He nodded. "I don't mean directly. Just that an awful lot of stuff might come out in the papers that shouldn't . . . gossip."

"About your uncle and Mildred Brexton?"

"Mainly, yes. You see, my hunch is that if they try to indict Brexton, he'll drag Fletcher and Allie into the case . . . just to make trouble."

It was uncanny. These were practically the same words I had overheard between Brexton and Claypoole the day of the murder. Uncle and nephew had evidently exchanged notes . . . or else there was a family secret they all shared in common which made them nervous about what Brexton might do or say in court.

"What did you intend to do?" I asked, curious about his own role.

He shrugged. "Whatever I can. I've been awfully close to Fletcher and Allie. I guess they're more like parents to me than uncle and aunt. In fact when my father died, Fletcher became my legal guardian. So you see it's to my interest to help them out, to testify in case there's . . . well, an accusation against them."

"What sort of accusation? What is Brexton likely to pull?"

Randan chuckled. "That'd be telling. It's not anything really . . . at least as far as this business goes. Just family stuff."

I had an idea what it was: the relationship between brother and sister might be misconstrued by a desperate man; yet what had that to do with the late Mildred Brexton? Randan was no help.

He shifted the subject to the day of the murder. He wanted to know how everybody behaved, and what I thought had actually happened in the water. He was keener than I'd suspected, but it was soon apparent he didn't know any more than the rest of us about Mildred's strange death.

I offered him a cigarette. I took one myself. I lighted his. Then I dropped the matches. Swearing, I felt around for them in the sand at my feet.

I retrieved them at last. I lit my own cigarette. It was then that I noticed that my fingers were dark with some warm liquid.

"Jesus!" I dropped both matches and cigarette this time.

"What's the matter?"

"I don't know . . . my fingers. It looks like blood. I must've cut myself."

"I'll say; you're bleeding." Randan offered me a handkerchief. "Take this. How'd you do it?"

"I don't know. I didn't feel a thing." I wiped my fingers clean, only to find that there was no cut. The blood was not mine.

We looked at each other. My flesh crawled. Then we got to our feet and pushed aside the metal swing.

At our feet was a man's body, huddled in its own blood on the white sand. The head was turned away from us. The throat had been cut and the head was almost severed. I walked around to the other side and recognized the contorted features of Fletcher Claypoole in the bright moonlight.

V

There was no sleep in that house until dawn.

Greaves arrived. We met by candlelight in the drawing room. It seemed that shortly after midnight the lights had gone out, which explained why there'd been no light in the house when Randan and I arrived. One of the plain-clothes men had been testing the fuse box in the kitchen for over an hour, without success.

Everyone was on hand but Allie Claypoole, who had caved in from hysteria. A nurse had been summoned and Allie was knocked out by hypo . . . a relief to the rest of us, for her shrieks, when she heard the news, jangled our already taut nerves.

No one had anything to say. No one spoke as we sat in the drawing room, waiting to be called to the alcove by detective Greaves. Randan and I were the only two dressed; the others were all in night clothes. Brexton sat in a faded dressing gown, one hand shielding his face from the rest of us. Mary Western Lung, looking truly frightened, sat huddled, pale and lumpy, in her pink, intricate robe. Mrs. Veering snuffled brandy with the grimness of someone intending to get drunk by the quickest route. Randan and I were the observers, both studying the others . . . and each other, for I was curious to see how he would take the death of a favorite uncle and guardian; he was the coolest of the lot. After his first shock, when I thought he was going to faint, he'd become suddenly businesslike: he was the one who had the presence of mind not to touch the body nor the long sharp knife which lay beside it, gleaming in the moon. He had called the police while I just dithered around for a few minutes, getting used to the idea of Fletcher Claypoole with his head half off.

The women were called first; then Randan; then me . . . Brexton was to be last, I saw. For the first time I began to think he might be the murderer.

It was dawn when I joined Greaves in the alcove. The others had gone to bed. Only Brexton was left in the drawing room. The lights were now on. Greaves looked as tired and gray as I felt.

I told him everything that had happened. How Randan and I had talked for almost twenty minutes before discovering the body beneath the swing.

"What time did you arrive at the house of"—he consulted his notes gloomily—"Evan Evans?"

"A few minutes before twelve."

"There are witnesses to this, of course."

"Certainly."

"What time did Mr. Randan arrive at this house?"

"About one-fifteen, I'd say. I don't know. It's hard to keep track of time at a party. We left at one-thirty, though. I remember looking at my watch." I was positive he was going to ask me why I looked at my watch, but he didn't, showing that he realized such things can happen without significance.

"Then you dropped off Miss Bessemer and came straight here?"

"That's right."

"At what time did you find the body?"

"One forty-six. Both Randan and I checked on that."

Greaves strangled a yawn. "Didn't touch anything, either of you?"

"Nothing . . . or maybe I did when I got blood on my fingers, before I knew what was under the swing."

"What were you doing out there? Why did you happen to sit down on that swing?"

"Well, we'd just come home from the party and there weren't any lights on in the house and Randan wanted to talk to me about the murder of Mrs. Brexton, so we walked around the house and sat down there. I suppose if a light'd been on, we'd have gone inside." I didn't want to confess I'd been scared to death of going into that house alone.

"Didn't notice anything odd, did you? No footprints or anything?"

"Nothing. Why were the lights out?"

"We don't know. Something wrong with the master fuse. One of our men was fixing it while the other stood guard." Greaves sounded defensive. I could see why.

"And the murder took place at twelve forty-five?"

"How do you know that?" He snapped the question at me, his sleep-heavy eyes opening suddenly wide.

"It fits. Murderer tampers with fuse box, then slips outside, kills Claypoole in the swing while the police and others are busy with the lights, then . . ."

"Then what?"

"Well, then I don't know," I ended lamely. "Do you?"

"That's our business."

"When did the murder take place?"

"None of your—" But for reasons best known to himself, Greaves paused and became reasonable; I was the press as well as a witness and suspect. "The coroner hasn't made his final report. His guess, though, was that it happened shortly after the lights went out."

"Where's the fuse box?"

"Just inside the kitchen door."

"Was a policeman on guard there?"

"The whole house is patrolled. But that time there was no one in the kitchen."

"And the door was locked?"

"The door was unlocked."

"Isn't that odd? I thought all cooks were mortally afraid of prowlers."

"The door was locked after the help finished washing up around eleven. We have no idea yet who unlocked it."

"Fingerprints?"

Greaves only shrugged wearily.

"Any new suspects?"

"No statement, Mr. Sargeant." He looked at me coldly.

"I have a perfect alibi. I'm trustworthy." I looked at him with what I thought were great ingenuous spaniel eyes. He was not moved.

"Perfect alibis are dirt-cheap around here," said the policeman bitterly.

2

I found out the next morning what he meant.

I awakened at eight-thirty from a short but sound sleep. I spent the next half-hour scribbling a story for the *Globe* . . . eyewitness stuff which I telephoned to the city desk, aware that I was being tuned in on by several heavy breathers. Then I went downstairs to breakfast.

Through the front-hall window I caught a glimpse of several newspapermen and photographers arguing pathetically with a plain-clothes man on the porch . . . I had, I decided, a pretty good deal, all in all . . . if I stayed alive, of course. The possibility that one of the guests was a homicidal maniac had already occurred to me, in which case I was as fair a victim as anyone else. I decided the time had come to set my own investigation rolling . . . the only question was, where?

In the dining room a twitchy butler served me eggs and toast. Only Randan was also down. He was radiant with excitement. "They asked me to stay over, the police asked me, so I spent the night in my uncle's room."

"Wasn't that disagreeable?"

"You mean Allie?" His face became suddenly gloomy. "Yes, it was pretty awful. But of course the nurse stayed with her all night, knocking her out, I guess, pretty regularly. I didn't hear anything much, even though the walls around here are like paper. It was also kind of awful being in Fletcher's bed like that . . . luckily, the police took all his things away with them."

"You see anybody yet this morning?"

He shook his head, his mouth full of toast. "Nobody around except the police and the reporters out front. They certainly got here fast."

"It'll be in the afternoon papers," I said wisely. "Have they found out anything yet about the way he was killed?"

"Don't know. I couldn't get much out of Greaves. As a matter of fact, he got sore when I asked him some questions . . . said one amateur detective was enough for any murder case. Wonder who he meant?"

" 'Whom' he meant," I said thoughtfully, aware that Harvard's recent graduates were not as firmly grounded in Fowler's *English Usage* as my generation. "I expect he meant me."

"You're not a private detective, are you?" He looked at me fascinatedly, his eyes gleaming behind their thick lenses.

"No, but I'm an ex-newspaperman and I've been mixed up in a couple of things like this. Nothing quite so crazy, though."

"Crazy? I've got a hunch it's perfectly simple."

"Well, that's good to hear. Why keep us in suspense any longer?" My sarcasm was heavy; I am not at my best at breakfast.

"Maybe I won't." He looked mysteriously into his coffee cup. I found him as irritating as ever. He was my personal choice for murderer, with Mary Western Lung a close second.

"I suppose you think Brexton did it because he's jealous and wanted to kill not only his wife but her lover too, selecting a weekend at his wife's aunt's house as the correct setting for a grisly tableau?"

"I don't see what's wrong with that theory . . . even if you do try to make it sound silly. There's such a thing as spur-of-the-moment murder, isn't there? And this was the first chance he had of getting them both together." Randan was complacent.

"Why wasn't he cleverer about it? I know most painters are sub-average in intelligence but, if he wanted to get away with these murders, he couldn't have picked a worse way of going about it."

"Well, I'm not saying I think he did it. I'll make you a bet, though: that I figure this out before either you or Greaves." I told him I'd take him up on that: twenty dollars even money.

The morning was sunny and cool outdoors; the sea sparkled; the police were everywhere; and Greaves, it developed, had moved over from Riverhead and was now staying in the house, in Brexton's downstairs room (the painter was assigned a room upstairs) and we were all told to stay close to the premises for the rest of the day.

I set to work on the alibis.

Both Mrs. Veering and Miss Lung, it developed, had gone to bed at the same time, about twelve-thirty, leaving Allie and Brexton together in the drawing room. Randan was at the club. Claypoole took his last walk at midnight. None of the ladies had, as far as I could tell, an alibi. Allie, of course, was still knocked out and no one had been able to talk to her. I was beginning to wonder what Greaves had meant by perfect alibis being cheap. I discovered after lunch.

Brexton was treated like a leper at lunch. Everyone was keyed up, and frightened. It was easy for me to get him away from the others.

"Let's take a walk," I said. We were standing together on the porch overlooking the ocean.

"I wonder if they'll let us . . . or me," said the painter.

"We can try." We strolled out of the door, pausing a moment on the terrace. New sand had been raked over the dark blood beneath the swing. The sea was calm. No visible sign of death anywhere to mar the day.

We walked, a little self-consciously, past the swing and down on to the sand. A plain-clothes man appeared quietly on the terrace, watching us. "I feel very important," Brexton smiled dimly. "We'd better not walk far."

In plain view of the detective, we sat down on the dunes a few yards from the house. "You're a newspaperman, aren't you?" Brexton was direct.

"Not exactly. But I'm writing about this for the *Globe.*"

"And you'd like to know how I happened to drown my wife and murder an old family friend on a quiet weekend at the beach? That would be telling." He chuckled grimly.

"Maybe something short of a confession then," I said, playing along.

"Do you really think I did it?" This was unexpected.

I was honest. "I don't know. I don't think so, for a number of reasons that would be of no use to you in court."

"My own approach exactly."

"Who do *you* think did it?"

He looked away. With one hand he traced a woman's torso in the sand; I couldn't help but watch the ease with which he drew, even without watching the lines—not at all like his abstractions. "I don't think I'll say," he said finally. "It's only a hunch. The whole thing's as puzzling to me as it is to everybody else . . . more so since most of them are quite sure I did it. I'll tell you one thing: I couldn't have committed either murder."

This had its desired effect. I looked at him with some surprise. "You mean . . ."

"Last night when Claypoole was killed, assuming it happened before one-fifteen, just before your arrival on the beach with Randan, I was with Allie Claypoole."

This, of course, was the big news—the reason for Greaves's gloom early that morning. "You told the police this?"

"With some pleasure."

"And they believed you?"

"All they have to do is ask Allie."

"But she's been hysterical or unconscious ever since, hasn't she?"

He frowned slightly. "So they say. But when she's herself again they'll find out that there was no way on earth I, or Allie for that matter, could have killed her brother."

We were both silent. I recalled as closely as I could everything which had happened the night before: had there been any sound when Randan and I circled the house? Any marks upon the sand? All I could see in my mind, though, was that great dark house in the wild moonlight. Dark! I thought I'd found a hole in his story.

"If you were talking to Miss Claypoole, how come you were in the dark? There wasn't a light on in the house when we got there."

"We were on the porch, in the moonlight."

"The porch overlooking the terrace?"

"No, on the south side, the golf-course side."

"I wonder where the police were."

"One patrolled the house regularly while the other was looking for extra fuses, which the butler had mislaid. The policemen had flashlights," he added, "to round out the picture."

"Picture of what is the question."

"Picture of a murderer," said Brexton softly and with one finger he stabbed the torso of the figure in the sand. I winced involuntarily.

"Is there anything you'd like me to say?" I asked, trying to make myself sound more useful than, in fact, I was. "I'll be doing another piece tomorrow and . . ."

"You might make the point that not only was I with Miss Claypoole when her brother was killed, but that my wife was in the habit of taking large quantities of sleeping pills at any time of the day or night, and that four was an average dose if she was nervous. I've tried to tell the police this, but they find it inconvenient to believe. Perhaps now they'll take me seriously."

"Mrs. Brexton was not murdered? She took the pills herself?"

"Exactly. If I know her, her death was as big a surprise to her as it was to the rest of us."

"You don't think she might have wanted to kill herself? To swim out where she knew she'd drown?"

"Kill herself? She planned to live forever! She was that kind." But he wouldn't elaborate and soon we went back to the house while the plain-clothes man watched us from the shadow of the porch.

That afternoon Liz paid me a call and we strolled along the beach together to the Club; apparently the policeman didn't much care what I did.

Liz was lovely and mahogany-dark in a two-piece affair which wasn't quite a bathing suit but showed nearly as much. I was able to forget my troubles for several minutes at a time while watching her scuff along the sand; her long legs were slender and smooth with red paint flaking off the toenails as she kicked shells and dead starfish.

But she wouldn't let me forget the murders for one minute. She had read my piece in the *Globe* which was just out, and all the other papers too. "I don't think it's safe," she said after she'd breathlessly recited to me all the bloody details she'd read that afternoon.

"I don't think so, either, Liz, but what can I do?" I was willing to milk this for all it was worth . . . the thought that she might be erotically excited by danger to the male (cf. behavior of human female in wartime) was appealing, but not precise. Liz, I think, has no imagination at all, just the usual female suspicion that everything's going to work out for the worst if some woman doesn't step in and restore the status to its previous quo.

There wasn't much room for her to step in, though, except to advise. "Just leave, that's all you have to do. They can't stop you. The worst they can do is make you appear at the trial, to testify." The dramatic possibilities of this seemed to appeal to her; her knowledge of the technicalities was somewhat vague, but she was wonderful when she was excited, her eyes glowing and her cheeks a warm pink beneath her tan.

I maneuvered her into the dunes just before we got to the Club. She was so busy planning my getaway that she didn't know until too late that we were hidden from view by three dunes which, though they didn't resemble the mountains of Idaho, did resemble three pointed smooth breasts arranged in a warm triangle. She started to protest; then she just shut her eyes and we made love, rocking in the cradle of white hot sand, the sky a blue weight over our heads.

The Ladyrock by day is a nautical-looking place with banners flying, a pool where children splash around, a terrace with awning for serious drinkers, rows of lockers and cabanas, a model club on a model coast and full of model members, if not the pillars, at least the larger nails of the national community.

I was a little nervous of being introduced to Liz's aunt, who sat with a group of plump middle-aged ladies in pastel-flowered dresses and white hats, all drinking tea under a striped umbrella. I was sure that our lust marked us in scarlet letters but, outside of the fact that on a fairly cool day we were both flushed and dripping sweat, there was apparently no remarkable sign of our recent felicities. Liz's aunt said we were both too old to be running races on the sand and we were dismissed.

"Races, she calls it!" I was amused as I followed Liz to her family's cabana.

"I'm sure that's what she thinks sex is, anyway." Liz was blithe. "They had no sense of sport in those days." I don't know why, but I was shocked by this. I realized from hearsay that, although Liz was occasionally willing, she was far from being a sexual gymnast like so many girls of her generation. The real rub of course was to hear her talk the way I usually did. I resented her lack of romance, of all the usual messiness which characterizes even the most advanced of modern lovers. I wondered if she was trying deliberately to pique me; if she was, she was succeeding. I was willing to do almost anything to get a rise out of her; just one soulful look, one sigh, one murmured, "I wish this could go on for ever" would have made me feel at home. Instead, she was acting like a jaded high school boy in his senior summer.

We washed up carefully in the shower of the cabana and then I put on a pair of her uncle's trunks which hung sadly from my pelvis, to her delight. "I wish all men would wear them like that," she said, pouring herself into a bright-green creation which fitted her like scales do a snake. "Leaves more to the imagination." And then she was off in a lightning break for the ocean. I didn't overtake her until she was well into the first line of breakers.

We weren't back on the beach until the cocktail crowd had arrived. Hundreds of brightly dressed men and women were gathering beneath the umbrellas. They formed into separate groups like drops of oil in a glass of water. Certain groups did not speak to others. Those with too much money were treated as disdainfully as those with too little. Even here in paradise you could tell the cherubim from the seraphim.

Liz's aunt belonged to the top-drawer-but-one old guard: a group of middle-aged ladies who played bridge together, deplored the wicked influences which each year gained ground in the village, whispered about the depravities and bad taste of those richer than they, smiled tolerantly at the nervous carefulness of those poorer, and, in general, had themselves a good time while their husbands, purple of face, slow of mind, wheezed about golf scores in the bar.

Liz spared me her aunt and we found ourselves a vacant table close to the pool where we drank a newly invented cocktail, the work of the club bartender, who was obviously some kind of genius: gin, white mint, mint leaves, a dash of soda. I looked forward to getting drunk. The sun was warm, though late. The salt dried with delicate tickle on my skin. Liz was beside me . . . everything was perfect except Dick Randan, who joined us, wearing a jazzy pair of plaid trunks which set off the sallowness of his skin, the millions of visible sharp bones in his skinny body.

"Playing hookey, I see," he said with a boom of heartiness in imitation of the old bucks at the bar. Uninvited, he sat down. "How are you today, Miss Bessemer?" He turned his spectacles in her direction. I wanted to kick him.

"Fine, thank you," and Liz gave him her best Vivien Leigh-as-Scarlett O'Hara smile.

"I suppose you heard about what happened to us last night after we left you."

"Yes," said Liz softly and she fluttered her eyelids shyly; she was giving him the business and I almost burst out laughing.

Randan fell deeply. "It's been a terrible strain," he said tensely, flexing one minuscule bicep.

"You must have nerves of absolute steel!" Liz trilled.

"Well, not exactly, but I guess Pete here has told you a little what it's like."

"I should crack up in five minutes,' said that girl of stone with an adoring glance at both of us.

"It's not easy," said Randan with lips heroically thinned.

I intervened. "Was I missed at the house?"

"No, the guard saw you coming over here with Miss Bessemer."

"Oh?" I waited to hear more of what the guard saw, but evidently he was a man of discretion. Randan went on, "So I thought I'd come over and see who was around. I was getting a bit tired of that atmosphere. You know Allie is still knocked out, don't you?"

"I thought she was up by now."

Randan shook his head. "No, she's been raving, in an awful state. Nobody's allowed near her except Greaves. I finally went to him—you know, as next of kin—and demanded a report on her condition. He told me she hadn't made sense since early this morning. I told him her place was in the hospital, but he said she was under expert medical care, whatever that is around here."

Liz stopped her teasing at last, enthralled as usual by our situation. "Do you think they'll really arrest Mr. Brexton?" she asked.

Randan shrugged. "It's hard to say. Some of us aren't entirely sure he's responsible," he added weightily.

"Oh, but it *has* to be Mr. Brexton."

"Why is that?" I was surprised by her confidence.

"Because only a man could have cut Mr. Claypoole's throat. Peter hadn't any reason to do that, so that leaves just Brexton."

"And me," said Randan, nodding. "I'm a suspect too."

"Oh, but you were out that night; besides, you wouldn't kill your uncle . . . anyway, even if you could've, there was no way for you to kill Mrs. Brexton, since you were in Boston."

"Spending the day with friends," added Randan stuffily. "Don't think I didn't have to prove to Greaves that I was up there when it happened."

"So then you have two alibis, which rules you out. Only poor Mr. Brexton could've done both murders."

"Very neat," I said. "But suppose 'poor Mr. Brexton' has an alibi for the second murder and a good explanation for the first?"

"What's that?" They both looked at me curiously.

"I have no intention of telling either of you anything until you read it tomorrow in the *Globe*. But I will say that I happen to know Brexton was with Allie Claypoole at the time of the murder."

Randan looked at me with some interest. "Are you sure of this?"

"Certainly. And I think it rules him out."

"Unless..." Liz paused. We both looked at her, a little embarrassed by the sudden consequences of what I'd said.

"Unless what?" Randan's voice was edgy.

"Unless, well, they did it together... which might explain why she went to pieces afterwards." This fell cold and unexpected between us.

"Miss Claypoole is my aunt—" began Randan dryly.

Liz cut him short with luminous apologies. "I didn't mean anything really; I was just talking. I don't know anything about anything; just what I've read and been told. I wouldn't for the world suggest that she or anyone—" Liz brought the scene to a polite end. But we left her, after another round of drinks, with the definite sensation that something shocking had happened, that some strange vista had been unexpectedly opened.

We were halfway down the beach to the house before either of us spoke. It was Randan who broke the silence. "I can't believe it," he said finally.

"About your aunt and Brexton? Well, it was just one of Liz's more harebrained theories."

"But the damned thing is, it might make sense to that fool Greaves; I couldn't let that happen."

"I'm sure it won't occur to him."

"Won't occur to him? What else will occur to him when he hears they were together? It leaves only three other possibilities: myself, Miss Lung and Mrs. Veering. I wasn't around and I don't think the two ladies have any motive. Brexton was trying to bluff you."

I nodded. "I've taken that into account. It's more than possible."

Randan shook his head worriedly. "But that doesn't make sense because when Allie recovers she'll deny his story... if he's made it up."

I was soothing. "There's probably more to the murder than we know. Maybe he was killed before the time supposed. Maybe Brexton zipped out of the house, murdered him and then came back in again, all under the pretext of going to the bathroom."

"Too complicated." But his face brightened as he considered these complexities. "Anyway, we've got to look after Allie now. I'm going to suggest they put an extra guard on duty just to look after her."

"Why?"

"Well, if he was bluffing, he won't want her to come to, will he?" The logic was chilling, and unarguable.

We found Greaves standing in his crumpled gray business suit along the terrace, studying the swing.

"How's my aunt?" asked Randan.

"Where the hell have you been?" Greaves looked at him irritably. "I wanted to talk to you."

"I went over to the Club. Is she—"

"Still the same."

"What did you want to ask me?"

"We'll go into that after dinner."

Randan then demanded a full-time guard for Allie, which was refused on the grounds that two plain-clothes men in the house and a full-time nurse was quite enough. When Greaves demanded to know why protection was needed, Randan clammed up; then, with a look at me to implore silence, he went into the house to change for dinner.

Something occurred to me just as I was about to go inside myself. "I was wondering," I said, "why you haven't asked me any more questions about that note you found, the one you thought I'd manufactured for your amusement."

"You said you didn't, so that's that." But this fell flat.

"You think you know who fixed it, don't you?"

"That's possible."

"The murderer?"

Greaves shook his head. "Claypoole," he said.

I was more surprised by his admission than by his choice. "Why? Did you find fingerprints or something?"

"Just plain horse sense." Greaves was confident. "Claypoole suspected all along that Brexton was the murderer. He didn't dare come out in the open and accuse him because of family connections, scandals, things which would affect him too. So he sent the note to give us a clue. Unfortunately, it gave Brexton a clue too, and he was able to kill Claypoole before he could tell us the inside story of what went on between the three of them, or maybe even the four of them. A story which we're unraveling pretty fast right now."

This left me breathless to say the least. "You realize you're accusing Brexton of murder?"

"That's right." Greaves was almost frivolous. I wondered what new evidence the police had unearthed. Greaves enlightened me. "It seems that Claypoole was first knocked unconscious, then he was dragged up to the terrace where his throat was cut."

"How do you know he was dragged? Were there any marks on the sand?"

"Sand in his clothes. The tracks, if there were any, got rubbed out by the tide."

I didn't follow his reasoning. "Why do you think this indicates Brexton?"

Greaves only smiled.

I thought of something. "If Claypoole was first knocked unconscious, it means that a woman could've done it, doesn't it? Isn't that what a woman would do? And since she wasn't strong enough to carry him, she'd be forced to drag the body up to the terrace, where she'd then cut his throat with . . . with . . ."

"A knife belonging to Brexton. A knife covered with his fingerprints." Greaves looked at me slyly, his case nearly done.

VI

I'm quite sure now that Greaves was bluffing. He suspected Brexton was the murderer and he had enough circumstantial evidence to turn the whole thing over to the District Attorney's office, but he knew that many a good minion of the law has hanged himself with circumstantial evidence which a bright defense has then used to embarrass the prosecution. Greaves had no intention of moving for an indictment which would not stick. His bluff to me was transparent: he wanted to create in everyone's mind a certainty of Brexton's guilt; if this could be done, the case would certainly be strengthened psychologically . . . and Greaves, I'd already discovered, was a devoted if incompetent amateur psychologist.

I went up to my room and took a long bath, reconstructing the revelations of the day. There had been a number, and none seemed to fit the picture which was slowly beginning to form in my mind.

I had tracked down most of the alibis. Anyone could have put sleeping pills in Mildred Brexton's coffee. Randan, who was in Boston that day. The two Claypooles and Brexton knew where the sleeping pills were located. Miss Lung could not have known. Mrs. Veering might have known, since she was undoubtedly one of those hostesses who enjoy snooping around their guests' possessions.

Alibis for the second murder were all somewhat hazy, excepting Allie's and Brexton's; if they had really been together at the time of the murder, it either ruled them both out as murderers or, worse, ruled them in as joint killers for reasons unknown . . . at least in her case. Mrs. Veering had no alibi, nor did Miss Lung. Randan did; he was at the Club. Who then, logically, was in the best position, motive aside, to have committed both murders, allowing of course that all alibis were truthful?

The answer was appalling but inevitable: Mrs. Veering.

I dropped the soap and spent several minutes chasing it around the bathtub while my mind began to adjust to this possibility.

Of all the suspects she alone had no alibi for either murder . . . other than a possible claim of ignorance as to the whereabouts of the various bottles of sleeping pills. If Brexton and Allie were not joint murderers, then the only person left who might have killed both Mildred and Claypoole was Mrs. Veering, who, as far as I knew, had no motive.

The thought of motives depressed me. The "how" of any murder is usually a good deal simpler than the "why." These people were all strangers to me and I had no way of knowing what tensions existed between them, what grievances were hidden from the outside world. But at least Greaves and I were in the same boat. He didn't know any more than I did about the people involved. He had the advantage, though, of a direct mind: Brexton was quarreling with his wife, Brexton killed his wife. Claypoole threatens to expose him out of love for the dead woman. Brexton kills Claypoole, using his own knife, which he thoughtfully leaves beside the body to amuse the police.

At that point, I ruled Brexton out. He hadn't done the murder. I had a hunch, though, that if anyone knew who had done it, he did. Meanwhile, there was the problem of motives to sort out, and Mrs. Veering was now my primary target. She would be a slippery customer, since, even at best, she didn't make much sense.

I was just pulling on my trousers when Mary Western Lung threw the door between our rooms open and stood before me, eyes burning with lust and bosom heaving. I realized too late that the bureau which I had placed between our connecting door had been moved to its original position by some meddling servant.

With great dignity I zipped my fly. "You were looking for me, Miss Lung?"

She pretended embarrassment and surprise, her eagle eyes not missing a trick. "I don't know what I'm doing, honestly!" She moved purposefully forward. I pulled my jacket on and shoved a chair between us, all in one dazzling play.

"Sit down, Miss Lung."

"My friends call me Mary Western," she said, sinking disappointedly into the chair. "I was so immersed in "Book Chat" that, when I finished, instead of going out of the door to the hall, I just barged." She gave a wild squeak which was disconcerting . . . it was obviously intended to reproduce a ripple of gay laughter at her own madcap derring-do; it was awful.

I mumbled something about the perils of authorship.

"But of course *you* would understand. By the way I read with great interest your account of our tragedies in the *Globe*. I had no idea you were a past master of the *telling* phrase."

"Thanks." I tied my tie.

"But I think you should have consulted some of us before you went ahead. There are wheels within wheels, Mr. Sargeant."

"I'm sure of that."

"Yes, wheels within wheels," she repeated, relishing her own telling phrase. Then she got to the point. "I must tell you that I do not altogether agree with your diagnosis of the case."

"Diagnosis?"

She nodded. "It was perfectly clear from your piece in the *Globe*—between the lines, that is—that you feel Brexton did *not* kill either his wife or Fletcher."

"And you feel he did?"

"I didn't say that." She was quick, surprisingly so. "But, in the light of what evidence there is, I don't see any basis for your confidence."

"I'm hardly confident . . . anyway, it was, as you say, between the lines."

"Perfectly true, but I thought I should talk to you about it if only because you might, without meaning to, of course, make trouble for the rest of us."

"I don't—"

"I mean, Mr. Sargeant, that if Brexton did not do the murders, then one of us must have . . . it's perfectly simple."

"That's logical. I had even thought that far ahead myself."

She was impervious to irony. "And if it is one of us, we are all apt to be dragged *very deep* into an unpleasant investigation which might seriously affect us all, personally and professionally. You follow me?"

I said that I did. I also said that I could hardly see what the famous author of "Book Chat" had to fear from an investigation.

"No more perhaps than the rest of us who are innocent . . . and no less." She was mysterious. She was also plainly uneasy.

"I'm afraid we're all in for it, anyway," I said, sounding practical. "I don't think my reporting makes much difference one way or another. We're all in for some rough questioning—that is, if Brexton doesn't confess or something dramatic happens."

"Why make it worse? I'm convinced he killed Mildred."

"You weren't originally."

"Only because I couldn't believe that such a thing had happened, *could* happen. Now my only hope is to see this thing quickly ended and Brexton brought to justice. He was tempted . . . God knows; *I* know. Mildred had not been herself for a year. She was becoming simply impossible. The night before she died she got hysterical . . . at darling Rose, of all people, and attacked her with a knife . . . the very same knife Brexton used to kill Fletcher. Oh, it was terrible! Her attacking Rose, I mean. Rose screamed—it woke us all up, remember? And then, of course, Brexton came rushing in and stopped . . ."

I was now listening with, I must confess, my mouth open with surprise. I didn't want to arrest her incoherent flow for fear she might clam up; at the same time I knew that what she was saying was extremely important.

When she paused for breath, I asked with affected calm, "That's right, Mildred and Mrs. Veering stayed in the drawing room after we went up to bed, didn't they?"

"Why, yes . . . that's when the quarrel started. Rose told me about it later. Brexton had gone to bed and I suppose Rose was scolding Mildred about her behavior when Mildred just lost her head and rushed at her with a knife . . . poor darling! Rose was *out of her mind* with terror. She screamed and Brexton came rushing in and slapped Mildred. It was the only thing to do when she was in one of her passions. Then he took her off to bed and Rose came upstairs, telling us not to worry . . . you remember that."

"I wonder how Mildred happened to have the knife—it's a kind of palette knife, isn't it—in the drawing room?"

Miss Lung shrugged. "With a madwoman, you never know. Rose, of course, was positive Mildred wanted to kill her. She has been like that for years about many people and we've always humored her . . . I mean, you know how Rose is: impulsive and, of course, her little vice doesn't make for one hundred percent rationality, does it? But it seems that this time Rose was right and Mildred did attack her."

"Why?"

"That is none of our business," said Miss Lung coldly. "But I will say that they were great friends *before* her breakdown. Rose was loyal to her afterwards when many people didn't want to have her around. She even invited them here for the weekend so that Mildred might have a chance to relax and get a grip on herself. Then, of course, the girl attacks her. It's hardly fair. My point is that things like that are no one's business but Rose's . . . they shouldn't be written about by gossip columnists, especially since I'm convinced the whole terrible thing is really very simple. I only hope the police act quickly before . . ."

"Before another incident? Another murder?"

She looked almost frightened. "No. I didn't mean that exactly." But she wouldn't go on. "I hope we're not too late for dinner." She made a production out of studying the heart-shaped gold watch she wore on a chain over her heart. Then, talking "Book Chat," we went downstairs and joined the other guests.

Greaves sat in the center of the sofa, looking like an unsuccessful experiment in taxidermy. He had changed to a blue serge suit which smelled of mothballs and was strewn with lint like snow upon a midnight clear. He was being a member of the party tonight, not a policeman, and he was, figuratively speaking, watching every fork. The others played along as though he were an old friend. No mention was made of the murders. The conversation was forced but general. Brexton was in excellent form which, considering the fact his head was well in the noose, was surprising. I wondered if he was saving up a surprise or two.

I found out one significant bit of news right off. Mrs. Veering, over the martini tray, said, "Poor Allie is still unconscious. I'm sick with worry about her."

"Hasn't she come to at all?"

"Oh, yes, regularly . . . it's only the dope which keeps her out. You see, when she comes to, she starts to rave! It's simply horrible. We're so helpless . . . there's nothing anyone can do except pray."

"Have you seen her?"

"No, they won't let anyone in except the doctor, and the nurse. I have demanded a consultation and I think perhaps they'll have to have one. Mr. Randan's agreed, of course, as the next of kin."

"Consultation?"

"To see what's wrong with her."

"You mean . . ."

"She may have lost her reason." And on that cheerful note, we went in to dinner.

I remember looking around the table that night with some care. The odds were that the murderer was among us, quietly eating stewed tomatoes and lobster Newburg. But which one? Brexton was the calmest, no doubt banking heavily on that perfect alibi. If he was telling the truth—and we'd soon know from Allie Claypoole herself—he would be safe . . . unless, of course, the business was even more bizarre than any of us suspected and the two of them, like the Macbeths, had together done in her beloved brother for reasons too lurid for the family trade.

Just as the dessert was brought in, Mrs. Veering, with a strange bland smile, got to her feet and pitched head-forward onto the table.

There was a stunned silence. Her tumbler landed on the thick carpet with a hollow sound. Flowers from the centerpiece splattered everywhere.

Miss Lung shrieked: a thin pale noise like a frightened lovebird.

The rest of us sat frozen in our chairs while Greaves leaped from his chair and pulled her chair back from the table. "Don't anybody move," he said.

2

But this was not the crisis he or anyone had anticipated. The butler came rushing in with digitalis and Mrs. Veering recovered sufficiently to say, with a ghastly parody of her social smile, "I'll be all right . . . heart . . . bed."

She was carried upstairs and the trained nurse undressed her while Greaves ordered a doctor.

Our ever-diminishing party then sat rigidly in the drawing room, drinking brandy and waiting for Greaves, who, with one of his plainclothes men, was investigating Mrs. Veering's glass, her food, the table, the servants.

Miss Lung was the most affected. I was afraid she might have a stroke herself. "Poor Rose! Knew it would . . . told her . . . never listens . . . the strain, the awful strain . . . can't be helped . . . everything possible, always, from the very beginning . . . alcohol . . ."

Greaves joined us within the hour. He seemed genuinely puzzled. "Mrs. Veering is all right, we're happy to report. She has a cardiac condition, a chronic one. She had an attack and—"

"Drugged!" Miss Lung looked at him, her eyes wide and glassy. "I *know* she was drugged—like poor Mildred—or worse: poison!"

This is what we had all been thinking.

Greaves, without hesitation, went to the table where the whiskey was kept and, regulations or no regulations, poured himself a stiff drink. Then he joined our tense circle. "She was not drugged and she was not poisoned. She is resting comfortably. Her doctor is with her now. She may have to stay in bed a day or two, but that's all."

There was nothing for us to say. Miss Lung obviously did not believe him. The rest of us didn't know what to think. "No one can see her until tomorrow," said Greaves just as Miss Lung got purposefully to her feet. "Rose is my oldest friend and when she is in her hour of need I must go to her, *come what may.*" The authoress of *Little Biddy Bit* looked every yard a heroine.

"I'm sorry, but I can't allow it." Greaves was firm. Miss Lung sat down heavily, her face lowering with anger. Greaves looked at the rest of us thoughtfully. "This is going to be a difficult night," he said. "I will tell you right off that we're waiting for Miss Claypoole to recover and give us her story of what happened the night of her brother's murder. Until we have her testimony, we can do nothing but wait."

Awkward silence greeted his candor. Everyone knew what he meant. No one said anything; no one dared look at Brexton, who sat doodling with a pencil on a sketch pad. I half expected him to say something out of line, but he ignored Greaves.

"Meanwhile," said Greaves, with an attempt at heartiness, "you can do anything you like. We'd prefer you to stay here, but we can't force you exactly. Should you want to go out, please check with me or one of the men on duty. I know all this is unusual procedure, but we're in an unusual situation without much precedent to go on. It is my hope, however, that we will be able to call a Special Court by Friday."

"What is a Special Court?" asked Brexton, not raising his eyes from the sketch pad on his knees.

"It's a court consisting of the local magistrate and a local jury before whom our district attorney will present an indictment of a party or parties as yet unknown for the crime of murder in the first degree." He gathered strength from this legal jargon. It was properly chilling.

Then, having made his effect, he announced that if anyone needed him, he could be found in the downstairs bedroom; he went off to bed.

I went over and sat down beside Brexton, feeling sorry for him . . . also curious to find out what it was that made him seem so confident.

He put the pad down. "Quiet weekend, isn't it?" This wasn't in the best of taste, but it was exactly what I'd been thinking, too.

"Only four left," I said, nodding. "In the war we would've said it was a jinx company."

"I'm sure it is too. But actually it's six surviving, not four, which isn't bad for a tough engagement."

"Depends how you reckon casualties. Has Mrs. Veering had heart attacks before, like this?"

"Yes. This is the third one I know of. She just turns blue and they give her some medicine; then she's perfectly all right in a matter of minutes."

"Minutes? But she seemed really knocked out. The doctor said she'll have to stay in bed a day or two."

Brexton smiled. "Greaves *said* the doctor said she'd have to stay in bed."

This sank in, bit by bit. "Then she . . . well, she's all right now?"

"I shouldn't be surprised."

"But why the bluff? Why wouldn't Greaves let anybody go to her? Why would he say she'd be in bed a few days?"

"Something of a mystery, isn't it?"

"Doesn't make any sense."

Brexton sighed. "Maybe it does. Anyway, for some reason she wants to play possum . . . so let her."

"It's also possible that she might have had a worse attack than usual, isn't it?"

"Anything is possible with Rose." If he was deliberately trying to arouse my curiosity, he couldn't have been more effective.

"Tell me, Mr. Brexton"—I spoke quietly, disarmingly—"who killed your wife?"

"No one."

"Are you sure of this?"

"Quite sure."

"Then, by the same reasoning, Claypoole hit himself on the head, dragged his own body through the sand and cut his own head half off with your palette knife."

Brexton chuckled. "Stranger things have happened."

"Like what?"

"Like your knocking yourself out the other morning in the kitchen."

"And what about that? That, I know, wasn't self-inflicted."

Brexton only smiled.

"Your wife killed herself?"

"By accident, yes."

"Claypoole—"

"—was murdered."

"Do you know who did it?"

"*I* didn't."

"But do you know who did?"

Brexton shrugged. "I have some ideas."

"And you won't pass them on?"

"Not yet."

I felt as if we were playing Twenty Questions. From across the room came the high squeal of Miss Lung appreciatively applauding some remark of our young historian.

I tried a frontal attack. "You realize what the police will think if Allie Claypoole testifies that she was, as you say, with you when her brother died?"

"What will they think?" His face was expressionless.

"That perhaps the two of you together killed him."

He looked at me coolly. "Why would they think that? She was devoted to him. Look at the way this thing hit her. The poor child went out of her head when they told her."

"They might say her breakdown was due to having killed her own brother."

"They might, but why?"

"They still think you killed your wife. They think Claypoole had something on you. They think you killed him. If Allie says you were with her, then they'll immediately think she was involved too."

"Logical, but not likely. Even allowing the rest was true, which it isn't, why should she help me kill her brother?"

I fired in the dark. "Because she was in love with you."

Brexton's gaze flickered. He lowered his eyes. His hands closed tight on the pad in his lap. "You go too far, Mr. Sargeant."

"I'm involved in this too," I said, astonished at my luck; by accident I had hit on something no one apparently knew. "I'd like to know where we stand, that's all."

"None of your business," he snapped, suddenly flushed, his eyes dangerously bright. "Allie isn't involved in any of this. There'll be hell to pay if anybody tries to get her mixed up in it . . . that goes for the police, who are just as liable to court action as anyone."

"For libel?"

"For libel. This even goes for newspapermen, Mr. Sargeant."

"I had no intention of writing anything about it. But I may have to

... I mean, if Greaves should start operating along those lines. He's worried, the press is getting mean. He's going to have to find somebody to indict in the next few days."

"He has somebody."

"You mean you?"

"Yes. I don't mind in the least. But there won't be a conviction. I'll promise you that." He was grim.

I couldn't get him to elaborate; I tried another tack. "If neither you nor Allie killed Claypoole, that leaves only three suspects: Miss Lung, Mrs. Veering and Randan. Why should any of those three have wanted to kill Claypoole?"

Brexton looked at me, amusement in his eyes. "I have no intention of giving the game away, even if I could, which is doubtful. I'm almost as much in the dark as you and the police. I'll give you one lead, though." He lowered his voice. "Crime of passion."

"What do you mean?"

With one quick gesture of his powerful right hand he indicated Miss Lung. "She was in love and she was spurned, as they say."

"In love with whom?"

"Fletcher Claypoole, and for many years."

"I thought she was in love with the whole male sex."

"That too. But years ago, when I first met her, about the same time Fletcher did, she was a good-looking woman. This is hard to believe, I know, but she was. All the fat came later when Fletcher wouldn't have her. I painted her once, when she was thin . . . it was when I was still doing portraits. She was quite lovely in a pale blond way. I painted her nude."

I could hardly believe it. "If she was so pretty and so much in love with him, why didn't he fall for her?"

"He . . . he just didn't." The pause was significant. I thought I knew what he didn't want to say. "But she's been in love with him ever since. I think they quarreled our first day here."

"About that?"

"About something."

"I can't see her committing murder fifteen years after being turned down."

"Your imagination is your own problem," said Brexton. He got to his feet. "I'm going to bed," and with a nod to the two on the couch, he left the drawing room.

This was the cue for all of us. Randan asked me if I wanted to go to the Club with him. I said no, that I was tired. Miss Lung waited to be invited to the Club herself but, when the invitation did not come, she said she would have to get back to her auctorial labors . . . the readers of "Book Chat" demanded her all.

I went upstairs with her. On the second-floor landing one of the plain-clothes men was seated, staring absently into space. Miss Lung bade us both good night cheerily and, with a long, lingering look at the servant of the public, she oozed into her room, no doubt disappointed that his services did not include amatory dalliance with Mary Western Lung.

I went to my own room and quickly shoved the bureau against the connecting door. Then I telephoned Liz, only to find she was out.

I went over and looked out of the window gloomily and thought of Liz, wondering whether or not I should join Randan, who was just at that moment getting into his car, and make the round of the clubs. I decided not to. I had an idea there might be something doing in the next few hours, something I didn't want to miss out on.

Fully clothed, I lay down on my bed and turned the light out. I thought about what Brexton had told me, about what he *hadn't* told me. Very neatly, he'd provided Miss Lung with a motive. Not so neatly, he'd allowed me to discover what would, no doubt, be an important piece of evidence for the prosecution: that Allie Claypoole and he were in love, that the two of them, as easily as not, could've killed her brother for any number of reasons, all ascertainable.

3

I wakened with a start.

I had gone to sleep and not moved once, which explained why my neck ached and my whole body felt as though I'd just finished a particularly tough set of calisthenics. I don't know what awakened me. I won't say premonition . . . on the other hand, a stiff neck sounds prosaic.

The first thing I did was look at my watch, to see how long I'd slept: it was exactly midnight according to the luminous dial.

I switched on the light beside my bed and sat up, more tired than when I'd dropped off to sleep.

I had half expected a call from Liz. The fact I hadn't received one bothered me a little. I found I was thinking altogether too much about her.

Suddenly the thought of a stiff shot of brandy occurred to me, like a mirage to a dying man in the Gobi. I had to have one. It was just the thing to put me back to sleep.

I opened the door and stepped out into the dimly lit hall. At the far end the plain-clothes man sat, staring dreamily at nothing. He shook his head vigorously when he saw me, just to show he was awake.

"Just going to get something," I said cheerfully.

He grunted as I passed him. I went downstairs. The lights were still on in the drawing room. I remember this surprised me.

I had just poured myself some brandy when Miss Lung, pale and flurried, arrayed in her pink awning, materialized in the doorway.

"Where is the nurse? Have you seen the nurse?"

"What nurse?" I looked at her stupidly.

"The nurse who—"

"Someone looking for me?" A brisk female voice sounded from the main hall. Miss Lung turned as a nurse, white-clad and competent, appeared with a covered tray.

"Yes, I was. A few minutes ago I went into Rose's room to see how she was . . . I know that nobody's allowed to do that, but I just didn't care. Anyway, she wasn't in her bed. I rapped on Allie's door and there wasn't any answer there either and I was afraid—"

"I'm the night nurse," said the white figure. "We change at midnight. I was in the kitchen getting a few things ready. As for Miss Claypoole, she is under morphine, and wouldn't be able to hear you."

"But Rose? Where on earth can she be?"

"We'll find out soon enough." We made an odd procession going up those stairs. The angular angel of mercy, the billowy plump authoress of "Book Chat" and myself with a balloon glass of brandy in one hand.

The guard stirred himself at the sight of this procession. "I told her she wasn't supposed to go in there, but—"

Miss Lung interrupted him curtly. "This is Mrs. Veering's house, my good man, not the city jail."

We went into Mrs. Veering's room first and found our hostess, handsome in black lace, sitting up in bed reading a detective story. She was dead sober for once and not at all like her usual self. She was precise, even formidable. "What on earth is everybody doing—" she began, but Miss Lung didn't let her finish.

"Oh, Rose, thank heavens! I was terrified something had happened to you. I was in here a few minutes ago and you were nowhere in sight; then I rapped on Allie's door,"—she indicated the connecting door—

"and there wasn't any answer. I couldn't have been more terrified."

"I was in the bathroom," said Mrs. Veering, an unpleasant edge to her voice. "I'm perfectly all right, Mary. Now do go to bed and we'll have a nice chat tomorrow. I still feel shaky after my attack."

"Of course I will, Rose, but before I go you must . . ." While the two women were talking, the nurse had opened the connecting door and gone into Allie's room. She had left the door half open and I maneuvered myself into a position where I could look in. I was curious to see how Allie looked.

The nurse was already on the telephone. "Doctor? Come quickly. An injection. I don't know what. I think she'll need an ambulance."

Before the law intervened to keep us all out, I was at Allie's bedside.

She lay on her back, breathing heavily, her face gray and her hands twitching at the coverlet. The nurse was frantically examining a hypodermic needle.

"What happened?"

"Someone's given her an injection." The nurse managed to pump a last drop of fluid from the hypodermic on a piece of cotton. "It's . . . oh, God, it's strychnine!"

4

This time the questioning was general. There were no private trips to the alcove.

Greaves joined us an hour to the dot after the ambulance took Allie to the hospital.

Mrs. Veering was on hand, pale and hard-eyed, her own attack forgotten in the confusion. Miss Lung was near hysteria, laughing and giggling uncontrollably from time to time. Brexton was jittery. He sat biting his knuckles, his old faded dressing gown pulled up around his ears, as though to hide his face. Randan, who'd arrived during the confusion, sat with a bewildered look on his face while Greaves explained to us what had happened.

"She'll be all right" were his first words. He paused to see how the company responded: relief in every face . . . yet one was acting. Which?

Greaves went on, not looking at anyone in particular, "Somebody, at midnight exactly, got into Miss Claypoole's room and attempted to give her an injection of strychnine. Luckily whoever did this did a sloppy job. Very little was introduced into the artery, which saved her life."

He pulled out a tablet of legal-size paper. "Now I'm going to ask each of you, in order, to describe where he or she was at midnight. Before I start, I should say for those who are newcomers to this house that on the second floor there are seven bedrooms, each with its own bath. The hall runs down the center of the floor with a window at either end. On the west side of the staircase are three bedrooms. On the north, farthest from the stairs, is Mr. Sargeant's room. Next to him is Miss Lung. Next to her is an empty room, and south of that, of course, is the stairs. Three bedrooms and a stairwell on the west side." He paused a moment; then: "All contiguous bedrooms open into one another, by connecting doors in the rooms themselves . . . *not* through the bathrooms, which do not connect."

"I can't see what all this has to do with what's happened," said Mrs. Veering irritably.

"It has a great deal . . . as I hope to show you in a few minutes." Greaves made some marks none of us could see on the tablet. "Now, on the other side of the hall, the east side overlooking the ocean, there are four bedrooms. The north bedroom belongs to Mr. Randan. The next to Mrs. Veering. The next to Miss Claypoole and the last to Mr. Brexton. Both Mr. Brexton and Mrs. Veering are in bedrooms which have doors which open into Miss Claypoole's room."

"The door in my room is locked," said Brexton suddenly. His voice made us all start.

"That's correct," said Greaves quietly. "It was locked this morning by me, from Miss Claypoole's side of the door; the key was not in the lock, however."

"What do you mean by that?" Brexton's voice was hard.

"All in good time. And don't interrupt, please. Now, I hope you will all be absolutely honest. For your own safety."

There was a grave silence. Greaves turned to me. "Where were you at midnight?"

"In bed, or maybe just waking up."

"Do you always sleep fully dressed?"

"Not always. I just dozed off. I hadn't intended to go to sleep but I did, probably around eleven or so."

"I see. And you say you woke up at twelve."

"That's right. I looked at my watch. I was surprised I'd been asleep. I turned on the light and decided that a drink of brandy might be just the thing to get me back to sleep."

"And you went downstairs?"

"As you know." I was aware that, while I talked, Greaves was recording everything in shorthand; this was an unexpected talent. I described to him what had happened.

He then turned to Miss Lung. "We'll move from room to room, in order," he said. "Yours is next. Where were you at midnight?"

"I . . . I was in Rose's . . . in Mrs. Veering's room, looking for her."

"Are you sure it was midnight?"

"No, not exactly; but I guess it must've been because I was only in there a few minutes and I saw Mr. Sargeant right afterwards. I was *terrified* when I didn't find her. Then, when I knocked on Allie's door and got no answer, I knew something *must* be wrong; I rushed off to find the nurse. The policeman on duty saw me."

"Unfortunately, he didn't see you go in. He *did* see you come out. He was standing on the top stair, it seems, talking to the nurse going off duty, his back to the hall, when you went into Mrs. Veering's room, at ten minutes to twelve."

"I . . . I was only in there a *very* few minutes."

"Yet the nurse went off duty at ten minutes to, or rather, left Mrs. Veering's room at that time to meet her relief who was arriving downstairs. She paused to chat with the man on duty. While this was happening, you went across the hall from your room to Mrs. Veering's, isn't that right?"

"Well, yes. I did notice the policeman was talking to somebody on the stair. I couldn't see who it was . . ."

"Miss Lung, did you try to open the door between the two rooms?"

There was a tense silence. Miss Lung was white as a sheet. Brexton sat on the edge of his chair. Mrs. Veering's eyes were shut, as though to blot out some terrible sight.

"I . . ."

"Miss Lung, did you or did you not try to open that door?"

The dam broke. The cord of silence snapped. Miss Lung wept a monsoon. In the midst of her blubberings we learned that she *had* tried to open the door and that it was locked, from the other side.

It took several minutes to quiet Miss Lung. When she was at last subdued, Greaves moved implacably on. "Mr. Randan, will you tell me where you were at midnight?"

Reluctantly Randan tore his gaze from the heaving mound which was Mary Western Lung. "I was in my room."

"What time did you come back to the house?"

"I don't know. Quarter to twelve or so. The night nurse and I arrived at the same time. We came in the house together. We both went upstairs; she met the other nurse who was on duty and I went to my room. I was just about to get undressed when the commotion started."

"When were you aware of any commotion?"

"Well, I thought something was up even before I heard anything definite. I heard Sargeant's door open and close. It's right opposite mine, so I could tell he was up. Then I heard somebody stirring next door to me . . . it must've been Miss Lung. I didn't pay much attention until I heard them all running up the stairs."

"What did you do then?"

"I went out in the hall and asked the man on duty what was happening. He said he didn't know. Then you appeared and . . ."

"All right." Greaves turned to Mrs. Veering. "And where were *you* at—"

"I was sitting on the toilet." The crude reply was like an electric shock. Miss Lung giggled hysterically.

"You were there from ten minutes to twelve until twelve o'clock?"

"I don't carry a stopwatch, Mr. Greaves. I was there until I finished and then I went back to bed. The next thing I knew, three maniacs were in my room." This was a fairly apt description of our invasion.

"Did you see or hear anything unusual during those ten minutes?"

"No, I didn't."

Evidently Greaves hadn't been prepared for such prompt negatives. He started to ask her another question; then he decided not to. She was looking dangerously angry. I wondered why.

Greaves turned to Brexton and put the same question to him he had to the rest of us.

"At twelve o'clock I was sound asleep."

"What time did you go to bed?"

"I don't know. Eleven . . . something like that."

"You heard nothing unusual from the next room, from Miss Claypoole's room?"

"Nothing in particular."

"Then what in general?"

"Well . . . moving around, that's about all. That's before I went to sleep."

"And when you awakened?"

"It was around midnight—I thought I heard something."

"Something like people running? Or shutting doors?"

"No, it was a groan . . . or maybe just my imagination or maybe even the noise of the surf. I don't know. It's what awakened me, though.

Then, of course, everybody started to rush around and I got up."

"This sound that you heard, where did it come from?"

"From Allie's room. I thought it was her voice too. I think now maybe it was."

"What did you do when you heard it?"

"I . . . well, I sat up. You see, there was only a few seconds' interval between that and everyone coming upstairs."

Greaves nodded, his face expressionless. "That's very interesting, Mr. Brexton. You didn't by any chance try to open the door, did you —the door between your room and Miss Claypoole's?"

"No, I knew it was locked."

"How did you know that?"

"Well, I . . . I tried it sometime ago . . . the way you do with doors."

"The way *you* do, Mr. Brexton."

"It's a perfectly natural thing to do." Brexton flushed.

"I'm sure, especially under the circumstances." Greaves reached into his pocket and pulled out a handkerchief which he unwrapped. It contained a key which he was careful not to touch. "What is this, Mr. Brexton?"

"A key."

"Have you ever seen it before?"

"How do I know! All keys look alike."

"This is the key to the door which leads from your room to Miss Claypoole's."

"So what?"

"It was found twenty minutes ago, hidden in the pillowcase of your bed. Mr. Brexton, I arrest you on suspicion of an attempted murder in the first degree. You may inform your attorney that a Special Court will be convened this Friday in East Hampton. I am empowered by the State of New York—"

Miss Lung fainted.

VII

Brexton was arrested and taken to jail at two o'clock on Tuesday morning. The Special Court was scheduled for Friday. This gave me two days to track down the actual murderer for the greater glory of self and the blind lady with the scales. Forty-eight hours in which I was apt as not to find that Brexton was indeed the killer.

I got up the next morning at nine o'clock. I was barely dressed when the managing editor of the *Globe* was on the phone. "Listen, you son of a bloodlouse, what d'you mean by slanting those damned stories to make it sound like this Brexton wasn't the murderer?"

"Because I don't think he is." I held the receiver off at arm's length while my one-time employer and occasional source of revenue raved on. When the instrument quieted down, I put it to my ear just in time to hear him say, "Well, I'm sending Elmer out there to look into this. He's been aching to cover it, but no, I said, we got Sargeant there— you remember Sargeant? bright-eyed, wet-eared Sargeant, I said—he'll tell us all about it, he'll solve the goddamned case and what if the police do think Brexton killed his wife, Sargeant knows best, I tell him, he'll work this thing out. Ha! You got us out on a sawed-off limb. Elmer's going to get us off."

"Flattery will get you nowhere," I said austerely. "Neither will Elmer. Anyway, what would you say if I got you the real murderer, exclusively, and by Friday?"

"Why don't you . . ."

I told him his suggestion was impractical. Then I told him what he could do with Elmer, if he was in the mood. I hung up first.

This was discouraging. Elmer Bush, author of the syndicated column "America's New York," which, on television, became the popular weekly résumé of news, *New York's America,* was my oldest rival and enemy. He had been a renowned columnist when I was only assistant drama editor on the *Globe.* But, later, our paths had crossed and I had managed twice to get the beat on him news-wise, as we say. This was going to be a real trial, I decided gloomily.

I called Liz, who sounded wide awake, even though I was positive she'd only just opened her eyes.

"They arrested Brexton last night."

"No!" She made my eardrum vibrate. "Then you were wrong. I thought he did it. Of course, that's just woman's intuition, but even so, it means *something.* Look at all the mediums."

"Medium whats?"

"The people who talk to the dead . . . they're almost always women."

"Well, I wish you'd put in a call to Mildred Brexton and—"

"Oh, don't tease. Isn't it exciting! Can I come over?"

"No, but I'll see you this afternoon if it's all right."

"Perfect. I'll be at the Club after lunch."

"What happened to you last night?"

"Oh, I was at the Wilsons' dance. I was going to call you, but Dick said you'd gone to bed early."

"Randan? Was he there?"

"Oh yes. He's sweet, you know. I don't know why you don't like him. He was only there for a while, but we had a nice chat about everything. He wanted to take me up to Montauk for a moonlight ride in his car, but I thought that was going too far."

"I'm glad you have limits."

"Don't be stuffy." After a few more cheery remarks I hung up. This was apparently going to be one of those days, I decided. Elmer Bush was arriving. Randan was closing in on Liz. Brexton was in jail, and my own theories were temporarily discredited.

Whistling a dirge, I went down to breakfast.

The sight of Randan eating heartily didn't make me feel any better. No one else was down. "See the papers?" He was beaming with excitement. "Made the front pages too."

He pushed a pile toward me. All the late editions had got the story.

"Painter Arrested for Murder of Wife and Friend" was the mildest headline. By the time they finished with the relationships, it sounded like something out of Sodom by way of Gomorrah.

I didn't do more than glance at the stories. From my own newspaper experience. I've learned that newspaper stories, outside of the heads and the first paragraph, are nothing but words more or less hopelessly arranged.

"Very interesting," I said, confining myself to dry toast and coffee —just plain masochism. I enjoyed making the day worse than it already was.

"I guess neither one of us got it," said Randan, ignoring my gloom. "I suppose the obvious one is usually the right one, but I could've sworn Brexton didn't do it."

"You always thought he did, didn't you?"

Randan smiled a superior smile. "That was to mislead *you* while I made *my* case against the real murderer, or what I thought was the real murderer. But I didn't get anywhere."

"Neither did I."

"That business of the key clinched it, I suppose," said Randan with a sigh, picking up the *Daily News,* which proclaimed, "Famous Cubist Indicted: Murders Wife, Cube's Friend."

I only grunted. I had my own ideas about the key. I don't like neatness. I also respect the intelligence of others, even abstract painters: Brexton would not have left the key in his pillow any more than he would have left his palette knife beside the body of Claypoole. In my conversations with him he had struck me as being not only intelligent but careful. He would not have made either mistake if he'd been the killer.

I kept all this to myself. Accepting without comment Randan's assumption (and everybody else's) that justice was done and murder had out.

Mrs. Veering and Miss Lung came down to breakfast together. Both seemed controlled and brisk.

"Ah, the gentlemen are up with the birds!" exclaimed the penwoman brightly, fully recovered from her dramatic collapse of some hours before.

"I'm afraid it's been something of an ordeal, Peter." Mrs. Veering smiled at me. She was pale, but her movements were steady. Apparently she had, if only briefly, gone on the wagon; she was quite a different person sober than half lit.

I mumbled something inane about Well, things could've been worse.

"And I'm afraid we won't be able to carry through our original project either."

I had already given it up, but I pretended to be thoughtful, a bit disappointed. "Yes, I think you're right under the circumstances," I said, nodding gravely. "It might not be the wisest thing to do."

"I knew you'd understand. I'm only sorry you've wasted nearly a week like this."

"Not *all* wasted."

She smiled. "That's right. You got several stories out of it, didn't you?"

Miss Lung chimed in. "Thrillingly presented, Mr. Sargeant. I can't wait to see what your account of the *murderer at bay* will be like."

"Tense," I said, "very tense."

"I can hardly wait! Though heaven knows any reminders of what we've just gone through will be unpleasant, to say the least. Rose, we have been tested, all of us, in the furnace of experience."

"And emerged bloodied but unbowed," said Mrs. Veering, who could scramble a saw with the best of them. I asked to be excused, pleading work.

"Certainly." Mrs. Veering was amiable. "By the way, Mr. Graves, or whatever his name is, called me this morning to say he'd like us all to stay together—in East Hampton, that is—until after the Special Court. I hope it won't inconvenience you; you're welcome to stay here, of course, till then."

I said that was fine by me.

I went to my room and telephoned my secretary, Miss Flynn.

"The Case Has Broken Wide Open," she said in the tone of one who follows crime at a careful distance.

"Looks like it." I had no intention of saying anything over that phone which would give anyone listening in an idea of my private doubts. "I'll be back Friday afternoon. Any news?"

She gave me a precise summary of what had happened in my absence. I told her what should be done for the various clients. I then asked her to check a few things for me. Though they sounded odd, she was, as usual, reticent; she made no comment.

"I shall, as you know, exert every effort to comply with these Requests," she said formally. "Incidentally, a Mr. Wheen has been calling you every day. Has he attempted to Contact you yet?"

I said no, and she said he hadn't stated his business, so that was that.

My next move, after hanging up, was strategic.

In the room next to me, Miss Lung's, I could hear a maid vacuuming. The entire second floor was empty, except for the one maid. Stealthily I left my own room, crossed the hall and entered Dick Randan's room.

It was a fair duplicate of my own. He hadn't bothered to unpack and his suitcase lay open and full of rumpled clothes. I went through everything quickly. Aside from the fact that he wore Argyle socks with large holes in them, there was nothing unusual to be found. I was looking for nothing in particular, which naturally made my search all the more difficult. I *did* want to get the layout of the rooms clear in my mind, though.

I cased the bathroom and found the usual shaving things; I also found a woman's handkerchief with the initials R.V. It was wadded up and stuck in a glass on the second shelf of the medicine cabinet. R.V. was Rose Veering, but why Randan had her handkerchief in his bathroom was a mystery. It was unmarked . . . no bloodstains or anything interesting, just a lace-type handkerchief, as they say in bargain basements. Puzzled, I put it back. Could he be a kleptomaniac? Or a fetishist? Or had Mrs. Veering made love to him in the night, leaving this handkerchief as a token of her affection? Or had he just happened to find it and picked it up and stuffed it in the nearest receptacle, which was, in this case, a drinking glass? I decided I was going out of my mind, ascribing significance to everything.

I went back into his bedroom and looked at the two windows, both of which were open. Being a corner room, it had two views: one of the dunes to the north with a half-glimpse of beach, the other of the terrace directly below and the umbrellas; the sea was calm, I saw. On this side, directly beneath the window, the roof of the first-floor porch sloped. The window screens, I noticed, were the permanent, all-year-round kind.

Then I opened the door between Randan's room and the next bedroom, Mrs. Veering's. This was the largest of all the rooms with three windows overlooking the ocean. It was expensively furnished, very pink and silken and lacy. It was also full of bric-à-brac, clothes . . . too much stuff to do more than glance at.

I did find something fairly interesting in her bathroom. On a metal table was a small autoclave, on which were placed several hypodermic needles and vials of medicine, all neatly labeled with her name and the contents. Two of the vials contained strychnine, which, I knew vaguely, was the stuff to be given a failing heart in an emergency. Obviously Mrs. Veering was prepared for anything . . .

The door to what had been Allie Claypoole's room was unlocked. It smelled like a hospital. Her clothes were still there, all neatly arranged in the cupboard and in the drawers of the bureau. If there was anything remotely like a clue, the police had doubtless found it by now. I skimmed hurriedly through everything and then went on to Brexton's room. It was a mess, with the mattress on the floor and the sheet and pillows scattered around on the floor. Someone had come for his clothes apparently; and there was no longer any sign of his residence. I found nothing . . . except that the window to his room, the window which looked east on the ocean, was directly above the metal swing beneath which I'd found the body of Fletcher Claypoole. Since there had been a full moon that night, Brexton *could* have seen the murderer if he had looked out of that window . . . his view was the only one from the second floor which allowed an unobstructed view of the swing; the others had their view of it blocked by umbrellas and awnings.

Not much to go on, but still a possibility . . . and it might explain Brexton's seeming confidence: he had actually witnessed the murder of Claypoole. Yet, if he had, why had he kept silent? It was a puzzle. I had no idea the solution was already at hand.

2

I waited around until eleven-thirty for Greaves to show up, but it developed that he was about the state's business in Riverhead, and wallowing in a sea of official approbation. The legal machinery was now being set in motion by the District Attorney's office and the doughty Greaves could rest on his laurels.

When I was sure that he wasn't going to pay us a visit, I asked Randan if I could borrow his car. He was gracious about it, only asking me if I was sure I had a driver's license. I said I was and took the car.

The day was crisp and clear, more autumn than summer. Along the main street of East Hampton the elms had begun to yellow a bit at the edges. Winter was near.

I drove straight to the Hospital of St. Agatha, where I knew Allie Claypoole had been taken. With an air of confidence which I didn't feel, I walked into the gloomy Victorian brick building, told the receptionist that I was Dick Randan, Miss Claypoole's nephew, and that I wanted very much to see her.

To my surprise, after a few minutes of whispering into telephones, I was told that I could see her, for ten minutes, but that I must not in any way excite her. She had been, it developed, conscious and collected for some hours.

She lay propped up in a hospital bed, her face white as paper, but her eyes clear and bright. She was completely rational. She was startled to see me. "I thought Dick—" she began.

I interrupted her quickly. "Wanted to come, but sent me instead. I wonder if I could talk to you alone." I glanced at the nurse, who was fumbling efficiently with various sedatives on a tray.

"Against doctor's orders. *And* police orders," said the nurse firmly. "Don't worry; I won't listen."

Allie smiled wanly. "I'm afraid we'll have to obey orders. Why do you want to see me, Mr. Sargeant?"

I sat down close to her bedside, pitching my voice low. "I wanted to see how you were, for one thing."

"Nearly recovered. It seems the strychnine, instead of killing me, provided just the jolt I needed. They tell me I was in some danger of losing my mind." She said all this matter-of-factly. She was in complete control of herself.

"You don't remember anything? I mean about the strychnine."

She shook her head. "I didn't come to until in the ambulance."

"You were with Brexton when your brother was killed?"

She nodded. "I've already told the police that, this morning when that awful little man came to see me."

"They didn't want to believe you, did they?"

"No, they didn't. I can't think why."

"Did you know they've arrested Brexton?"

Her eyes grew wide; she skipped a breath; then she exhaled slowly and shut her eyes. "I should have known," she whispered. "No, they didn't tell me, but that explains why they seemed so disappointed when I told them. I think they wanted to cross-question me, but the doctor told them to go. Paul *couldn't* have done it. He had no reason to do it. He was with me."

"We haven't much time." I spoke rapidly. "I don't think Brexton did it either, but the police do and they've got a good deal of evidence, or what they think is evidence. Now you must help me. I think this thing can be solved, but I've got to know more about the people involved, about past history. Please tell me the truth. If you do, I think we can get the charges against Brexton dismissed."

"What do you want to know?"

"Who had any reason to kill your brother?"

She looked away. "It's hard to say. I mean, what exactly is *enough* reason? There are people who have grievances, but that doesn't mean they would kill."

"Like Miss Lung?"

"Well, yes, like her. How did you know about that?"

"Never mind. What actually happened between her and your brother?"

"Nothing. That was the trouble. She was in love with him. He was not in love with her. We all lived in Boston then, as you know. We saw a great deal of each other. I suppose you know she wasn't fat in those days . . . she was rather good-looking. It nearly killed her when he took up with Mildred. About that time, she began to get fat . . . I don't think it was glandular, just neurotic reaction. She never went with another man, as far as I know, and she never stopped loving Fletcher."

"Could she have drugged Mildred, do you think?"

"I . . . I've wondered that all along. She hated Mildred. I think she hated Mildred even more when she turned down Fletcher . . . one of those crazy things: hates her for being a rival and then hates her even more for rejecting the man she herself loves. Yes, I think she might've drugged Mildred, but it seems odd she should wait fifteen years to do it."

"Perhaps this was her first opportunity in all that time."

"Perhaps. I don't know. Even if she did, why would she then kill Fletcher?"

"Revenge for his having turned her down?"

"I wonder. At first I thought it was an accident, that Mildred had just taken an overdose of pills and gone in swimming, but then, when the police got involved, why, it occurred to me that Mary Western Lung gave Mildred those sleeping pills if only because no one else there really hated poor Mildred."

"Not even her husband?"

Allie shrugged. "He was used to her. Besides, he had plenty of better opportunities; he wouldn't pick a weekend party to kill his wife."

"You disliked Mildred, didn't you?"

"She was not a friend of mine. I disliked the way she tried to hold on to Fletcher after she'd married Brexton. We quarreled whenever we met, usually about my keeping him in Cambridge when she thought he should live in New York, where she could get her claws into him."

"*Did* you keep him in Cambridge?"

She smiled sadly. "There was no keeping him anywhere except where he wanted to be. He was never interested in Mildred after she married. In fact, she bored the life out of him."

"Yet she went right on . . . flirting with him."

"If that's the word. She was possessive, certainly."

"Would your brother have wanted her dead?"

Allie looked at me with startled eyes. "What do you mean?"

"I'm just trying to cover all the motives, that's all. I wondered if for any reason he might've had a motive."

"I can't think why. Of course not. You don't kill old girl friends just because they bore you."

"I suppose not. Now for your nephew. Would he have had any reason to want to kill Mildred?"

She shook her head. "I don't think he ever met her more than once or twice. Besides, he was in Boston. I happened to talk to him the night before she died, long-distance."

"Family business?"

"In a way. I also invited him to come down here. Rose had said it would be all right."

"Then that rules him out as far as Mildred goes. Did he have any reason to want your brother dead?"

She shook her head slowly. "No, not really. They weren't very sympathetic. Two different types. Fletcher was his guardian, you know. I don't think they openly quarreled, though last winter there was some kind of flare-up, over money. Fletcher controls Dick's estate and Dick wanted to get it all in his own name. But Fletcher was firm and that was the end of that. They've seen very little of each other since."

"Then I gather Randan wasn't eager to come down here."

She smiled. "He refused when I telephoned him. He was nice about it, but I could tell he didn't want to see Fletcher. I thought he should . . . I'm the peacemaker, you know."

"I suppose curiosity about Mildred brought him?"

She nodded. "He's fascinated with crime."

I had to work fast. "And Mrs. Veering?" Across the room I could already see the nurse getting restive.

"We met her about the same time we met Mildred . . . we had mutual friends. Rose and I have always been close; Rose was more upset than anyone when Mildred didn't marry Fletcher."

"Would she have any motive, do you think, for either murder?"

Allie shook her head. "None that I know of. Mildred was a trial, but then, she didn't have to see her if she didn't want to. For the last year, she hadn't wanted to . . . I was surprised when Rose asked us down and told us the Brextons would also be in the house. I thought she'd stopped seeing her. It seemed odd . . . Fletcher and I weren't sure we wanted to come. Oh, God, how I wish we hadn't!" This was the first sign of emotion she'd displayed during our talk. The nurse looked disapprovingly at me. Allie bit her lower lip.

I was relentless; there was little time. "Mrs. Veering was friendly with your brother?"

"Of course. No, there's no motive there. I can't think of any possible reason for Rose to want to—"

"Then you'd rule her out altogether as a murderer?"

Allie only shook her head, confusedly. "I don't know what to think. It's all so horrible."

The nurse said, "Time for you to go, sir."

I asked my last question. "Are you in love with Brexton?"

She flushed at this. "No, I'm not."

"Is he with you?"

"I . . . you'd better ask him, Mr. Sargeant."

3

I found Liz on the terrace of the Club guzzling contentedly in the company of several distinguished members of the international set, including Alma the Marchioness of Edderdale, a raddled, bewildered creature with dark-blue hair who had inherited a Chicago meat fortune with which she'd bought a string of husbands among whom the most glamorous had been the late Marquess. She wandered sadly about the world, from center to center, set to set, in a manner reminiscent of a homing pigeon brought up in a trailer.

She looked at me with vague eyes when we were introduced; I've known her for years. "Charmed," she sighed, her face milk-pale beneath the wide hat she wore to protect herself from the sun. On her arms elbow-length gloves, circled at the wrist by emeralds, hid the signs of age. Her face had been lifted so many times that she now resembled an early Sung Chinese idol.

Liz quickly pulled me away. She was delighted with the news. "It's all just as I said, isn't it?" Only the fact she looked wonderful in red kept me from shoving her face in.

"Just as you said, dar."

"Well, aren't you glad? You're out of that awful house and the thing's finished."

"I'm holding up as well as possible."

"Oh, you're just being professional! Forget about it. People make mistakes. Everybody makes mistakes. I read your pieces in the *Globe* faithfully . . . of course, it was perfectly clear you thought Brexton didn't do it, but I'm sure the *Globe* won't be mad at a little thing like that. I mean, look at Truman that time."

"Truman who? At what time?"

"Truman the President the time when he got elected and they said he couldn't. Nobody minded everybody being wrong."

I maintained her innocence. Heads had fallen that dark year. One head might fall this year. Of course, I could live without the *Globe*, but even so, an old alliance would be forever gone if I didn't dish up something sensational.

At that moment my nemesis, Elmer Bush, wearing canary-yellow slacks, a maroon sports jacket, alligator shoes and a smile such as only the millions who watch him on television ever get from his usually flintlike face, moved resolutely toward me, hand outstretched, booming, "Long time no see, Brother Sargeant!"

I forced down a wave of nausea and introduced him to the table; everyone seemed more pleased than not to have this celebrated apparition among them.

"Quite a little to-do you been having in these parts," said the columnist, slapping me on the back in the hopes I had a sunburn. I didn't. I punched his arm fraternally, a quick judo-type rabbit punch calculated to paralyze the nerves for some seconds. But either he was made of foam rubber or I've lost the old magic. He didn't bat an eye. "*Globe* felt I ought to come down for a look-see."

"A what?" I still kept my old-buddy smile as a possible cover-up for another friendly jab in his arm (I'd figured I'd missed by an inch the nerve center), but he moved out of range.

"A look-around . . . always the kidder, Pete. Ha! Ha! Been reading those pieces you write. Some mighty good on-the-spot coverage, if I say so myself."

"Thanks." I waited for the blow to fall; it did.

"Of course you backed the wrong horse. Got them sort of peeved at the city desk. You know how sensitive they are. Course, I never figure anything you say in the papers makes a damned bit of difference, since everybody's forgot it by the next edition, but you can't tell an editor that." This was the columnist's credo, I knew. I had often wondered how Elmer had avoided a lynching party; his column is in many ways the dirtiest around town—which puts it well into the province of the Department of Sanitation, Sewer Division.

"He hasn't been indicted yet."

"Friday." Elmer smacked his lips. "Had a little chat with Greaves . . . old friend of mine. Used to know him when I covered Suffolk County in the old days." This was probably a lie. Elmer, like all newsmen, tends to claim intimacy with everyone from Presidents to police officials. "He's got a good little old case. That key! Man, that's first-class police work."

I groaned to myself. Liz, I saw, was enchanted by the famous columnist. She listened to him with her pretty mouth faintly ajar. I said wearily, "You're right, Elmer. It takes real cunning to search a man's room and find a key. They don't make policemen nowadays like they used to in Greaves's day."

Elmer sensed irony . . . something he doesn't come in contact with much in his line of snooping in the wake of elopements and divorces and vice raids. "Don't sell Greaves short," he said slowly, his face solemn, his manner ponderous. "There aren't too many like him around . . . clear-headed thinkers. That's what I like about him. You could've picked up a lot from him. I did. I'm not ashamed to admit it . . . I'll learn from any man." There was a pause as we all considered this.

Then I asked gravely, innocently, "You also find out why Brexton used the key to get into Miss Claypoole's room?"

Bush looked at me as though I'd gone off my head. "You been in publicity too long," he said at last, contemptuously. "He stole the key from Mrs. Veering—it was kept in her desk, by the way, right in the top drawer where anybody could've swiped it—and he unlocked Miss Claypoole's door when he heard the nurse go off duty. Then he tiptoed in, took a hypodermic, filled it with strychnine, tried to give her a shot, failed . . . ran back to his room and locked the door, hiding the key in his pillowcase."

"Oh, isn't that fascinating!" Treacherous Liz was carried away with excitement.

"The strychnine," I said quietly, "was kept in Mrs. Veering's room, not in Miss Claypoole's. How could he've got it?"

"Any time . . . any time at all." Elmer was expansive.

"Perhaps. That leaves only one other mystery. I'm sure you and Greaves have it worked out, though: *Why* did Brexton want to kill Allie?"

"Keep her from testifying."

"Yet she has already testified that she was with Brexton at the time her brother was killed, isn't that right? Well, it doesn't make sense, his trying to destroy his only alibi."

Elmer only smiled. "I'm not at liberty to divulge the prosecution's case . . . yet."

I was appalled at the implications. Neither Elmer nor Greaves was a complete fool. Did this mean that the state was going to try to prove that Allie and Brexton *together* had killed her brother? That Brexton might've then wanted her dead to clear himself? . . . No, it didn't add up; the police weren't that stupid. They knew something I didn't, or they were bluffing.

Alma Edderdale invited us all to her cabana. Liz and I followed her, leaving Elmer to circulate importantly among the important members of the Club.

Lady Edderdale's cabana was a choice one on the end of the row, with a bright awning, a porch and a portable bar. A half-dozen of us arranged ourselves in deck chairs. The afternoon was splendid with that silver light you only get in the autumn by the sea.

Lady Edderdale talked to me for some minutes. At last she began to place me. She seemed almost interested when I told her I was staying with Mrs. Veering.

"Poor dear Rose," she murmured. "What a frightful thing to have happen! Brexton was my favorite modern old master too. Why should anyone want to have murdered him?"

I tried to explain that it was not Brexton, but his wife who'd been murdered; but Alma only nodded like a near-sighted horse confronted with oats in the middle-distance. "His wife, Peggy, was always a trial, wasn't she? But, poor darling, what will she do without him now? She was Rose's daughter, you know."

I gave up. Lady Edderdale's confusion was legendary. She ambled on in her rather British dying-fall voice. "Yes, it must be a strain for all of them. I'm sure the person who killed him must be *terribly* sorry now. I should be, shouldn't you? Such a fine painter, I mean. How is Rose, by the way? I haven't seen her yet."

I said she was as well as could be expected.

"Yes, I'm sure she's very brave about it all. It happened to me, you know. Right out of a clear sky, too. They came one day and said, 'Lady Edderdale, we'll want a new accounting.' Of course I didn't know what they were talking about, so I told them I *never* did accounts, but my lawyer did. They went to him and, before you know it, I had to pay over a hundred thousand dollars."

I had the sensation of being caught in a nightmare. Either Lady Edderdale had gone completely off her rocker or I had or we both had. I looked desperately at Liz, but she was sunning herself wantonly beside a thick white Swede.

"Hundred thousand dollars?" I repeated the one thing which I'd managed to salvage from her conversation.

"More or less. I don't know the exact sum, but it was simply *awful* trying to get that much in such short time. They are relentless. I hope they gave Rose a little more time than they gave me."

"Time?"

"Yes, to pay them."

"Them?"

"Those awful income tax people."

Then it was all clear. "How long ago did Rose find out she'd have to pay all that money?"

"Well, not too long ago. I'm awfully bad about time. We lunched at the Colony, I remember, with Chico Pazzetti . . . you know Chico? His wife's left him, by the way."

"She told you this at the Colony? Recently?"

"A month ago, yes. I remember she was in town for several days; she'd come down to talk to them, to the Bureau of Internal Revenue people, about the thing."

"Just what kind of . . . thing was it?"

Alma sighed and waved her emerald-laden arms helplessly in the air. "I don't know, really. I know she was awfully upset and she wanted to talk to me because I'd gone through the same thing. I was no help, I fear. I think she said a hundred thousand . . . or was that what *I* had to pay? No, we *both* had to pay that much and on short notice. I remember saying we were in the same boat except, of course, Rose, poor darling, really hasn't much money any more."

4

I told Liz I'd call her later that day if I got a chance. Then, excusing myself, I went back to the North Dunes.

The house looked peaceful and strangely empty, as though no one lived there any longer. A prophecy? It was nearly empty too, I found, when I went inside. Everyone was out for the day except Miss Lung, who sat at Mrs. Veering's desk with the proofs of the penultimate "Book Chat" in her hand. "You see me at my labor," said the penwoman, removing her glasses with a smile equally compounded of lechery and silliness. Yet she was not really a fool; I was beginning to see that.

"I went to see Allie," I said, sitting down in the chair next to the desk, where I had had so many interviews with Greaves.

"Oh? I didn't know anybody was allowed to see her."

"They let me in. She's much better."

"I'm glad. I'm devoted to Allie. By the way, I'm doing Pearl Buck this week. I think her Indian phase so fascinating . . . especially after all the China she's done. I mean, there's just so much China to do and then one wants a change." She read me the entire column of "Book Chat." I applauded weakly.

"Hard at work?" Mrs. Veering, looking businesslike and steady, appeared in the alcove; she removed a sensible hat. "What a day! The first chance I've had to get any work done."

Miss Lung got to her feet. "I was just having the *nicest* chat with Mr. Sargeant. I was testing my column; you know how I am about 'reader response.' If only more writers would attempt, as I do, to gauge exactly the average response and then strive to that goal, as I do. I believe in making a direct contact with the average mind on *every* level."

I excused myself, average mind and all.

I took a short walk on the beach in front of the house. The light was dimming; the silver day was becoming gold. I realized that no one had yet found the spot where Claypoole had been killed. It would probably be impossible to tell now; he had been dragged on the beach, probably close to the water so that the surf would hide the murderer's footprints. I had a hunch the murder had taken place close to the house, probably just out of sight, behind the dunes. Yet why wouldn't the murderer leave the body where it was? Why drag it to the terrace . . . a risky business, considering the house was full of police?

Something kept eluding me; it was like a word temporarily forgotten which the tongue almost remembers but the mind refuses to surrender up.

It was no use. Two gulls circled the sea. In the north the blue sky was smudged with gray—a storm approaching? the first blast of winter?

I shivered and went into the house. I had one more errand to perform that day.

5

Brexton was seated gloomily on a bunk in the rather picturesque jail of East Hampton. He wore civilian clothes (I'd half expected to see him in a striped suit) and he was sketching with a bit of charcoal on a pad of paper.

"Therapy," he said with a smile as I came in. "You don't look much like my lawyer."

"It was the only way I could get in. I told the police I was a junior partner of Oliver and Dale. You look pretty comfortable."

"I'm glad you think so. Sit down."

I sat down on a kitchen chair by the barred window. The branch of a green-foliaged tree waved against the window; I felt like a prisoner myself.

"I don't think you did it," I said.

"That makes two of us. What can I do for you?"

"Three. I talked to Allie this morning. I don't see how they could possibly arrest you in the light of her testimony."

"But they have." He put the pad down on the bed beside him and wiped charcoal smudges off his fingers with an edge of the blanket.

"I'm doing a piece about this for the *Globe*. I guess you've been following them."

He nodded, without any comment.

"Well, I'm trying to solve the case on my own and I think you know who murdered Claypoole. I think you might even have watched the murderer roll the body under the swing. Your window looked directly onto the terrace, onto the swing."

He chuckled softly. "If that's an example of your detective methods, I'm lost. For one thing, I wasn't in my own room until a good deal later and, for another thing, I was still sleeping in the room on the ground floor."

"Oh." I looked at him stupidly. I had missed on that, all right—missed cold. I began to feel a little shaky about my deductive powers. "Well, that rules that out." I rallied. "Where were you exactly at the time of Claypoole's death?"

"Sitting in the dark mostly, with Allie, on the porch."

"Did either of you leave the porch at that time, while the lights were out?"

"Yes, as a matter of fact both of us did, for short periods. I went to see the man on duty about the lights, but I couldn't find him. I guess he was hunting for the fuse box. Then I came back and Allie and I talked for a while. She left the room to get a book she'd brought me, but forgotten to give me, an art book . . ."

"All this in the dark?"

"There was a lot of moonlight. You could see perfectly well. She got the book from her room. We talked for a bit and then went to bed. The rest you know."

"What did you talk about?"

"Mildred mostly."

"You didn't talk about the possibility of marriage, did you? I mean between you and Allie."

"That's nobody's business," said Brexton sharply.

"I'm sorry." I shifted ground. "What do you know about Mrs. Veering's tax problems?"

He gave me a slow, amused smile. "You know about that?"

"Not much . . . just gossip. I gather she's being stuck for a great deal."

"Quite a bit." Brexton nodded. "Over a hundred thousand dollars."

"Can she pay it?"

"I suppose so, but it'll wreck her income."

"How does she happen to have to pay all that?"

"Well, the Veerings have a foundry out West. It does well enough and her interest in it pays her a large income. Her late husband's brother runs the business and looks after everything. Rose has got a good business head herself. She started out as a secretary to old man Veering, the president of the company. He married her, died and left her his share. Now it seems that recently the brother pulled some fast business deals . . . mergers, that kind of thing. I'm not much on business . . . I *do* know it had something to do with a capital-gains tax which really wasn't, if you follow me. The government found out and now Rose and the brother both have to cough up a hundred thousand cash."

"And Mrs. Veering hasn't got it?"

"Not without selling most of her interest in the foundry."

"Then you'd say she was in a tough spot?"

"Yes, I'd say she was in a very tough spot." Brexton spoke slowly, his eyes on the green branch which softly scraped the bars of the window.

I played my hunch. "Was your wife a wealthy woman, Mr. Brexton?"

He knew what I was up to, but he gave no sign; he only looked at me without expression. "Yes, she was."

"She was wealthy on her own . . . not through Mrs. Veering? Not through her aunt?"

"That's right. My wife's money came from the other side of the family."

"Did Mrs. Veering try to borrow money from your wife?"

Brexton stirred restlessly on the bunk; his hands clasped and unclasped. "Did Allie tell you this?"

"No, I'm just playing a long shot."

"Yes, Rose tried to get Mildred to help her out of this tax settlement. Mildred refused."

Neither of us said anything for a moment; then: "Why did your wife refuse?"

"I don't know. I suppose it was too much money, even for her. They had a terrible scene the night before she was drowned. I guess you heard the screams. Both had awful tempers. Mildred attacked Rose with my palette knife (by the way, I never saw it again after that night —until it was found beside Fletcher's body). I broke it up and calmed Mildred down."

"I would've thought it was the other way around: Mrs. Veering should have been the hysterical one, for having been turned down."

"They both were. They were a good deal alike, you know, meantempered, unbalanced. Mildred wanted to leave the house right then, but I talked her out of it; by the next morning she was all right again."

"Do you think that was why your wife was invited—you were both invited for the weekend—to help Mrs. Veering?"

Brexton nodded. "I know it. I think that's why Mildred got so angry. She knew Rose was getting tired of her behavior. Rose had dropped us flat for almost a year. Then, when this invitation came, Mildred was really kind of bucked up; she always regarded Rose as the social arbiter of the family and it hurt her when Rose wouldn't see us any more. But then when she found out after dinner that first night that we'd only been asked down because Rose needed money, she blew up. I'm afraid I didn't altogether blame her."

"Do you think your wife, under ordinary circumstances, would have let her have the money?"

Brexton shrugged. "She might have. It was an awful lot, though. But then, I never did know how much money Mildred had. She always paid her bills and I paid mine. That was part of our marriage agreement."

"You had a written agreement?"

"No, just an understood one. Mildred was a good wife for me—strange as that may seem to anybody who only knew her during this last year."

I shifted to the legal aspects of the situation. "What line do you think the prosecution will take?"

"I'm not sure. Something wild, I think. My lawyers are pretty confident, but then, considering what I'm paying them, they ought to be." He chuckled. "They should be able to buy all the evidence they need. But seriously, they can't figure what Greaves has got on his mind. We thought Allie's testimony would convince even the District Attorney's office. Instead, they went right ahead and called the Special Court for Friday and stuck me in here."

"I suppose they are going chiefly on motive; you killed your wife because you didn't like her and wanted her money . . . Maybe they'll prove you wanted to marry Allie, which would explain why she gave you an alibi."

"Except why should I want to kill her brother—the one person she was really devoted to?"

"I think they'll just pick a motive out of the air . . . whatever fits . . . and use the presence of your knife beside the corpse as primary evidence."

"Thin," said Brexton, shaking his head.

"Fortunately, the prosecution doesn't know about the quarrel you had with Claypoole after your wife drowned. They probably know what we all know—that he cursed you when she died—but they don't know about the fight you had in your room, the one I heard while sitting on the porch."

Brexton's self-control was admirable. He showed no surprise, only interest. "You heard that?"

"Most of it, yes. Claypoole blamed you for killing your wife. Not directly . . . at least I don't think that's how he meant it. I couldn't be sure. The impression I got was that he was holding you responsible, in some way, and that he was going to expose you."

"Well, that was about it." Brexton's tone could not have been more neutral, less informative.

"I haven't any intention of telling the District Attorney this."

"That's very nice of you."

"But I'd like to know what it meant . . . that conversation. What you meant when you said you'd tell everything too."

Brexton paused thoughtfully before answering; his quick, shrewd painter's eyes studying me as though I were a model whose quality he was trying to fix exactly with a line. Then he said, "There's not much to tell. Mildred hounded Fletcher for the last few years, trying to get him to marry her. He wasn't interested, though he'd been in love with her before she married me. Then, during the last year, he began to change. I think I know why. He started to see her. They took a trip to Bermuda together under assumed names. I found out . . . people always do. I gave Mildred hell, just on general principles. She promptly had a nervous breakdown; afterwards she asked me for a divorce and I said not yet. I guess that was a mistake on my part. I wasn't in love with Mildred, but I liked her and I was used to her and I suspected Claypoole was interested in her only on account of her money. Allie had told me how their income had begun to shrink these last few years, like everybody else's. I think Fletcher decided the time had come to get himself a rich wife. He was furious with me for standing in his way. Then, when Mildred drowned, he was positive I had something to do with it, to keep her money for myself, to keep her from marrying him. That's all there was to it. He blew up and threatened to accuse me of murder . . . I have a hunch he did, before he died, and I think that's what Greaves is counting on to get me indicted—Fletcher's accusation of me before he himself was murdered."

Now it was making sense. "One other thing: what did you mean when you told him you'd bring Allie into the case if he accused you?"

Brexton actually blushed. "Did I say that? I must've been near the breaking point. I'd never have done a thing like that . . . I was just threatening, trying to warn him off."

"In what way could she have been brought into the case?"

"She couldn't ever; what I said had to do . . . well, with other things, with her and me and her brother. I was only threatening; it was the worst thing I could think to say to him. Funny, I'd even forgotten I'd said it, until you mentioned it."

I was now fairly sure of the line the District Attorney would take. This was a help.

Then the jailer appeared, a fat policeman who waggled some keys and told me my time was up.

"Good luck," I said as we parted.

Brexton chuckled. "I'll need it." He picked up his sketch pad again. "I think you're moving in the right direction, Mr. Sargeant." But the policeman had me out of the cell block before I could ask him what he meant.

It was sundown when I got back to the house and parked Randan's car in the drive. It was pleasant not to be observed by policemen. They were all gone. Only Miss Lung, Mrs. Veering, Randan and myself were in the house, not counting servants.

I found Randan alone in the drawing room, writing furiously in a notebook, a highball beside him. "Oh, hello." He looked up briefly to make sure I wasn't all broken up from an automobile accident. "Car all right?"

"Car's fine . . . ran over a small child, but you'll be able to square it with the parents; they seemed a broad-minded, modern couple." I fixed myself a martini.

"I'm writing up the case," said Randan, dotting a period firmly and shutting the notebook. "Going to do a serious piece on it."

I changed the subject. "Where are the beautiful ladies?"

"Making themselves more beautiful. Dinner's early tonight, in half an hour. Oh, your friend Liz called and asked me to ask you to join her at the party they're giving Alma Edderdale in Southampton tonight. I said I'd drive you down."

"And got yourself invited too?"

Randan looked pained by my bad taste. "I was only trying to be helpful."

"I'm sure of that. By the way, I saw Brexton this afternoon."

"In jail? I didn't know they'd let anybody in."

"I have influence. Did you try to see him too?"

Randan nodded. "Yes. I wanted to check on something. I'm beginning to get a little doubtful about the case," he added importantly.

"Doubtful? I thought you agreed with Greaves that Brexton—"

"I'm not so sure now. I . . . well, I overheard something this afternoon, here in the house. I don't like to appear to be an eavesdropper, but—"

"But you listened to a conversation not meant for your ears. Perfectly common human trait . . . after all, what is history but a form of eavesdropping?" Fortunately, this was a rhetorical question. Randan ignored it. "I heard Mrs. Veering talking to a lawyer."

"To Brexton's lawyer?"

"Yes . . . but they weren't talking about the murders. They were talking about a will, about Mrs. Brexton's will. It seems she left half her estate to her aunt, to Mrs. Veering. The other half she left to Claypoole. Her husband didn't get anything. Seems he even agreed to the will beforehand. Now, what I was wondering . . ."

VIII

Dinner was a forced affair. Luckily Miss Lung was in an ebullient mood and kept us in stitches with her "Book Chat." I tried not to look at Mrs. Veering, who had decided to have just a touch of Dubonnet against doctor's orders. She was so well lit by the time coffee was served that Randan and I were able to slip away without much explanation to anyone, except Miss Lung, who was roguish.

It took almost half an hour to get from East Hampton to Southampton.

The moon was down and the night sky was partly obscured by clouds moving in from the north.

We didn't talk much, both occupied with our thoughts. At one point Randan tried to pump me about the tax case, but I wasn't giving him any of my cherished leads. This was one story I intended to have all to myself.

It was just as we were getting out of the car in front of the mansion on Gin Lane where the party was being held, that Randan said, "I guess we both know who did it."

I nodded. "We should've figured it out sooner. There were enough loose ends left flapping."

"I thought it was skilfully done." He switched off the ignition. "When did you catch on?"

"With Alma Edderdale yesterday. She let the cat out of the bag, talking about Rose's tax problems."

Randan nodded. "It ties in. You going to tell Greaves? Before the Special Court?"

I shook my head. "No, I'll try and work it out for the *Globe* first. Then, when I think I've got it plotted just right, I'll talk to Greaves . . . that way I'll be sure to have the story before anybody."

We went to the party. I was feeling just fine, walking on clouds of fatuity.

The ballroom (it was, so help me, a ballroom) was a vast affair with parquet floors and huge pots of ferns and three chandeliers and a gallery where musicians played soft music. Everybody, as they say, was there.

I paid my respects to Lady Edderdale, who stood with a bewildered expression beside her host, a man who had made his millions mysteriously in World War II . . . no doubt stealing tires and selling them to the black market.

"Ah yes, Mr. . . ." she sighed as we shook hands, my name forgotten. "I have such an awful time with names, but I never forget a face. When did you leave London?"

I got away as soon as I could and went through the milling throngs to a dining room where a buffet, complete with four chefs, had been prepared, and here, as I expected, was my light of love, gorging herself on smoked turkey and surrounded by a circle of plump, bald, dimpled bachelors.

"Peter! You could make it."

"With you any time," I said in my best vulgar Marlon Brando voice. The bachelors looked at me nervously: a stud trotting through a circle of horses to the nearest mare.

The mare looked particularly radiant in white and gold, wearing family diamonds, which made me wonder if perhaps a marital alliance might be in order.

I glared at the bachelors and they evaporated. We were left with smoked turkey and champagne and Cole Porter from the orchestra in the ballroom and no one but people to interrupt our bliss.

"Why did you go running off like that this afternoon?" Liz looked at me curiously; I prayed for a jealous scene. But there was none. In fact, she didn't even wait for an excuse. "I hear it's all over. Somebody told me Brexton won't have a chance; that they got a full confession."

"Are you sure?" This would be, as they say, the ultimate straw.

"No, I'm not really. It's just the rumor going around."

"What're you doing after this, hon?" I spoke out of the side of my mouth; the other side was full of food.

"Tonight? Well, I'm going home, as every proper girl should."

"Let's go to bed."

"Bed?" She said this in such a loud startled voice that one of the chefs noticeably paled. "Bed?" she repeated in a lower voice. "I thought you only liked to romp among the cactuses . . . or maybe you mean a bed of nails somewhere."

"Young women should never attempt irony," I said coldly. "It's not my fault that, through bad management, you haven't been able to provide me with the wherewithal to make love properly, preferably in a gilded cage. You do have an income, don't you?"

"I want to be loved only for my money," she said, nodding agreeably. "After all, beauty passes. Characters grow mean. But money, properly invested, is always lovable."

"Yours *is* properly invested? In gilt-edged or at least deckle-edged securities?"

"Yes, but I didn't know you cared."

"So much that I'm willing to put you up for the night at the New Arcadia Motel, a center of illicit sexuality only a few miles from here."

"What will my family say?"

"That you are wanton. The money's in your name, isn't it?"

"Oh, yes. Mummy had her second husband make me a trust fund . . . sweet, wasn't it?"

"Depends entirely on the amount." I started to put my arm stealthily around her when Elmer Bush came roaring down upon us.

"How's the boy? . . . Say now! Is this the same pretty little girl I met today on the beach, Miss Liz Bessemer?"

"The same pretty little girl," agreed Liz with a dazzling smile. "And this, I suppose, is still the famed Elmer Bush, who, through the courtesy of Wheatmushlets, is heard over NBC once a week?"

That slowed him up. "Quite a bright little girl, isn't she, Pete? You're some picker, boy. Well, I guess lucky in love, unlucky in crime. Ha! Ha!" While we were doubled up with merry laughter at this sally, Liz stole quietly away.

"Say, didn't mean to barge in on you and the girl friend." Elmer positively smacked his lips as he followed Liz with his eyes as she strolled into the ballroom; all eyes were upon her, her shoulders bare and smooth above the white and gold dress.

"No, Elmer, I'd rather see you any day."

"Some kidder." Elmer was perfunctory now that there was no one around to impress except me, and he knew, of course, I wasn't one of his fans. "Want you to do me a favor."

"What's that?"

"I'd like to get an interview with Mrs. Veering. I can't get through to her. She's playing hard to get . . . God knows why, since she's a real publicity hound. Now, if you would—"

"But, Elmer, we're rivals." I pretended surprise. "After all. I'm still trying to get myself out of a hole."

"This is for the *Globe*. Not for me." He stood there, noble, self-sacrificing . . . I half expected to hear the soft strains of the *"Marseillaise"* in the background.

"Well, I'm sorry, Elmer, but you'll have to get to her on your own."

"Now look here, Sargeant, I've been sent here by the *Globe*, same paper that's been paying you for those dumb articles on why Brexton didn't do the murder. I can tell you one thing: you don't stand any too well around the office. Now, if I tell them you've been co-operative, really helpful, they might not write you off as a complete loss." He stared at me, hard and menacing, the way he does when he attacks the enemies of a certain senator who is trying to root out corruption and Communists.

"Elmer," I said quietly, "I hate you. I have always hated you. I will always continue to hate you. There is nothing I would not do to show you the extent and beauty of my hatred. I would throw you a rock if you were drowning. I would—"

"Always the kidder," said Elmer with a mechanical smile to show that he knew I was joking. "Well, I'm not kidding. The paper expects you to co-operate. If you don't, you might just as well give up all ideas of ever working for them again."

"Suppose I'm right?" I was getting tired of him fast, but I realized my situation was hopeless, anyway, if I didn't produce the real story, and soon. He was out to cut my throat, as they say in the profession.

"That Brexton didn't kill his wife and Claypoole?" Elmer looked at me pityingly.

"I wouldn't bank too much on Claypoole's accusation before he died." My shot in the dark hit the target.

Elmer blinked. "Know about that, eh?"

"That's right. I also know the prosecution is going to build its case on Claypoole having said Brexton murdered his wife . . ."

"He told the whole story to the police the day he was murdered." Elmer looked smug, just as though he had done it all himself with his little hatchet. I was glad to hear my guess confirmed. Elmer had served his purpose.

2

"I'm sure they'll check up on me, just to be unpleasant." Liz sat with nothing on in front of the dressing table, arranging her hair; she is one of those women who do their hair and face before dressing. I lay on the bed, blissful, enjoying the morning sun which fell in a bar of light across my belly. It had been an excellent night . . . morning too. Nothing disturbed me.

"What do you care?" I said, yawning.

"I don't really." I watched her shoulder blades as she made mysterious passes at her hair and face, her back to me. "It's just that when I said I was staying with friends in Southampton, I shouldn't've mentioned Anna Trees. They're bound to see her, and my aunt will ask her about my overnight stay and . . ."

"And you're worrying too much. Besides, I'm sure your aunt would approve of the New Arcadia. Clean sheets. Private bathroom. View of a roadhouse and U.S. Route One as well as the company of a red-blooded American boy . . . Come here."

"Not a chance in the world, Peter." She rose with dignity and slipped on her silk pants.

I wanted her again, but she had other plans. Sadly, I got up myself and went into the bathroom to take a shower. When I came out, Liz was fully dressed and going through the wastebasket in the preoccupied way women have when they are minding someone else's business.

"Ah, ah," I said sharply, the way you do to a child. "Might find something dirty. Don't touch."

"Nonsense." Liz pulled out a newspaper and a cigarette butt. "Just as I thought: marijuana. I thought I smelled something peculiar."

"Well, don't touch it. I thought all women were mortally afraid of germs."

"Stop generalizing." Liz dropped the butt back into the wastebasket and opened the newspaper absently. I got dressed.

A sharp sound from Liz halted me. "Is *this* Claypoole?" she asked, holding up the paper for me to see.

I took it from her. It was a Monday edition of the *Journal-American*. There were several photographs of the principals involved in our local killing. One was of Claypoole. I nodded, giving her the paper back; I combed my hair in the dusty mirror. "What about it?"

"Well, I know him."

"*Knew* him. So what? A lot of people did."

"No, but I saw him only recently. I didn't really know him, but I think I met him . . . or ran into him, or something." She paused, confused, poring over the newspaper intently. "I know!" She squealed.

"Well?"

"It was Sunday night, at the Club . . . before I went on to Evan Evans's party. I dropped in with some people, with a boy I know. We looked around just to see who was there. It was dead, you know the way Sunday night is, so I had my escort drive me over to Evan's . . . Anyway, before I left, I remember seeing him, Claypoole, ever so distinctly. He was awfully good-looking, in an older way; I noticed him because he was by himself, in a plain suit. Everybody else was dressed. He was standing all alone in the door which opens onto the terrace."

"You didn't speak to him?"

"No, I just caught the one glimpse."

"What time was it?"

"Time? Well, not much after twelve-thirty."

I was excited. "You realize that you may be the last person to've seen him alive?"

"Really?" She was properly impressed. "I don't suppose it proves anything, does it? He must've strolled over from the North Dunes . . . Peter, I'm starved, let's get some breakfast."

Stealthily we left the New Arcadia Motel, the way hundreds of couples every week did, their unions blessed only by the gods of love, the sterner bonds of society momentarily severed or ignored.

We found a pleasant inn just south of the village of East Hampton where we ate a huge breakfast. It was an odd morning, with a white mist high overhead through which the sun shone diffused, bright but not concentrated.

"I love those spur-of-the-moment adventures," said Liz, eating more eggs than I've ever seen a slender girl eat before.

"I hope you don't have a great many of them."

"As many as I can squeeze in without being untidy," she said comfortably, leaving me to guess whether she was serious or not.

"I suppose, next thing you'll tell me you do this all the time, in motels."

"There's an awfully disagreeable streak of Puritanism in you, Peter. I worry about it."

"I just want to be able to think of you as being all mine, clean from the word go."

"From the word go, yes." Liz beamed at me over coffee. She was a beautiful creature, more like an act of nature than a human being ... I thought of her in elemental terms, like the wind or the sky, to wax lyrical. Usual laws of morality didn't apply to her.

I changed the subject . . . just looking at her upset me. "How much longer do you intend to stay down here?"

Liz sighed. "Tomorrow I go back. I tried to talk them into letting me stay longer, but they wouldn't. I don't think any magazine should try to put out issues in the hot weather. Nobody'll read them."

"Who reads fashion magazines? Women just buy them to look at the pictures of clothes."

"Well, it's an awful strain working in New York in the hot weather. I was supposed to go back yesterday, but I got an extra day. When will you be back?"

"Friday. I'll have to stay here for the Special Court, to testify. I'll go back to New York right afterwards."

"What an interesting weekend it turned out to be," said Liz, putting ice from her drinking glass into her coffee cup. "I don't know why I never ask for iced coffee when I hate it hot. Peter, do you really think Brexton's innocent?"

I nodded.

"But if he didn't do it, who did?"

"Somebody else."

"Oh, don't be silly! Who could possibly have done it?"

"Somebody with a motive."

"Well, you must have some idea who it was if you're so certain it wasn't Brexton."

"Oh, I know who did it, all right." And I did. I had known for nearly half an hour.

Liz's eyes grew round. "You mean you're sitting right here having breakfast with me like this and you know who killed Mrs. Brexton and Claypoole?"

"I can't see what having breakfast with you has to do with it, but, yes, I know who the murderer is. Thanks to you."

"To me? What have I done?"

"I'll tell you later."

Liz looked at me as though she wasn't sure whether or not to telephone for a squad of men in white. She tried the practical approach. "What're you going to do about it now that you think you know everything?"

"Now that I know, not think. I'm not sure. I have to tie up some ends first. Even then I may not be able to prove what I know."

"Oh, Peter, tell me! Who is it?"

"Not on your life." I paid for breakfast and stood up. "Come on, dear. I've got to take you home."

"I have never in my life known such a sadist." Liz was furious and persistent, but I wouldn't tell her anything. She hardly spoke to me when we pulled up in front of the North Dunes and I got out. She slid haughtily into the driver's seat. "It's been very nice, Mr. Sargeant."

"I've had a swell time too."

"Beast!" And Liz wheeled out of the driveway on two wheels, the gears screeching with agony. Smiling to myself, I went into the house. I had a tough day ahead of me.

3

No one but the butler was in sight when I arrived. He bade me good morning and made no comment about my night out. I went upstairs to my bedroom and immediately telephoned Miss Flynn.

"I have undertaken the tasks assigned," she said, in her stately way. "The following are the results of my Herculean Labors." She gave me several pieces of information; one was supremely useful. I told her to expect me Friday afternoon and, after a bit of business, we rang off.

I was surprisingly calm. The identity of the killer had come to me that morning with Liz. Something she had said acted like a catalyst: everything fell into place at once . . . all those bits of disconnected information and supposition had, with one phrase, been fused into a whole and I knew with certainty what had happened, and why.

I packed my suitcase; then I went downstairs and left it in the hall. I was not going to spend another night in this house.

On the terrace, watching the mist grow dense, become fog, was Miss Lung. She was sitting quite alone with a brilliant Guatemala shawl around her shoulders.

She jumped when I approached. "Oh, Mr. Sargeant. What a start you gave me! A little bird told me you didn't come home last night."

"The little bird was on the beam," I said, sitting down beside her. "Looks like a storm coming up."

She nodded. We both looked out to sea, or rather at the line of gun-metal-gray breakers: the horizon was gone already and fog was rolling in from the sea in billows. It was suddenly chilly, and uncomfortably damp.

"We have had such lovely weather," said Miss Lung nostalgically. "I suppose this must be the end of summer. It comes like this, doesn't it, all at once."

"Not until later, about the time of the equinox," I said absently, watching her out of the corner of my eyes. She was unusually pale, her "Book Chat" manner entirely discarded. I could almost imagine the slender, good-looking woman imprisoned beneath the layers of fat and disappointment. "You were very fond of Mr. Claypoole, weren't you?"

"What makes you ask?" She looked at me, startled.

"I'm curious about this case, that's all. I've always thought there were some very important facts the police didn't know."

"I'm sure there's a great deal of importance the police don't know," said Miss Lung sharply. "And I'm in favor of keeping them ignorant, aren't you?"

"In general, yes. That was what you meant, though, wasn't it? About not wanting too close an investigation . . . You remember the other day when you told me."

"Yes, I remember. I have nothing criminal to hide. It's certainly no secret about Fletcher and me. I'm sure if it hadn't been for Allie (whom I adore, believe me), we might have married once. She wouldn't let him; then Mildred tried, and failed too . . . that's all."

"Yet why should that bother you? I mean what difference would it make if it should all come to light, about you and Fletcher?"

Miss Lung paused before answering; then she said, with an odd look in her eyes, "I'll tell you exactly what I feared, Mr. Sargeant, but you must promise me never to refer to this to anyone, certainly never to write about it in the press. Do you promise?"

"Well . . . yes, I promise."

"I was afraid that if the police should start prying around in our past —Fletcher's, Paul's, mine—they would sooner or later discover that Paul Brexton painted me, fifteen years ago, in the . . . well, the altogether. You must know that I have fans everywhere in the United States and Canada, and if that painting should ever come to light and be reproduced in the Yellow Press, I would be absolutely finished as an authoress of 'Book Chat.' You see now my fear of investigation?"

It was all I could do to keep from laughing. "I see exactly what it is you feared. As a matter of fact, I did hear about the painting."

"You see? Already people have begun to talk about it! Ever since this hideous business started I've been in mortal dread of someone unearthing that picture. In my last conversation with Paul before he was taken to jail, I implored him to keep silent on that subject, come what may."

"I'm sure he will. I hear, by the way, it was quite a good painting."

"I was not ever thus," said Miss Lung, with a brief return to her sly-boots self.

We chatted a while longer. Then I went into the house. Everything was shaping up nicely. So nicely that I was scared to death.

On the second floor, I slipped into Brexton's old room. No one saw me. The room had been straightened and now looked perfectly ordinary. I checked the lock of the door to what had been Allie's room (another key replaced the one the prosecution had taken for an exhibit); the lock worked smoothly. Then I went to the window and examined the screen. As I expected, there were scratches on the sill, at either corner. Long regular scars in the weathered wood. Tentatively, I pressed my finger against the screen: it was loose. I was not able to check the other windows, for, as I was about to enter Allie's room, Mrs. Veering appeared in the doorway.

"Mr. Sargeant!" She seemed genuinely surprised. "What are you doing in there?"

"I . . . I was just looking for something," I stammered stupidly.

"In *this* room? I can't think what," she said flatly, as though suspecting me of designs on the silverware. "Mary Western told me you were back. I'd like to talk to you."

"Certainly." We went downstairs to her alcove off the drawing room.

She was all business, a tumbler of Dubonnet on the desk in front of her. "I've decided to go ahead with the party," she said.

I was surprised. "I thought . . ."

"At first I thought it would be in bad taste. Now I think I can't afford to back out of it. People expect one to carry on." She took a long swallow of Dubonnet, carrying on.

"You may be right," I said. "I'm afraid, though, I won't be able to handle it. I'm due in New York Friday."

"Oh. Well, I'm sorry. If it's a matter of fee . . ." She seemed disturbed by my refusal.

"No, it's not that at all. I just have an awful lot of work piling up and . . ." I made a series of glib and, I hoped, plausible excuses. I couldn't tell her my real reason; she would find out soon enough.

"I'm very sorry. I hope at least you'll still be kind enough to advise me now."

I said that I would and we had a brisk business talk in which I confided to her what I'd felt all along: that she was quite capable of mapping out a publicity campaign on her own. She took this without elation or demur.

"Thank you. I do my best. As you probably know, I have had certain tax difficulties lately." She looked at me shrewdly to see how I'd react. I didn't bat an eye; I looked at her as though it were the first I'd heard of these troubles.

She continued, satisfied apparently with my silence. "People have actually started a rumor that I've been wiped out financially. Well, it isn't true and, for that reason, I don't dare *not* give this party. I sent the invitations out this morning."

So that was it. She was spending Mildred's money before she got it. I couldn't blame her under the circumstances . . . it was an act of God.

4

To my surprise Allie Claypoole and Greaves showed up together for lunch.

She was pale and she walked as though she were unsure of her legs, like an invalid new-risen. Greaves was jubilant in a restrained, official way.

"Certainly is nice to see everybody like this," he said. "Not official or anything like that."

"We're always happy to see *you*, Mr. Greaves," said Mrs. Veering smoothly from the head of the table. The butler passed champagne around. It was quite a luncheon.

Randan and Allie sat next to each other and talked in low voices through most of the lunch while the rest of us either listened to Mary Western Lung or drank our champagne in silence.

It wasn't until dessert that I was able to turn to Greaves, who was on my left, and ask a question which could not be heard by the rest of the table; Miss Lung was loudly recounting a bit of scandal which had taken place at a meeting of the Ladies' Paintbox and Typewriter Club.

"What did the knife look like?" I asked in a low voice.

Greaves looked surprised. "Knife?"

"Yes, the one they found beside Claypoole. I never got a close look at it."

"Just an ordinary knife, very sharp. A kind of kitchen knife with a bone handle and Brexton's initials on it."

"Initials?" That was it! "Were they prominent?"

"Yes, they were pretty big. What're you up to, Sargeant?" He looked at me suspiciously.

"I may have a surprise for you."

"Like what?"

"Like the real killer."

Greaves snorted. "We got him and don't you go rocking the boat. We have enough trouble without your interference. Elmer Bush's told me about the way you operate. I told him if you tried anything—"

"Elmer is my best friend," I said, hardly able to contain my delight. "One other question and then I'm through. Sunday morning Claypoole said he went to the John Drew Theatre to look at the paintings. Well, I happen to know the theater was closed that morning. I figure he went to see you."

"What if he did?" Greaves squirmed uncomfortably.

"I have a hunch he drove over to Riverhead and told you Brexton murdered his wife. I believe your district attorney, misled by you, is building his case and political ruin on that visit."

"I don't like your tone, Sargeant." Greaves had turned very red. "But since you know so much already, I'll tell you that, yes, Claypoole came to see me and he accused Brexton. I don't think Brexton knew it . . . that's why he killed him that same night, to keep him quiet, not knowing it was already too late. I should've acted right away. I realize that now, but I didn't think anything could happen in a house with two M.C.I. men on hand. Anyway, it's all over. Nobody can save your friend Brexton," said Greaves, quietly folding his napkin and placing it beside his plate.

"He's not my friend; he's also not your clay pigeon, Greaves."

"Now, look here—" But Mrs. Veering had got to her feet; she led us all into the drawing room for coffee.

I got Allie Claypoole away from Randan for a moment. "You're not giving in, are you?"

"About Paul?" She sighed and sat down shakily. I sat down beside her. "I don't know what to think. Greaves has been with me all morning. He's trying to make me believe Paul tried to murder me, but I can't . . . I just *won't* believe it."

"Good," I said. "You stick by what you feel. You're right."

She clenched her slender white hands into two fists. "But if Paul didn't, who *could've* done it?"

"The same person who killed your brother."

"Do you know who it is?"

I nodded. She looked at me with real terror in her eyes. Then Greaves, suspecting I might be intimidating a valuable witness, joined us and I excused myself.

I was about to go telephone 1770 House to see if they might have a room for the night when Randan, with a smirk, said, "What happened to you and Liz? Suddenly you both just disappeared and Miss Lung tells me you didn't come home at all last night. I looked around for you when I left, but you'd gone by then."

"Miss Bessemer and I spent the night with the *Times* crossword puzzle at the New Arcadia Motel," I said and walked away.

I made a reservation for that night by telephone. Then I slipped out of the house by way of the front door. I wanted one more look around before I finished my case.

I walked among the umbrellas on the terrace, sad-looking in a gray fog, which had already blotted out the ocean only a few yards away. It was as thick a fog as I'd ever seen. The umbrellas looked like monsters, looming in the mist.

Then I took out my watch and began to walk, at a good pace, down the beach to the Club.

Five minutes later I reached the Club.

It was a strange walk. I couldn't see more than a few feet in front of me. If it hadn't been for a cluster of rotten black pilings which marked the beginning of the Club beach I wouldn't have known where I was. The clubhouse was invisible. There was no sound from its general direction.

I had the impression of being packed in cotton wool. I almost felt that if I put my hand out, I could touch the fog, a gray heavy damp substance.

Far out to sea, I heard the horn of a ship, lonely and plaintive. Well, it would soon be over, I told myself. I was oddly depressed. I had solved the case, but there was no elation, only relief and perhaps a certain fear.

I made my way back slowly. I followed the edge of the water, which eddied black upon the white sand. If I hadn't, I would've got lost, for there were no landmarks—nothing but white sand and gray fog.

I timed my return trip so that I'd know when I was abreast the North Dunes. Otherwise I knew I might keep on until Montauk without ever knowing where I was.

I was three minutes and two seconds from the Club when a figure appeared, tall and dark. We both stopped at the water's edge; each had been following the water line. Then Randan approached. He was carrying my suitcase. "I thought you were taking a walk," he said amiably. "I followed you."

"You thought I'd walk to the Club?"

He nodded. "It's a nice walk, isn't it? Perfect for a foggy day."

"I like the fog." I glanced at the suitcase in his hand; this was it at last. I knew what was coming. "Not such a good walk, though, if you're carrying something."

"Like your suitcase?" He grinned.

"Or like your uncle."

The smile faded from his face. We were only a yard apart, yet his features were faintly blurred by the intervening fog, white and enveloping. We stood within a circle of visibility whose diameter was not more than a yard. Somewhere far above, in another world, the afternoon sun was shining. We were like the last survivors of a disaster, alone with our secrets.

A wave broke close to us. Water swirled around our shoes. Simultaneously we moved farther up the shore, each keeping the other in range. Was he armed? The question repeated itself over and over in my brain. If he was . . .

"You know a great deal," said Randan. He put the suitcase down. He was wearing a trench coat, I noticed . . . very sensible, I thought inanely, keep the damp out; fog caressed us like damp cotton; my clothes were soaked, and not only from fog.

"I have my suspicions," I said, trying to sound casual. "But they don't do me much good, since there's no evidence of any kind." Anything to throw him off the track. I was positive he was armed. I planned a sudden break up the beach, into the fog. One leap and I'd be out of sight. But if he was armed . . .

"You're not stupid." Randan sounded somewhat surprised.

"Thanks. Unfortunately, neither are you. There's no way of making a case against you. I think I know exactly what happened, but there's no proof of any kind. You thought of everything." But he was too smart for such flattery. I was talking fast, to no point. My suitcase in his hand meant this was the payoff.

"Tell me what you know, Sargeant." The question was put quietly, without emphasis.

"Not enough."

"Tell me anyway." He put his hand in the pocket of his coat. I went death-cold: Was he armed? Was he armed?

I decided to talk, my legs tensed for a spring into the whiteness around us, into the protecting, the murderous fog. My mouth was dry. Sweat trickled down my side. With difficulty I kept my voice steady. "I think you made your plan in Boston, the night before you came here. You heard about the murder on the radio . . . or rather the mysterious death of Mildred Brexton. You knew her husband would be held responsible. You also knew of Fletcher's dislike of Brexton, on Mildred's account. On a wild chance, you thought there might be an opportunity for you to kill your uncle, making it look as though Brexton had killed him."

"All this from having heard over the radio that Mildred Brexton drowned accidentally?" He sounded amused.

I nodded. "Also from a conversation with Allie, by telephone, the day before. I think she told you pretty much the situation down here. You knew what to expect." This was a guess. It was accurate.

"I didn't think Allie would mention that telephone call," said Randan. "Yes, that gave me the . . . the background of the weekend party. Go on."

"Just in case, you prepared, in Boston, the note saying Brexton was the killer. I had my secretary check the Boston papers for your last day there: none carried an account of Mildred's death . . . too soon. Because of that you weren't able to get an X or a K out of the headlines. This bothered me when I first saw the note. I figured that any one of us preparing such a note would have had no trouble finding Xs and Ks, since the papers were full of references to Brexton, to Mildred's death."

"Good, very good." Randan seemed pleased. "I was worried that the police might discover my note was made from Boston papers. Fortunately, they were so positive Fletcher fixed the note that they didn't bother tracking it down. Then what happened?"

"You arrived in the early morning, Sunday, by car. You went straight to the house. The guard was asleep. You looked around. In the living room you found Brexton's palette knife with his initials on it, left there after Mildred attacked Mrs. Veering Friday night. You took it, for future use. You were in the kitchen . . . perhaps examining the fuse box, when I arrived. You struck me with—"

"Of all homely items, a rolling pin." Randan chuckled. "Not hard enough, either." A gull shrieked. The surf whispered.

"You then left the house, making your official appearance later on that day. You found out soon enough what was going on. Your uncle no doubt told you he suspected Brexton of murdering his wife. He might even have told you of his denunciation of Brexton to the police. If he did, and I think he did, the moment was right. Your uncle had accused Brexton of murder. Your uncle is murdered. Brexton, without a doubt, would be held responsible. The rest was comparatively simple."

"I'm all ears."

I watched his face while I talked, reading his responses in his expression rather than his words. I recapitulated quickly. "Mildred died by accident. Brexton knew this. The rest of us did too until that policeman, prodded by your vindictive uncle, scenting an easy case, decided to make something out of it. Both he and your uncle played your game to perfection . . . to their regret."

"Greaves will certainly benefit. He's already a hero." Randan was smug. I played right along.

"That's right. I don't suppose Greaves will ever know that he's sent an innocent man to the chair."

"No, he'll never know," Randan agreed cheerfully. "There'll be no one to tell him he was wrong."

I pretended not to get this, but I did, and I was ready; he was armed, all right. Under cover of fog he would commit his last murder, destroy the only witness of his cunning. I made plans while we talked.

"You fixed two alibis for Sunday night, the night you killed your uncle. First was at the Club. The second was at the Evans's party, where you ran into us . . . an unexpected meeting, I'd say. You made a date to meet your uncle at the Club around twelve-thirty. You drove over. He walked . . . along the beach. You met on the beach, I think, probably near the cabanas, in the dark. You talked. Perhaps you strolled away from the Club, toward the house. At some point you both sat down. You struck him on the head with some object."

"Very like a stone."

"And dragged him to the house, where you knew the police would be busy with the tampered fuse box and the others would've gone to bed. You then cut Claypoole's throat with Brexton's knife and rolled the body under the swing, leaving the knife nearby to implicate Brexton. Aware that friend Greaves would be sufficiently simple to think that a man of Brexton's intelligence would leave a knife with his own prints and initials on it beside a dead body."

"Pretty good, Sargeant. You've missed a few subtle touches here and there, but you have the main points. Go on."

"Then you went back to the Club, putting in a second appearance, pretending you were there all along. After that you went on to Evans's party. You didn't make a single mistake." I laid it on. I had two alternatives. One was to disappear into the fog and run the risk of being shot; the other was to try a flying tackle before he could pull the trigger of that pistol which, I was sure, was pointed at me in his trench-coat pocket.

While I made up my mind, I talked quickly . . . flattered him, made it appear that I thought he was in the clear, that I was only an appreciative audience, not dangerous to him. He was too smart to fall for this, but he enjoyed hearing me praise him. "After all," he said, "you're the only person I'll ever be able to talk to about this. Tell me how you happened to suspect me. No one else did."

"Just luck. I told you something you didn't know, remember? I told you Allie had been with Brexton at the time of Claypoole's death. I knew this was something the murderer couldn't know and that the others hadn't heard. You acted quickly, as I thought you would. Allie must never regain consciousness. Her testimony would save Brexton. Her death would incriminate him once and for all. You had to kill her. At this point, though, you brought up a second line of defence which I admired particularly. Rose's tax difficulties. No doubt your uncle or Allie had told you about them. You knew she was a potential candidate for murderer of Mildred . . . she had the best motives of all, really. You took one of her handkerchiefs with the idea of planting it in Allie's room in case something went wrong. It would've implicated Rose, but either you forgot to use it or else you were too sure of success. You came back to the house when the nurses were changed, at midnight. You had less than five minutes to give Allie the strychnine which you'd already got from Mrs. Veering's bathroom. You pushed the screen out of your window. You walked along the top of the porch to Allie's room. You pushed that screen in. You turned the key to Mrs. Veering's room, which was lucky, because you nearly had a visit from Miss Lung. You started to give Allie a hypodermic, but there wasn't time to do it properly. Miss Lung had sounded an alarm. You unlocked the door between the two rooms, went back out the window to your own room and then made an appearance."

"Excellent." Randan was pleased to hear from me the story of his cleverness. "Couple of good details involved. One was planting the key to Allie's room in Brexton's pillow the day before . . . just in case. The other was the business of the screens. Had to loosen them with a knife . . . I thought I'd never get them right. Fortunately, they were all warped from the damp weather and they stuck in place even after being loosened. You're right about the handkerchief bit too. I was going to use it if Allie got Brexton off the hook."

"Your mentioning the murder of Sir Thomas Overbury helped put me on to you." I moved a millimeter closer to him. "The case was somewhat the same."

"Not at all the same. Did I mention him? I'd forgotten that. A slip. What else put you on to me?"

"A remark . . . you said something about 'spur of the moment.' It stuck in my head; I don't know why. I never believed, frankly, that Mildred was murdered. Claypoole, of course, was. It could only have been a spur-of-the-moment murder, improvised on the spot, under cover of a suspected killing and arranged to fit in with the details of the first, the false murder. Then, last night, Liz gave me a piece of information I needed: she'd seen Claypoole at the Club a few minutes before he died. Nobody knew he'd gone there. She got a glimpse of him only by chance. We knew that you had been there at the same time. Everything began to add up. Then, when I found out about the Boston newspapers . . ."

"It's been nice talking to you." He stepped back a pace.

Soon. Soon. Soon. I braced myself. I talked fast. I inched toward him as I did. My plan decided upon. "Why did you kill him, though? That's one thing I could never figure out. I could never fix a proper motive."

"Money. He was permanent executor of my trust fund. As long as he lived I couldn't touch my own money until I was forty. I didn't want to wait until then. He was severe. I always hated him. When Mildred died I saw my chance. There'd never be another opportunity like it. I improvised, as you said. It was fascinating, too. I've always studied murders. Planned them in my head, just for sport. I was surprised how easy it was to commit one . . . how easy to get away with it." I had moved, without his noticing it, a foot closer to him.

"But now," he said quietly, "Mr. Sargeant will unexpectedly leave East Hampton before the Special Court, baggage and all. By the time he is reported missing in Manhattan, Brexton will be well on his way."

I hit him low and hard. There was a pop, like a cork being blown from a bottle. A smell of gunpowder. For a moment, as we wrestled, I wondered if I'd been hit. Sometimes I knew, from the war, you could be shot and not know it.

But I was not hit. We fought hand to hand grimly at the water's edge. Randan swore and gasped and kicked and struggled like a weak but desperate animal; it was no use, though, and in a moment he lay flat on the sand, breathing hoarsely, barely conscious, a hole the size of a silver dollar burned in his coat where he'd fired at me . . . his revolver a yard away in the sand. I pocketed it. Then I picked him up and carried him back to the house . . . sea foam, frothy as beer, in his hair as I followed the same route he himself had taken three days before when he had dragged the unconscious body of Fletcher Claypoole to the house.

5

"A Miss Bessemer is in the Outer Office." Miss Flynn looked at me with granite eyes. "She has No Appointment."

"I'll see her, anyway. Poor child . . . she was involved in a white-slave ring in Georgia. I'm trying to rehabilitate her."

Miss Flynn's reply was largely italics. She disappeared and Liz bounded into my office, her face glowing. "A hero! Darling Peter a hero! When I read about it I didn't believe it was the same one I knew . . . the same Peter Sargeant who . . ." Words for once failed her. I allowed her to kiss my cheek.

"I had no idea you were so brave . . ."

"Ah."

"And so right." Liz sat down in the chair beside my desk and stared at me.

I waved modestly. "I was merely doing my duty, ma'am. We here in southern Ontario feel that duty's enough without any of this horn-blowing . . ."

Liz's eyes narrowed thoughtfully. "I must say I suspected him too. Oh, I didn't say anything about it, but I had a hunch . . . you know how it is. Especially that night at Evans's party, right after he killed his uncle . . . his eyes were set too close together."

"Eyes?"

"You can always tell; eyes and hands . . . set too close together means a criminal."

"His hands were set too close together . . ."

"Now, don't be maddening! He shot at you, didn't he?"

I nodded calmly.

"Then you threw him on the ground and used judo to make him confess."

"A somewhat highly colored version of what happened," I said. "I was very brave, though. Since he has the build of a somewhat frail praying mantis, you might say I had the edge on him."

"Even so, he had a gun. I suppose he'll get the chair." She sounded matter-of-fact.

"Never can tell. They'll probably plead insanity . . . especially after they read those notebooks of his. He gives the whole thing away . . . writes about a perfect crime which resembles the one *he* committed. I think he was a kind of maniac."

"Oh, you could tell that just by looking at him. I knew the first time I ever laid eyes on him. Not that I ever thought he'd done it . . . I won't say that."

"Yet."

"No, I won't say that, but I *did* think him peculiar and you see how right I was. I've never seen so much space as the *Globe* gave you . . . that Mr. Bush must've been livid."

"I think he was distressed." It made me feel good, thinking of Elmer's column being all chopped up because the issue which had contained my story had had a particularly well displayed "America's New York" telling how Elmer himself had helped gather the evidence which was to send Brexton to his just reward.

"Where's Brexton now?"

"I don't know. I think he's gone off somewhere to hide . . . also to marry Allie when this thing dies down." I got up and went over to a corner of the office where, face to the wall, was a large painting. "Brexton, with tears in his eyes, said he would give me anything I wanted: money, paintings . . . anything. I asked him for this." I turned the canvas around and there, triumphantly nude, reveling in her own golden skin, was the young Mary Western Lung, not yet a penwoman, not yet the incomparably, fertile source of "Book Chat."

Liz shrieked with pleasure. "It's Miss Lung! I can tell. You know she wasn't at all bad-looking."

"I intend to keep this one in the office for all to see. I shall collect a small but useful sum each month to keep it out of the hands of her competitors and enemies."

"Her breasts were too big," said Liz critically, that sharp slanted mean look on her face that women assume when examining one another.

"Many people like them that way," I said, turning the picture back to the wall.

"Shall I go?"

"No, as a matter of fact there is an exercise which I've only just submitted to the Patent Office: it will make a pair of water wings out of the most nondescript—" I was heading purposefully toward Liz when the little box on my desk spluttered, exactly like Miss Flynn. I answered it.

"That Mr. Wheen who has been trying to contact you . . . he is on the Wire." Miss Flynn's voice dripped acid . . . she knew what was going on in the Inner Office.

"I'll talk to him," I said.

Liz came and sat on my lap. "Stop that!" were the first words of mine Mr. Wheen heard.

"Stop what?" The voice was harsh, gravelly. "I just now got you, Mr. Sargeant."

"I didn't mean *you*, sir," I said smoothly. "I understand you've been trying to get in touch with me . . ."

"Yeah, that's right. I think I got a job for you. It's about Muriel Sandoe."

"Muriel Sandoe? I don't think—"

"She was an associate of mine. You know her maybe by her professional name in the circus: 'Peaches' Sandoe. Well, you see, this elephant . . ."